THE
PAUPER
FIELD

THE PAUPER FIELD

TREVOR G. JACKSON

IZZARD INK
PUBLISHING®

IZZARD INK PUBLISHING
www.izzardink.com

Library of Congress Cataloging-in-Publication Data

Names: Jackson, Trevor, 1976- author
Title: The pauper field / by Trevor Jackson.
Description: First edition. | [Salt Lake City] : Izzard Ink Publishing, 2025.
Identifiers: LCCN 2025005386 (print) | LCCN 2025005387 (ebook) | ISBN
   9781642281187 hardback | ISBN 9781642281170 paperback | ISBN
   9781642281163 ebook | ISBN 9781642281194 ebook other
Subjects: LCGFT: Thrillers (Fiction) | Novels
Classification: LCC PS3610.A3554 P38 2025 (print) | LCC PS3610.A3554
   (ebook) | DDC 813/.6—dc23/eng/20250303
LC record available at https://lccn.loc.gov/2025005386
LC ebook record available at https://lccn.loc.gov/2025005387

Designed by Daniel Lagin
Cover Design by Andrea Ho

First Edition

Contact the author at thepauperfield@gmail.com

Hardback ISBN: 978-1-64228-118-7
Paperback ISBN: 978-1-64228-117-0
eBook ISBN: 978-1-64228-116-3
Audiobook ISBN: 978-1-64228-119-4

SUMMER

CHAPTER ONE

IN TERRA LIOS

TUESDAY, AUGUST 7, 1:13 AM

"**W**ho's there!" Braxton's voice cracked the stillness of the night, fists clenched in reflex. There was nothing there. His booze-addled brain was playing tricks on him. Again. Silence. He plodded on.

The sticky nighttime air clung to his skin as he continued, stumbling through the labyrinthine streets of the small Oregon town. Even after a few weeks of living in Jacksonville, he remained a hapless wanderer, easily lost with each twist and turn he took. A lone drunken figure drifting through the shadows. Then he heard it again.

In Terra Lios, In Terra Lios. . .

The words seemed to appear from nowhere and everywhere at once, a whispering chant that ebbed and flowed with the wind, snaking through the surrounding narrow streets. The rustic town's charm had turned into a maze of confusion, each twist and turn drawing him closer to the voices beyond. Every step Braxton took led him further into the invisible web of disembodied chanting, his mind tangled between the urge to flee and the need to understand.

In Terra Lios, In Terra Lios. . .

The warm nighttime air shrouded him as a shiver ran down his spine, each haunting repetition of the phrase pulling him deeper. He stumbled, the paving beneath his feet seeming to shift and slide as the distant chant morphed into a hypnotic rhythm, guiding his steps to a narrow, brick-lined pathway leading to an empty park.

In Terra Lios, In Terra Lios. . .

Braxton tried to shake the eerie mantra from his mind, but it clung to his thoughts like a specter, refusing to be dispelled. The pathway wound through the park, bordered by dim lanterns that cast a pale, yellow-orange glow, flickering like ghostly sentinels amidst the whispering trees.

It wasn't long before he found himself in a small square, where a small stone bench waited for the weary. He glanced around, half-expecting to see the bearers of the cryptic message materialize from the shadows. But there was nothing—only a dirt path that disappeared into the shadowy wilderness beyond.

And just like that, the voices stopped.

Braxton sighed. Yet another auditory hallucination. Shaking it off, he pulled out a metal flask and took a swig of bourbon. Then he lit a smoke, took a long drag, and looked up at the stars pinpricking the darkness above.

"Smoky Way Galaxy. . .aw, shit." he nearly lost his balance. "Yeah, don't look up." He swerved and collapsed onto the bench.

Settled in, Braxton took another long drag, the smoke curling into the night sky before being swallowed by the vast emptiness above. His mind whirled, thoughts coming fast and lucid, splintering in a dozen different directions until returning to the ominous voices that had lured him there. After another moment of silence, Braxton stubbed out his cigarette and with a deep, steadying breath, hoisted himself back onto his feet.

In Terra Lios, In Terra Lios. . .

The voices returned, louder than ever. Emanating from the dark outer reaches. The path ahead beckoned, a trail of possibilities and hidden perils that melted into the unseen depths of the wilderness beyond.

As he stepped toward the enveloping shadows, he couldn't shake the feeling that something unseen, unheard, was watching, waiting.

In Terra Lios, In Terra Lios. . .

The chanting was hypnotic, pulling him toward its source. His heart skittered, and his breathing became uneven. The narrow beam of moonlight filtering through the trees seemed to play tricks on his eyes, casting long, dancing shadows on the dirt path ahead.

The path twisted and turned, taking him deeper into the wooded area. And as he went, the voices grew louder, their cadence more haunting.

In Terra Lios, In Terra Lios. . .

He felt drawn to it, an invisible force compelling him forward. Fear gnawed at him, yet he could not turn back. The chanting beckoned, drawing him deeper into the woods. It was as if he understood what they were saying without knowing the words.

The chanting reached its climax as Braxton stepped into a small clearing. Before him stood a large, ancient tree. Its gnarled branches clawed at the heavens, holding a dark secret beneath.

Braxton's legs gave out, his body colliding with the ground. Fuzzy gray stars danced into view as he lay there, enduring the pain surge through his body. And then there was silence.

Total silence. Nothingness. Then some sounds. Like a leaking spigot. Or those big plops of rain right before the sky explodes. A sickly wind stirred. Leaves rattled and shimmered, pines whispered. As the branches started swaying, he heard the disquieting creaking of branches and ropes. He raised his head.

Then he saw it.

Ghost-white figures, like limp marionettes, dangled eerily, swaying ever so slightly in the night breeze. Moonlight cast an otherworldly sheen on the bodies. Braxton's mind struggled to process the horror before him.

He looked up at the sky. The stars swirled around him as a tunnel collapsed in on him. Braxton lay there, unable to breathe. Paralyzed by the realization that he had ventured into a realm where darkness ruled, a place meant for hiding the most sinister of secrets.

"Holy shiii—" he heard as everything faded into darkness. The words echoed as if from a distance, his voice reacting to the bodies swinging beneath the tree's bough.

And then, Braxton knew no more.

FIVE HOURS LATER

The cold tile pressed against his cheek, its unfamiliar texture drawing him back into consciousness. A steady dripping sound echoed in his ears, sharper and more defined than before. This was a persistent, metallic tap of leaky faucet on porcelain. Not the uneven plops he remembered from. . . where had he been?

The air felt different too. Still and muffled. A stark contrast to the muggy night air he recalled from the deep recesses of his mind. As his fragmented memory started rebooting, Braxton's confusion veered into panic.

Blinking, he took in his surroundings—it was a bathroom, and he was wearing nothing but his skivvies. The dim glow of morning light peered through a small window above him. A rush of panic, of confusion, forced him to sit up. He looked around for a moment, trying to find anything that could ground him. He took in the water-streaked mirror, the vintage tiles below, and the navy-blue shower curtain. Recognition flickered; it was his bathroom, the one in the house he'd only recently started to call home.

He moved to his hands and knees, noting the scrapes on his limbs, evidence of a night he didn't fully remember. With effort, he rose, using the sink to steady himself, and grimaced at the scabbed-over dirt and splinters embedded in his palms. Sighing, he shook his head and took stock of things. This wasn't his first rodeo after all.

It looked like his knees and elbows took most of the night's damage. Ordinary and usual cuts and bruising. He gauged his nausea-to-head-ache hangover ratio at seven-to-three, signaling minimal head trauma. Familiar with the program, he let go of the sink and stood on his own two feet, catching his reflection in the mirror. He looked like hell.

Braxton turned on the cold faucet, letting the water blast into the basin before splashing handfuls of it onto his face, through his hair, and into his parched mouth. The icy coldness of the water made his scalp tingle, triggering yet another memory—the one about ghostly porcelain-white bodies swaying in the night.

A shiver racked through him as he struggled with the remnants of the night. Braxton couldn't shake the feeling that this particular hang-over was far from ordinary. The events of the night remained hazy, obscured by noise and the fog of intoxication, but the unnerving image of the swaying white figures clung to his thoughts like an uninvited guest refusing to leave.

Retching, Braxton went to all fours and thrust his head over the toi-let. He knew better than to throw up in the sink where things could get clogged up.

Again, this wasn't his first rodeo.

THREE HOURS LATER

Later that morning, Braxton was in the Jacksonville Saloon, an old-timey barroom with worn wooden flooring, comfy barstools, and no-frills table settings. As Braxton sipped his Jack and Coke, memories of his failed marriage stirred, sharpened by the sting of a botched legal career. He wallowed in the self-pity. Anything was better than the disturbing mem-ories from the previous night.

"All things considered," Braxton began, voice still a touch unsteady, "the litigation lottery could have been worse. But losing that case on the back of my failed marriage? That's a double blow." He paused, swallowing hard to keep himself together. Jason, the owner, watched as Braxton finished his drink, his hand poised over the ice box with a scooper.

Braxton downed the last of his drink and pushed the empty tumbler forward. "Double, but on the rocks please." Jason reached for a glass, his other hand diving into the ice box. "No need for a fresh glass," Braxton said, "just add ice to that one."

Jason shook his head, placing the new drink in front of Braxton with practiced ease.

"Do they teach ambidexterity at mixology school?" Braxton teased.

"Never took any mixology courses. I'm self-taught," Jason replied, wiping the counter. "You looked a bit rough this morning from last night. Everything okay?"

Braxton chuckled, nodding toward his beverage. "Rough night. Crazy dreams." He paused, taking a moment to shake off eerie remnants of the night seeping from his subconscious. The midmorning sun streamed through the windows of the empty barroom. Just dreams, he reassured himself. They were just dreams.

"Anyhow," Braxton continued, his voice a shade heavier, "the courtroom gives me anxiety now. Hard to step into a place that forced your bankruptcy after trying to uphold a kid's rights. Especially when you've sworn to protect its principles."

Jason leaned in, genuinely curious. "You never gave me the full story, so I want to get it straight. This kid drew a war scene at school and got arrested, right? You sued the school and lost. And then you, the lawyer, ended up paying the school district's legal fees?"

"Yeah, pretty much." Braxton sighed. "The sixth-grade teacher's name was on the drawing, so he was arrested for making criminal threats. I took the case thinking that free speech would prevail. The judge disagreed. So, under the Government Code, I was held jointly liable for the district's defense fees. Guess that's the price for challenging the system."

Jason shook his head, pouring another round. "That's harsh. I once faced a bogus fine for a minor liquor license issue, but nothing close to six figures."

Braxton managed a wry smile. "Well, bankruptcy had a silver lining. Cleared all credit card debts. But student loans? That loophole was shut tight. Got a bit of a break later from an unexpected settlement, so thought I'd change scenes. So, here I am in Jacksonville. And that's pretty much 'the rest of the story' as it were."

Jason refilled Braxton's glass, raising an eyebrow. "Jacksonville isn't exactly a hotspot for young single guys. You sure about this move?"

Braxton took a sip, relishing the burn. "Been visiting Ashland since high school. Love the Shakespeare Festival and Lithia Park. The cost of living is cheaper, and I found a good rental deal. Thought I'd give writing a shot here."

Jason nodded. "Not bad timing. We've been seeing more tourists. The music festival is drawing a crowd. Things will slow down in winter, but Medford's just fifteen minutes away. It's fine, so long as you stay away from terra incognita when conditions are bad."

Braxton's gaze grew distant. "Terra incognita, huh?" A small shudder jolted through his body as the words uttered out, an inexplicable sense of foreboding. Something stirred in him, a sense of dread. As if everything was about to collapse into darkness.

"Sorry, throwback term from my military days. Unfamiliar ground." Jason watched him, concern evident. "You alright?"

Braxton shook off the unease. "Yeah, all good. What's the damage?"

"For you? Ten bucks," Jason replied.

Braxton left three fives on the counter. "Thanks, might drop by later."

"You mean, like what you've been doing every night recently?" Jason grinned, calling out as Braxton reached the front door, "Need some water for the road?"

Braxton paused, the door half open, the bourbon soothing but the eerie sensation still present. "No, I'm good. Thanks."

He stepped out into the bright sunlight and started walking through Jacksonville's quaint nineteenth-century downtown center. With each step, Jason's "terra incognita" remark sunk deeper into his mind until the chanted words emerged, echoing like a dark mantra: *In Terra Lios.*

The unsettling memories began to flood back—the eerie plopping, the dead bodies hanging beneath the gnarled old oak, the haunting chant. The oppressive warmth amplified his terrifying recollections, making every moment feel suffocating. Desperate for some relief, Braxton slipped into the shade of an alley to take a quick bolt from his flask. But the refrain wouldn't leave him.

In Terra Lios, In Terra Lios. . .

It became an oppressive weight, pulling at the fringes of his sanity. He began to sweat coldly, his steps wavering as he neared home. The gag reflex threatened to overcome him.

Holding onto a tree for support, he tried to steady his racing heart. He gulped air, trying to push the chilling images and voices into the back of his mind. But as his vision began to tunnel and white, staticky stars danced around, the chanting grew louder and clearer in his head.

In Terra Lios, In Terra Lios. . .

His limbs felt like they were wading through thick mud, but he forced himself to move, driven by the need to escape the otherworldly voices and the macabre visions they conjured.

Reaching his front door felt like an eternity. His trembling hands struggled with the lock, and as the edges of his vision darkened, the world seemed to collapse around him, enveloping him within the realm of lost souls that were echoing from the abyss.

And then there was silence.

Regaining consciousness, Braxton found himself on the bathroom floor again. Confusion reigned. How had he gotten there? He went to the kitchen, gulped down water, and noticed the front door securely locked, with no recollection of having done it.

He didn't know what was going on, but he did know one thing: this called for a cold beer. Stat. The unsettling feelings were already shedding once he got to the fridge, attributing the strange episode to the bourbon and stress. But, deep down, he couldn't deny the power it held over him.

Fifteen minutes and two beers later, Braxton had mellowed. He read up online that "in terra lios" technically translates to "in the land of riots." But, just like *illegitimi non carborundum*, it isn't real Latin. He also found out that drunken hallucinations can happen to even the most seasoned of drinkers, particularly when hard liquor is involved. He closed his laptop, rubbed his eyes, and reclined on the couch.

"Just a weird day," he reassured himself as the eerie chanting faded into silence. "Just a weird day."

CHAPTER TWO

AN UNINTELLIGIBLE ECHO

WEDNESDAY, AUGUST 8, 11:03 AM

B raxton had already called it a day, and it wasn't even noon yet. Since moving to the Rogue Valley area, he had claimed he was on a sabbatical to write a novel and maybe delve into the Oregon Shakespeare Festival scene in Ashland. Sometimes, when feeling particularly bitter, he'd add a snarky comment about recapturing the dreams his parents had robbed him of (e.g., "That's great that you enjoy writing and acting, but what are you REALLY going to do with yourself?"). Deep down, though, he wasn't sure who he was fooling more: himself or everyone else.

His routine in the small cottage near downtown Jacksonville typically revolved around three activities: (a) staring at a blinking cursor, lost in thoughts; (b) aimlessly browsing Facebook and other websites; and (c) taking shots of whatever liquor was handy for purposes of "inspiration." On occasion, he would venture out for a walk or drive, attempting to jot down some coherent thoughts in his notepad, only to return and fall into the familiar pattern of opening a bottle, starting a Word document, and losing himself online.

He was about a third into the Bulleit bottle and two-thirds through the coffeepot, the cursor on his Word document blinking mockingly amidst a sea of white space. He closed the document to remind it who was boss, and browsed the internet. That's when a local news headline snagged his attention:

YOUNG FAMILY REPORTED MISSING

Aug. 8—Jacksonville, Ore. Jackson County law officials have issued an emergency missing persons report for Medford police officer Aaron Stewart (26), Elena ("Elle") Harris (28), and their child Hunter (3). Harris, owner of Insouciant Gallery, Stewart, and their child reportedly visited family and friends in Grants Pass on August 6 to plan their upcoming wedding. Neither has been seen since. Jackson County police authorities request the public's assistance in reporting any information concerning the family's potential where-abouts.

Bile surged into the back of Braxton's throat as recognition flickered in his mind. He had met her, Elle, right in front of her art gallery, next to the realtor's office where he had signed his lease. Her vibrant presence and the gallery's artistic pulse had briefly lifted his spirits that day.

Braxton's stomach twisted into knots as he reread the article, making sure that he hadn't missed anything. He reached for the bottle, downing at least a finger's worth before coming up for air. The article stirred the torrent of memories he wanted to erase—swaying silhouettes under a gnarled oak tree, their ghostlike forms disturbingly vivid. Whispers of "In Terra Lios" from that night echoed in his mind, as if resonating with the fate of the missing family.

But those were just weird post-blackout dreams you had, Braxton tried to convince himself, pouring a generous shot into his coffee. He gulped it down to the bitter dregs. "Dude, that's some crazy shit," he muttered, an attempt to brush off the growing sense of unease. While the alcohol provided a temporary haze, he felt the disquiet lingering in the fringe.

With a heavy sigh, Braxton filled his flask, the ritualistic act a temporary respite from his swirling thoughts. He picked up his notepad, its blank pages a stark reminder of his stalled aspirations, and headed out the door.

As he walked, the familiar path to the Saloon took on a different hue. Cringing, he hoped it wasn't due to yesterday's near-collapse-in-broad-daylight episode. He waved at a couple of neighbors talking on their front porch. Much to his relief, they smiled and waved back. But their faces seemed more distant, muted by the news of the family's disappearance.

Braxton found himself grappling with the reality of Elle's absence, a stark contrast to the brief, lively encounter he'd had with her some weeks back. It wasn't just another headline. It felt personal, as if he knew Elle before talking to her at the gallery—like he had glimpsed a part of her world before it abruptly and inexplicably vanished.

With each step toward the Saloon, Braxton's mind churned with unwanted introspection. He navigated the familiar route, but his mind was elsewhere, weighed down by the unsettling news. The rhythm of his footsteps metered his thoughts, grounding him in the present yet echoing with the undercurrents of his past.

Braxton's introspective bubble was burst by the bustling scene on the main street. Several news vans were parked along the street, and reporters were staking their claim. Cables snaked across the sidewalks. Bright lights and flashbulbs cut through the day. Camera crew members were wiping their brows in the midmorning heat, trying to capture every angle of the unfolding drama. Much to their chagrin, local police had already cordoned off Elle's gallery across the street from the Saloon, where an officer dutifully stood guard. Another officer was on traffic patrol, instructing a news van where to park.

Taking in the police presence, Braxton instinctively popped a mint strip into his mouth before reaching the Saloon. This was quite a departure from the Jacksonville he knew—a town marked by its slow-paced rhythm and understated charm. The intrusion felt almost surreal, as if the town had been thrust onto a stage it never sought, every resident looking over their shoulder, unwittingly trapped in a story they did not write.

"Dude, this is some *real shit* going down," Braxton mumbled, a sense of disbelief coloring his tone. In a bid to regain some composure, he adjusted his cap, ran a hand through his hair, and pushed open the door to the Saloon.

Inside, the atmosphere was abuzz. People huddled around the wooden tables, their conversations a mix of speculation and concern. Braxton caught fragments as he navigated his way to an open stool: "Could it be something sinister?" "What if they just ran off together?" "She seemed so grounded. . ." "That guy, he's the last person you'd suspect. . ." The theories were as varied as the patrons voicing them, each adding their own spin to the unfolding mystery.

Settling into his usual spot at the bar, Braxton picked up a menu. He glanced at his smartphone—no bars. The network was jammed.

"Hey, Braxton, what'll it be today?" Jason's familiar voice came from behind the bar, a welcome anchor in the midst of all the chaos.

"Any chance of Wi-Fi in here?" Braxton asked, raising his voice over the bar's hum. With a half-smile, he hoisted his phone above his head, as if to catch a signal from a distant satellite. "Maybe a stronger drink will help boost my signal," he quipped, "so how about a double Buffalo on the rocks."

"Keep it under your hat, but connect to the 'SLN' network," Jason said, his voice low as he reached into the ice machine. He gestured toward a sign behind the bar. "Password's our phone number, skip the area code." Placing Braxton's drink before him, he added, "How about a club sandwich with a free craft beer on the side?"

"I'll go with that. Good call," Braxton agreed, appreciating the suggestion. He took a hearty sip and swiveled in his stool to observe the room. It was a blend of the familiar and the unfamiliar: locals interspersed with business-casual types engrossed in their laptops and phones, intermittently stepping outside for private conversations. Outside, a Jackson County sheriff's vehicle prowled California Street, its methodical patrol a silent reminder of the town's unrest.

Braxton let out a low whistle as his gaze drifted over the eclectic mix in the Saloon and the frenzied scene outside. *Dude,* he thought while entering the Wi-Fi credentials, *this is some seriously real shit going down.*

With his phone now connected, he paused, his finger hovering over the screen. He had come to Oregon to get away from the chaos, to find some semblance of peace. Yet here he was, on the brink of diving back into the kind of turmoil he sought to avoid. Steeling himself with another bolt of liquid courage, he resolved to face whatever lay behind that first search result.

MISSING FAMILY WELL KNOWN TO COMMUNITY

Aug. 8—Jacksonville, Ore. Intensified search efforts are underway for Medford police officer Aaron Stewart (26), Elena "Elle" Harris (28), and their son Hunter (3), reported missing since the early hours of August 8.

Elle Harris, revered in Jacksonville as an accomplished artist and philanthropist, owns Insouciant gallery. Her family's roots trace back to the early days of the town's founding. Since opening her gallery in 2007, Harris has been instrumental in showcasing the talents of Rogue Valley artists and has actively supported local art and educational initiatives, particularly in the wake of the 2008 economic downturn.

Aaron Stewart, serving as a detective with the Medford Police Department since 2010, is a respected figure in the legal community known for his integrity and dedication. Following his military service in Iraq and Afghanistan, Stewart's law enforcement career began in 2007 as a bailiff for the Jackson County Circuit Court. While the Medford PD has yet to issue a formal statement, sources close to the department describe Stewart as a model officer deeply committed to community service.

The family, last seen on August 6 in Grants Pass while preparing for their upcoming August 11 wedding, disappeared under mysterious circumstances. Their vehicle, a dark-blue 2011 Audi Q5 SUV, was noted leaving the area around 9:30 PM. Statewide alerts have been issued, with law enforcement urging the public to come forward with any information that might aid in the family's location.

A waitress emerged from the small back kitchen and served Braxton's order. "*Bon appétit,*" she said before grabbing a water pitcher from behind the bar. She disappeared into the crowded dining area before Braxton could thank her.

Settling in, he placed his phone on the bar, the screen lighting up with a photo from the news article. He immediately recognized Elle standing next to Aaron at some fancy event, both of them smiling, clearly in love. They were a very attractive couple.

She was petite and well proportioned, with wavy, almost jet-black hair that framed an alabaster complexion, large bright-green eyes, and high cheekbones that narrowed into a full mouth and a pointed chin. Elle's artistic flair, evident even in a still photo, reminded Braxton of the passion he'd once had for the arts as a youth, now buried under layers of law school brainwashing and unfulfilled ambitions.

Aaron was the gold standard of rugged Pacific Northwest good looks. Tall, strong chin, and a wiry build, with brown hair and inquisitive hazel eyes. Just by looking at him, Braxton could tell that (a) the guy was no dummy and (b) he could handle himself if things went sidewise.

He took a bite of the sandwich. Like most food served in the area, it was pretty damn good. After a few more bites, the room's atmosphere shifted. Phones buzzed and conversations hushed as Jason, fumbling slightly, switched the TV from a baseball game to a news broadcast. "Breaking News" flashed across the screen, the anchor's words scrolling below his canary-yellow blue-striped tie in urgent subtitles.

Turning, Braxton absorbed the scene: patrons' eyes locked on the TV, expressions ranging from concern to disbelief. The reporters outside set up their cameras under the hot sun, the street now a flurry of activity and anticipation. The sudden overlap of the broader world into the Saloon's cocoon became overwhelming. He needed a smoke. ASAP.

"Can you keep an eye on this?" he asked Jason, gesturing toward his half-finished meal and handing over his debit card. "Need to step out for a bit." Jason, still half-focused on the broadcast, nodded in understanding. Braxton drained the last of his beer and made his way outside, seeking a momentary refuge from the town's collective anxiety, yet feeling an inexplicable pull toward the very unrest he aimed to avoid.

"Thank you, Dan," a lively young Asian reporter in a bright jacket said into her microphone. "We're live in downtown Jacksonville, covering the search for Medford police detective Aaron Stewart, artist Elle Harris, and their young son Hunter. Breaking news just in: Some eighty miles south of us, California Highway Patrol has located a dark-blue 2011 Audi SUV in Weed, California, abandoned in a vacant lot. Details are scarce, but it matches the description of the family's vehicle."

Braxton walked past the reporter, her heavily applied makeup a vivid touch of Technicolor against the seriousness of her report. He continued along, listening to the array of journalists broadcasting their pieces to the cameras.

A seasoned mustachioed reporter, his wool suit ill-suited for the heat, added, "No word yet on federal involvement. All we know is the family's car has been located. The town clings to hope for their safe return."

A slender, bottle-blond reporter added, "Sources report that the young family were regarded as local royalty in the community." Braxton felt a wave of disgust. Shaking his head, he turned down the next street.

Seeking solitude, Braxton found a quieter spot, took a discreet swig from his flask, and lit a cigarette. Fragmented catchphrases like "tragedy" and "thoughts and prayers" filtered through the cacophony until merging into an unintelligible echo fading into the backdrop of Jacksonville's time-worn brick facades.

He frowned and inhaled deeply from his cigarette, feeling a mix of disdain and resignation at how quickly the news seemed to transform from informative reporting into a ratings-driven spectacle. With a sigh, Braxton resumed his walk, choosing a street that ran parallel to the media frenzy.

After snubbing out his smoke and tossing it into a nearby trash can, it dawned on him how quick he was to throw shade on the reporters. No need to be judgy. They were just doing their job. And it really *was* a tragic story. The missing family seemed like wonderful people. He knew their type, was friends with their type, the kind of smart, beautiful people that he wished he could be like, but couldn't really resent because they were genuinely cool, nice people.

With these thoughts swirling in his head, Braxton snuck another pull from his flask as he headed back toward the bar. However, the alcohol only seemed to intensify the uneasy sensation in his stomach. He dismissed it as hunger and quickened his steps, eager to return to his meal and the familiar confines of the Saloon.

As Braxton returned to his barstool, he was enveloped by the bar's typical, more relaxed atmosphere. The clamor of the day's events had receded, leaving behind the low murmur of conversation and the sound of the baseball game playing on the TV. The familiar, comforting smells of aged wood and the remnants of spilt beer mixed with the faint notes of whiskey greeted him. The bar's worn dark wood, polished over the years, shone softly under the dim, inviting light of vintage filament bulbs. The media crowd, their intense energy dissipated, were quietly settling their tabs, their day's work merging into the fabric of the Saloon's daily life.

Jason, ever the attentive bartender, offered a nod toward the taps. "How about a complimentary craft beer?" he suggested, presenting a selection from a local brewery. Braxton appreciated the gesture; it was small things like this that made the Saloon feel like more than just a bar.

"That sounds perfect," Braxton agreed, comfortably easing back into his seat. "And let's add a Jameson on the rocks to accompany those hops. Anyway, not sure which reporter you watched, but I had NO idea that they caked on so much makeup! Nevertheless, I prolly wouldn't kick that younger one out of bed." Jason's response was a smile tempered with a discreet hand motion, reminding Braxton to keep it down a notch.

Realizing his voice might have carried, Braxton quickly lowered his volume. "Oh, shit, inside voice. My bad." A quick glance around confirmed his remark hadn't disturbed the other patrons, who seemed engrossed in their own conversations.

"Dude, seriously," Braxton continued in a softer tone, "that couple seem like really decent people. Now that I think of it, I met Elle briefly right over there. By that realtor's office when I secured my place. We chatted a bit. Really chill and down to earth. She went to art school in San Francisco, right?"

Jason's nod came with a tinge of nostalgia. "Yeah, you can imagine how many guys got all butthurt when she and Aaron hooked up. But I was nothing but happy for them. The guy she was with before was sort of infamous for being full of himself. But you know," he said, casting a glance around the bar and lowering his voice, "that's not uncommon for the legacy families around here. As for Aaron, the dude is rock-solid, unflappable, no ego. Deadpan sense of humor. You'd like him. And I know for a fact that he can handle himself. He was a corpsman with Marine Recon. Definitely the kind of guy you want by your side if shit ever hits the fan."

Braxton's interest was piqued as Jason shared his insights. "Recon, huh?" he responded with a low whistle of respect. "That's like Marine Corps special forces, right?"

"Right," Jason confirmed with a nod. "Ballsy crew to roll with, that's for sure. Believe it or not, I served as an Army Ranger for a bit before an injury shifted me to Military Police. During my MP time in the Bosnian War, I heard all sorts of wild stories about covert operations from my Ranger buddies—which, by the way, never happened. So, I can only imagine what Aaron dealt with over in Iraq and Afghanistan."

Braxton nodded in recognition of Jason's experiences. "No doubt. And hey, thanks for your service."

Jason flashed an appreciative smile. "Thanks, Braxton. Luckily, I didn't see as much direct action as some of the others in our little ragtag Rogue River vet group. We often get together for rafting and fishing trips. That's how I got to know Aaron. There's something about sharing stories over a few beers after a long day on the river. And you wouldn't believe what some of those guys went through. Aaron wouldn't share much, but I could tell— he had this edge to him. It seemed like he had a death wish while shooting the rapids. Then he started chilling out after meeting Elle. Now everyone wants to be in his raft." A light chuckle escaped him as he reminisced. "Anyhow, that's a little backstory for ya. I know you're just peering in on this from the periphery, but this is kind of a big deal. For all of us."

Braxton took in the information, his view of the tragedy deepening. "Sounds like a solid guy," he mused while reflecting on his own situation. "And here I am, the shady, dejected outcast who moves into town within weeks of the"—noting the malfunction in his brain-to-mouth filter, he switched tracks mid-sentence—"well at least you know I've been around here the last few nights!"

Jason chuckled at the comment, shaking his head in amusement as he went back to managing the cash register.

Braxton idly dipped a few fries, now at room temperature, into the custom aioli blend and popped them into his mouth. Despite losing their initial heat, they retained a satisfying crunch and were surprisingly fla-vorful with the dip. With a beer in one hand and a sated appetite, he turned his chair to face the front window.

The scene outside had quieted down. The reporters had retreated to their vans, and the police officer who had been stationed outside Elle's gallery was no longer there. Glancing at the clock, Braxton noted it was past noon; the sun was high in the sky, casting its midday glow.

Sitting there, Braxton's mind wandered. He thought back to his evenings at the Saloon since he'd moved to town. Initially, he had tried the tavern down the street, but it hadn't felt right. The Saloon, with its authentic vibe and more reasonable prices, suited him better, especially given his tight budget. He distinctly remembered being here on Monday night, but the details of how he got home remained blurry.

Memories surfaced of lively chats and laughter with his new cadre of drinking buddies. He remembered ordering mineral water toward the end of the night, maintaining the appearance of moderation while secretly taking swigs from his flask in the restroom. He was sure he had left the Saloon without incident, Jason's appreciative nod for the generous tip still clear in his memory.

Then his recollections took a darker turn. Fragmented images haunted by eerie voices and unsettling visions before waking up in his bathroom with bruises, vomit breath, and a massive hangover attesting to a night gone bad.

"How things looking?" Jason asked, snapping Braxton back into reality. "If you liked that IPA, I can recommend something else along those lines." Braxton, feeling the weight of the day, decided it was time to wrap things up.

"Rain check that, *por favor*. Let's settle up," he said, reaching for his wallet. A moment of panic set in as he noticed his debit card missing, but he quickly remembered handing it over to Jason. "Ah, right," he said, masking his brief lapse, "wanted to make sure I had enough cash for your tip. You know, to give you some liberty in your income-reporting duties and what-not. Run the card, please."

Jason chuckled, handing back the card and receipt. "Fuckin' Braxton. Deny it all you want, but you are SUCH the lawyer," he jabbed.

Braxton grinned, adding an extra five-dollar tip to the already discounted bill. "Thanks, man. Might drop by later," he said, folding the receipt into his overstuffed wallet. "And I'll keep this for my own expense-reporting purposes."

Feeling the buzz, Braxton stepped out into the warm embrace of the afternoon sun. He popped a mint strip, feeling his mouth tingle as his gaze swept over the street. The prowling sheriff's vehicle was shepherding the last of the news vans along California Street, while police officers at key intersections directed the flow of traffic, maintaining a semblance of order amidst the day's unexpected developments.

"Serious, serious shit," Braxton thought out loud. Realizing that talking to himself in front of a bar wasn't the best of looks, he pivoted left and headed home.

The off-putting feeling from earlier had settled somewhat. The alcohol had loosened his movements, and the heat of the day accelerated his pace, a welcome distraction from the lingering effects of his hangover. His strides took him past old town into a blend of architectural styles, a contrast that mirrored the day's events—a mix of the old and the new, the expected and the unexpected.

Ambling along, Braxton took a left turn and continued for a couple of blocks until he reached a shopping center. The center was an eclectic mix of concrete, brick, and logs, its facade an attempted homage to the town's rustic aesthetic. Finding a spot where the architectural styles from the nineteenth and twentieth centuries merged in an uneasy alliance, Braxton pulled out a cigarette. He lit it, the flame briefly illuminating his face in the shadow of the building. Leaning against the cool shade, he took that first long drag, the smoke curling into the air. A wave of relief washed over him as the nicotine hit his system, easing the tension in his shoulders and allowing a momentary escape from the whirlwind of thoughts and emotions that had accompanied the day's revelations. In that instant, with the weight of the day lifted, Braxton found a brief respite in the simple act of smoking, standing at the crossroads of the town's architectural history.

As the comfort of the smoke filled his lungs, Braxton's attention naturally shifted from the ember of his cigarette to the life unfolding before him at the shopping center. The front parking lot was mostly vacant. Braxton watched as a middle-aged woman in a Lexus maneuvered out of the space, her attention divided between the phone pressed to her ear and the task of driving. Nearby, a young mother and her son, hand in hand, made their way from the grocery store. The child held a banana in his other hand, beaming with pride about his adult duty as his mom cradled two heavily laden shopping bags against her chest.

An elderly man stepped out of the hardware store, carefully inspecting an item wrapped in clear plastic. He turned it over in his hands, considering it from every angle, before placing it back in his bag and moving on. This slice of everyday life brought a soothing touch of normalcy to Braxton's surroundings, a welcome relief from the earlier chaos of the day.

As the mother and her young son made their way to their SUV, still holding hands, the tranquil scene abruptly shifted. Two unmarked Crown Victorias sped in, disregarding the speed bumps. They screeched to a stop, effectively encircling the mother and son. A detective in plain clothes stepped out of the first vehicle, quickly flashing his badge to the surprised pair. His partner exited the other car, holding a radio, ready for communication.

The little boy came to attention and saluted the detectives with his free hand, the banana obscuring most of his face.

Captivated by the scene, Braxton felt the sear of his cigarette as it burned down to his fingers. He flicked the butt to the ground, stamping it out underfoot. Lighting another, he mused to himself that a bag of popcorn would be the perfect accompaniment to the unexpected drama unfolding before him.

The woman put her purse on the hood of the unmarked car and pulled out her wallet. She handed her license over, still taken aback.

The other detective approached, trying to keep a straight face as the child did an about-face, puffed up his chest, and banana-saluted him as well. After a brief exchange, the second detective took the license and walked back to his car to relay the information.

Upon his return, the first detective assisted the woman with her groceries, placing them in her SUV as she remotely unlocked it. He leaned in, took a few deep sniffs, and inspected the interior cabin—a clever, if not sly, way to check out her car without explicit permission. As the detective stepped back from his sneaky little looky-loo, the little boy, no longer saluting, stood at ease, banana now hidden behind his back.

Watching the scene, Braxton pondered the nature of this stop. She had a decent SUV, but it was several years old and by no means flashy. Their attire was unremarkable, and there was no evident sign of distress or intoxication. So that ruled out drug dealing.

A sudden realization zinged through his head. If he wasn't preoccupied with lighting another cigarette, he might have dramatically smacked his forehead once it dawned on him—the little boy might be the missing Hunter. From his vantage point, it was hard to be certain, but the resemblance to the photos he had seen online was uncanny.

Just then, the boy snapped to attention again, saluting as a black Suburban screeched to a halt behind the SUV. The driver remained at the wheel as two agents, embodying the classic FBI image with their sleek suits and slick shades, stepped out with an air of authority. They confidently approached the group, badges prominently displayed, taking charge of the situation.

A brief yet intense conversation ensued between the agents and the detectives. The mother and child, after a few words with the agents, were ushered into the backseat of the Suburban. The vehicle, along with the detectives' cars, departed as swiftly as they had arrived, leaving a wake of unanswered questions.

Looks like the Feds are involved, Braxton surmised, the thought merely skimming the surface of his concerns. He finished off his flask with a practiced tilt, the last drops a brief respite in the midst of the day's dramatic events. Gathering his cigarette butts, he crossed the street, his mind more occupied with the scenes he'd witnessed than with any reflections on his habits. His need to replenish his flask was just another part of the day, as routine as the cigarettes he smoked.

Stepping into the liquor store, the familiar chime of the door greeted him like the opening note of a well-rehearsed song. The cool air inside, laced with the rich, heady aroma of distilled spirits, enveloped him like a comforting shroud. This was a place where worries could be temporarily set aside, where the pervasive scent of alcohol promised oblivion, offering to momentarily erase the haunting images and the tight knot of tension ensnaring his thoughts.

Armed with a bottle in hand, Braxton's thoughts turned to the unfolding drama around him. The day's events, including the FBI's dramatic full-on rendition, were a clear indication that there were deeper, more complex layers to the story yet to be revealed. Jittering from both nicotine and adrenaline, Braxton felt a compelling urge for another drink, his mind a whirlwind of anticipation and trepidation, simultaneously eager and apprehensive about what revelations tomorrow might bring.

CHAPTER THREE

SHE LOOKS REALLY FAMILIAR

THURSDAY, AUGUST 9, 8:56 AM

Sipping his morning coffee, Braxton scrolled through the latest news on his laptop. By the second day, the national media had latched onto the story of the missing family. The FBI, now leading the investigation, underscored the seriousness of the situation. Teams of volunteers, aided by helicopters equipped with infrared technology, methodically searched the vast wilderness from Grants Pass to California's Shasta region. But amidst the escalating concern, a faint yet persistent thread of optimism glimmered.

Given Elle's family's considerable wealth, kidnapping emerged as the leading theory. The idea was that some bad actors pretended their car broke down, or some other ruse, to rob a good Samaritan. But upon being recognized, they were taken captive for a hefty ransom. However, Aaron's combat expertise made it equally plausible that the family had evaded their captors and either lost their bearings or were still hiding from their would-be abductors. Hopes remained high. Aaron was an elite military veteran with a proven record of surviving hostile environments. And Elle, equally formidable in her own right, also had a history of resilience.

Braxton read on about Elle's past environmental activism—a point of contention within her family. During her college years, she'd been arrested for staging protests at old-growth logging sites. Her most notable act was occupying a treehouse for an astounding six weeks, the last two of which while subsisting on rainwater and bugs, until being airlifted to the nearest hospital for urgent medical care.

After absorbing the news, Braxton closed his laptop and stood up to stretch. He'd been trying to ease off the morning sauce, especially after noticing his expanding waistline. Resolved to reverse this, he decided to get back to his exercise regimen starting today.

Before becoming a day drinker, Braxton had once aimed high, applying to join the FBI. He had reached the final stage of testing but was ultimately rejected, primarily due to his lack of combat and law enforcement experience. Among the other candidates, only one other lawyer had made it that far, a congenial woman already employed as an analyst at the bureau. Despite his qualifications, Braxton knew his chances were slim, so the rejection, although disappointing, wasn't a shock.

While he didn't get the job, he did get in shape. And his legal career had started to blossom, financially speaking, softening the blow of the rejection. Then came the six-figure judgment, total bankruptcy, and wholesale loss of faith in a system to which he was bound by nondischargeable student debt.

Braxton began with some warm-up crunches and push-ups in his living room. Two years ago, he could knock out sixty crunches a minute for a solid three minutes. Aware of his current limits, though, he let his count drift and his mind wander.

His thoughts meandered back to that time in his life—the period leading to the amicable divorce from his wife. When his law practice began attracting more clients who actually paid for his all-nighters. Then all his hard-earned success, the progress and recognition, was simply wiped away with a single stroke of a judge's pen.

Some memories from that era were crystal clear, while others were murky. He recalled days filled with confusion, not understanding why his wife was upset until she tearfully recounted the hurtful things he had said the night before. His initial denials crumbling as he realized his memory had betrayed him again, leading to tearful apologies and silent gratitude that his blackout alter ego hadn't turned violent.

The beep of his watch snapped Braxton back to the present. He rolled onto his haunches, pausing for a moment before stepping outside. The burn in his chest and stomach from the exercise dulled the remnants of his hangover, and a few extra stretches added to the relief. He began jogging at a leisurely pace, heading toward Britt Gardens, about three-quarters of a mile away.

The morning air was a pleasant seventy degrees, refreshed by a cool breeze that had swept away the early drizzle. As his legs warmed up, Braxton increased his pace, feeling a sense of contentment. His breath was steady, and his knees were holding up well. He ran down his street, took a left onto North Third, and soon reached the main street, where he observed dozens of newspeople setting up shop along the sidewalk.

He turned right onto West Main, then left onto South Oregon, and finally right onto Fir Street, where the road began to incline toward the forested trailhead. At the gravel parking lot, Braxton finished his water and tossed it into the recycling bin posted at the trail base.

This is good, he thought, starting up the trail. *I should do this more often.* But after a quarter mile of uphill jogging, he had to slow to a near walk, gasping for breath. *No need to overdo it*, he reminded himself as his heart pounded in his ears.

Braxton continued at a more manageable pace for another half mile until he reached Panorama Point. There, he caught his breath and admired the stunning view: the eastern Siskiyou Mountains rose majestically behind the homes nestled along Roxy Peak's base, all set against the dramatic backdrop of Mount McLoughlin's steep granite peak.

The way back down was easier, though he had to concentrate on his footing and couldn't enjoy the view as much. Upon reaching the trail base, Braxton felt a surge of renewed energy. He embraced this second wind and quickened his stride for the final stretch back home.

Jacksonville's streets buzzed with activity due to the media presence. Braxton jogged along California Street, casually waving at Jason, who was unlocking the Saloon for the day. Reaching his neighborhood streets, Braxton recited the NATO phonetic alphabet to keep himself distracted from his burning lungs and exploding eardrums.

By the time he reached "Mike November," his mind drifted to other memories from the recent past. Like waking up at a friend's house next to a girl he'd known since high school, with no memory of how he ended up in her bed, and how grateful he was to hear that blackout-Braxton wasn't a rapist and just wanted to spoon.

Then his thoughts inevitably veered back to the unsettling events of that eerie night. The voices chanting "In Terra Lios," and the harrowing sight of ghostly figures hanging beneath the tree. The memory was like a cold shadow over his mind, reminding him of the night's terrifying uncertainty and his own vulnerability during such blackouts. This time around, he couldn't shake the feeling that his blackout alter ego might have landed him in some serious trouble.

Determined to push away these haunting thoughts, Braxton resumed with the phonetic alphabet. "Oscar! Papa! Quebec! Romeo!" he called out loud, each syllable punctuating his strides. The rhythmic recitation helped crowd out the dark memories, allowing him to focus on the present moment. He increased his pace, sprinting the last two hundred yards, feeling the rush of air and the steady beat of his heart as he reached his driveway.

Once inside, Braxton downed a glass of water, then took a few swigs from the Wild Turkey bottle left over from the night before. Holding the bottle, he made his way to the bathroom to prepare for the day.

Two hours later, he sat staring at a blinking cursor, unable to shake his writer's block despite his stash of liquor, energy drinks, and snacks. Admitting defeat, Braxton logged onto Facebook instead.

The Baader–Meinhof phenomenon seemed at play as Braxton thought about his ex-wife, only to find a message from her pop up with the quirky title, "What's up, chicken butt?"

Ironically, their relationship had actually improved post-divorce. After more than a decade together, and with their diverging views on children becoming clear, they had both come to realize that their marriage was more about meeting societal expectations than genuine compatibility.

The divorce was both amicable and swift, with no financial obligations exchanged between Braxton and Erika. Yet, despite the dissolution being as agreeable as possible, Braxton couldn't shake off a deep-seated feeling of failure. This feeling only intensified after the harsh legal judgment led him into a downward spiral of bankruptcy and binge drinking.

He shuttered his small practice, turning to full-time drinking while managing to work part-time legal jobs. Financially, he was just getting by, until a stroke of luck in the form of a five-figure referral fee paved the way to Jacksonville.

Despite Braxton's own disillusionment with the legal profession, Erika continued her work as a paralegal in the Bay Area, while also studying for the LSAT. Her message to Braxton was light-hearted yet sincere.

"Hey," it began, "I trust you're on your way to writing the next 'great American novel' up there ;). Same old stuff down here. Thanks for the LSAT course help, by the way. The test is six weeks away, and the pressure is mounting, but I'm hanging in there. Just wanted to express my gratitude again. Oh, and about that missing family in the news—crazy stuff! The woman looks so familiar. Didn't we meet her a few times at that bar near your law school? The artsy one who dated that Spanish bartender for a hot second? Or am I mixing her up with someone else? Anyway, just checking in, hope all's well with you."

Braxton nearly choked on his bourbon, forcing it down with a deep, steadying gulp. He took a moment to gather his thoughts, wrestling with the urge to reveal everything—the blackout, the disturbing visions, even their possible link to the missing family. But caution prevailed; he understood that venturing into those dark memories was both risky and unwise. Opting for a more light and casual tone, he began typing his response.

"Holy shit! I think you're onto something, Erika! Her look was different back then, but yeah, that's definitely her. We chatted last month; she mentioned SF and her art school days, but I totally missed the connection. But in all fairness, that bartender was seeing like three girls at the same time, so you gotta cut me some slack there :P No worries about the LSAT class. Just don't hold it against me later! lol. Thanks for checking in. Hope all's good with you too. :-)"

As soon as Braxton hit Send, an epiphany struck him. The reason Elle had seemed familiar during their chat last month became clear—their brief encounters from the past had unconsciously stayed with him. Shaking his head in a mix of disbelief and newfound understanding, he took another swig of bourbon. Deciding not to wade further into his murky troubled thoughts, he poured the last of the whiskey into his flask and tucked it into his cargo shorts, ready for a change of scenery.

"Smells like a frickin' distillery in here," Braxton grumbled, navigating around the well-worn furniture that had come with the cottage. Each piece told a story of previous tenants, from the faded comfortable sofa in the living room to the sturdy, scratched kitchen table that had seen better days. As he collected the empty bottles scattered across these surfaces, he reflected on the lived-in feel of the place, which somehow made his own existence feel even more transient, more impermanent.

Yanking a bin from under the sink—its exterior adorned with peeling stickers from bygone local festivals—he dumped the bottles into it. The bin quickly overfilled, the glass clinking together in a chorus that felt oddly accusatory in the quiet of his home. With a resigned sigh, he hauled it outside to the recycling cart, wincing as the noise of clattering bottles echoed through the quiet neighborhood.

SEVERAL HOURS LATER

By four o'clock, the Saloon was buzzing with anticipation over a scheduled press conference regarding the missing family. Online, speculation about new developments in the case was rampant.

Nursing his sore muscles with a stiff Michter's Rye, Braxton blended into the mix of locals, reporters, bloggers, and tourists. All eyes were on the wide-screen TV, where the "BREAKING NEWS" logo flashed, signaling the start of live coverage.

Jason, sensing the room's focus, turned up the volume. The broadcast shifted to a live exterior shot of the Medford Police Department. A group of both uniformed and plainclothes law enforcement officials gathered, setting a somber tone. The chatter in the Saloon quieted down as a burly police chief with salt-and-pepper hair approached a lectern, marked with the City of Medford seal.

"Hello, everyone," the chief began, his voice weary, "and thank you for your patience. While we can't discuss the specifics of our ongoing investigation, I can confirm our collaboration with the FBI on the case of Aaron Stewart, his fiancée Elle Harris, and their child."

Murmurs and a flurry of excited whispers rippled through the crowd, punctuated by the sound of news alerts from various devices. "Holy shit," someone mumbled under their breath, "Jesus Christ," another voice whispered in awe. Braxton's gaze drifted to the window, where he saw reporters scrambling to set up for their post-announcement coverage.

He turned his attention back to the TV. "Let me hand this over to Edward Richter," the chief continued, "who is the special agent in charge of the investigation." The chief stepped back as the lean fifty-something white-haired agent made his appearance from stage left.

With his gaunt, authoritative presence and striking white hair, he looked perfectly cast as the guy who would play the special agent in charge (SAIC) in a movie. The chief offered a supportive pat before stepping aside, joining the other uniformed officials to the right of the stage.

"Thank you, chief," Richter commenced, his voice carrying a polished, matter-of-fact tenor tinged with a northeastern accent. "As stated by my colleague, we're not at liberty to share all the details at this stage. Our foremost priority is to respect the privacy of the families involved and maintain the integrity of our investigation."

Braxton's attention meandered to the set of suited officials standing to the left of the stage, even recognizing the two FBI agents from yesterday's shopping center incident, until landing on a female agent who looked around his age. She looked kind of irritated, and he could have sworn she subtly rolled her eyes before Richter went on.

"So," Richter said, "we have a formal statement that I will provide in a moment, and then I'll hand this back over to Chief Williams."

A hush fell over the Saloon. SAIC Richter methodically smoothed the prepared paper statement on the lectern, soaking in the moment before clearing his throat.

"At approximately 0617 PDT this morning, local authorities in Weed, California, responded to a call about an unaccompanied male child on North Weed Boulevard," SAIC Richter announced, his voice smooth and confident, relishing the gravity of the moment. "The minor child was disoriented but healthy, and after welfare services' clearance, he was brought to a medical center in Medford, Oregon."

Richter's gaze, icy blue and sharp, captured the camera's attention. "We can officially confirm that the child is Hunter Harris." His announcement unleashed a maelstrom of relief, confusion, and a chorus of murmurs throughout the Saloon.

Caught in this storm of reactions, Braxton wrestled with the news. His own mixed feelings—a sense of relief for Hunter, but deep-seated unease over the absence of his parents—became entangled with the restlessness of the female agent standing behind Richter. Her impatience, silently echoing the bar's tumult, made it too difficult for Braxton to absorb the rest of Richter's statement.

MOMENTS EARLIER

At half-past three that afternoon, Special Agent Riley McAvoy found herself caught between frustration with SAIC Richter for arranging a 4:00 PM press conference and self-irritation for not anticipating it. She was deep in a crucial conversation with Aaron Stewart's mother when the announcement came. Hastily confirming a follow-up interview and accounting for the time difference in Missouri, McAvoy swore under her breath and hurried to gather her things.

Richter, while very smart and capable, had a penchant for prioritizing media presence and his own image in high-profile cases, often at the cost of sensitivity toward the victims' families. It would also lead to some brash decision-making. McAvoy had lost count of how many times she had to clean up after his missteps, the most recent one involving an unwarranted detention of a young mother and son who had nothing to do with the case.

Despite his flaws, Richter had a knack for reinforcing the bureau's polished image, assembling strong teams, and leveraging his agents' skills effectively. McAvoy, preferring a more discreet approach, often found herself at odds with his camera-focused methods.

Climbing into a black Suburban with four other agents, McAvoy headed toward the police station a few miles away. In the vanity mirror, she tied her light brown hair into a ponytail, noting the fatigue reflected in her bloodshot eyes. She had been burning the midnight oil, and it showed. With the relentless schedule, she hadn't removed her contact lenses since leaving Portland. She slipped on her sunglasses, offering some respite from the glaring afternoon sun as they sped to their destination.

"Lose the shades, McAvoy," Richter's sharp voice cut through the din as she joined the other agents on the press stage. She complied, revealing her tired, blue-green eyes rimmed with red.

"You smoke some contraband on the way here?" Richter's deadpan query was met with a restrained smile from McAvoy. "Ditch the contacts when you're pulling all-nighters," he added with a small wink. McAvoy nodded, adjusting her blazer as she moved to her position on stage.

After Richter's comments about respecting the victims' families, McAvoy found herself rolling her eyes, a reflex she couldn't suppress in time. She straightened up and squinted, internally grumbling about Richter's rule against sunglasses during press events and her own discomfort with being in the media spotlight rather than actively working the case.

By 5:30 PM, when McAvoy got back to the resident agency office bustling with technicians and support staff, her eyes felt like they were ablaze. She removed her contact lenses and applied some saline solution to soothe them.

After dabbing away the residual drops and checking her mascara in the mirror, she put on her wire-framed glasses. Heading out the back exit, she felt the burning in her eyes simmer down to a more tolerable level. Climbing into her personal vehicle, she set off toward Jacksonville, her mind shifting to the tasks ahead.

A FEW HOURS LATER

Braxton leaned against the bar at the Saloon, stretching his legs and observing the dwindling dinner crowd. "Looks like you're left with the hard-core crew here, Jason," he commented. The kitchen had stopped taking orders, and only a few tables remained occupied. At the far end of the bar, two older locals were deep in conversation over their drinks.

There was a subtle shift in the atmosphere as a pair of middle-aged locals entered, holding the door for a professionally dressed woman behind them. The men joined their companions at the far end of the bar, and Jason began pouring PBR drafts for the group.

The woman, looking a bit out of place, took a seat near Braxton. She pulled out her Blackberry and, after briefly massaging the bridge of her nose, placed her glasses on the bar.

Jason was quick to attend to her. "What's your well vodka?" she asked, putting her glasses back on. After a brief pause, she added, "Actually, just make it an Absolut vodka martini. Very dry, with a twist, no olives, please." As Jason set about crafting her drink with practiced ease, the woman turned her attention back to her phone, scrolling through its contents.

Braxton couldn't help but be intrigued. He estimated her height to be around five-nine, with a lean, athletic build. Her face was elegant, marked by high cheekbones and a distinctive long nose that lent character to her otherwise symmetrical features. Her hair, worn loose, cascaded just past her shoulders. He averted his gaze as she began to stretch and survey the room.

Lost in thought, Braxton peered into his glass, watching the interplay of light with the ice and bourbon. With a swirl of his drink, he took a small sip. His movement caught her attention, and she turned to him, offering a brief smile before refocusing on her phone.

When Jason placed her martini on the bar, she paused to take a small sip, elegantly swirling the glass by its stem. Braxton's eyes drifted to her hand, noting the absence of any jewelry. Seizing the moment, he spoke up as she took another sip. "You're FBI, right?"

Her reaction was unexpected—a snort followed by a chuckle. "No, not even close. I'm a pharmaceutical rep. Just needed a break from a convention in Medford. But you're not the first to make that guess," she replied, adjusting her glasses. "It's the glasses, isn't it? Left my contacts back at the hotel."

Braxton played along, hiding his surprise. "That was my second guess. And yeah, the glasses. They're unique, not your typical drug rep look."

She laughed. "You'd be surprised. Geek chic is in. So, are you in the industry?"

"No, but my folks are," Braxton replied, sidestepping. "Anything exciting? I mean, like Viagra or Cialis? Or something more obscure?"

"The latter. Our latest is for macular degeneration, but," she leaned in conspiratorially, "off the record, it's being pitched for diabetic retinopathy too."

"Ah," he said, "well, your secret's safe with me." Braxton finished his beverage and sought out Jason who was standing by the locals. "¡Uno más, por favor!" he ordered once within earshot.

"How about you?" she asked. "You live here or just visiting?"

"I guess a bit of both. Kind of on a sabbatical, you could say."

"Oh?"

"It's a bit of a long story," he replied with a hint of evasion. "But I just moved up here. Came up from the California North Bay Area. You know, wine country?" he pointed his index finger upward and swirled it in a circle as if to say "ooh la la."

"Sure," she nodded. "I was in the Napa Valley a few months ago for a bachelorette party. Beautiful area. So, do you work in the wine industry?"

"Well, sort of incidentally," Braxton responded. "You know, this area has a similar vibe to Napa's, albeit on a larger scale and with fewer vineyards. Not sure how much you know about each place, but the cities are kind of the same too. I mean, you have Medford and Napa, which are the most populous towns but not really tourist hotspots. Then there's Ashland, akin to Napa's St. Helena—picturesque, clean, and touristy. And Jacksonville? It's got a Calistoga-like quaintness," he mused before trailing off.

Braxton realized he was a bit out of practice with spontaneous bar conversations. His post-divorce dating life, arranged largely online, allowed him to finesse his attorney persona ahead of time. Here, face-to-face with an attractive, apparently single woman, he felt his current backstory lacked substance. He wasn't keen on making something up, knowing that any drunken slip-up would unravel the narrative. Thus, he chose a more toothless version of the truth.

"So, yeah," he resumed, "I'm an attorney. Not here in Oregon, though. Had a bit of a windfall in the litigation lotto, enough to afford me a break to reassess things."

"You seem a bit young for a midlife crisis," she quipped with a light-hearted tone.

Braxton laughed it off. "And you? Originally from? I'm going to guess. . . Illinois?"

"Close. Wisconsin," she responded, intrigued. "How did you guess that?"

"Ah, WisCAAAnsin," Braxton playfully exaggerated the accent. "I've got family around Chicago. Your accent's subtle. It showed when you mentioned retinopathy."

Noticing a flicker of annoyance on her face, he started backpedaling. "I'm not knocking it, honestly. It's unique. I mean, my Californian accent is basically non-existent, just bland American English."

She shot back, "Whatever. Sounds like you're just being *hella* mean about it, *dude.*"

"Oh-hoh! *Touché.*" Braxton chuckled and gave her a friendly slap on the back before realizing it might have been too forward. "Sorry, that was just way too awesome to not acknowledge."

"No worries," she reassured him. "So, how have things been here? Were you around when that family disappeared?"

"Well, yeah, I've been here for about a month now," he replied. "Actually, it's been brought to my attention that I hung out with the mom a few times in San Francisco. Back when she was an art student. Weird how I didn't make that connection. But in my defense, she was barely in her twenties and looked a lot more 'Bohemian' back then." He air-quoted Bohemian.

"Brought to your attention?" she queried, raising an eyebrow.

"Yeah, by my ex-wife earlier today. She was always better at that kind of thing. I can be pretty clueless with names and faces, actually. It's like, 'have I seen this person before, or am I tripping?' Best not to embarrass myself and get into the awkward 'do I know you?' conversation. Anyways, I didn't make the connection when I bumped into Elle before inking my lease last month." Braxton nodded in the general direction of the real estate office across the way. "But hey, at least they found the kid, Hunter, right? Jesus, how crazy is that? I hope he's going to be okay."

Realizing that he was rambling again, Braxton shifted the topic. "So, where are you based out of?" he asked, looking to steer the conversation in a new direction.

"Portland," she took a few swallows of her drink, making a slight face at the vodka's sharpness. "And you were almost right about Illinois. I moved from Chicago to the West Coast around two years back."

"Nice," Braxton. "Hey, let me get the next one for you."

She paused with a hint of playfulness. "Well, if you insist. . ." Braxton caught Jason's attention, and the bartender made his way over.

"I'll go with a Bulleit on the rocks," Braxton announced. "And for you. . .another martini?" He waited for her nod before instructing Jason, "Alright, a Stoli martini then, very dry, twist, no olives." He turned back to her with a slight grin. "Live a little and go with the Stoli."

She responded with a brief smile and a small shrug.

Braxton found himself captivated by her smile, brief as it was. It was fleeting, yet there was something familiar about it, an echo of something he couldn't quite recall.

"Thanks again," she said. "Nice to escape the convention scene for a bit. The things that go on there, you wouldn't believe."

"Oh, I might. Been to a fair amount of conventions in the family law racket, and believe it or not, things can get pretty wild." Her expression showed curiosity. "You know. Family law," he elaborated. "Like divorce, custody, property division, support, the occasional 'you're NOT the father'—stuff like that."

Braxton paused as Jason refreshed their drinks. "To be honest, if I could go back in time and tell my law school self that he'd become a divorce lawyer, he probably would've quit on the spot. But, hey, if it pays the bills. . ."

"I'll drink to that," she said with glass raised.

"Cheers," Braxton replied, clinking his glass against hers. "I'm Braxton, by the way." He extended his hand.

"Riley," she responded, offering a firm handshake. Braxton noticed a slight tension in her expression, a brief tightening of her grip after saying her name. Like she had accidentally given something away.

"That's quite the handshake," he commented with a hint of amusement. "Did they cover that in pharmaceutical rep training?"

She let out a genuine chuckle. "Oh, it's an art form, honed over years."

"LOL," Braxton said the acronym out loud. "Oof. That's kinda cringe that I just said el-o-el IRL. . ." He caught himself drifting again. "Mind watching my drink for a sec? Need to use the restroom." She nodded, and he slid off the bar stool. "Back in a flash."

Emerging from the bathroom after a comically long pee, followed by a few discreet flask shots, Braxton nearly collided with Jason who was standing just outside.

"Whoa, hey there," Braxton exclaimed. "Sorry about that, almost ran you over. My bad."

Jason, unfazed and absorbed in his phone, replied without looking up. "No worries. Hey, that woman you were just talking to at the bar, she looks really familiar, don't you think?" He continued scrolling through his phone as if searching for an answer.

Braxton shrugged. "Maybe, but you know I'm not great with faces," he replied.

Jason held up his phone, showing a photo from the press conference. "See her? To the left of the speaker, in the middle of the group. Doesn't she look like your bar friend?"

Jason's suspicion seemed to mirror Braxton's own. He squinted at the photo, noting the agent who had rolled her eyes at the press conference. "Sort of," Braxton admitted with a hint of reluctance. "The picture's a bit grainy, though. Could be her, but she says she's in pharmaceuticals, and she seems to know her stuff. Maybe we're just being a little paranoid?"

"The guys and I have been speculating since she walked in. She's a new face around here. Just thought I'd run it by you. Would appreciate it if you didn't mention—"

"Mention what?" Braxton interrupted with a playful smile.

"That she looks like the FBI agent from—"

"Dude, you're not getting it. Mention what? I seriously have no idea what the hell you're even talking about." Braxton's smile broadened into a shit-eating grin.

Jason laughed. "Right, right. Plausible deniability. Ever the lawyer."

"Not in Oregon, my friend," Braxton quipped, tipping his cap as he turned back to the bar.

Jason's laughter receded as Braxton returned to his bar stool. Their conversation picked up again seamlessly, flowing through a range of topics. The warmth of the whiskey heightened his awareness, sharpening his focus on every nuance of their interaction. Riley was more than just attractive; there was something really familiar about her, as if they had crossed paths before.

As they reached the end of their drinks, Braxton took the plunge.

"How long does your convention run?" he inquired.

"Ugh, it's a whole thing," Riley replied with a slight exhale of frustration. "Ends Monday, but there's more to it. My company's eyeing a satellite office in this area, and I'm at the helm of that project. There's a lot of health care money in Medford—believe it or not—so we're finding ourselves down here more and more often." She took a thoughtful sip, gently swirling the remnants of her drink.

"Interesting. So, you might be around here again soon?" Braxton ventured, his tone light yet hopeful. "Guess I can hold off on asking for your number for now. Adds a bit of mystery to life, doesn't it?" He touched his heart, playing up the melodrama for effect.

Riley's reaction was encouraging. A soft chuckle escaped her lips, her eyes rolling in mock exasperation, but her smile was genuine.

"Perhaps. This place has its charm, a nice break from the usual. Who knows, maybe we'll run into each other again?" She finished her drink, standing with a sense of purpose. "It's been fun." She extended her hand.

"Fun?" Braxton's voice carried a hint of playful sarcasm. "I mean, let's not get ahead of ourselves. 'Interesting' or 'pleasant' might be more apt." Torn between his interest and not wanting to seem too eager for her contact details, Braxton stood and extended his hand, playing it cool. "Next round's on you should we meet again," he said, his tone more formal.

"Fair enough." She lingered for a moment, her eyes conveying a mix of curiosity. "Do you have a card or anything?" she asked.

Braxton felt a surge of excitement at her showing interest, but it was shadowed by a subtle unease. Was her inquiry merely casual, or could there be an investigative motive behind it? Concealing his internal tug-of-war, he replied with a casual air, "Fresh out, unfortunately."

An idea then sparked in his mind. "How about this: we simultaneously exchange details the next time we meet and confer. Agreed?" His proficiency in legalese, even while tipsy, made the words flow smoothly.

"So stipulated," Riley replied, her handshake firm but momentarily tightening. The legal jargon slipping out seemed to catch her off guard, causing a fleeting look of embarrassment to cross her face. Noticing this subtle reaction, Braxton couldn't help but grin as he released her hand. Hiding her blush, Riley mumbled a hasty farewell and walked out the front door, leaving Braxton with a mix of intrigue and amusement.

Outside the Saloon, Riley paused, her thoughts racing. "'So stipulated?' Really, Riley?" she scolded herself. Frustrated by her lapses and the fatigue clouding her judgment, she hoped her unintended reveals hadn't been too obvious.

Back inside, Braxton approached the corner where Jason and the locals were gathered. "Gentlemen," he began, "what's the over-under? Because I'm ninety-nine percent sure that she's fed. One with a law degree." The men exchanged knowing looks, amused by the recent exchange they had overheard.

Jason chuckled. "I've got to admit it, Braxton. You're actually kind of smooth in your own offbeat, geeky kind of way."

One of the regulars, Donnie, chimed in with a grin. "You know what? I could've sworn that there were diamonds on her back. She definitely shined brighter while on the way out." The group erupted into laughter at the quip.

As the laughter subsided, Braxton finalized his tab, still chuckling to himself. The evening's unexpected encounter had left him with a curious blend of amusement and intrigue.

LATER THAT EVENING

As Braxton left the Saloon, the cool night air greeted him, quickening his steps along the dimly lit streets of Jacksonville. With each stride, a refreshing vigor replaced the day's weariness, his thoughts clearing as he walked the familiar path back to his place. He arrived at the cottage, its quaint silhouette emerging under the moon's glow, and felt an unexpected surge of motivation ripple through him, an urge to harness the night's remaining hours to be productive.

He opened some windows, letting in the cool night air. The living room and kitchen were first on his list, so he set to work tidying up. His next task involved gathering the dead soldiers scattered about his room, ranging from pint-sized to full handles, followed by a full round of vacuuming. It took two trips to carry all the empty bottles to the outside bin. This time he made a point of gently placing each overstuffed bag into the bin, one by one, so as not to disturb his neighbors.

He rummaged once more for the shorts, shirt, and flip-flops he hadn't seen since Monday, but they remained elusive. Laundry was next on the list, but he dismissed the idea. Knowing his habits all too well, he'd either forget about it or pass out before moving the wash to the dryer. And the last thing he wanted was clothes with that sat-in-the-wash-too-long funk.

Settling into his evening, Braxton mixed himself a Manhattan and sprawled on the living room couch. He opened up his laptop and flipped through the TV channels, landing on a main network for some background noise. Scrolling through Facebook, he noticed a lot of his friends were still active. Some were out at the bars, others lamenting the little sleep they got thanks to their kids.

After dropping a few witty comments here and there, Braxton sipped his drink and attempted to locate Riley's Facebook page through various search filters, but to no avail. He bandied with some mutual friends on different updates, including his own, when the evening news caught his attention.

The intro faded, revealing a fifty-something anchor with suspiciously youthful brown hair. A still from the day's press conference hovered over his shoulder. The broadcast cut to the perky Technicolor reporter in Jacksonville, her on-screen makeup noticeably less vivid than in person.

The report offered no significant updates on young Hunter's discovery. The narrative was supplemented with local footage, images of the missing couple, and clips from the press conference. He scrutinized the individuals behind SAIC Richter, particularly the female agent standing centrally. Her hair neatly pulled back, sans glasses, the image was distant but unmistakable. It was Riley, the same woman he had met at the Saloon. The realization that he had just shared a drink and possible sparks with her amplified the allure of their encounter, blending intrigue with a newfound thrill.

After the reporter concluded, the news shifted to another story. "In other local news," the female anchor announced, "Jacksonville businessman Mitchell Emerson was arrested for disorderly conduct at the Medford Medical Center. At thirty-two years old, Emerson is a well-known figure in real estate and the wine industry. He founded Emerson Family

Wines in 2005 and, more recently, opened Forest Creek Vineyards. Despite the controversies and praises his ventures have sparked, specific details surrounding his arrest remain undisclosed."

As the male anchor cheerfully pivoted to the weather forecast, a tangible shift occurred in the room. Braxton glanced over at his laptop, its screen now a quiet portal to a world still spinning outside. The buzz of his social feeds had dulled to a whisper. With a thoughtful furrow of his brow, Braxton reached for the bottle, pouring another drink as he sank deeper into reflection.

"Man," he scoffed, the bitterness not entirely directed at the whiskey swirling in his glass, "I just passed the bar exam in 2005. Dude obviously came from money. Must be nice." He took a generous sip, letting the warmth of the liquor momentarily fill the spaces between his thoughts.

Shaking his head, Braxton wrestled with the envy gnawing at the edges of his conscience. He allowed himself a moment to consider the contours of his own life, the privilege of a supportive, if unconventional, family. His father, a man of profound faith and discipline, emerged from a working-class background to earn the rare combination of a PhD and an MD. Raised with a stern but loving hand, Braxton knew his path had been eased by sacrifices he'd never had to make. His father's journey from the cloistered life of a seminary school and monastic devotion to the seismic shift brought on by love—meeting Braxton's mother had redefined his understanding of calling. Or, as he put it, "I came to realize that my spiritual calling was less a command and more an echo."

Braxton's mother, hailing from a more affluent background, carried the legacy of her own parents who navigated the tumult of World War Two with resilience and pragmatism. Her father, a dedicated military dentist, and her mother, a nurse known for her spirited wit and resolve—including the threat of high colonics to deter overly familiar patients—set examples of strength that culminated in their move to California, where they built a life marked by both success and eventual tragedy due to prolonged X-ray exposure.

The serendipitous meeting of his parents at a family reunion of all places, a kind motorcycle-riding monk and a UCLA college student, laid the groundwork for Braxton's existence, a testament to life's unpredictable ironies.

Despite his mother's recurring claims about their limited finances, rooted in the genuine struggles of his father's medical school days, the family eventually settled in a comfortable three-bedroom home nestled on a cul-de-sac amidst the undulating hills of the Napa Valley. Braxton's father spent countless hours at the California Medical Facility, while his mother balanced part-time nursing with raising Braxton and his older brother. Yet, even amid her continued claims of financial hardship, a few years later they all moved into a nearby brand-new four-bedroom tract home located on a couple of acres.

Braxton's childhood was basically an eighties kid's dream. The endless open fields were perfect for aimless wandering, and cowpies served as makeshift frisbees. Oak-studded creeks begged to be explored, and the rural landscape was dotted with countless targets for his BB gun. Dirt and street ramps were irresistible for catching air on his BMX bike, and impromptu street football and basketball games lasted until the familiar calls for dinner echoed from home.

His brother Chase, four years his senior, often cast a shadow over this idyllic time. Not keen on delving into those memories, Braxton took a deep drink, feeling the need for a distraction. "Shit, might as well," he muttered to himself, standing up to shake off the encroaching thoughts.

In his room, Braxton rummaged through his dresser drawer, retrieving his dwindling weed stash, now reduced to a quarter ounce. He packed a small green nugget into his glass pipe and lit up. After a series of tokes interrupted by a couple of coughing fits, he stepped outside for some fresh air.

On his modest back deck, Braxton stood enveloped by the night, the gentle valley breeze stirring around him. As he emptied the ash from his pipe and lit a cigarette, his gaze wandered into the darkness beyond his yard, eyes gradually adapting to the night's embrace. He recalled how his vision always took a bit longer to adjust, often presenting waves and strobes of greenish-white blobs during the transition. He recalled when this peculiarity had been a topic of conversation during a family camping trip when he was about seven years old.

On that trip, walking to the communal bathroom with his brother, Braxton had inquired if Chase experienced the same visual phenomenon. Chase, seizing the moment to further mess with Braxton's mind, stopped and turned to him with a serious expression.

"I'm not supposed to tell you this," Chase intoned solemnly, hands-on Braxton's shoulders, "and I hate to break it to you, but your eyes are bionic. Your real eyes were defective, so Mom and Dad enrolled you in an experimental program for bionic replacements. They're waiting until you're twelve to tell you."

Braxton looked around the campsite, noting how the slackening strobes were outlining trees and rocks that were invisible moments earlier. "Cool!" Braxton exclaimed, "I have cyborg-enhanced night vision?! That's awesome!"

Unsatisfied with Braxton's reaction, Chase escalated. "Also, you were born a girl. To qualify for the bionic eye program, you had to be a boy, so Mom and Dad put you in an experimental sex change program when you were two weeks old." Braxton shot Chase a skeptical look.

Chase doubled down. "Don't believe me? That red strip between your scrotum and butthole? Those are stitch marks from your surgery."

Braxton was stunned into silence, fighting back tears to adhere to "the laws of Chase" which dictated that "only baby girls cry." The rest of their walk to the bathroom was silent, Braxton internally wrestling with the news as they took their place at the side-by-side urinals.

Unaware of Chase's silent comparison as they did their business, which confirmed the hard truth that his little brother was packing more heat, Braxton's stream continued drilling away at the pink half-eroded urinal cake as Chase washed his hands.

"Hmm," Braxton remarked after finishing up several moments later, "I guess the doctors didn't just make my eyesight better."

At the time Braxton was referring to taking a longer pee. It wasn't until decades later, while digitizing old family photo albums, that Braxton understood why his comment had resulted in Chase's silent treatment for the remainder of that trip.

Braxton's laughter broke the silence of the night as the memory faded. Finishing the smoke, he flicked the cigarette butt into an empty beer can doubling as an ashtray. Back inside, he poured himself a quadruple bourbon on the rocks, the clink of ice echoing in the quiet kitchen. With a long, satisfying gulp, he carried his drink to the living room, the weight of the night's events mingling with the warmth of the bourbon. Trying to relax on the couch, he let the day's encounters and revelations wash over him in the dim light of his home.

"Meh. Screw it," Braxton grumbled, returning to the kitchen to grab the bourbon bottle. "And hydration's always key," he reasoned, pouring a glass of water.

After downing the water, he compulsively sorted through his dirty laundry in his room again, frustrated at not finding the clothes he wore the other night. A quick check of the garage laundry machines likewise yielded nothing. "Oh well," he sighed, making his way back to the living room.

As Braxton sank back into the couch, the glow from his laptop casting flickering shadows across the room, he noticed the digital buzz starting to crescendo again. The night had reached that point where the inhibitions of his single friends dissolved into a stream of drunken revelations and live scenes captured by the ever-present eye of smartphones.

Clicking through the updates, a string of private messages caught his eye. He clicked open the message window, thinking, *She looks really familiar*, as he scrolled through her profile, each detail pulling him deeper into a web of digital anonymity.

The final coherent moments of Braxton's night melded together: the allure of the online encounter, the soothing burn of another drink, and the crafting of a message that felt both daring and dismissive of tomorrow's consequences. As the night wore on and their conversation began to fade into the hazy edges of consciousness, a sense of casual recklessness took hold. It was a familiar dance for Braxton, this flirting with the unknown, a way to blur the lines of his reality and escape into a world where actions felt free of their weight, if only for the night.

Braxton leaned into the indulgence of the moment, letting the digital exchange and the promise of oblivion dissolve the sharp edges of his day-to-day reality. As he faded into unconsciousness, he couldn't help but revel in the thought that, sometimes, diving headfirst into the night's embrace was exactly what he needed to forget the rigid confines of his so-called real life.

CHAPTER FOUR

WHEN IT RAINS, IT POURS

SUNDAY, AUGUST 12, 2:55 PM

In a fluid, practiced motion, Riley drew her sidearm, aimed, and fired. A three-round burst hit the target's chest. She paused, inhaled deeply, and exhaled before firing three more rounds, this time aiming for the head. Three more bursts to the top, three to the chest and a final shot, precisely aimed, to the groin.

Sundays were sacred for Riley, reserved for her time at the gun range. It was more than practice; it was a ritual, a form of prayer. Among the best marksmen in her class, she took pride in her tactical prowess. She examined the target as it slid back toward her. Most shots were on point, though a couple veered a little wide for her tastes. The groin shot, though, was perfectly centered.

As Riley patched up the holes in her target, her mind was awash with a tumult of thoughts, crashing against the shores of her personal and professional life. The recent investigation, with its fleeting leads that dissolved into frustrating dead ends, loomed large in her mind. She remembered the transient hope when remnants of a campsite were found on the Rogue River shore near Grants Pass, only to discover there was no direct evidence linking it to the missing person's case—likely just a stop for river rafters or detouring Pacific Crest Trail hikers.

Her thoughts shifted to the night of the press conference and her unexpected encounter with Braxton. His presence lingered in her mind—not just because of his wit and charm but an unplaceable familiarity. The irony wasn't lost on Riley; having a man in her life seemed as out of place as an assault rifle at a peace summit. Yet, there he was, infiltrating her thoughts with the precision of a well-trained sniper. She reattached the target to the hanger and watched it retreat to the end of the lane.

They always end up going the same way, she thought, filling her magazine almost absentmindedly. After a string of bad-to-worse relationships, Riley had lost confidence in her picker. And then there was Braxton—a blunt contrast to the men she typically encountered. He wasn't just another guy with a law degree; there was a uniqueness about him that set him apart somehow. Maybe it was how he represented a refreshing change of pace, a deviation from her norm that piqued her curiosity. But what really intrigued her was the sense of familiarity he exuded, a nagging feeling that they shared a common thread she couldn't quite pinpoint.

Riley inserted the magazine into her handgun and chambered a round with practiced ease. She stilled her mind, focusing on her breathing—in and out, in and out. Two shots to the head, two to the chest, one to the groin.

As she executed the pattern, her mind wandered back to her days as an FBI analyst in Chicago, living with her then-boyfriend. He was a police detective, a man who had harbored bitter resentment after being rejected by the FBI. He concealed his envy and anger under a veneer of normalcy, all the while belittling Riley for her career ambitions and lack of desire for a traditional family life. His toxicity had pushed her to transfer to San Francisco, a move to escape his suffocating control and rebuild her sense of worth.

Riley alternated her shots until the magazine was empty. In two smooth motions, she ejected the spent mag, inserted a new one, and readied her handgun again. Focused and methodical, she repeated her firing pattern, the sound of each shot echoing in the range. Once finished, she felt a sense of relaxation wash over her. She cleared her weapon, collected the empty magazine, and pressed the button to retrieve the target. Examining the target, she noted the tight groupings around her intended marks, a testament to her skill and focus.

As she began packing up, a thought struck her, a connection emerging from her subconscious. It brought her back to that time in her life in San Francisco, when she had applied to become a Special Agent. She remembered the intense interviewing process, the group of applicants she was with, faces blending into one another during a period filled with both anxiety and anticipation.

Could that be it? Riley thought, *is that why he's so familiar?* The possibility intrigued her, adding a layer of mystery to the familiar yet elusive figure of Braxton.

TWO DAYS LATER

Braxton entered the Saloon, the familiar ambiance enveloping him as he approached the bar. Spotting Jason behind the counter, he offered a grin that was part satisfaction, part mischief. "Hey, Jason," he said, easing onto his usual stool. "It's been a minute."

"There he is," Jason said, already lining up Braxton's drink. "Seems like you've got some stories to tell. What's new?"

"You wouldn't believe it if I told you," Braxton replied, raising his glass in a half-toast. He glanced outside, noting the diminishing number of reporters and news vans on California Street. With the media's focus shifting to international affairs, the local missing persons case seemed to have receded into the background. The past several days had blurred together, and Braxton wondered if his unplugging from the media stream had anything to do with that.

Jason leaned forward, intrigued. "Do tell. You vanish for a bit and come back looking like you ran a marathon and won the lottery."

Braxton took a sip, the ice cubes clinking against the glass. "Alright, so you've heard of drunk dialing, right? Well, I guess I did the social network version of that." He launched into his story, detailing the unexpected reconnection with an old friend from middle school—a series of events ignited by a hazy night resulting in an impromptu multi-day rendezvous.

"Apparently we were on the phone for like an hour that night," Braxton said, a hint of disbelief in his voice. "Didn't remember a thing about it. So you can imagine my confusion when she started texting location updates the next morning." He paused, taking a thoughtful pull from his drink. "Had to go through our Facebook messages to piece it all together, and then it was like, 'Damn! I guess this is happening.'"

He chuckled, deciding not to share the more explicit details of their exchange. "I don't know about your situation, seeing as you're not wearing a ring. But it's been an eye-opener for me. People I haven't thought about in years are suddenly reaching out. Old crushes confessing after two decades? It's surreal." He raised his glass in a casual toast before taking a deeper drink.

"Anyway, the whole experience was something else," Braxton's grin widened, a mix of amusement and disbelief at his own tale. "She used to be this quiet bookworm, but let's just say she's. . .evolved. I mean, I thought I heard some crazy stuff from my dad's intern days at SF General—like the kind of things one can find lodged way up there—but this was another level. We're talking kinks I didn't even know existed."

Braxton wrapped up his story with a chuckle. "We parted ways as quickly as we reconnected. No strings, no drama. It's a brave new world out there, my friend."

Jason couldn't help but laugh, shaking his head at Braxton's narrative. "Fuckin' Braxton, man. Only you, bro," he said, his voice filled with amusement and a hint of disbelief, as he moved on to serve another customer.

Braxton, engrossed in *Onion* articles on his phone, was about a quarter-way through his drink when she entered. He kept his focus glued to the phone, re-reading the same lines while his peripheral vision detected her approach.

She took the seat right next to him. "Do you have Summer Shandy here?" she inquired.

"That's one of my favorites on a day like this," Jason responded. "You got great taste. In a tall glass with lemon?" Riley nodded, and Jason left to prepare the drink.

"Hello." She turned toward Braxton, who was doing his best to appear nonchalant despite his rapidly beating heart. He raised his eyes from his phone, offering a nod, and then feigned sudden recognition.

"Oh, *hello!*" he blurted out, perhaps a bit too startled. "Hey, I almost didn't recognize you in your casual gear. How are you?" he added, attempting to smooth over his initial start.

All things considered, Braxton thought that he played off the blood rushing in his head, rapid heartbeat, shortened breath, and an earth-shattering internal voice screaming, *She's here! She just looked over! She's walking up next to you! She just took a seat right next to you! She just said something! She's looking directly at you! She just said something to you!*" rather well.

Jason returned with Riley's drink, placing it on a coaster before taking her twenty-dollar bill to the register. Riley, with sunglasses atop her head and hair flowing down, radiated a natural beauty in her skirt, light blouse, and Birkenstocks. The look accentuated her effortless charm, Braxton observed, a style that highlighted her allure even on what appeared to be her day off.

"I've been fine," Riley said. "The convention's over, thank God, so it's a little less hectic." She dropped the lemon slice into her glass. "How's the sabbatical life been treating ya?"

Braxton let out a sigh, "Oh, just another shitty day in paradise." His gaze shifted to her drink. "Haven't tried that one yet, is it any good?" he asked, nodding toward her glass. "If so, that's a great choice for a day like this. Did you know there's a story behind Radler?"

Riley, intrigued, shook her head. "No, what's a Radler?"

"Well, Summer Shandy is an American version," Braxton dove into the tale. "There was this bar in Bavaria, southern Germany, back in the 1920s, when cycling was becoming popular. Cyclists would ride through the Alps, stopping at pubs for refreshments. This one bar owner, running low on beer, mixed it with lemon soda and called it 'Radler,' which means 'cyclist' in German. It's a mass-produced brew now." Braxton pondered for a moment. "How does that saying go? 'Necessity is the mother of invention'?" He took a quick sip of his drink.

He continued, a note of wistfulness in his voice. "That aside, what I really like about the story is the image it conjures. Imagine biking through Bavarian countryside, fresh air, the Alps all around, stopping at little pubs along the way. Sipping on a Radler, just enough to maintain that perfect buzz under the sun. Sounds like an incredible way to spend a day, doesn't it?"

"That's a random bit of trivia," Riley remarked, smiling. "Where did you learn that?"

"Well, I have a degree in German Literature and I spent a summer there. Plus, you know, the internet helps," Braxton replied with a grin.

As the hours passed, Braxton found himself on his second shandy, its effects enhanced by visits to the bathroom for extra flask shots. Deciding to share appetizers, they continued chatting, with Riley insisting on getting the last round. She then handed Braxton her Blackberry, asking him to input his contact information.

Riding the wave of "when it rains, it pours," plus the alcohol, Braxton felt a sense of ease as their conversation flowed. He decided to steer the dialogue into more playful territory.

"Okay," Braxton ventured, "let's talk pet peeves. What are your top three?"

Riley raised an eyebrow. "That's quite the question. You first, since I bet you've already got yours lined up."

"Fair enough," Braxton conceded. "First up, mildew-smelling laundry. It's like expecting spring meadows but getting a swamp monster's embrace instead. And bath towels? Wrap yourself in the scent of marshland. Add scented dryer-sheets, and it's a whole new level of funk!"

Riley couldn't help but chuckle, intrigued by his detailed disgust.

"Next, decorative pillows. They look nice but are utterly pointless. Can't sleep on them, they just end up tossed aside. Why not make them both functional and stylish?"

His annoyance was amusingly clear, sparking another chuckle from Riley.

"And number three," Braxton went on, "decorative towels in the bathroom. You know the kind, right? They're so fancy that they're practically untouchable. You wash your hands, and then there's this dilemma of finding a towel that's actually meant for drying. And by this time, water's dripping down your arms, soaking into your sleeves. You end up desperately searching for a usable towel, but all you find are more decorative ones. So, you're left with no choice but to wipe your hands on your pants. Honestly, what's the point of having towels if you can't use them to dry off?"

Braxton concluded his rant with a thump on the bar, the sound echoing his fading exasperation. He inhaled deeply, letting the air escape slowly, a ritual of calm. "Sorry about that." He chuckled, a sheepish grin spreading across his face. "Now it's your turn."

"That's not really fair," Riley countered, her tone playful yet contemplative. "I mean, I haven't had time to categorize things yet. Even then,

I think you're stretching it since two of your peeves fall under the same category: decorative items. But I'll let it slide."

She thought for a moment. "Alright, keeping with the bathroom theme: toilet paper rolls that unroll from the back. Obviously they should come from the front. Less contact, less mess."

Braxton raised his glass in agreement. "Hear, hear!"

"Then, there's those sloppy store displays," Riley continued, noticing Braxton's puzzled expression. "At grocery stores, you know? They set up these displays, but half the time labels are all over the place, or there's a glaring typo. Drives me nuts."

Braxton nodded, a smirk playing on his lips. "Gotcha," said Braxton, now getting it. "Nothing to do with bathrooms. Come to think of it, that's totally a good one!"

Riley cleared her throat, "Exactly. Last one—people in lines."

Braxton leaned back. "First two, spot on. But the last one? It's a bit on the generic side, no?" He paused, a twinkle in his eye, careful not to push her buttons too hard. "Unless, of course, there's more to it?"

With a roll of her eyes and a hint of mischief, Riley retorted, "Oh, there's more. It's those who stand in line, totally unprepared. Like the guy who's had all day to fill out the paperwork but waits until he's at the counter, or argue about policies as if the world revolves around him. Or at Starbucks, where they chat on their phone instead of ordering, holding everyone up. It's the complete lack of awareness for anyone else that really gets to me."

She took a breath, her frustration simmering. "And don't get me started on the ones who make custom orders, substituting this for that, and then claiming they got the order wrong. Seriously," her voice sharp, "that shit *seriously* drives me nuts."

Riley's hands went to her temples, finding her sunglasses. With a quick, fluid motion, she swiped them off her head, letting them clatter onto the bar.

"Whoa. Tell me how you really feel," Braxton said, leaning back and raising his hands in mock surrender, a playful grin on his face.

Riley let out a light giggle, the tension from her rant dissipating. She picked up the glasses from the counter and slid them into her purse.

"Generic criticism totally withdrawn," Braxton declared, his voice carrying a tone of genuine amusement. "You absolutely nailed that last one. Completely concur."

Riley's gaze wandered around the bar. "I'm looking for a change of pace. How about we head out?"

Braxton's eyebrows shot up, a mix of excitement and wariness in his voice. "Uh. . .yeah, might as well," he replied, attempting to sound nonchalant. "Let me just take care of the bill and visit the restroom, no particular order," he said, rising from his seat.

As Braxton settled the tab, his mind was a whirlwind. Riley, still shrouded in mystery, was an enticing enigma. He mused over the unpredictability of life, like a sudden downpour on a clear day.

LATER THAT EVENING

"Well, here's to me and that fucking ex-husband of mine!" a woman exclaimed a few tables down, her cheer slicing through the room's hum. The others at her table, a lively group of women, raised their glasses in unison of celebration, their collective "woooo!" filling the room.

Braxton, sitting a few tables away, couldn't help but snicker at the raw enthusiasm of the toast. He glanced over at the woman, noting the spirited energy of the group. It was a divorce party, clearly a night of libation and liberation for the women involved, especially the one leading the toast.

Before this unexpected interruption, Braxton and Riley had been immersed in their own world at the cozy Italian restaurant, a block from the Saloon. The ambiance was warm and the dishes were homestyle—comfort food with generous portions. They had shared a Caesar salad and struggled to finish their generous entrées.

As their plates were cleared, Riley opted for a cappuccino, while Braxton chose an Irish coffee, savoring the rich blend of coffee and whiskey. It was around this time that the group celebrating the divorce was seated, their arrival coinciding with a subtle shift in Riley's demeanor.

Braxton noticed her attention drift over to the boisterous table. Her eyes narrowed slightly, not with annoyance, but with a keen, investigative focus. Turning back to Braxton, she offered a quick, polite smile. "Excuse me for a moment, I need to powder my nose," she said, her tone casual yet with an undercurrent of urgency that Braxton couldn't quite place.

Left alone, Braxton took the opportunity to soak in the atmosphere of the restaurant. The lively chatter and laughter from the divorce party added a vibrant energy to the place. He couldn't help but observe the women, especially the one who had made the toast, her presence commanding and full of life.

Their eyes met unexpectedly. Braxton, caught like a deer in headlights, managed a sheepish yet sincere smile and raised his glass in a silent toast. The woman mirrored his gesture, a knowing smile playing on her lips.

Interrupting this exchange, the server approached with a bag of their boxed leftovers. Braxton, hoping to alleviate any lingering awkwardness, checked his phone and found an unread message from an unknown sender:

What's taking u so long?

Puzzled, he was about to dismiss it when the waiter reappeared.

"Anything else I can help you with?" he inquired.

"Oh, the bill, please," Braxton responded, still distracted.

"Your date took care of it," he said with a chuckle, a hint of amusement in his tone.

Braxton couldn't decide what surprised him more—the fact that Riley had covered the bill or that she was referred to as his "date." A sense of warmth spread through him at the thought. "Oh, right, my bad," he replied with a laugh. "Thanks." Pocketing his phone, he collected the leftovers and made his way outside.

Once outside, Braxton caught sight of Riley standing by her car, her attention fixed on her phone. The warm evening air swirled around her, lifting strands of her hair in a gentle dance. As she stretched, the contours of her athletic frame were accentuated by her blouse, a sight leaving Braxton breathless and awestruck.

Her silhouette against the fading light of dusk was striking—she was more than just beautiful; she was captivating in a way that transcended the ordinary. Braxton felt a jolt of nervous energy, his heart racing. He was struck by the intensity of his attraction to her, a feeling that seemed to scramble his thoughts and words.

To regain his composure, Braxton turned away, taking a moment to himself. He cleared his throat, whistling a tune under his breath as a distraction. The few seconds felt like an eternity as he tried to steady his nerves.

Turning back around, Braxton grounded himself and found his voice, albeit with some effort. "Oh, there you are," he said, trying to sound more composed than he felt.

Riley turned toward him, her smile radiant in the dimming light. "Indeed. I am here," she responded, her tone casual, seemingly oblivious to the turmoil she stirred in him.

Braxton approached, each step feeling heavier than the last. "You live pretty close by, right?" Riley asked.

"Yeah, pretty close," Braxton answered, his heart still racing from the sight of her. "You sure you're okay to drive? It's an easy walk."

"I'm fine, hop in," she assured him, opening her car door with a fluid motion.

As Braxton settled into the passenger seat, he couldn't help but steal glances at her. Riley, apparently unaware of the deep impression she was making, fired up the engine. The car roared to life, the blaring sound of NPR news abruptly cut off by Riley.

"Now that you know what I jam to, try not to be too intimidated by how hip and cool I am," she quipped, her voice laced with playful humor.

Braxton chuckled, the tension easing slightly. "I'll do my best," he replied, his mind still spinning from her allure.

Riley's U-turn was as smooth as their evening had been unpredictable. Braxton, silent in his seat, mulled over Riley's secret life with the FBI, a revelation that intrigued yet complicated his feelings. Deciding against sharing this hidden truth, he let the silence between them grow, a choice that felt right yet heavy with unexplored potential. The drive to his place, though brief, was thick with the anticipation of words left unspoken.

They arrived outside Braxton's cottage, the car coming to a soft stop in the tranquil night. Here, away from the night's earlier buzz, the quiet around them seemed almost reflective, mirroring the complexity of their silent exchange.

As they entered, Braxton, relieved that he had tidied up earlier, played the gracious host and offered Riley a nightcap. She accepted with a nod, her eyes subtly scanning the room, her gaze sharp yet discreet.

Pouring whiskey into two glasses, Braxton noticed Riley's careful scrutiny of his cottage, her training evident in her observant manner. Handing her a glass, their fingers brushed, sending a jolt through him. "To unexpected evenings," he toasted, his voice steady.

"To the unexpected," Riley echoed, her voice low with a trace of mystery. She sipped her drink, her intense gaze on Braxton stirring a blend of desire and caution within him.

Excusing himself, Braxton retreated to the bathroom. Riley, seizing the moment, drifted through the cottage to the kitchen. A quick survey of the fridge revealed Braxton's bachelor habits: a half-empty jar of craft cocktail cherries, pizza boxes from last night's dinner, several craft beers nestled beside a carton of orange juice, and a somewhat aged block of cheddar cheese. Silently closing the fridge, she turned her attention to his laptop. The sight of the password-protected login screen brought a brief flash of frustration to her eyes before she closed it with a deliberate, gentle click.

The quaint home, in its quiet intimacy, seemed to whisper tales of Braxton's life. Riley absorbed each detail—the books, the cocktail accessories, each item offering a glimpse into the man who intrigued her.

Upon his return, Braxton found Riley on the sofa, her presence weaving an aura of allure and mystery. Approaching her, the air pulsed with an electric tension. Their kiss, tentative at first, blossomed into a fervent expression of their mutual fascination, their embrace weaving together unanswered questions and unspoken desires.

Yet, at the peak of their connection, Riley pulled away. Her breath was unsteady, her eyes stormy with conflicting emotions. "I should go," she declared, her voice firm despite the evident reluctance.

Braxton, immersed in the intensity of the moment, managed only a nod. "I understand," he murmured, his voice a mix of admiration and unspoken longing.

Riley gathered her belongings smoothly, her swift departure masking an undercurrent of turmoil. Pausing at the door, she shared a look with Braxton that spoke of both farewell and a recognition of the unexplored depths between them.

Then she left, the door closing softly in her wake. Braxton stood in the ensuing silence, the echo of her presence and the lingering secrets hanging in the air like a haunting melody.

Man, when it rains, it pours. . .

CHAPTER FIVE

THAT WAY LIES MADNESS

WEDNESDAY, AUGUST 15, 3:32 PM

Braxton cradled his drink, letting the ice clink softly against the glass as he took a thoughtful sip. The Saloon was alive, pulsing with the energy of those seeking refuge from the day's blistering heat. Laughter and conversations swelled, filling the space with a dynamic hum that made this Wednesday afternoon feel like a weekend peak. As the triple-digit temperatures scorched the world outside, the Saloon transformed into a haven, bustling with patrons whose shared escape wove a vibrant backdrop of connection and shared respite.

"Talk about mixed messages," Braxton lamented, his voice carrying over the clinking of glasses and animated chatter, as Jason worked behind the bar slicing lemon wedges. "Granted," he continued, leaning in to share his tale, "we're playing a bit of cat-and-mouse. I don't think she knows that I know she's FBI. But there were some definite sparks. And there's this weird sense of familiarity between us. Anyhow, we went to that Italian place down the way. It was a pretty lively scene, even more so after dinner when a party of women celebrating a divorce came in. That was quite amusing."

Braxton chuckled at the memory before elaborating further. "Come to think of it, Riley excused herself right around the time that party was seated. So, she missed a hilarious toast the divorcee made about 'that fucking ex-husband of mine.' Who, by the way, totally caught me checking her out."

Jason raised an eyebrow, his eyes flashing a mix of amusement and curiosity. "The just-divorced woman caught you scoping her out while you were on a date with another woman?" he remarked, a touch of humor in his tone. "That's a bit awkward."

Braxton grinned, unapologetic. "Well, yeah. But she was cute, funny, and had a great laugh. What can I say? She really didn't seem to mind, though. Anyways, it turns out Riley had paid the bill and was waiting for me outside."

Jason leaned in, a knowing grin on his face. "Well, that's an interesting turn of events," he remarked, not the least bit surprised. "You and the divorcee making eyes at each other while the FBI is footing the bill? Classic Braxton."

Braxton chuckled, appreciating Jason's nonchalant reaction, before continuing his narrative. "Then Riley basically told me to get in her car so we could go to my place. She was in quite a hurry, too. And, yeah, once we got to my pad we messed around a little. Basically PG-13 stuff. And she was really into it, we both were, it was amazing. But then she pulled back. Like, I could tell that the flesh was willing—the spirit was definitely there. But something held her back, and just like that, she headed out the door."

"Did you check your place for bugs?" Jason asked, a hint of amusement in his voice.

Braxton took a thoughtful sip of his drink before responding, "Given who she works for, that crossed my mind. But I'm almost certain she would need approval for that. Judging from her non-domestic car and how much she had to drink, I don't think this was a sanctioned operation. But, like a dumbass, I didn't check to see if my laptop was closed or open when I went to the bathroom."

He leaned in a bit closer, his tone more conspiratorial. "I don't have any weird or criminal stuff on there. But even if I did, it would be inadmissible 'fruit from the poisonous tree.' I won't get into the collateral source rule, as that really doesn't apply."

Braxton paused for a moment, looking around the bar before continuing, "Sorry, guess you really don't need to know the blow-by-blow minutiae that run through my head concerning the rules governing the interface between civilians and law enforcement. But I find it fascinating."

Jason nodded at another customer, then flashed Braxton the universal "one-inch" sign, indicating he'd be back in a moment.

Braxton couldn't resist a smirk as Jason returned. "Bro," he teased, "I think it's great that you're cool with having a small peen and all, but do you really want to advertise that to the whole place?" Braxton raised his hand and playfully demonstrated the "one-inch" gesture, erupting into laughter at his wisecrack. Jason rolled his eyes but couldn't help but chuckle in amusement.

"Anyways, where were we? Oh, right, bugs and warrants. So, I have a pretty solid antivirus suite, which I ran like a mofo. Nothing unusual. Changed my credentials to be safe. Haven't seen any random surveillance vans around my place or anything," Braxton grinned, "so, I think I'm good."

"Soo. . . maybe she didn't want it to be like a one-night thing, and she's actually into you?" Jason's suggestion hung in the air, stirring something deep within Braxton.

The idea sent a subtle ripple through him, a mix of hope and apprehension. He harbored strong feelings for Riley, yet the possibility of unrequited affection loomed in his mind. He dismissed it with a light-hearted scoff, though a trace of sincerity lingered. "Yeah, right," he responded, his heart quietly yearning for it to be true.

Then, a sudden thought struck him, less like a thunderbolt and more like the flicker of a long-forgotten light. "Hold on," he said, a note of realization in his voice. "Actually, Riley might have been there at the FBI interviews in San Francisco. We could have met back then!" This new insight, subtle yet profound, gently tugged at his memories, hinting at a deeper thread woven into their shared past. "You know I'm not the best with names and faces, but the only other applicant with a law degree was a woman who already worked there as an analyst. I doubt they're the same person, but who knows?"

Braxton took another swallow and sifted through his memories of the FBI interview process, again drawing a blank as to what the other applicants looked like. The agents who interviewed him, though, he could pick them out of any lineup.

"I have a really weird kind of memory, FYI," Braxton remarked. "Some things are crystal clear, photographic, verbatim. Other stuff I barely even remember unless someone or something triggers it. I wish I had control of that on/off switch, you know?"

"For sure," Jason acknowledged. "Hey, by the way, I have a question for you. Hang out for a bit?"

"Sure. But if it's a legal question, I can't give you any advice under Oregon law—"

"You've made that abundantly clear over the last several weeks, Braxton," Jason smiled and shook his head. "Nothing legal, more of a proposition."

"Ooohh, scintillating," said Braxton. "Guess I'll have to wait with bated breath along with a Jack and Coke if that's okay."

Jason retrieved a tumbler from the rack, generously poured Jack Daniels over ice, and added a dash of Coke. "On the house," he said before turning to attend to another patron.

"Cheers," Braxton chimed in, raising his glass in acknowledgment. With nothing else to do, he unlocked his phone to pass the time.

"Hey." Jason had returned.

Braxton looked up from his phone and reoriented himself. Judging by the remnants of his drink, the gaming app had absorbed him for at least fifteen minutes.

"Yo," Braxton replied, placing the phone face-down on the bar. "Can I get Michter's Rye on the rocks when you get a chance, please?"

"Sure," Jason nodded, reaching for a bottle on the upper shelf. "So, basically, you ever work a bar?"

"Front-end at weddings only," Braxton replied, "but I did a little bar-back and kitchen work back in the college days. Why do you ask?"

"Okay, cool," Jason said. "I figured you might know a thing or two from this side of the bar. Basically, I'm taking off in a few hours for a week-long trip. I've arranged to have someone, her name is Stacey, to sub for me here. Tony and Amanda will be doing their usual kitchen service. I think everything's covered, but I'd appreciate it if you could hang around the place for the next week just to keep an eye on things. Like make sure the tills are balanced, opening, closing, keeping the peace, stuff like that," Jason grabbed a pen and notepad as Braxton took it all in.

"Dude. . .you SURE about that?" Braxton was still wrapping his head around the ask. It seemed like a pretty big responsibility, but it's not like he had anything else to do. Jason tore a piece of paper from the pad, folded it in half, and slid it over.

"Obviously I'm trusting that you won't party too hard or anything while on duty," said Jason. "I know that you lawyer types can handle your booze. But, you know. . ."

Braxton unfolded the note and found the terms of compensation more than reasonable.

"Yeah, dude, for sure," Braxton grinned. "I can handle all that stuff. When do we start the debrief?"

"Stacey will be coming in in about twenty minutes." Jason checked his watch. "So, we can start then?"

"Perfect. If I'm not here, I'll either be out having a smoke or in the crapper," Braxton over-disclosed. "I guess you didn't need that level of specificity. . ."

"Fuckin' Braxton," Jason sighed with mock exasperation. He grabbed a bottle of Michter's Rye and poured a double. "Here you go. Maybe this will help dumb down that big brain of yours."

"I'll drink to that." Grinning, Braxton raised his glass. "Here's to new adventures, and many more."

Jason raised his water bottle. "Hear, hear. And here's to being careful what you wish for."

Finding Jason's comment a bit odd, Braxton shrugged and went along with it. "That too," he said. "That too."

ONE DAY LATER

Late morning had already brought searing heat to the mountainous evergreen wilderness of the Rogue Valley, casting a relentless blaze upon the landscape. Riley finished up her last witness statement at the campground and was walking to her unmarked sedan. The back of her blouse was soaked with what had felt like rivers of sweat cascading down her back, all of which pooled at the base of her spine.

Keeping the sedan's door open, she reached into the sunbaked cabin to start the car and crank the AC. She peeled off her sweat-soaked blazer and draped it on the passenger seat.

After taking in the view of granite peaks and towering evergreens to clear her mind, Riley eased into the driver's seat, grimacing as her damp blouse sandwiched between her skin and the upholstery. She took another moment to gather her thoughts and notes.

Circumstantial pattern at best. Forensics were doing their thing. But without any bodies, there wasn't much they could do by way of comparison. All victims were white. The male victims were in public service, and the female victims were from local legacy families. All lived in the

Rogue Valley area. She made a tertiary-level note to check out local archives for some legacy context.

The AC was starting to chill the cabin, and Riley felt her sweat start to evaporate. She put her small notepad back into her blazer pocket and tossed her legal pad onto the passenger seat. After massaging her temples, Riley eased the car from the gravel lot and headed to the remote windy road that connected to the highway. A deputy sheriff flagged her through the exit.

"Man, I could actually use a drink right now," she heard herself say. Riley steered onto the main road heading toward Highway 199 and cell reception.

As Riley continued driving, she couldn't help but feel a sense of relief wash over her. The temporary respite from the intense heat and connectivity was kind of nice, and for a moment, she felt centered and at peace. The winding road ahead seemed to stretch on forever, leading her deeper into the wilderness.

But just as she began to relax, thinking she might enjoy a peaceful moment of solitude, her Blackberry sprang to life with spasms of buzzes, alerts, and notifications. The unexpected cacophony of electronic interruptions shattered her newfound sense of calm, and she let out a sigh of exasperation.

It seemed that the demands of the modern world had found a way to intrude into even the remotest of wilderness regions. With a resigned shake of her head, Riley focused her attention on the buzzing device, knowing that whatever awaited her on the other end would inevitably pull her back into the chaos of life and work.

MOMENTS LATER

Braxton's first day stepping in for Jason found him perched at his usual spot by the bar, swapping his regular bourbon on the rocks for a glass of mineral water. In light of his new responsibilities, he restricted his day drinking to incognito shots from the flask.

The Saloon operated with its usual weekday cadence, not bustling but far from empty. The regular clink of glasses and the steady hum of conversations created a comfortable, familiar backdrop. The staff, adept and unhurried, attended to patrons with a practiced ease, their movements reflecting the day's unruffled pace. It was business as usual, the Saloon's rhythm undisturbed by Jason's absence.

In the midst of observing the Saloon's activity, Braxton's phone intruded with a missed text, quickly followed by a series of notifications from his chosen news outlets. The buzzes momentarily diverted him from the bar's gentle ebb and flow. Yielding to curiosity, he tapped the hyperlink of the third message, letting the world of news reel him in.

RETIRED COUPLE REPORTED MISSING

August 16—Rogue Valley, Ore. Jackson County Sheriff's Department has issued the following public alert: Andrew Holman (71) and Susan Holman (67) were reported missing on August 16. The couple left on August 4 for a camping trip and have not returned. Their vehicle, a blue 2010 Dodge Ram 3500, and Airstream trailer were recovered near the campsite. Jackson County law officials request the public's assistance in reporting any further information concerning their whereabouts.

Braxton let out a concerned sigh, muttering to himself, "That's not good, that's not good at all." Without overthinking it, he headed to the bathroom, seeking solace in a few swigs from his flask.

Upon his return, he addressed Stacey, the new bartender. "Mind if I change the channel real quick?"

Braxton reached behind the bar to grab the remote and settled back onto his stool. Landing on the local stations, Braxton saw that the usual daytime TV programs were preempted by breaking newscasts.

He went with the Technicolor reporter, mostly to see whether her makeup was more obvious on the Saloon's HD wide screen (it wasn't, surprisingly). Behind the newscaster, a nearly empty gravel parking lot stretched out, framed by majestic mountains and dense forest.

"Thank you, Dan," the reporter acknowledged. "As you can see, we are near the Holman's Siskiyou Forest campsite. It's a family-friendly location, not too far from the main highway. But phone and internet service are virtually nonexistent. The couple were scheduled to return home yesterday afternoon. After checking in on their campsite, local authorities reported them missing."

Braxton increased the volume as the reporter's words outpaced the subtitles.

"The retired couple were reported to be in good health and were active travelers. Andrew Holman, former chair of the Jackson County Board of Commissioners, retired from decades of public service last year. His wife, Susan Holman, is a retired school teacher and principal. Both are natives of Jacksonville, with family lines dating back to the town's founding.

"This would be the second missing persons case since the disappearance of Elle Harris and Aaron Stewart last week. Their three-year-old son Hunter, who was found in Weed, California, is reported to be in good health at 'an undisclosed safe location.' Both local and federal authorities have no comment as to whether the two disappearances are related or not."

Of course they're related, thought Braxton. It seemed quite obvious to him. Both women came from legacy families. And both men were in public service. The reporter continued to discuss the missing couple's abandoned truck and trailer but had no further details beyond that.

"Pretty crazy, huh?" Braxton remarked to Stacey.

"For sure," she replied, pulling her blond-on-black hair into a ponytail. She appeared to be in her late twenties, sporting an alternative look that would be considered tame in Portland. "Andrew Holman's been a local fixture since way before I was born. So much so that it was a pretty big deal when he retired after his wife got cancer. She beat it though. Man, that really sucks. I hope they're okay."

Braxton sympathized with Stacey's concern for the missing couple, but as he listened to her talk, an eerie sensation began to creep over him. It was a feeling he hadn't experienced in several days, ever since he had successfully pushed those haunting memories to the back of his mind.

"Hey, you all right if I head out for a little bit? Call me if anything crazy happens, obviously," Braxton asked, his voice slightly distant as his thoughts drifted back to that terrifying night. He tried to hide the tremor in his hands by casually adjusting his glasses.

"Yeah, no worries," Stacey replied, seemingly oblivious to Braxton's change in demeanor. "I think we're good here for the rest of the day, to be honest."

Braxton nodded absentmindedly, his mind preoccupied with the disturbing images and ominous chanting that had plagued him since that fateful night. In an attempt at false bravado, he flashed a confident grin. "Well, I'll be back. Shouldn't be gone for too long." He started gathering his things, his hands trembling slightly. Out of habit, he pulled out his wallet to square up. "Wait, never mind." He forgot that his nonalcoholic drinks were on the house. "Okay, see you." He waved at Stacey and headed out the front door.

A blanket of heat enveloped his body as he stepped into the daylight. It felt pleasant at first, but as he walked away from the Saloon, his thoughts were consumed by the memories he'd managed to keep at bay for the past few days. The gnawing feeling had returned, triggered by the news of the second missing couple, and he knew he needed something stronger to suppress those issues—with immediate effect.

LATER THAT EVENING

The Saloon was a hive of activity that evening, buzzing more intensely than usual. Its regulars, a loyal cadre familiar with every creak of the floorboards, found their routine camaraderie interspersed with the influx of media personnel, tourists, and curious onlookers. These newcomers, drawn by the unsettling allure of the month's second missing persons case, lent a peculiar energy to the place. As the evening newscasts flickered to an end across various screens, a palpable shift occurred. The crowd, a mosaic of concern, intrigue, and the need for distraction, sought refuge in the Saloon's welcoming dimness.

Braxton, now in a more relaxed state compared to earlier that day, observed the additional crowd with mild amusement. He had managed to push aside his troubled thoughts through the liberal application of liquid courage, a few bowls of weed, and a touch of Adderall. For the time being, his personal struggles were tucked away, and he had taken the opportunity to replenish his provisions and booze inventory. He even tidied up the place before returning to the Saloon. As he sat in his usual spot, he couldn't help but feel a sense of accomplishment, knowing that he would return to a clean, well-stocked home later that night.

Braxton took another look around at the bustling scene, reveling in the luxury of having a couple of reserved stools at the bar. He casually sipped from his mineral water and scrolled through his phone, finding no major updates, just additional background information about each victim's political and philanthropic accomplishments.

He was perplexed by what he considered a glaring omission in the media coverage. It seemed that no one was willing to connect the dots, even though it appeared so obvious to him. The pattern was crystal clear: each female victim came from a legacy family, and the male victims held prominent positions in public authority. While the media reported that each couple was well-known in the community, this distinct and, in his mind, glaring pattern seemed to elude reporters, bloggers, and podcasters alike.

Braxton's contemplation was abruptly pierced by the sound of Riley's voice. "Hey," it cut through his thoughts, "is this seat taken?" Braxton's heart raced as he looked up and saw her standing there. He blinked at her a couple of times and even pinched himself under the bar, just to confirm he wasn't lost in a dream.

"Oh, hey," he responded, trying to regain his composure. "Sorry, was spacing out there for a second," he said with a sheepish smile. "Have a seat if you like. I have VIP executive privileges here now." Braxton stopped talking to prevent his heart from leaping out of his mouth.

"VIP executive privileges? Fancy." She eased onto the stool next to him.

"I know, right?" Braxton couldn't help but feel a rush of excitement. "The head honcho is out, and he asked me to basically keep an eye on things. Pretty good gig, considering that Stacey over there knows what she's doing."

He nodded toward the lanky, tattooed bartender and caught her eye as she turned around. "You rolling with the Stoli martini?" he asked Riley, relaxing now that alcohol became the topic of discussion. He might as well imbibe too, now that he had a guest. And for all Stacey knew, he'd only been drinking sparkling water that day.

"Sure, but let's make it Grey Goose, and *I'm buying*," Riley emphasized the latter part as Stacey approached. Braxton's heart skipped a beat at her generous offer. "Vodka martini," she directed to the barkeep, "you guys have Grey Goose, right?" Stacey nodded. "Okay, vodka martini, very dry, with a twist and no olives. And he's going to have a Michter's Rye Manhattan. Make it a double. And. . .what kind of cherries do you guys have?"

"We use Luxardo for the upper shelf drinks, and—"

"Okay, he'll want one of those," Riley went on. Braxton watched in amazement as she stuffed a twenty-dollar bill into Stacey's hand before he could protest.

"Sure thing, I'll be right back," Stacey turned around to make the beverages.

"Uhhhh." Braxton's mouth started before his brain. "Wow," he managed. "I mean, is it weird that I found that whole thing kind of arousing?

I mean first, points for style. No stumbling there. But second, how did you know I wanted the cherry?"

Her laugh relaxed him. Maybe things weren't as awkward as he thought. It wouldn't be the first time that he had overthought things, that's for sure.

"An educated guess," Riley said with a mischievous glint in her eye. "You just don't seem like a standard maraschino kind of guy."

"Well, very impressive," Braxton remarked, still pleasantly surprised. It occurred to him that she must have seen his stash of craft cherries in the fridge when she went through his kitchen the other night. But it worked out, as his genuine flummox seemed to throw her off.

He was finding it increasingly difficult to toe the line between her being a federal agent versus her as a romantic interest. Yet, he couldn't help but sense mutual sparks flying between them.

"Are we celebrating something?" he asked after Stacey served their cocktails.

"Well, we just closed on a commercial office in Medford, and it looks like I'll be down here for the foreseeable future. So, that's something." Riley raised her drink. "Cheers," she toasted Braxton, maintaining eye contact as they clinked glasses.

"Hey. You know that rule, too," Braxton said after taking a swallow. He felt the concoction creep down his throat and trigger relaxing warm tingles in his belly. Aside from the hits from his hip flask—now half empty since its last refill—he had not yet had a proper cocktail that day.

"You mean about the eye contact?" Riley replied. "It's a European thing, I think. Means bad luck otherwise."

"Wellll," Braxton made a maybe/maybe not wobbling hand gesture. "Generally, yes. But at least in Germany, it's more specific. Apparently, if you don't make eye contact while clinking glasses, it's something like seven years of bad sex."

Riley cocked her head, as if to either fact-check her memory or to make a mental note that Braxton had made two sexual innuendos—arguably three, including the cherry—within minutes of their conversation.

"Hey," he continued, leaning in a bit closer, "I told you about my dad being a psychiatrist, right?"

"Yeah," said Riley, her curiosity piqued but not quite tracking.

"Right, so he would tell us some general stuff—broadly, all privileges maintained—and one of them was about this one-off patient he assessed when he worked at the California Medical Facility prison in Vacaville. You know, like where they hold people like Charles Manson and Ed Kemper?"

"Sure, gotcha." Riley waited for a beat. "I mean, I know about Charles Manson."

Braxton found her attempts to not act like an FBI agent endearing. She knew more about serial killers than he did. Of course she knew who Ed Kemper was.

"Right," he continued, lowering his voice somewhat, "well, I'm not talking about those kinds of guys right now. So, anyways—compared to super-max—CMF is actually not too bad. And a lot of inmates try to transfer in there by claiming that they're criminally insane. And doing those intakes was one of the things that my dad would do."

"Anyways," Braxton wet his whistle with a sip of his cocktail, "this one guy comes in, swearing up and down that he's a sex addict. My dad basically tells him there's no such thing and proceeds with the psych testing. You know what the Rorschach test is, right? The inkblot thingies that the patient looks at and tells the therapist what he sees?"

"Sure, like the butterfly blobs and stuff like that, right?" Riley tracked, intrigued.

"Exactly. So, my dad holds up the first inkblot, and the guy says it's him masturbating. The second one is him having sex with two women. By the third one, the guy is kind of offended, asking why my dad is showing him bestiality porn. At this point, my dad puts everything down and says, 'You know what? I think you're right. You're the first sex addict I've ever evaluated.'" Braxton couldn't hold back a chuckle, stifling his laughter as he continued. "Well, now the guy is really worked up, exclaiming, 'Look who's talking! *You're* the one showing me all the dirty pictures!'" Unable to contain himself, Braxton completely lost it.

Riley's expression was priceless. "Wait. . .soo. . ." she started laughing, realizing that it was a joke setup. "Oh god, you're terrible," she giggled.

"So, you get my point," he went on with an abashed smile. "I mean, in case there was any awkwardness about—"

"Dude. Brax. You think too much," Riley said. "You need to relax, buddy."

She gently patted and stroked his back for a couple of seconds, the result of which had quite the opposite effect on Braxton. His smile widened, and he took another swig to calm himself down.

"So, pretty crazy stuff going on with these missing couples, right?" Braxton remarked, setting down his drink. "Have you been keeping up with that, or has big pharma been taking up all your time?"

"You're right, it's quite unsettling," Riley responded. "I've heard bits and pieces about it. Tragic, for sure."

Braxton swirled his glass, his tone becoming more serious. "It's frustrating, though. I've lost even more faith in modern media reporting. I haven't come across a single article that acknowledges the obvious pattern between the two cases." He continued, emphasizing his point. "I mean, in both instances, the man was in public service, and the woman was from 'old' money." He added air quotes around the term. "Wouldn't it be wild if there was some sort of 'Hatfield and McCoy' blood feud going on or something like that?"

A brief silence followed as Riley regarded him with an intrigued expression, and then a brief chuckle escaped her lips. "Are all lawyers as conspiratorial as you?" she teased with a playful grin. "Okay, I got a question for you." She switched gears. "Would you rather be able to time-travel to any point in your lifetime or have Jedi mind-trick powers?"

"Whoa, hold up," Braxton interjected with a playful grin. "You can't just drop a bomb like that without some ground rules. For the mind control, is it a one-on-one deal, or am I controlling everyone on the planet?"

Riley, amused, replied, "Let's say it's limited to those in your immediate vicinity or anyone you're directly communicating with."

Braxton nodded, quickly moving on. "And for time-travel, am I aging, or is it a 'Back to the Future' scenario?"

"Always 'Back to the Future'," Riley responded with an exaggerated sigh, "You don't age. Now, choose."

"Okay, okay." Braxton waved his hands as if to beg her off. "Mind control. No regrets," he answered.

"That's it?" Riley said after a pause. "No explanation whatsoever?"

"Quid pro quo, madam," Braxton said with a dramatic air.

"Time-travel, of course," she said without hesitating. "The possibilities are endless. Fix mistakes, foresee problems, and well, financial freedom. Plus, I'd worry about going overboard with mind control should I come across any particular assholes. So, that one's easy for me."

"Hmm," Braxton began, a playful glint in his eye, "I like how you have a 'particular' asshole in mind. But we need not unpack that now."

"I wasn't saying that about anyone in partic—" Riley protested.

"I know, I know," Braxton reassured her with a gentle pat on her back. "It was just a side comment. But no. It's not just because a mind control lawyer would be worth millions per day. It's mostly about not wanting to know too much about my future, like my death date. And there's the matter of immortality. Could be tempting to stick to one decade, say the nineties, which would totally rock by the way, but then you're faced with choosing your own end. Nope, I'd rather navigate my fate with mind control." He took another pull from his nearly empty glass, which he pointed out to Stacey as she did her rounds.

"Okay," Riley said as the bartender approached, "you get a hundred-year range from when you're born."

"Hah," Braxton scoffed, "is this how the pharma-industrial complex works? Sweeten the pot on the back end? Oh, and are you good for now?" He pointed at Riley's half-full drink. "I guess just a bourbon on the rocks, please."

"And I'll have another one of these, please," Riley said, having downed her drink while Braxton ordered.

"Jesus," he quipped. "That's a hell of a trick, making your drink disappear like that. But yeah, the hundred-year thing doesn't change my mind. I'd rather go through life using mind control until its unpredicted terminus," he concluded.

"Hmm," Riley acknowledged, "I see your point there." Stacey returned with change, and Braxton left a few bucks on the counter. "But knowing when I'm ready to go seems okay to me. Guess we'll agree to disagree."

"For sure," Braxton said. "And I'm not trying to convince you otherwise. Just saying that mind control is obviously the better choice"—he delayed for a moment as Riley started to scowl—"for me, that is," he snickered. The ice cubes danced about in his glass as he took another drink. Riley rolled her eyes and took a drink herself, aping him.

"Well," Riley scoffed, "obviously it's not the best choice when you can do both."

"What do you mean," said Braxton. "It was one or the other, right?"

"Right," she confirmed. "But the beauty of the time-travel option is that you can select it first. Then when you're done with it, you can time-travel back to the moment of decision and choose mind control."

"Ah, man!" Braxton admitted defeat. "Touché. Well played." His expression must have amused Riley because it took a while for her to stop giggling. It was nice to see her more relaxed.

"That's an interesting theory about the blood-feud thing," said Riley. "But I thought you didn't have any experience in criminal work, right?"

"Not really. Well, you're going to laugh. I actually applied to the FBI a couple of years ago. Special Agent, you know, suits with guns and badges? The recruitment process has multiple phases, and I made it through phase two. But alas, it was not meant to be. To be honest, I may not have passed the PFT for all I know."

"Right," Riley nodded along. "Understandable."

Braxton smiled and paused. Most pharmaceutical reps wouldn't know what PFT stood for, and she knew exactly what it meant.

"You know, what PFT stands for? It's the Physical Fitness Test." Braxton took a sip and licked his lips. "Are you sure you're not FBI?" he taunted.

Riley chuckled, her cheeks blushing slightly. "Ha-ha, you got me there. Actually, I didn't know what that meant, but I didn't want to interrupt. I just know it's tough to get into the FBI, that's all. So, you applied? How does that even work?"

"Well, I guess being a lawyer helps get your foot in the door," Braxton let it slide. "Then I did a lot of running and got a gym membership. Started reading up on polygraph techniques because—like many Californians our age—I smoked weed within the past five years. Never made it to the polygraph, though. I guess they didn't like my phase two exam or interview answers. Makes sense, as I have zero law enforcement background. And the only other attorney in the applicant pool already worked there as an analyst. But it is what it is."

Braxton chose not to mention how the FBI's rejection ultimately resulted in his bankruptcy and wholesale loss of faith in the jurisprudential system to which he remained handcuffed by virtue of crushing student loan debt. It seemed a bit too early in the game to broach that subject.

Lost in thought, Braxton didn't notice the subtle change in Riley's demeanor as her eyes widened and she took a sharp breath.

"Where did you interview?" she asked, her curiosity palpable.

"Depends on where you live," he replied, refocusing on the conversation. "In my case, it was San Francisco. In the federal building. Same place as the federal court, just a different floor."

"I knew it!" Riley blurted out, her eyes briefly brightening with recognition before she quickly masked her excitement. "I mean, how they break it down geographically. That's how my company does it, too. Oh well, their loss for not hiring you." She took a sip of her drink, settling her nerves before changing the subject. "So, how's the playwriting coming along?"

"Oh, swimmingly," he said, brushing off the previous topic. "Actually, I'm sticking with straight prose for now. Screenwriting requires a lot of character arc and plot planning before you can dive into the actual scriptwriting. I prefer to start with an idea and then see where it goes. That's harder to do with a screenplay." He took another drink, steering clear of how he hadn't been able to finish anything he started.

"So, what's going on now with your writing, then?" she prodded.

"Well, I have a few different things in play. But lately, I've been working on a dystopia-like story about a global virus pandemic. Kinda like the Spanish Flu, but in the twenty-first century. It's interesting to think about. I mean, things were still pretty brutal in 1918. People's life expectancy was like early fifties to mid-fifties, and dying from diseases like measles was still a thing. That was still the industrial age. So, it's kind of fun—while also terrifying—to think about how a pandemic like that would go down during the information age. I mean, just for starters, can you imagine what quarantine orders would do to the global economy? Anyways, that's sort of the setting I'm working with." He chose not to mention that he was only two pages into that story.

"That sounds pretty interesting, actually. Dark. But interesting," said Riley. "So, I know you've mentioned it in passing before, but was there anything in particular that made you decide on this sabbatical thing that you're on?"

"I don't know," Braxton said after some contemplation. "It just felt like the right thing to do. I've spent most of my life doing things based on societal expectations. That's why I pursued a law degree, became a lawyer, and married my long-term girlfriend. On the surface, everything looked great. But deep down, not so much.

"My spouse and I started having different expectations as we entered our thirties. We ended up getting divorced and, thankfully, it was amicable. Still, I couldn't shake the feeling of failure. Then I started hating the legal work, dealing with other people's problems without dealing with my own. And like manna from heaven, I received a referral fee for a personal injury case that was finally settled. Nothing ludicrous, but enough runway for a lean year. So, here I am. Trying to break society's mold by following my dreams," he gave a halfhearted thumbs-up.

Again, Braxton left out the part about losing all faith in the judicial system and the resultant chronic drinking. Too soon, he surmised, too soon.

"I understand that," Riley nodded empathetically. "Dealing with someone going through a tough time can be challenging, especially when you're constantly handling other people's problems without addressing your own. That way lies madness."

"Hey, I'll drink to that. And to good conversation," Braxton raised his glass with a broad smile. They clinked their glasses, gazing into each other's eyes. It was one of those moments forever captured by Braxton's haywire photographic memory.

The mental snapshot triggered something in him. It was her! The FBI analyst who was also applying for the special agent position in San Francisco. He didn't remember her being this attractive—she looked different back then. But he did recall thinking she was the coolest person in the room.

"So, about the other night—" Braxton navigated into awkward waters.

"Seriously, Brax," she interrupted, "you think way too much. So, tell me about your other stories."

Braxton smiled. "You know, my laptop's at home if you want to take a look at them."

"Are you trying to get me to come home with you tonight, Mr. Hayward?" asked Riley with a playful tone.

"You've really gotta stop with those dirty pictures," Braxton grinned. "I just like your company is all. No pressure or anything. Fine either way."

He held his breath, unsure what fate had in store. A pregnant pause. Then two more.

"Okay." Riley flagged Stacey. "Can you close us out please?"

"Sure," said Stacey. Riley gathered her things, and Stacey returned her card. "On the house." She turned her head and gave Braxton an encouraging wink.

"Wait, are you sure?" asked Riley.

"And don't you need me to help close tonight?" Braxton chimed in.

"Yep, I'm sure," Stacey said to Riley. "And nope, we're good tonight," she answered Braxton. "Have a nice night!"

"Thank you, that's really sweet of you." Riley turned to Braxton. "Ready?" He nodded and stood up, ready to follow her anywhere. Braxton remembered to breathe again once he got into her car.

Elated by the growing connection with Riley, he cast aside all of his worries and concerns. Being with her not only ignited his passion, it made him feel like he could navigate any unexpected twists and turns that lay ahead, even the mysteries the universe had in store for him. Then, a lingering thought from Jason's toast about being careful what he wished for echoed in his mind. Shrugging it off, he admired Riley's profile against the backdrop of the city lights. Her radiance captivated him.

Caught by his gaze, Riley questioned, "What is it?"

Braxton averted his eyes momentarily, watching as they entered his neighborhood. "Oh, nothing," he replied with a smile. "Just enjoying the view, and eagerly anticipating where this story will lead us, is all."

Riley chuckled, shaking her head affectionately. "Relax, Brax. Stop overthinking and savor the moment."

"Enjoying the moment," Braxton agreed with a grin. "That's the first thing I'll toast to once I'm home."

CHAPTER SIX

KIND OF A WEIRD
BREWERY NAME

FRIDAY, AUGUST 17, 5:16 AM

R iley's eyes snapped open, her sleep-fogged mind jolted by the persistent buzzing of her phone. She fumbled for it on the night-stand, her heart racing as she saw the FBI alert flashing on the screen. With a quick glance at the time and a throbbing headache, she cursed under her breath. It was still dark outside, the world cloaked in the predawn silence.

Slipping out of bed, Riley moved with practiced stealth, careful not to disturb Braxton, who was still lost in peaceful slumber beside her. She couldn't afford him waking up, not now. His questions about her abrupt departure could lead to explanations she couldn't provide.

Padding out of the room, Riley went outside and retrieved her backup change of clothes from her car. A quick glance in the bathroom mirror confirmed that she looked like a mess, but there was no time for a proper shower. She settled for hitting the hot spots, washing away the remnants of sleep and any traces of the night.

Dressed in her FBI attire, she took in her reflection in the mirror again. Her eyes were resolute, her expression determined, but there was an undercurrent of unease that no amount of preparation could dispel.

Leaving a note for Braxton on the kitchen counter, she scrawled a hasty message: "Had to rush. Will explain later. Sorry. Riley." She attached it to the fridge with a sigh of hope that he would understand.

Feeling oddly guilty about departing without a word, Riley headed to her car. As she zoomed in on the coordinates provided by the FBI dispatch alert, her stomach twisted in knots. The grim news displayed on her phone screen made bile from the previous night rise in her throat. This was no false alarm. It was a gruesome discovery, and she might be one of the first to get there.

Riley gripped the steering wheel as she sped toward the scene. She dialed the command dispatch number on her phone, her voice steady despite the urgency in her heart.

"This is McAvoy. I have an ETA of approximately five to six minutes," she reported.

Dispatch responded promptly, "Roger that, Special Agent McAvoy. Standby."

A moment later, SAIC Richter's voice crackled through the line. "Ah, Agent McAvoy I presume. You're one of the first responders, and I'm about five minutes out as well."

"Understood, sir," Riley replied, her tone professional.

Richter's voice carried a hint of playful condescension. "Well, McAvoy, you certainly are quick on your feet, but remember, this isn't one of your solo gigs."

"Of course, sir," Riley responded with an unfettered eyeroll.

Richter's tone became more intense. "Since you're so on the ball, you'll be leading the initial securing of the scene for the search and forensics teams. They're about twenty minutes out. I need you to ensure everything remains pristine until they arrive."

Riley nodded, even though Richter couldn't see it. "Understood. I'll make sure the area is locked down."

"Just be vigilant, McAvoy. Keep an eye out for press and other looky-loos." Richter's condescension took a lighter tone. "And for the love of god, make sure that the local boys don't get their filthy paws all over my crime scene."

Riley chuckled softly at Richter's version of levity. "Don't worry, sir. I'll keep them in line."

Richter added with urgency, "By the way, the black and whites are on their way too, so hit the gas."

As she reached her destination, Riley parked about a block away. She knew she had to approach the cemetery's alternate entrance carefully. It was typically used by groundskeepers and maintenance crews, and the entrance itself might hold valuable clues.

Riley checked her firearm, ensuring a round was chambered and the gun was snugly holstered. With her heart pounding, she stepped out of the car, ready to face the grim scene that awaited her.

LATER THAT MORNING

When Braxton woke up, he found that Riley had already left. He began his morning with a mid-level workout and a run, although his hangover limited the intensity. During his run, his mind drifted to a dreamlike memory of Riley taking a shower and kissing him goodbye while it was still dark out. But he quickly shifted his thoughts to more pleasant memories, like the way the nighttime light shimmered off Riley's skin as her taut body rhythmically pulsed above his own. The way she would arch her back just before climaxing. And how the caress of her silky hair would gently tease and arouse nerve endings he never knew he had. . .

To avoid undue chafing—among other reasons—Braxton terminated that particular train of thought and deposited it into the spank bank.

After showering and making himself presentable for the day, Braxton went to the kitchen and poured himself a strong brew of bourbon-coffee. Before opening the fridge to retrieve some half-and-half, he saw that Riley had left a note on it with her private email.

In summary, aside from the usual hangover shit, Braxton was feeling pretty good. Having properly titrated the coffee, he took an ambitious swallow and winced at its scorching heat.

"Woo! I'm gonna feel that in a couple of hours." He unstopped the bourbon bottle and took several long pulls until coming back up for air. "Yowza," he gasped.

Being with Riley had triggered some thoughts on his dystopian pandemic story. In this grim tale, an incompetent president takes zero measures as a virus spreads from Asia to the rest of the globe. Health care resources are immediately overwhelmed, and quarantines are implemented state-by-state. Then the supply chain grinds to a halt. Martial law is imposed, and troops are deployed to secure supplies for the populace using an untested private-enterprise drone-delivery system. Society collapses into factions as local militias shoot down the drones and raid federal supply depots . . .

He took a less aggressive drink from his spiked coffee and opened his laptop. After logging in, he opened the Word file (generically titled "Dystopia") to input his stream of thought.

Braxton was surprised to discover that he had been at it for more than an hour. He took a swallow from his coffee and grimaced. It was cold and bitter with a boozy aftertaste. Never one to waste good bourbon, he took a deep breath and downed the rest.

"Well, that was productive." Braxton unplugged the laptop and dropped it on the living room couch. After pouring himself a drink, he Googled the *Medford Gazette* and went to its home page. A red "BREAKING NEWS" banner caught his attention, and he clicked on it instinctively.

HUMAN REMAINS DISCOVERED
AT JACKSONVILLE CEMETERY

August 17, Jacksonville, Ore. The discovery of human remains this morning has resulted in the total lockdown of the historic Jacksonville Cemetery. All access to the cemetery is prohibited pending further notice. Law enforcement officials advise that any unauthorized individual(s) in the area may be subject to immediate detention and/or arrest. Further updates will be provided as they become available.

"Holy shit," Braxton uttered. "Holy fuckin' shit." A haunting memory gripped him as he stared blankly at the laptop screen. It was as if a dark veil had descended upon his thoughts, transporting him to a place he'd tried to forget.

A place shrouded in an eerie darkness, with the shadowy tree canopy ominously blotting out the stars. The air was thick with silence, broken only by the disquieting sound of creaking rope and haunting chants that seemed to emanate from the depths of his subconscious.

His mind's eye painted a vivid yet unsettling picture: lifeless ivory figures swaying in the sluggish breeze, their bodies suspended from gnarled branches by taught, creaking ropes. The sight of those haunting specters, suspended in midair, sent a shiver of dread coursing through him, turning his bowels into jelly.

Then the plopping sound echoed in his ears, each uneven repetition driving home the gruesome reality of the scene. It was a place where time seemed to stand still, and the boundaries between dreams and nightmares blurred into an indistinguishable haze.

Braxton recoiled from the vividness of the memory, his heart pounding in his chest. He shook his head vigorously, as if trying to dislodge the haunting images that had resurfaced. "Snap out of it, mofo," he scolded himself, the harshness of his voice a stark contrast to the haunting recollection. "That was just a bad dream! That didn't really happen."

Taking refuge in the bottle of bourbon, he downed three consecutive gulps, attempting to drown out the disquieting echoes of that distant night. It took three more swigs for him to finally shake off the shadows and regain his composure.

"Ahh, there we go," he muttered, his voice laced with a mixture of relief and desperation. He shook his head one last time, as if to clear the lingering remnants of the unsettling memory, and headed to his room.

"Time to smoke a bowl," he declared, seeking solace in the familiar rituals of the present to banish the ghosts of the past.

A FEW HOURS LATER

The sun was high in the sky, casting a relentless heat over Jacksonville. Braxton found himself back at the Saloon, seeking solace from the sweltering day. It was just before noon, and the Saloon, with its comforting air-conditioning, was about half full. The atmosphere inside was a welcome relief from the scorching outdoors as the temperature climbed into the eighties. The cemetery remained under lockdown, and the press had set up camp in a parking lot nearby, casting a shadow of anticipation over the town.

As Braxton settled into his customary spot, nursing a refreshing sparkling water, he felt a sense of calm wash over him. Greetings and pleasantries were exchanged with Stacey, the cute ever-friendly bartender, and some of the regulars who had become his drinking buddies. Conversations flowed effortlessly, touching on topics ranging from the mundane to the extraordinary. The herb he had indulged in earlier helped soothe his mind, the Xanax eased his nerves, the Adderall provided an extra boost for sociability, and his hip flask, now about three-quarters full, remained a steadfast companion.

Braxton leaned in closer to the two older regulars he had grown fond of over time, Earl and Donnie, and shared his musings. "You know," he began, his voice carrying a note of contemplation, "these are indeed peculiar times we're living in. But what I'm starting to realize is that when life gets crazier than usual, it has a funny way of shifting your priorities around."

Earl, a white widowed Oregon native in his early sixties but appearing older due to his distinct appearance, was the type who didn't mince words. His bushy gray hair and sideburns flowed from beneath an oversized derby cap, and he wore thick plastic-rimmed glasses reminiscent of NASA engineers from old space-race documentaries. Retired with full benefits from a municipal water job, Earl was set for life.

Donnie, a Black man in his later sixties but looking considerably younger, sported a summery straw fedora that complemented his lean, tall frame. Donnie had left behind the hustle of California and relocated north to cut his cost of living. He had retired from a successful career selling high-end luxury cars and had even struck it rich during the home-flipping craze of the mid-2000s, only to face a divorce. From his perspective, it was the best thing that had ever happened to him.

With a shared unspoken understanding of life's quirks, Earl exchanged an amused glance with Donnie. "You're starting to see it, huh?" Earl replied, his tone hinting at the many stories they had shared over drinks.

"I guess I don't have to tell *you guys* that," said Braxton, a thoughtful expression on his face, "but I just flashed on something that happened about five years ago when I was living in San Francisco." He took a sip from his seltzer water, letting the coolness wash over him. "I was a brand-new attorney, already stressing about the way my boss was handling things at the practice. And my then-wife was stressing about some work-related shit, too.

"I had picked her up from the Financial District, and we were driving to our Richmond District apartment. Traffic was EXTRA slow, and we were just fuming. I started taking side routes and saw how all streets feeding into Fulton were jamming up. I took a left on the first street that wasn't congested and zipped toward Fulton, thinking I had outsmarted the traffic. Or so I thought.

"Even though the light was green, these SFPD motor cops rolled to a stop in the middle of the intersection, forcing us to yield. Which I did, right at the traffic light. We were absolutely seething by then, cursing whatever fucking bigwig was forcing us to wait. Then these guys in blue uniforms started riding by on these Enduro-style motorcycles, flanking a burnt-sienna mid-eighties Lincoln Town Car. And in the backseat of that car was the frickin' Dalai Lama, waving and smiling at us with child-like exuberance."

"You mean, the Buddhist guy?" Earl asked, raising an eyebrow.

"Yeah, like the Buddhist guy," Braxton confirmed. "So, we sat there like deer in the headlights and waved back at him. Then we turned to each other, silently confirming that that had just happened. We were suddenly in this calm, serene mood. And I came to realize that all the things we were stressing over were basically chickenshit. It was like the wake of the dude's spiritual aura lapped through us as he passed on by. Later that night, we decided to move to my hometown and hang up my shingle there."

Braxton omitted the part about how this decision resulted in spectacular failure.

"Not saying whether that was the right decision or anything," he continued, "but it's crazy to think about how things may have been different if I didn't have that experience, you know? It definitely realigned things, that's for sure."

"Well, either way, that's a pretty cool experience, if you ask me," Donnie said with a chuckle, while Earl nodded in agreement. "Reminds me of my experience with Pastor Fuzz, actually."

"Who?" Braxton asked, intrigued.

"Pastor Fuzz," Donnie repeated. "He was one of the local pastors at a little town I was living in back in the day. So, I was hanging out at the local watering hole, having my usual. And I notice this woman sitting at the bar who was on a real tear. Sloppy drunk. Next thing I know, Pastor Fuzz comes in and approaches the drunken lady."

"'Mary,' the pastor says, 'I noticed you weren't in church this morning and, frankly, I'm surprised to see one of my parishioners in such a state on this wonderful Sunday afternoon. Is everything okay?'

"Mary slurred an apology and tried to get up from her stool. Losing her balance, she falls into the good pastor, who also loses his footing, and both end up on the floor. After some further tussling about, the pastor found himself mounted atop her spread-open legs, with her back on the floor and skirt hitched up over her waist. All the while, he's trying to lift her up by her shoulders, but she keeps flailing back onto the ground." Donnie's hand slapped the bar top for additional effect. "Noting the commotion, the bartender came over to them.

"'Hey, you two,' the barman said after taking in the scene, 'I can't have this sort of thing happening in my bar. This isn't that kinda establishment.'"

"'No, no!' the pastor exclaimed, realizing what it must look like. 'You don't understand!' he said. 'I'm Pastor Fuzz!'"

"'Oh, I see,' said the bartender. 'Well, I guess if you're that far along, you might as well finish the job.'"

After a moment of processing, Braxton lost it. "Oh, my God," he said, wiping away tears of laughter. "Oh, Jesus Christ. Terrible. I haven't heard that one before. You had me going there for a second."

The men were still laughing at Braxton's expense when someone else walked into the Saloon.

She was a straight-haired brunette of about five-three and wearing low, chunky two-inch heels. Braxton estimated her to be in her early thirties. She walked up to the middle of the bar and put her oversized bag on the counter. Braxton recognized her immediately.

"Can I help you?" Stacey asked the new patron.

"I was looking for Jason." She rummaged through her large gray leather purse.

"He won't be back until next week. I'm filling in right now," said Stacey. The woman pulled out a growler-sized bottle and put it on the bar. "Ummm," Stacey eyed Braxton for an assist.

"Hey, there," Braxton got up from his stool. "Hi, I'm Braxton," he extended his hand. "I'm sort of keeping an eye out here for Jason until he gets back. But you can't bring your own alcohol in here."

"Oh, I know," she said. "it's a gift for Jason. And I'm Emily, nice to meet you," she gave him a firm, professional handshake. "My family dabbles in craft brewing and distilling, and we're giving him a sampler. He'll know what it's about. Can you make sure he gets it?" She picked up the bottle and thrust it toward Braxton, which he instinctively received. "Sure, that's fine," he replied. "I'll put it in the back. Does it need to be chilled or anything?"

"I think it's best at cellar temperature, but everyone has their preference," she responded. "It leans on the stout side."

"Do brewers call these things a 'shiner' or is that a wine thing?" Braxton turned the unlabeled bottle from side to side.

"No," she said, "it's just a growler. I don't get why the wine folks call their bottles shiners. Anyway, can you let Jason know that Emily dropped by with a sample of the latest batch?"

"Yeah, sure, no problem. Certainly does look stout." Braxton looked into the opaque dark brew suspended in the brown glass bottle. "It looks like black coffee from here."

"Yeah, it's pretty strong stuff, that's for sure. Anyhow, please make sure Jason gets it. And it was very nice to meet you," Emily said as she grabbed her oversized bag from the bar. Now much lighter without the growler, the bag appeared deflated as she lifted it and walked toward the front door.

"Likewise, and sure thing. Oh, and congrats on the divorce!" Braxton said, playfully raising an eyebrow. Emily came to a dead stop and turned around.

"I'm sorry?" she asked. "Have we met before?"

"Not formally. But I think I overheard some of the toasts shared at your divorce party table the other day." Braxton raised his glass and grinned, his tone laced with flirtatious humor. "What was it again?" he teased, "Here's to you and that *charming* ex-husband of yours?"

"Oh my god," her hand went to her forehead, partially hiding a sudden blush. "I thought I recognized you!" Her infectious laugh echoed throughout the Saloon. "Honestly, I don't remember much of what happened that night, so don't hold it against me!"

"Ha, ha, no worries," Braxton chuckled, his smile showing genuine interest. He liked her. He found her cheerful, no-bullshit attitude refreshing. He even thought he felt a spark of mutual attraction, but held back a bit, considering his situation with Riley. "Mum's the word, and I'll make sure Jason gets this," he jostled the growler. "Cheers."

"Cheers." She flashed him a captivating smile before turning back around, leaving Braxton with a lingering sense of intrigue.

Braxton made his way down the hallway toward the restroom, taking a right turn into Jason's cramped office—a space cluttered with stacks of invoices and a small, well-worn wooden desk tucked against the wall. The dim lighting created a cozy atmosphere, and Braxton carefully placed the brew on the desk, its contents casting a warm, inviting glow. He grabbed a Post-it note and pen, quickly scribbling "TO: JASON / FROM: EMILY" before affixing the note to the bottle, snugly wedging it into the corner.

As the day transitioned into evening, law enforcement continued to maintain a lockdown on the cemetery, restricting access to local residents only. During this brief downtime, Braxton made a pit stop at home to refill his hip flask, indulge in a relaxing joint, and take another dose of Adderall (in that precise order).

Upon his return to the Saloon, Braxton caught wind of some rumors circulating among the locals and media types at the bar. First, the Holman family had plans to make a public statement at 6:00 PM. Second, there were whispers of more than one body being discovered. The ringing of the Saloon's landline phone in the background prompted Stacey to answer it.

Amidst the chatter and uncertainty, Braxton couldn't help but wonder about Riley's current situation at the cemetery. A sense of envy washed over him, imagining himself in an alternate universe where he was the special agent on the case. However, the thought of being out in the scorching heat without access to a drink quickly dispelled any envy. Stacey broke his reverie by thrusting the Saloon's phone into his view.

"It's Jason," she said. Braxton grabbed the phone, gave Stacey a nod of gratitude, and worked his mouth, tongue, and lips to avoid slurring any words.

"Hey, Jason, what's going on?" he began. "Hello?" he inquired as he heard Jason's voice on the other end. "Okay, I hear— sorry," he attempted to sync up with the phone lag. More silence followed, and just as Braxton was about to give up, Jason's voice finally came through.

"Hi, Braxton. Doing good. Just checking in on things while I have some reception. How's everything going at the Saloon? All good?" Braxton waited for Jason to finish his transmission.

"Yeah, well, things are fine here. That whole missing persons thing and cemetery shutdown added an extra layer of excitement, so it's been a bit busier. But Stacey and the kitchen staff have everything under control. How are you?"

"Good, good, thanks for asking," Jason replied after a slight lag. "Yeah, I heard some updates about that cemetery stuff while I was on the road. Pretty crazy. But things are going well there? No major bar brawls, drug busts, nothing like that?" Jason's sarcasm was evident in his tone.

"Nope, things have been pretty smooth," Braxton chuckled. "Front-end and kitchen tills have balanced each night. I heard the inventory order you placed the other day will arrive tomorrow morning."

"Oh, yeah," Braxton recalled, "Emily dropped by earlier today with a growler for you. And guess what, she was the divorcee who caught me checking her out!" Braxton wasn't sure if the delay was due to the phone lag or if Jason's call had actually dropped.

He was about to ask "Are you there?" when he heard Jason's voice again. "Ah, dude, no way. That's hilarious. So, Emily came by with a what?"

"A growl-er," Braxton enunciated, "of some craft brew. She said it 'leans' stout, but if you ask me, the stuff looks darker and thicker than your average Guinness. Anyway, she wanted to make sure you knew that she dropped it off. I put a note on it, and the bottle's on your desk," pleased that he had recalled all of that from memory. Braxton checked off that to-do item from his mental list.

"Oh, cool, okay. Thanks for the heads up. Is it any good?" Jason asked.

"Wasn't about to take the liberty without your permission, dude," Braxton said. "Do they make good stuff?"

"Yeah, they do actually," said Jason. His voice carried a hint of concern, though Braxton didn't seem to pick up on it. "Her family has been in the distilling and brewing industry for ages. And they did particularly well during the Prohibition days—if you get what I'm saying. Anyways, they're in the process of opening up a retail brewery and distillery soon here. That's what's being built on that hill you live next to. So, Emily likes to drop by with samples here and there. So, the beer she brought. . .it's like a super-dark stout, huh?"

"Yep," Braxton confirmed. "I'll go ahead and pour myself some, let you know how thick and frothy the head is, and then stick it in the cooler so you can have sloppy seconds." The weed was clearly having its effect on him, as Braxton couldn't stifle a juvenile giggle at his own crude joke.

"You're really cracking yourself up over there with that one, huh?" Jason said. "Okay, well, cool. Thanks for the update. I should have some reception on Sunday, so text me if anything crazy happens. But it sounds like things are all good. So, assuming that you've got a handle on everything, we'll touch base once I get back on Wednesday. Thanks for doing this, man. Sounds like I hired the right non-Oregon lawyer for the job."

"No sweat, dude," Braxton said, noting Jason's more relaxed tone. "I'll text you if anything above my pay grade happens, but assume no news is good news."

"Okay, great. I've got some fish to catch, so I'll let you go. Have a good one," Jason signed off, and Braxton ended the call, a sense of intrigue and camaraderie between them strengthening with each conversation.

Braxton grabbed the remote from behind the bar and walked back to his stool. Looking around, no one seemed to notice or care about the game on TV as he punched in the local news channel with the Technicolor reporter.

The TV screen cut to a somber shot of the grieving Holman family, numbering at least twenty, standing behind their spokeswoman. All of them stood in front of an ivy-covered trellis at the Holmans' stately home. Braxton turned up the volume a bit.

"We are all praying for the family and our community during these difficult times," the spokeswoman continued, her voice heavy with emotion, "and we ask for dignity and respect for the Holman family's privacy." Braxton estimated her age at about fifty years old. Her rounded figure was professionally dressed, and not one strand strayed from her chin-length dark-brown hair.

Braxton stared at the screen as the camera panned over the grieving family members. He watched the faces, one by one, his curiosity turned into intrigue.

Then, it happened. Second from the right, standing among the Holman family, was Emily. The divorcee. The one who had dropped off the growler earlier that day.

Braxton's eyes widened in shock, and his hand twitched, causing him to lose his grip on his glass. The cocktail glass thunked on the bar top, nearly spilling the drink. He couldn't believe what he was seeing. His mind raced with speculation, and his pulse quickened.

This was no ordinary coincidence. Emily, the woman who had casually delivered beer to him earlier, was somehow connected to the Holman family, the very family at the center of a murder case that was consuming the town. It was a shocking revelation for Braxton.

Unable to process the full implications of this discovery, Braxton finally tore his gaze away from the screen. He had to get out, clear his head, and figure out what to do next. Puzzle pieces were falling into place, and connections were being made that he'd rather forget. He couldn't shake the feeling that he was getting closer to something intriguing and far-reaching. And he wasn't sure if he wanted to find out where that would lead him.

Braxton flicked the TV back to the sports channel, put a coaster over his half-empty drink, and headed outside for a smoke and a walk. But that did little to calm his nerves. Time to up the bourbon dosage.

Braxton had issued the last call at eleven o'clock and it was almost midnight. Business was good and no major drama. From what he could tell, the tills were balanced and the amounts were properly logged into Jason's bookkeeping ledger. He got up from the small desk chair, being mindful not to bump into anything in the cramped space. He went out front and let Stacey know that he'd close up and she was free to go. They exchanged goodbyes and Braxton locked the front door.

"Meh, what the fuck." He grabbed a pint glass and went back to the office where he cracked open the growler and poured himself a quarter. He held it up to the light, noting its darkness even through clear glass. Raising the drink to no one in particular, he took a long draft of the thick brew.

"Woo!" he exclaimed. "That'll put a bomb in your gut!" It was quite tasty, but a tad too rich for his preference. He drained the glass, and carried it and the growler to the kitchen.

Having washed and returned the glass, Braxton picked up the bottle from the counter. He held it to the light again, with the base just above eye level. From that angle, he saw what looked like a triangular logo embossed on its concave base.

"*Prime Ascendant*," he traced his finger over the small-font words inscribed over the inverted triangle. "Huh. Kind of a weird brewery name," Braxton mused. "Sounds more like the name of a cult, if you ask me."

Snickering at his comment, Braxton put the bottle in the cooler. But his amusement was short-lived. Just as he turned to leave the kitchen, a sudden, jarring clatter made him jump. He spun around to see a large metal bowl eerily spinning face-down on the kitchen tile. It had fallen from a rack he had been standing under only moments earlier. Time seemed to stretch as he waited for the noisy bowl to settle. Then, with tremoring hands, he bent down to pick it up.

As he did, he glanced at its shiny surface and froze in terror. Reflected in the polished metal, he saw them. Two ghost-white, desiccated figures with their mouths sewn up, each swinging like a limp marionette from a rope. Their hollow eyes stared back at him, devoid of life yet brimming with intensity. His heart raced, and a cold sweat broke out on his forehead.

Unable to comprehend what he was witnessing, Braxton tossed the bowl into the sink, the loud clang echoing through the empty Saloon. Without wasting another moment, he rushed to lock up and left the establishment, his mind a whirlwind of fear and confusion, haunted by the gruesome images he'd been working so hard to dispel from his mind.

As he walked home, flask in hand, Braxton started to rationalize what he had seen in the kitchen. *It had to be a trick of the light*, he thought. *Just the overhead kitchen lights reflecting strangely in the metal bowl. Yes, that had to be it.*

By the time he reached his front door, his flask was almost empty. He stepped inside and went straight to the drawer where he kept his stash. With trembling hands, he retrieved a Xanax, downing it with the last drops of bourbon from his flask. It was the last thing he remembered from that night as sleep and darkness overtook him, temporarily pushing aside the fear that had gripped him earlier. But for how long? The unsettling events of the evening still lingered in his mind, casting a long shadow over his restless sleep.

THE NEXT MORNING

Riley muttered a curse under her breath as she read the blast alert on her Blackberry: "AUG. 18 PRESS CONFERENCE RESET FROM 09:30 TO 09:00. ASSIGNED SPECIAL AGENTS: APPEARANCE REQUIRED." Richter's obsession with publicity never failed to infuriate her. She recognized the importance of a media presence, but it often felt like an extravagant waste of resources.

Collecting her belongings from her cubicle, Riley's frustration simmered just below the surface. In the motor pool parking area, her colleagues were already piling into the black transport SUV. She waved them off, choosing her unmarked sedan for the trip to the Medford police station. "Cutting it close, McAvoy," Richter chided as she approached her designated spot.

"Apologies, sir," she replied, slipping her shades into her jacket pocket. Riley had struggled to find parking, but she kept that annoyance to herself. She knew Richter's predictable response would have been, "That's why you take the transport vehicle."

"Well, you're here, shades off, and in position. Just try not to squint too much this time," Richter remarked before turning to face the cameras. The police chief stepped up to the lectern.

Following the standard privacy warnings and restrictions on discussing ongoing investigations, the chief introduced SAIC Richter. Richter adjusted his tie and retrieved his note cards, exchanging pleasantries with the chief while reporters, armed with smartphones and recording devices, anxiously awaited his words.

"First, I want to express my gratitude to the chief and our local authorities. The professionalism of Medford and Jackson County's law enforcement is beyond commendable. The community can rest assured they are in capable hands," Richter began, pausing dramatically. This time, Riley resisted the urge to roll her eyes at his theatrics.

"I'm sure you all have questions," Richter continued, "and I'll do my best to address them. However, as you know, we cannot comment on ongoing investigations. Now that the victims' families have been notified, I can share the following:

"Yesterday, two homicide victims were discovered in Jacksonville Cemetery. With a heavy heart, I confirm the remains belong to the couple reported missing on August sixteenth, namely: Andrew and Susan Holman."

CHAPTER SEVEN

A TWISTED REMINDER

FRIDAY, AUGUST 24, 8:43 PM

Riley sat alone in the dimly lit FBI office, her gaze anchored to the expansive array of case files sprawled before her. Hours melded into one another, marking the third time that day she had meticulously combed through each detail. Despite her unwavering dedication, the elusive breakthrough she yearned for remained just beyond her grasp.

Rising with a heavy sigh, she navigated the quiet of the office toward the coffee machine, her movement echoing softly in the nearly deserted space. The office held only herself and Richter now, its silence in direct contrast to the storm of thoughts raging in her mind. She poured herself a mug, grateful for the solitude provided by her boss's closed office door. Current progress was thin, and the last thing she needed was to report the stagnation of their investigation or engage in empty pleasantries.

This moment of pause, however, wasn't just about evading an unwelcome conversation. It was a crossroads for Riley, a tangible reflection of the internal conflict she faced between professional duty and personal truth. She found herself questioning not just the integrity of the evidence but the very fabric of her motivations. What did she truly seek—justice, or something more profound?

Standing in the quiet office, she realized that her involvement with Braxton was clouding her usual sharp focus. The cases on her desk demanded a detachment she found increasingly difficult to muster, her professional resolve tested by the emotional undercurrents of her past.

Her history with love was a series of lessons in caution, each relationship starting with a fervor that swiftly spiraled into a vortex of control and toxicity. Braxton, with his own set of complexities, appeared quite different from the men she'd known. He was an enigma, a blend of humor and darkness, stirring in Riley a hope she dared not fully embrace. The fear of history repeating itself cast a long shadow over her judgment, leaving her to grapple with the distinction between intuition and insecurity.

In this late-hour solitude, as she grimaced at the taste of stale coffee, Riley faced the challenging balance of guarding her heart while navigating the treacherous waters of new intimacy. Could she afford to let Braxton in, or was her attraction to him a risk to the objectivity critical to her badge? The more she pondered, the more she realized that her struggle wasn't just about maintaining professional integrity; it was about learning to trust again—not just in others, but in her own ability to trust her instincts.

Returning to her cubicle, Riley began organizing the case files, a desperate attempt to regain a semblance of control over the ever-expanding chaos of her life and the investigation. As she slid a folder into place, a series of photographs slipped out, cascading onto her desk.

The grim images portrayed the autopsies of the Holman couple, their lifeless bodies ghostly pale, their mouths grotesquely sewn shut. A twisted reminder of the dreadful secrets they had carried, secrets that would never pass their lips again.

Riley's thoughts drifted back to the chilling discovery at the cemetery, where the couple lay at rest beside the grand mausoleums housing the town's affluent families. Shrouded beneath linens, one of which had been disturbed by a curious groundskeeper.

Summoning her courage, Riley approached the covered bodies, her gloved hands trembling as she cautiously peeled back each sheet. The grotesque tableau—a meticulous reassembly of disemboweled corpses, preserved chemically, their mouths sewn in eternal silence—was indelibly imprinted in her memory.

The onslaught of these memories, coupled with the haunting photographs and the frustration of an unresolved case, surged over her. The anxiety swelled within, clawing at her chest, tightening its grip.

She thrust the macabre photographs back into the file and shoved it into a nearby cubbyhole, as if attempting to bury the horrors it contained. Desperate to leave the oppressive atmosphere of the office, she bolted from her chair, making it to her car just before her legs gave way.

Sitting in her car, her heart raced, the beat so loud it drowned out the world, save for a momentary, haunting impression of distant chanting. She battled for control, each breath a jagged struggle against the tide of her anxiety.

When she could finally coax the engine to life, its steady hum was a temporary balm, a brief reprieve from the chaos inside her. Directionless, she was driven by a deep, gnawing need to flee.

She found herself pulling into the lot of a dimly lit diner, its neon sign flickering like a beacon in the dusk. Inside, the scent of coffee and fried onions hung heavy, a contrast to the sterile tension of the FBI office. Riley chose a secluded booth by the window, her movements mechanical, her mind miles away. She ordered without looking at the menu—a simple cheeseburger and a cup of coffee, her attempt at comfort food. But the meal passed in a blur, the flavors and textures lost to her preoccupation with the cases that haunted her.

Leaving the diner behind felt like abandoning a brief attempt at normalcy, stepping back into the chaos that awaited. She drove to the extended-stay business suite that served as her current home, a place that felt both alien and confining. The walls of the suite seemed to close in on her, echoing her loneliness and amplifying the despair that gnawed at the edges of her resolve. In this impersonal space, the weight of her isolation and the darkness of her work converged, leaving her yearning for an escape she couldn't seem to find.

Under the warm embrace of the shower, she washed away the day's memories and changed into fresh clothes. Her solitude still weighed heavy, though, compelling her to take to the road in search of human connection.

Driving aimlessly, the clock neared 11 PM as she found herself in Jacksonville. Braxton's house came into view, bathed in the soft glow of lights, and his car sat parked in the driveway. She pulled over on the quiet street and approached his front door. Anxiety, trauma, and helplessness resurfaced, threatening to push her away. But then Braxton opened the door, clad in shorts and a graphic tee adorned with a parody Mastercard logo reading "Masturbate." Riley couldn't help but crack a fragile smile.

Laughter and tears intertwined as she stumbled into his arms, finding solace in his embrace. She clung to him, burying her head into his chest, grateful for the refuge he offered. Braxton welcomed her inside, preparing a vodka martini as she sank into the comfort of his couch. The TV played a childhood favorite, "Labyrinth," in the background. Braxton, sensing her need for distraction, remarked that she hadn't missed the best musical sequence yet.

He handed her the cocktail, and she patted the seat beside her. Braxton joined her, and she nestled into his embrace, her head resting on his shoulder. In that rare moment of human connection, warmth enveloped her, and an unexpected feeling tugged at her heart—a sensation that bordered on love. Their faces drew closer, and their lips met in a tender kiss. Braxton's concern shone in his eyes as he gently wiped away one of her tears, prompting him to ask if she was okay. Riley responded with a small but genuine smile, assuring him that she was.

As they settled in together, the playful banter continued, the movie playing on in the background. It felt as though a heavy weight had been lifted, and for once, she followed her own advice and savored the moment.

Deep down, she knew that the inevitable moment loomed when she would have to end things with Braxton. She couldn't continue lying to him, and the truth was too dangerous for both him and the investigation. She took another sip of her drink, grateful for the fleeting moment of solace they had found.

THREE DAYS LATER

The early morning sun bathed the Jackson County Circuit Courthouse in a gentle glow as Braxton made his way toward the imposing structure. Unable to focus on his writing, he felt a growing compulsion to piece together the threads of the murder and disappearance cases he had been pondering. Especially after seeing how distraught Riley was when they were last together, a part of him hoped there might be a chance for him to tell her that he knew who she really was, and to share his far-fetched theories with her, to support her emotionally and solidify their relationship. With these thoughts in mind, Braxton started his quest with online case-law research to determine what records he needed from the courthouse.

The courthouse, a product of the late seventies, occupied a central spot in Medford, nestled within meticulously landscaped grounds. Its exterior was a drab and unadorned three-story gray concrete structure, marked by horizontal windows and a flat roofline.

As he stepped inside, Braxton found the interior to be as utilitarian as the exterior. After passing through security, he discreetly fastened his belt and took a moment to familiarize himself with the courthouse's layout. His destination: the records division.

Entering the small waiting room, Braxton located the request form and settled into a chair to complete it. His professional experience had taught him the art of timing—show up early, but not too early, especially before the civil servants had had their morning coffee.

The clerk, a stout middle-aged woman with graying hair pulled back into a tight bun, regarded Braxton with a no-nonsense expression. Her glasses perched on the edge of her nose as she reviewed his request, her demeanor bordering on crankiness.

"This is going to take weeks to fill. And the fees will likely be steep, given how many cases you have listed here," the clerk admonished, her skeptical gaze lingering on Braxton. "What's this research for, anyway?"

Braxton's eyes lit up with enthusiasm as an idea dawned on him. "Well, I used to practice law, but now I'm working on a nonfiction book about the rich history and lore of the Rogue Valley region. It's a passion project, and I'm really diving deep into the local history. I just can't afford weeks of time and major court fees."

She regarded him for a moment and pursed her lips. Pouring on the charm, Braxton flashed a smile and leaned in while maintaining a respectful distance. "You know," he quipped with a playful glint in his eye, "they say the wheels of justice grind slowly. But I'm more than happy to help them speed up at no cost to the court."

Her lips twitched, and for the first time, her stern facade softened. Braxton could tell he was close.

"Not to mention," he went on, "and if it's okay with the powers that be, I'd be happy to give you and the court a special thanks in the acknowledgments once the book is published. I'll just need their permission and your name of course."

She leaned back in her chair, folding her arms. "Well, aren't you quite the smooth talker? We'll see what we can do," she said, her tone still gruff but now tinged with a hint of amusement. "But don't think I'm letting you off the hook for fees if you use up all of our toner and paper."

Braxton chuckled, appreciating her change in demeanor. "Deal. I'll be on my best behavior, I promise."

"My name's Linda, by the way. Let me buzz you through the door, it's right over there, and I can get you situated."

Braxton grinned. "Thank you, Linda. This means a lot to me, and I'm really grateful for your help." With a nod of approval, she buzzed the door and Braxton let himself into the records room.

Linda met him moments later, asked him to pardon the mess, and explained how they have been digitizing their records, but the cases he sought were still archived on microfiche. She led him to a bank of microfiche tapes meticulously categorized by year, and directed him toward the microfiche machine, her glasses slipping down her nose slightly as she did so.

"Go ahead. Take your time with those tapes. Just remember, you're doing the work here," she warned with a smirk and the tiniest of winks.

He examined his list of case titles by year and selected the relevant tapes from storage. With determination, he settled in front of the microfiche viewer. Curiosity and foreboding swirled within him as he studied the court filings, some painstakingly handwritten, dating back to the late 1800s. It was as though he stood at the threshold of a hidden world, one with the potential to unlock the long-buried secrets of the past—the missing pieces of the puzzle he desperately sought to quell the restless disquiet of his mind.

TEN DAYS LATER

"Hey, Braxton, how's the book coming along?" chirped the chipper volunteer at the front desk, her cheerful demeanor a stark contrast to Braxton's current state of mind.

"Oh, it's coming along. Just trying to stitch everything together," Braxton replied, forcing a smile. In truth, his once-promising pandemic story had hit a dead end, and it had been two weeks since he last heard from Riley. Despite his best efforts, the real-life missing persons cases constantly consumed his thoughts.

Each day blurred into the next as he spent his mornings in the dimly lit records division of the Medford courthouse, sifting through mountains of documents in a desperate search for answers. He felt trapped, unable to free himself from the grip of the mystery that had taken over his life. But his determination remained unshaken. Today, he had a follow-up visit to the Jacksonville historical society to cross-reference the records he'd managed to gather over the past couple of weeks.

Parking his car in the lot nestled between the cemetery and the old town, Braxton retrieved his trusted companions—a laptop and a legal pad. Today, he felt more like a lawyer on a mission than a writer. Embracing the role, he took three measured pulls from his flask, the warmth of the alcohol bolstering his resolve before he approached the unassuming gray building.

He had discovered that recordkeepers were remarkably willing to assist when they believed he was conducting research for a book about the area, so he ran with it. The volunteer ushered him inside, and Braxton settled into a small corner desk, ready to embark yet again on his search for answers. He opened his legal pad to a page filled with names, dates, and hastily scrawled notes—a cryptic spellbook unveiling his unwavering pursuit of the truth. After regaining his bearings, Braxton made his way to the library's stacks, determined to navigate the labyrinth of historical records in search of the elusive missing pieces of the puzzle.

THREE HOURS LATER

Braxton, emerging from a long stint in the suffocating archives room, felt a palpable relief as he pushed open the door to the Saloon, eagerly anticipating the blast of air-conditioning and the comfort of his favorite cocktail. Just as he stepped in, he nearly bumped into Stacey, who was on her way out, her shift having just ended.

"Escaping so soon?" Braxton teased, holding the door open for her, a playful grin spreading across his face. "And here I was, hoping for your magic behind the bar tonight."

Stacey laughed, the sound light and easy, matching the twinkle in her eye. "Magic's got a day off, Braxton. You'll have to settle for Jason's charm tonight. I'm sure you'll survive without me—barely."

"Guess I'll manage," Braxton replied with mock solemnity, stepping aside to let her pass. "But only if you promise to return and save us from his tyranny."

"It's a deal," Stacey shot back, her smile widening. "Keep an eye on him for me, will you? Make sure he doesn't burn the place down."

Their exchange, effortless and tinged with playful undertones, left a broad smile on Braxton's face. Indeed, he found himself genuinely looking forward to these moments of light-hearted banter with Stacey, appreciating the brief respite they offered from his research's solitude. And yes, he couldn't deny that her presence was also a visually pleasant addition to the Saloon's already welcoming atmosphere.

With a final smile shared between them, Braxton moved to claim his usual spot at the bar, catching Jason's attention in the midst of his own conversation with another customer.

"So, yeah," the man talking to Jason continued, "the latest launch numbers are looking pretty good."

"That's great to hear, man. Let me know if there's anything else we can do on our end," Jason replied. He then gestured toward Braxton. "Hey, have you met this guy yet? He's the lawyer guy I was telling you about earlier."

"No, I don't think we've met," the other man said, introducing himself, "Mitchell Emerson. Most call me Mitch." Based on the news report about his arrest around the time Elle and Aaron's son Hunter was discovered, plus further digging online, Braxton knew exactly who he was.

Braxton shook his hand with a firm grip, sizing him up at about six feet tall and noting his lean, sturdy frame. "Braxton Hayward. Either Braxton or Brax is fine. I'll let you play that one by ear. So. . . Emerson. . . why does that sound familiar?"

"Emerson Family Wines is my guess," Mitchell replied, displaying self-confidence without veering into arrogance.

"Ah, that's what it is." Braxton feigned ignorance.

"So, Jason says you practice law in the wine country, right?" Mitchell inquired.

"Well, it appears both of our reputations precede us," Braxton smiled, raising his voice slightly for Jason's benefit, "But I'm not a lawyer here." It was an inside joke that he ceased identifying as a lawyer the moment he left California.

"Jason was very specific about that," Mitch confirmed. "You practice California law, right?"

"That's where I'm licensed. Don't think I have it in me to take another state's bar exam," Braxton admitted.

"No, that's fine," said Mitch. "You ever do contract review, collections, things like that?"

"Yeah, that's something I generally handle. But only under California jurisdiction," Braxton reiterated.

"No, that's what I wanted to confirm. I have a good chunk of operating contracts based on California law. You want to drop by Forest Creek sometime next week to talk? Hey, Jason, you got a pen?" Mitchell reached for a card in a silver case and borrowed a pen from Jason.

"Call the main number," Mitchell instructed as he jotted down information on the card. "The launch has everyone pretty busy right now, so if no one gets back to you that day, just call my cell, which I'm writing down here." He handed the card to Braxton, who couldn't help but admire its quality.

"Well, I mean, no harm in me dropping by, I suppose. Let's circle back next week if that works for you?" Braxton was committed; already calculating the potential billables.

"Sure, that sounds good. Nice to meet you." Mitchell looked over at Jason. "Hey, I'm out of here. Thanks for having me by. It was good catching up."

"Yeah, no worries. Come by anytime," Jason replied.

Returning to his seat, Braxton ordered his usual bourbon on the rocks. Jason served it with a knowing look. "Hope you don't mind me mentioning you to that guy. And hey, if you make money, I make money," he said with a light jab.

Braxton chuckled, taking a sip. "I thought you weren't a fan of his, though? I mean, that's Elle's ex-boyfriend right?"

Jason shrugged, stacking glasses. "He's alright. Mellowed over the years, you know?"

"Mellowed enough to get arrested recently?" Braxton probed, his tone light but eyes sharp.

"Yeah, that was actually BS," said Jason. Braxton raised an eyebrow. "Well, think about it. One of Medford's finest goes missing. The police see Elle's jilted ex-boyfriend at the hospital. Everyone is running hot; pissing matches ensue. Then Mitchell is arrested for disturbing the peace. I understand the whole thing's been dismissed. Actually, I heard the arresting officer is still on unpaid leave," Jason said with a woeful laugh.

Braxton raised an eyebrow, swirling his drink. "Still, why was he there at all? Just seems odd, is all."

"Legacy families stick together," Jason remarked. "And hey, he's got a Stanford JD/MBA. Could be useful to know him."

Of course he does, Braxton seethed internally.

"Another round?" Jason offered.

"Yeah, why not?" Braxton agreed. "You know how I am with the first one: down the hatch."

There was a brief pause in their conversation, filled only by the ambient sounds of the bar. Then Braxton leaned forward, his voice taking on a reflective note. "Spent today buried in archives for my novel. Felt like I was back practicing law instead of writing."

Braxton rolled with it, taking the glass. "Yeah. Incorporating some of Rogue Valley's darker history. Turns out, there's a lot more to this place than meets the eye."

Jason's eyes sparkled with intrigue. "You mean the card game scandal right here in town? The guy they strung up on the porch? Must've been quite a sight before this area got all quaint and bed-and-breakfasty."

Braxton nodded, a wry smile on his face. "Exactly. Imagine the scene—a high-stakes game goes south, and suddenly it's an old-school frontier justice display on a front porch for like an entire day. The town's reaction? Just another Monday, another lost hand for Fred, apparently." He let out a chuckle, taking a slow, contemplative sip of his bourbon.

"Those archives must be full of gems like that. Fascinating, isn't it?" Jason said while turning away to attend to another customer.

Braxton pulled out a weathered manila folder and extracted a dense legal document. The title: "EMERSON et al. v. HOFFNUNG et al., 4 Or. 121 (1873)" promised a tedious dive into the hell that is antiquated legal writing. Braxton furrowed his brow as he navigated through the jargon-laden pages, his fascination with connecting the dots eclipsed by the tedium of legal prose. The document detailed a protracted dispute between two prominent community figures, their business entanglements mired in a labyrinth of legal proceedings.

As he waded through the text, Braxton's patience wore thin. Legal minutiae drowned the narrative, such as:

> fn 3. There was some confusion in the record consisting of percipient layman witness testimony regarding the term *"ab initio."* We agree with the Court of Appeals that we are not addressing any issues that may have arisen before the dates alleged in the third amended complaint. While not asserted by the litigants herein, upon remand we leave any remedies concerning such retroactive relief squarely within the ambit of the trial court's discretion.

Braxton sighed into his drink, exasperated by the antiquated fetish old-timey courts seemed to have with flowery, pedantic details. The term "ab initio" had surfaced during some witness testimony, prompting the Supreme Court to footnote that neither party was seeking retroactive (aka "ab initio") relief. He rolled his eyes, his thoughts meandering to the days of his first year in law school (1L) when such legal jargon was the bread and butter of their studies. *Ab initio: from the beginning,* he recollected, pulling out his phone to confirm his memory. A small smirk crossed his lips as he took a hearty sip of his bourbon, mentally congratulating himself for retaining that obscure piece of legalese.

Then, a curious thought struck him. A percipient witness, by definition, should have direct knowledge of facts, not legal theories. Why, then, would a witness—especially one who is called a "layman"—be testifying about complex legal doctrines? Could it be that they were referring to "ab initio" as if it were a tangible entity, perhaps a corporation or something akin?

"Ab Initio," he mused, the phrase rolling off his tongue. It sounded like the name of a secretive society or cult. The notion stirred a sense of déjà vu in Braxton; he had thought the same about "Prime Ascendant" when he first saw it on Emily's growler. The memory of the horrific images he had seen in the Saloon kitchen flashed briefly in his mind, but he quickly pushed it away.

Deciding to shift his focus, Braxton drained the rest of his bourbon and signaled to Jason for another. He needed to keep his thoughts clear, yet the enigma of "Ab Initio" and "Prime Ascendant" both intrigued and haunted him. He slid the document back into its folder and into his bag, stretching out in his seat. His gaze meandered around the bar, observing the patrons, the dim lights casting shadows that seemed to dance with the quiet hum of conversations.

The night was still young, and Braxton felt no rush to leave. The mysteries of the past, shrouded in legal jargon and hidden truths, weren't going anywhere. For now, Braxton chose to let the night unfold around him, embracing the moment's transient peace as a welcome respite from the cases consuming his thoughts.

SIX DAYS LATER

As Braxton was poring over the last set of Uniform Commercial Code transaction records at Forest Creek Vineyard's brand-new digs, his thoughts drifted to a story his law professor once shared. It involved

Abraham Lincoln, before his presidency, when he was a lawyer known for his integrity. Lincoln's partner had come back to find a man who had just been thrown out of their second-story office window. Upon questioning, Lincoln recounted rejecting a corrupt offer, despite being worth a small fortune. When asked why he threw him out the window, Lincoln's response was unequivocal: "I suppose it's because he was getting too close to my price."

Reflecting on this anecdote, Braxton found himself mulling over the legal work he was doing for Mitchell. Although necessary for financial reasons, he couldn't shake the feeling that, unlike Lincoln, his own price must have diminished over the past year.

At least for him, commercial and UCC transactional law was one of the most tedious, mind-numbing kinds of work out there. While the documents were littered with standard clauses, a lot can be buried in the fine print, warranting an additional level of analysis that Dante erroneously omitted from his *Inferno*. Despite the monotony, the financial gain was an undeniable boon.

The winery's office provided a marked contrast to the wearisome nature of his tasks. Opulent and fully equipped, it catered to his every need, complete with a private suite and a team of administrative staff at his disposal. The room was bathed in a warm, autumnal light filtering through the blinds, offering a small reprieve from the grind of his work. Despite everything, he had to admit there was a certain charm to the 'of counsel' aesthetic.

Determined to finish, Braxton shook off his daydreams and refocused on the document in front of him. Scrolling through the PDF, he arrived at the bills of lading section, meticulously cross-referencing numbers. A line caught his eye, triggering a thought, *What, this guy embalming bodies or something? That's a lot of methanol.* He chuckled at his own dark humor. With the end in sight, he pressed on, eager to conclude the day's work.

His official work concluded, Braxton had reached his limit with the tedium of commercial law. Yet, as he prepared to shut down for the day, he recalled a comment from the IT specialist who mentioned in passing that Braxton had full admin access to the network "to avoid bombarding me with requests for any deeper digging." Braxton hadn't thought much of it at the time, assuming it was standard procedure.

With a mix of curiosity and an aimless desire to procrastinate the inevitable return to his own thoughts, Braxton idly navigated through the network drives. He stumbled upon a peculiarly named folder, "EH_ Backup," hidden in a corner of Mitchell's personal directory. The directory was unusually networked to the server, a detail Mitchell seemed to have overlooked, mistakenly believing his personal files were secure on his hard drive alone.

Without any encryption to navigate, Braxton found himself delving into a series of documents and emails that were never meant for his eyes. They were between Mitchell's attorney, Jonathan Becks of Becks, Dalton & Pierce, and Cedar & Sterling Law Group. Both of which were based out of Portland and reeked of white-shoe elitism.

From: Jonathan Becks, Becks, Dalton & Pierce LLP
To: Mitchell Emerson
Subject: Re: Estate Inquiry

Dear Mitchell,

As per the attached correspondence, we've hit a standstill on accessing Elle's estate documents. Legally, we have solid ground to subpoena the records via probate court, bypassing the typical five-year wait. This would normally be our next logical step.

However, your adamant stance against any court action, despite the strength of our position, is frankly tying our hands. I understand your concerns about public perception and the need to respect Elle's memory, but our options outside of court are severely limited.

I'm frustrated because we're missing an opportunity to clarify significant aspects of Elle's intentions that you have a vested interest in. While I respect your decision, I want to make it clear that it significantly restricts how effectively we can represent your interests in this matter.

Let's regroup soon. It's crucial we find some common ground or alternative approach that meets your requirements without completely sidelining our ability to act.

Best,
Jonathan

The correspondence centered around inquiries from Becks, seeking information about Elle Harris's trust documents, specifically any guardianship nominations she may have made. "Given Ms. Harris's current status as missing, Mr. Emerson is seeking clarity on his position regarding her estate," Becks had written, a note of desperation hidden beneath the formal legal jargon.

Claire Sterling's response was direct and unyielding. "Oregon law requires a person to be missing for a period of five years before being legally declared deceased," Elle's attorney stated, refusing to release any details of her estate plan to Mitchell. Their firm stance was grounded in legal ethics and client confidentiality, rejecting further attempts by Becks to argue for an exception based on Mitchell's past relationship with Elle.

The exchange was not just a professional standoff but a poignant reminder of the real, unresolved human tragedy behind the legal procedures. Elle, once almost engaged to Mitchell and now vanished without a trace, was at the heart of a legal labyrinth that seemed to offer no immediate resolution or comfort to those she left behind.

Braxton sat back, disturbed by the desperation and legal barriers evident in the email thread. It painted a picture of Mitchell Emerson not as the successful vineyard owner he knew, but as a man grappling with the ghost of a past relationship, seeking closure through legal means only to be met with resistance.

With this new information, Braxton's perception of Mitchell shifted. The documents revealed a layer of complexity to Mitchell's personal life that Braxton hadn't anticipated. It was clear that the narrative woven into his front-facing ethos was more intricate and shadowed than the idyllic scenery outside suggested.

Deciding to keep his discovery confidential, Braxton realized he was now entangled in a web of moral and ethical dilemmas far beyond the scope of his contract work. The straightforward task of legal consulting had morphed into a narrative filled with unanswered questions and unresolved feelings, with Braxton inadvertently at its center.

The office's silence enveloped Braxton as he shut down his computer, a vivid contrast to the storm of thoughts raging within him. With each step he took away from his desk, the revelations of the day weighed heavily upon him, a tangible reminder of the vineyard's serene exterior masking a tumultuous history of loss, love, and legal entanglements. Now, Braxton found himself deeply intertwined in these narratives, a role he had never quite anticipated.

Crossing the threshold into the quiet evening, his path led him directly to Mitchell's executive sanctuary for a conclusive debriefing. The office, a reflection of refined taste with its large oakwood desk and tasteful decor, held Mitchell absorbed in the glow of his MacBook Pro. Braxton's knock on the open door was a gentle but firm announcement of his arrival.

Mitchell looked up, his expression shifting to one of casual interest. "Oh, hey there, Brax. How are things looking?" he asked, his voice carrying a hint of anticipation as he motioned toward a plush leather chair opposite his desk, inviting Braxton into the comfort of the meticulously curated space.

"Not too bad," Braxton replied, placing his files on one chair before taking the other. "Just to reiterate, my expertise is limited to California contracts. Regarding the Oregon ones, I can provide insights on the UCC, but not legal advice under Oregon law."

Mitchell nodded. "Understood. And you're always this particular with clients?"

"Necessary precaution, especially for clients with law degrees." Braxton chuckled. "And yes, I recommend having local counsel review the changes to those Oregon contracts. Just to be safe."

Braxton tactfully omitted his flask-assisted work process—that was an unspoken understanding. Alcohol was the only way he could endure such tedium.

"Understood, Braxton," Mitchell responded, his smile revealing perfect white teeth. "So, what do you have for me?"

Braxton opened his notes and began a detailed rundown covering each point, which lasted approximately eighteen minutes (0.30 hours).

"To sum up," Braxton concluded, "I've incorporated my suggested changes into your boilerplate templates and stored them as separate files for your review. That should cover everything. There weren't any major issues, just those few minor points we discussed." He paused, realizing it had been over half an hour since he'd had a drink.

"Oh, I guess one last thing," Braxton mentioned, breaking the rhythm of their conversation. "I noticed a significant increase in expenses with one of your vendors last month, related to additional supplies and materials." He retrieved the chemical purchase invoice from his work file and slid it across to Mitchell.

Mitchell took a moment, his face unreadable, before casually thumbing through the papers. "Yep, that lines up. We've been increasing our stainless-steel capacity recently. And cleaning all those tanks is no small task," he said, his tone almost too nonchalant as he handed the invoice back. "Anything else?"

Noticing the subtle shift in Mitchell's demeanor, Braxton changed topics. "About the payment—how would you like to handle that?" he asked, the discomfort of this part of the job lingering despite several years of experience.

Mitchell reached into his desk drawer and handed Braxton an envelope. Braxton accepted it with thanks, slipping it into his pocket without a glance.

"Aren't you going to check it?" Mitchell inquired.

"Should I?" Braxton quipped back.

"I included a two-hour bonus for the savings compared to what the Portland guys would have charged. Hope that's alright," Mitchell said, his grin suggesting a playful jab at Braxton's thoroughness.

Despite Mitchell's affable exterior and undeniable business acumen, Braxton found himself wrestling with a mix of professional admiration and personal envy. The guy had it all—charm, intelligence, and the advantages of a privileged upbringing. Nevertheless, Braxton extended a handshake, masking his internal conflict with a professional demeanor.

As he left the grandeur of the winery's château-style building, a nagging doubt clung to Braxton. Mitchell's reaction to the chemical purchases had been off—a brief flicker of masked alarm before he smoothly transitioned into his practiced, casual explanation. It felt rehearsed, too controlled. The addition of Mitchell's pointed inquiries about Elle's trust documents further complicated the picture, weaving a web of disquiet that Braxton couldn't easily dismiss.

In his car, Braxton was lost in a storm of contemplation. His hand reached for the hidden pint of liquor, each gulp offering a momentary escape from the escalating web of suspicions. The road back to Jacksonville stretched before him, each mile punctuated by the replay of his meeting with Mitchell. The brief but telling falter in Mitchell's demeanor was like an itch in Braxton's mind, insistent and unsettling.

As the familiar landmarks of Jacksonville began to emerge, Braxton's thoughts churned with intrigue and apprehension. There was a palpable sense that he was on the cusp of uncovering something deeply sinister, a narrative laced with danger that was just beginning to reveal itself, one that could change him in ways he couldn't yet fathom.

MOMENTS LATER

It was nearing five in the afternoon, and Riley had prepared herself for the meeting with SAIC Richter. Given the string of intense meetings he'd had all day, she anticipated he'd be rather stressed—a solid 4.5 on the Richter scale by her estimation.

As she rounded the corner to Richter's office, she found him and his assistant amidst a mountain of paperwork. They both looked up as Riley knocked lightly on the doorframe. "Here as requested, sir," she announced.

"Ah, McAvoy, good," Richter said, barely looking up as he continued to shuffle through files, passing them to his beleaguered assistant.

Riley hesitated. "If now's not a good time, I can come back later," she suggested.

"No, it's fine, come in," Richter motioned to a chair across from his desk. "Sit down, let's talk."

Riley took her seat, carefully arranging her own documents and notes. Richter barked a few last instructions to his assistant, who hurried out with the files, leaving them alone.

The door clicked shut, and Richter finally focused on Riley. "So, what's the situation with the kid?"

"Hunter?" Riley clarified.

"Yes. Anything new on that front?"

"Not much, I'm afraid. Elle and Aaron's estate lawyers are stalling, requesting a death certificate or a warrant. Hunter's been released back to family, and he's been placed at the Holman compound for the time being. It's unusual given there's no blood relation, but not unheard of according to County. He's being monitored by a social worker and seems to be coping."

"And has he provided any useful information?"

Riley almost let her sarcasm show. "No, sir. Their legal team is adamant about a warrant, and they're concerned further questioning might impede his recovery."

Richter, processing this, nodded. "Okay, we're at a stalemate then." He paused, clicking his tongue thoughtfully. "Well, I'll tell you what. Those two pickled stiffs are also well-connected. Because I'm getting heat from levels on high."

He leaned back, the weariness in his posture evident. "What's the latest on the Holman remains?"

Riley detailed their findings. "The autopsies and forensics are complete. We've archived everything on our end, but the condition of the bodies has made things. . .complicated."

Richter's interest peaked. "Anything unusual?"

"Their bodies were extensively embalmed—bone dry, no organs, filled with preservatives. It complicates matters." Riley handed over her summaries.

She continued, "The cause of death is undetermined. No trauma, no injuries. The embalming fluids have compromised most samples. We did get some insights from hair and bone tests—both had been on blood-pressure meds, and both tested positive for THC." Riley took a breath, "Also, Susan had advanced-stage cancer. Lymphoma."

Richter, digesting this, sighed. "So, they could have died from a number of causes. We're in the dark." He browsed through Riley's documents. "Should we release the bodies to their next of kin?"

Riley hesitated. "Well, I mean. . .that's kind of above my pay grade, sir. Respectfully."

"Fair enough." Richter offered a small smile. "The bodies are at the medical examiner's office, right?" Riley nodded. "A doctor is waiting to take custody. Credentials checked out. Here's the paperwork." He slid it across to her.

Riley reviewed the forms, noting the signature of "E.M. Andreas, M.D.," unfamiliar to her. "No red flags on my end, sir, but I don't know this Doctor Andreas."

"That's fine. Given the heat from upstairs, I'd rather get this off my desk." He signed the form and handed it back to her. "Drop this off at her desk, will you? And close the door on your way out."

Exiting Richter's office, Riley joked with his assistant about his mood. "Only a two-point-nine today?"

The assistant's weary laugh echoed in the office. "Feels more like a five-point-o here at the epicenter," she said as her phone began to ring.

Back at her desk, Riley was winding down for the day when a glance at her notes prompted a last-minute check. She entered Dr. Andreas's license number into the Oregon Medical Board database and discovered it belonged to Emily Marie Andreas, M.D. The doctor's profile appeared standard: licensed, long-standing practice in Medford. But a recent update caught her eye—a name change from her divorce judgment, reverting to her maiden name.

Riley's heart skipped a beat. Emily Holman!

Leaning forward in her chair, a soft chuckle escaped Riley's lips as she recalled ditching Braxton at the Italian restaurant a month earlier. Riley had recognized Emily from the art gallery's video feeds and didn't want to botch anything if she was brought in for questioning. While Emily wasn't a person of interest, the plot was definitely thickening.

Why would the Holman couple's remains be released to their nephew's ex-wife? She reached for the phone to share this revelation but hesitated, contemplating the potential fallout. Emily's divorce from Erik Holman was common knowledge, likely a familial courtesy. Deciding against causing any further stir, Riley set the phone down and logged off her computer. There was no need to further escalate tensions today—this could wait.

As she collected her things, Riley's mind was heavy with the day's findings. The stagnation of Elle and Aaron's cases contrasted sharply with the unraveling intricacies of the Holman case. Were these events interconnected, or merely a harsh coincidence? Though the answers eluded her, the urgency of uncovering the truth was undeniable. But, for now, there was little she could do but wait.

Taking one final glance around her workspace, Riley stepped into the tranquil evening. The mysteries at the heart of her investigations were deepening, their implications casting a profound shadow over her thoughts. Yet her determination did not waver. She was committed to unearthing the truth, regardless of the challenges it might present. The road ahead was shrouded in uncertainty, but Riley was certain of one thing: the journey, however arduous, was essential.

CHAPTER EIGHT

YOU'RE OUTTA CONTROL!

FRIDAY, SEPTEMBER 14, 8:47 PM

After depositing Mitchell's check, Braxton opted for a night out in Ashland. He started at a restaurant near Lithia Park, overlooking Ashland Creek. His evening began with a double Michter's Rye, leading into a meal of ribeye steak, truffle-infused parmesan polenta, and fire-roasted asparagus. Ignoring the old "wine before liquor" adage, he accompanied his meal with a glass of Emerson Family Wines pinot noir, which was decent enough. Enjoying his own company, Braxton took photos of his meal for Facebook, noting that the bill was substantially lower than what he was used to in the Bay area.

Post-dinner, he walked through Lithia Park, weaving through the regular crowd of hippies and dogs. The path, flanked by oak and ash trees, was perfect for a sunset stroll. He paused occasionally to photograph the creek, letting the serene environment sink in.

Passing a group of teens discreetly smoking weed off the main trail, memories from his high school drama class trips to Ashland surfaced, reminding him of the guy he was back in high school—full of sarcasm and smart-assery, so confident that he knew everything there was to know in life. He kept walking, shaking off the cringe and nostalgia with a few shots from his flask.

As the sun set behind the Siskiyou mountains, Braxton found himself reflecting on the differences between the long, hot summers of the Rogue Valley and the North Bay, still adjusting to this new phase of life. Feeling adventurous, he decided to check out the downtown bar scene.

He chose an Irish pub near the Ashland Springs Hotel. The selection of whiskey and bourbon immediately caught his eye. With the Shakespeare Festival stage performances in full swing, the pub wasn't crowded, ensuring quick service. He sat at the bar, flanked by a couple of women and a group of college kids who seemed to have just met.

The bartender, a tall woman with bold eye makeup, came over. Braxton ordered a double Bulleit on the rocks with a PBR beer back. While waiting, he observed the bar's mixed crowd. Once his drink arrived, he opened a tab and then headed to the back gaming room. After playing some pinball, with scores far from his college glory days, he returned to the bar for a double Jack and Coke, slowing down his drinking pace.

"Hey, I know you," a voice called from his right. Braxton turned, surprised to find the woman addressing him.

"Oh, hi," he replied, struggling to place her. Once she flashed her hard-to-forget smile, it clicked.

"Emily. We met at the Saloon last month. You helped Jason with that growler," she reminded him.

"That's right. I knew you looked familiar. Different lighting in here," Braxton explained. "Hey, I saw you on TV later that day. So sorry about you and your family's loss."

Emily brushed off the sympathy. "We're managing, but thanks," she said, her tone light. Braxton guessed she'd had a few drinks. "Here, have a seat." She gestured to the stool next to hers. "My girlfriend had a kid emergency right after I ordered this." She nodded toward the tall margarita on the bar.

"Sure," Braxton accepted, briefly setting aside his thoughts about her connection to the murder victims. Preferring conversation to solitude, he was relieved to move past the topic of death. As Emily checked her phone, he broached another potentially awkward subject.

"You don't have to rush off for a 'kid emergency' too, do you? I was just getting comfortable with the idea of you stalking me," he said with a playful tone.

"You're out of control!" Emily's giggle, light and carefree, broke through the hum of the bar. "No, they're with their dad tonight."

"That's good to hear. Co-parenting can be quite the challenge," Braxton said, tentatively probing.

"It's gotten better over time. The divorce centered mostly around financial matters. We make it work for the sake of the kids," Emily shared, her tone conveying a blend of realism and optimism.

"Good for the both of you," Braxton said. "May I ask how old they are?"

With a smile, Emily answered, "Three girls. My youngest are twins, eleven and six years old."

Braxton noticed her comfort in discussing her family. Her warm smile, poised demeanor, attractive figure, and the absence of a wedding ring suggested she was accustomed to such inquiries. Despite her connection to the murder victims, he found himself liking her straightforwardness. Her disarming tone wasn't an act, and her approach to life was a refreshing difference from what he was used to—at least in his professional experience.

"Seems like you've found a good balance," Braxton commented. "It usually gets a bit easier after the first year, doesn't it? The kids start to adjust, and you figure out which battles are worth fighting."

"Exactly," she agreed with a nod. "Have you been through a divorce yourself?"

"Yes, but we didn't have kids. One of the reasons why we split, actually. It was amicable, though, and we've stayed friends," Braxton explained. "Handled my fair share of family law cases, so I've seen all sides of it."

"Ah, so you're a lawyer?" Emily's question came with a hint of curiosity.

Braxton nodded. "Only licensed in California, though. I'm taking some time off, a sort of sabbatical, here in Oregon." He paused, then, driven by an impulse, he ventured further. "How are the kids handling the loss of their grandparents?"

Emily's response came with a slight hesitancy. "Well, they still have their grandparents, thankfully. My ex-husband is Andrew Holman's nephew," she clarified. "The family. . . we're managing. We're a pretty tight-knit group, so that's been our strength."

As she spoke, her gaze drifted away, fixating on a distant point beyond the walls of the pub. Her hand tightened around her cocktail glass, and she took several deep sips, as if seeking solace in the liquid courage. It was a fleeting glimpse into her concealed struggles, a subtle cry of a soul entangled in circumstances far beyond the ordinary.

Meanwhile, Braxton, lost in his calculations, remained oblivious. His mind was busy calculating Emily's age based on the ages of her children.

"So," he said after doing the math, "and I don't mean this as a cheesy pickup line or anything, but I'm guessing that you couldn't buy alcohol when you had your first kid?" Emily gave him a quizzical look, but upon sensing his genuine curiosity, she responded with a lilting, infectious laugh that echoed warmly in the room.

"Aww, thank you," she said, her cheer heartfelt. "I think you just made my day. I was twenty-nine when Zoe was born." Her broad smile lingered, reflecting amusement at Braxton's recalculations.

After a pause, Emily leaned in with a teasing glint in her eye. "So, was that your girlfriend you were with at the Italian restaurant? You know, during my wild divorce party?"

Braxton, caught off guard, responded with a hint of sheepishness, "Girlfriend? No, not exactly. We were on a date, but that's kind of. . . Well, it's been a while since I last saw her." He tried to keep the tone light, matching her playful approach, even as he internally acknowledged he might be over-sharing.

In fact, Braxton hadn't heard from Riley for the past few weeks, but he wasn't keen on diving into those details. Instead, he redirected the conversation back to a safer topic. "Anyway, how's the brewery doing? That stout was pretty solid. What other kinds of beers are you guys working on?"

Emily's mood brightened as she launched into a passionate description of the brewery's latest offerings. Braxton, grateful for the change of topic, waved down the bartender and ordered another round, steering them comfortably back into the realm of shared interests.

After about two hours at the bar, Braxton found himself assisting Emily into his BMW. Their conversation had been engaging, but as the evening wore on, Emily's energy waned, particularly after her fourth drink. Accepting Braxton's offer to drive her home, she slumped into the passenger seat. Braxton opened the sunroof for some fresh air and popped a breath strip, aware that the scent of alcohol was clinging to them both.

"Where to?" he asked as he started the car.

"I'm staying in the pool house tonight," Emily slurred, her words blending together. "It's up in the hills, near Britt Gardens."

Braxton's eyebrows rose in surprise, but he maintained his composure. "Do you have the address?" he asked, readying his phone.

Emily fumbled with her own phone, her fingers uncoordinated. "It's. . . Um, I always forget the exact address. I just drive there on autopilot. . ." Her voice trailed off as she scrolled through her contacts. "Ah, here," she handed him the phone, pointing to a contact labeled 'Auntie Sue.'

Braxton texted the address to his phone and set the GPS. "All set. You good? There's a window control right here," he said, gesturing to the car's amenities, "and I've got a plastic bag just in case I can't pull off the road in time."

"I'm fine," she insisted, cracking the window slightly. "I'll let you know if that changes. And sorry for this. . ."

"No worries, it happens," Braxton replied, pulling onto the road. He opted for back roads to Jacksonville, steering clear of the interstate.

The GPS estimated less than thirty minutes to their destination. Braxton streamed some upbeat music, letting the cool night air fill the car as he hugged the winding curves of the country roads. He had acquired the BMW at a bargain from a former client. It wasn't the latest model, but it was a significant upgrade from his old Acura, which had endured twelve years of wear and tear but, as his ex-wife often remarked, stubbornly refused to give up the ghost.

As the night enveloped the car, Braxton found himself embraced in a rare moment of introspection. This drive, with its smooth curves and open roads, resonated deeply with the dreams of his younger self—a boy who imagined adulthood as a series of adventures in sleek high-tech cars under starlit skies. For a fleeting second, he was that child again, unburdened and optimistic, his heart swelling with a nostalgic euphoria. But as quickly as the wave washed over him, it retreated, leaving him to face the waters of his current reality. His cynicism unraveled the moment—back into the complex weave of adulthood. The stress that shadowed every decision, the pressure of expectations—both self-imposed and from those around him—and the relentless juggling act of responsibilities.

Yet, in this introspection, Braxton found a poignant understanding of the irony and beauty that interlaced the path of growing up. Like, how his well-behaved, polite childhood might have robbed him of fully experiencing the adventures of youth, yet provided him with the foundation and wherewithal to pass the bar and become an attorney. These reflections were interrupted by the soft snores and head jerks of Emily, dozing off beside him.

"You okay?" Braxton asked softly, tapping her knee to check on her without taking his eyes off the road. Emily mumbled incoherently, shifted her position, leaned her head against the window, and slipped back into a light sleep.

The car glided smoothly through the night, the soft music and GPS directions the only sounds punctuating the silence. Braxton's thoughts wandered, a mix of contentment and introspection coloring the quiet drive to the Holman estate.

"Okay, we're here, Emily," Braxton said, trying not to startle her. They were at the front entrance of the Holman estate; the security gate was open. "Do you want me to drive you to the house?"

Stirring awake, Emily nodded and directed him up the driveway. "I'm at the pool house, just up a little ways. Do you mind?"

"No problem." Braxton started rolling up the private drive. He bore left per Emily's instructions, noticing numerous cars parked along the right-hand road leading to the main house, indicating a gathering. He stopped at the end of the driveway, where two barns sat. One, with faux-rustic garage doors, he assumed was the carriage house, making the other the pool house.

"Need any help?" Braxton offered as Emily searched through her purse for her keys, switching on the overhead light to assist her.

"I think I'm okay," she replied, her fingers finally locating the correct key, which she held up triumphantly.

"Very good," Braxton responded with an encouraging tone, watching as she gathered her belongings.

"Wait, do you need any help?" he asked again, his hand reaching toward the door handle. However, seeing her exit the car without difficulty, he relaxed. "Okay, cool. You're good. Awesome."

Emily paused, hand on the open passenger door, looking more steadier on her feet. "Thank you so much, sweetie," she expressed with gratitude. Braxton wasn't sure how to interpret the term of endearment, but he responded with a friendly smile and a thumbs-up.

As Emily shut the passenger door and waved goodbye, Braxton couldn't help but reflect on the evening. Any initial thoughts of a potential romantic connection had dissipated with her increasing inebriation. His priority had shifted to making sure she got home okay. He watched her make her way down the gravel path toward the pool house, ensuring she entered safely.

Once Emily was out of sight, Braxton started backing up when a buzzing noise from the passenger side caught his attention. He parked the car and turned on the cabin lights, discovering Emily's iPhone in the footwell. "Guess I'll have to drop this off at her door," he muttered, switching off the engine and stepping out into the night.

Approaching the pool house gate, Braxton found it securely locked with a keypad. He scanned the fence for any gaps but found none, and climbing over wasn't an option in his state. Deciding against leaving Emily's phone at the gate to avoid any damage, he headed toward the main house.

The house was well illuminated, but it seemed deserted. Reaching the covered porch, Braxton carefully placed Emily's phone in a corner next to the front door, opting not to ring the doorbell and intrude on any potential gathering inside. As he walked back down the driveway, faint voices caught his attention.

"I'll just let them know I left the phone out front," he muttered to himself, veering off toward the backyard. Crossing the front lawn, he confirmed his suspicion: there were indeed people in the back.

Braxton, steeling himself for a potential encounter, discreetly took a couple of swigs from his flask and popped a breath strip. He took a deep breath and ventured toward the backyard, passing a grassy knoll. The area beyond was lined with apple trees, creating a quaint orchard scene, but something felt unsettling. Just a few steps in, flickering lights at the periphery of his vision caused him to halt.

"Oh, Jesus, not fucking *now*," he whispered under his breath, feeling the onset of an unusual sensation. He knelt down as the shadows cast by the tree limbs began to swirl and cross around him. This wasn't a typical pre-blackout symptom for him; something was off. Closing his eyes and shaking his head, Braxton tried to dispel the disorientation.

When he opened his eyes again, his confusion turned to shock as the flickering lights revealed a scene unfolding just beyond the orchard. Braxton's heart raced as he realized this wasn't just a simple backyard gathering. The shadows and lights weren't mere tricks of his vision but indicators of something more ominous taking place.

About twenty feet away was a precession of dark-cloaked figures, each bearing a flaming torch. The person leading the forty-plus group was chanting in Latin or something else ancient, compounding the surreal nature of the moment.

Cautiously, he moved closer, staying low to the ground. The ritualistic nature of their actions was both fascinating and horrifying. The group formed a circle around a large fire pit, into which they began throwing their torches, one by one.

As the fire intensified, a wave of warmth reached Braxton, even from his vantage point a distance away. His eyes were inexorably drawn to a large wooden structure fueling the rising flames. It was then that he saw them—two lifeless bodies, bound to a beam and wrapped in white cloaks. One body's long hair hung limply, adding a hauntingly human element to the scene. It was clear these were not effigies, but actual human beings, now being consumed by the fire.

The fire's towering flames, initially a bright orange, started to shift into an unnatural blue, casting an eerie glow over the entire area. The fire's dance seemed to reach for the stars, engulfing the cloaked bodies in a hellish embrace.

For several seconds, he remained frozen, his mind grappling with the reality of what he was seeing. The realization that these were actual human bodies being consumed by flames jolted him into action. His survival instinct, strangely detached, was unambiguous in its command: *Time to get the fuck out of here.*

Quietly, he retreated from the clearing, the haunting sounds of the fire consuming the bodies echoing in his ears. As he moved away, the ritualistic chanting gradually faded, replaced by the intense crackling and popping of the fire as it sizzled through the cadavers. The air became thick with a pungent, acrid smell, a nauseating mixture of gasoline, burnt rubber and charred flesh.

Reaching the driveway, Braxton tried to calm himself. "It's okay, it's okay," he hummed under his breath. "You're just the guy who dropped off Emily. You didn't see jack shit."

He repeated this mantra, quickening his pace back to his car. His hands were steady as he slid into the driver's seat and twisted the ignition key. The engine sprung to life, and, as previously declared, he got the fuck out of there.

Braxton tore through the streets, his mind a whirlwind of thoughts and emotions. He pushed his car to its limits, driving like a bat out of hell, eager to put as much distance as possible between himself and the macabre scene he had just witnessed. When he finally got home his heart was racing and his hands trembled as he turned off the engine.

Stepping inside, Braxton's uneasy feeling intensified. The subtle disorder of his belongings hinted at an unwelcome presence during his absence. His writing pads, usually stacked and orderly, were in disarray, as if someone had rifled through them in a hurry. He rushed to his closet and found his locked handgun case—usually hidden on the top shelf—conspicuously on a different shelf.

His anxiety escalated upon noticing that his socks and underwear drawers had been switched. Oddly, his drug stash remained undisturbed. Fortunately, his laptop had been in his car that evening, so it was still safe. But these small mercies did little to ease the growing sense of intrusion.

But the most alarming discovery was the back door's deadbolt, unlocked and unlatched. Braxton was good about security, and he knew he had locked it before leaving. The realization that someone had been in his house, tampering with his belongings, sent waves of paranoia crashing over him.

Trying to steady his frayed nerves, Braxton grabbed a Xanax from his stash and chased it down with several large gulps of bourbon. He slumped onto his couch as he turned on the TV, a beer in hand. The flickering images on the screen blurred as his eyelids grew heavy.

In those last moments of consciousness, a dark thought crossed his mind. If things got too dire, if he found himself too deep in whatever mess he'd stumbled into, he had a way out. His gun, his final resort, offered a grim but definitive escape. With this thought echoing in his mind, Braxton succumbed to exhaustion and the effects of the alcohol and medication, drifting into an uneasy sleep.

FALL

CHAPTER NINE

THE MYSTERY AT ROGUE RIVER RANCH

FRIDAY, SEPTEMBER 21, 9:11 AM

The cramped FBI office was alive with a palpable sense of urgency that morning as SAIC Richter summoned everyone for an all-hands meeting. The overhead lights cast a sharp illumination on the agents gathered around, shadows flickering across their determined faces. Amidst her colleagues, Riley stood alert, the collective tension and focus tangible in the air. The space, usually filled with the low murmur of day-to-day operations, now held a concentrated silence, with agents drawn together, eyes fixed on Richter.

"Listen up," Richter's voice cut through the anticipation, echoing against the cool, hard floors and desks cluttered with the remnants of ongoing investigations. "We've got a code-red situation at Rogue River Ranch, deep in the wilderness, nearly three hours away by road."

Riley tensed at the mention of this remote and unfamiliar location.

Richter's gaze landed on Agent Reynolds, an ambitious Ivy Leaguer. "Reynolds, you're tasked with leading the ground investigation. Assemble your team and prepare to depart immediately."

Reynolds straightened up, a cocky smile playing on his lips as he relished the spotlight. "Yes, sir!" he replied with eager confidence.

Richter then turned to Riley. "McAvoy, I need you and three of our best forensic experts. You're coming with me. Chopper's spooling up and we're wheels up in ten."

Riley's pulse quickened. This was more than just an assignment; it could be a crucial lead. She noticed Reynolds' expression sour, his eyes briefly flickering with envy, but she couldn't afford to be distracted.

"Understood, sir," she responded, her mind already racing through the list of forensic experts. As she turned to gather her team, she felt the weight of Reynolds' glare. Yet her determination was unwavering. The mystery at Rogue River Ranch beckoned, and with it, perhaps, answers to the questions that had been haunting her.

In the helicopter the engine's roar melded with the whir of rotor blades, creating a cacophony that reverberated through the cabin. Below, the landscape was a tapestry of granite cliffs and dense evergreen forests, stretching out like a rugged, unending blanket. Across from Riley, SAIC Richter looked every bit the experienced agent, unfazed by the flight. In the back, the three forensic analysts sat huddled together, their faces tinged with airsickness.

Richter's voice, firm and clear, carried over the noise as he debriefed the team. "The discovery at Rogue River Ranch is significant, and it falls under our jurisdiction as it's federal land," he said. "It's not just any find; it's potentially game-changing. The ranger I spoke with couldn't give many details, but he was adamant about the severity of the situation."

Richter continued, "We need to be prepared for anything. This isn't a routine investigation. It's sensitive, and it's critical." His eyes met Riley's, conveying the urgency of the situation.

Riley nodded, absorbing every word. The gravity of Richter's tone and the seriousness of the discovery were not lost on her. She looked at the forensic analysts in the back as they exchanged uneasy glances, their earlier discomfort forgotten in the face of the unfolding scenario.

As the helicopter banked sharply, offering a view of the river winding through the valley, Riley's thoughts were on the mission. They were heading into the unknown, and their readiness for whatever they might find was paramount.

A FEW HOURS LATER

On the last afternoon of summer, a week after witnessing the unsettling funeral and having his home broken into, Braxton resorted to his familiar coping mechanisms: pretend it didn't happen, dive into work, and drink it into submission. To that end, he was walking to the Saloon for a midday refresher.

It looked like Mother Nature finally got the memo about the season changing. The air had that crisp, dry snap to it that he always enjoyed so much during that time of year. The autumnal splashes of auburn, yellow, and orange across the landscape were nice complements as well. It may be due to bias—as he was born in October—but fall was Braxton's favorite season.

Perched at the bar, Braxton unlocked his smartphone, his thoughts drifting to the rapid pace at which life changes and how seamlessly the world has shifted into the digital age. He found himself reminiscing about the 1990s and 2000s, times spent in bars without a smartphone, jotting down observations and musings in a notebook—à la Jack Kerouac—or just contemplating life's intricacies over a drink.

His trip down memory lane was interrupted as he opened a local news website for a weather update, only to have his attention captured by a striking "BREAKING NEWS" banner scrolling at the top of the screen.

EVIDENCE OF SUSPECTED CRIME SCENE
AT ROGUE RIVER RANCH

Sept. 21—Rogue River Ranch, Ore. As of 9:30 AM today, authorities have closed Rogue River Ranch due to an active crime-scene investigation. According to some sources, clothing and personal items were found at the National Historic Site near China Bear Rapids. The lockdown will remain in effect until otherwise notified. Updates will be provided as further information is obtained.

Braxton felt a chill. *Holy shit, this is not good*, he thought. With a sigh, he signaled Stacey and ordered a Michter's on the rocks. Her generous pour was more comforting than she realized. Drink in hand, he delved deeper online. Skimming through similar articles, his attention was finally caught by a tech news piece near the bottom of the page.

POTENTIAL CRIME SCENE DISCOVERED
BY OREGON DRONE PILOT

Sept. 21—Rogue River Ranch, Ore. A drone enthusiast may have just earned the dubious honor of being the first civilian to discover a potential crime scene using off-the-shelf unmanned aerial vehicle (UAV) technology.

Robert Reyes, an Oregon-based IT worker and drone hobbyist, had no idea what was in store for him when he flew his drone along a stretch of rapids near Rogue River Ranch, a National Historic Site maintained by the Bureau of Land Management.

According to Reyes, "I was having trouble with my Wi-Fi tether, so I was basically flying blind and had to land my drone on the shore where all the trees were. That was really nerve-racking because that thing isn't cheap! When I went to retrieve it, I saw some tattered clothes and a lady's handbag. So I told the rangers about it, and here we are."

It is unknown if any footage was captured and, if so, whether it would ever be released. According to Reyes, "I didn't have the chance to see what was recorded. But the nice FBI lady said that if they could keep the drone, they would pay me what I bought it for.

So, that was all good with me, because the latest model was just released at the same price I paid for the first one. Free upgrade."

The advent of consumer-ready drones raises many questions about privacy, air safety, and the need for comprehensive regulation, which has the Federal Aviation Administration running to catch up with the fast-growing industry...

Braxton paused, lost in thought. Rogue River Ranch was a remote spot, over two hours drive from Grants Pass. He sipped his drink, pondering.

The urge to share his discoveries with Riley was strong, but he resisted. It had been weeks since she had contacted him, and his calls were going straight to voicemail. He winced, recalling his drunken texts, and the follow-up apology he sent her to preserve a semblance of dignity. And come hell, high water, or even flaming cadavers—he wasn't about to meddle with that.

Imagining Riley at the crime scene, her analytical mind at work, the sun highlighting the lighter streaks of her hair as she took witness statements, he acknowledged his deep feelings for her. *It's over, move on*, he admonished himself. Finishing his drink, he headed to the bathroom to seek solace from his flask.

Returning from the bathroom, his spirits lifted by the flask, Braxton greeted Stacey with a playful tone. Stacey, who had her back to him and was busy with eyedrops, jumped slightly at his unexpected presence. She quickly composed herself, wiping away the last of the drops before turning to face him.

Stacey, attempting to mask her irritation, looked at Braxton. "Yes?" she asked.

Braxton, acting nonchalant, requested a Jack and Coke. "No straw, of course." As Stacey prepared his drink, he casually inquired, "So, how's it been growing with you?"

She replied in a matter-of-fact tone, "Oh, fine, you know. Just another day at the office."

Braxton, barely containing his amusement, responded, "Ah, well, that's a perfectly fine jay to roll if you ask me." He fought back a grin, while Stacey, pausing briefly, simply nodded and placed the drink before him. Braxton playfully continued. "Awesome. Dank you very much."

Stacey, pausing and tilting her head, scrutinized Braxton's smirk. "Wait, are you fucking with me?" she asked.

Braxton, feigning innocence, replied, "I don't grow what you're toking about." Unable to hold back, a wide grin took over his face. "But dooby honest, it's been a couple of jays since I dusted off the ol' reeferisms!" He laughed heartily. "Don't worry, your eyes are probably just red from the contacts. I'm not gonna jay anything. Seriously, though, you haven't herb me toke about my reeferisms with Jason?"

Stacey let out a sigh, rolled her eyes with a hint of amusement, and chuckled, "Fuckin' Braxton." She then turned back to her duties, while Braxton looked on, smiling.

Indeed, he was once known as "the guy who makes all the weed puns." Those times, back in his "college jays," seemed almost alien to him now. The puns started in high school as a code when scoring over the phone, a precaution against the imagined threat of wiretaps by the narc police.

It would go something like this:

BUYER: Hey man. I was wondering if you had anything growing on, and I can drop by?

SELLER: Sure, yeah. What were you thinking?

BUYER: Well, I'm kinda over the fun-guy. I was just thinking, you know, maybe something, you know, like OG? Bud?

SELLER: What the hell are you talking about, dude?

BUYER: Don't you green "What the hell are you toking about, doob?"

SELLER: [sighs audibly] Oh, my God. I get it. How much green bud do you want? Like an eighth?

That was back when you had to specify "green bud" as opposed to the brown, seedy "schwag" weed. Now he couldn't find schwag if he tried (not that he'd ever want to). His undergrad school in Santa Cruz was renowned for its high-caliber weed and spirited connoisseurs. There, the rumor of a guy who spoke only in weed-based euphemisms began, leading to the creation of "reeferisms."

The notion that he spoke exclusively in "reeferese" was exaggerated. Sometimes they would emerge at the onset (e.g., "How's it growing?"), but most often he reserved them for final salutations (e.g., "Toke it easy!").

It goes without saying that Braxton didn't include his undergraduate friends on the moral character application for the California State Bar.

His chuckle brought him back to the present. He tried again to divert his thoughts from the Rogue River crime scene but it proved futile. Finishing his drink, he stepped outside for a smoke.

The downtown scene, with its movie-like frontier setting, cool breeze, and skittering leaves, contrasted sharply with his mood. Even amidst the bustling tourists, as he walked to his usual spot, the cigarette failed to distract him. Darker thoughts, unmitigated by the nicotine, crept back into his mind.

Out of nowhere, Braxton's memory vividly brought him back to a morning with Erika, driving through San Francisco's Avenues. Attempting to synchronize with the traffic lights on Fulton Street, he failed and ended up first at Twenty-Fifth Avenue. It was there they witnessed a shocking scene: a young woman, darting in front of a bus into the crosswalk, was struck by an SUV whose driver rushed through the changing light. The impact was brutal, launching the woman into the air, her body tumbling before crumpling on the pavement.

Reacting instinctively, Braxton maneuvered his car to shield her motionless form, his mind racing as he shouted for Erika and others to call 911. As Erika directed the bewildered traffic, Braxton crouched beside the injured woman, urging her to stay still, reassuring her that help was on its way. Her response was weak and garbled, adding to the gravity of the moment. Around them, a spontaneous assembly of strangers came together in a collective effort to aid, covering her with a solar blanket and updating on the emergency calls they made. Braxton, meanwhile, stayed on the line with the dispatcher, providing details as sirens began to wail in the distance. Help was on the way.

In this critical moment, Braxton was deeply moved by the swift, compassionate response of passersby, a demonstration of humanity's inherent desire to help in times of crisis. A poignant reminder of life's fragility and the power of collective empathy. Later, learning of the pedestrian's likely recovery, he felt a sense of relief.

But the incident left a lingering impact. Driving down Fulton Street in the ensuing weeks, Braxton often experienced unsettling visions of shadowy figures darting in front of his car, a residual effect of the trauma. The thought of these phantoms triggered the more recent visions of ghostly figures and eerie sounds that seemed to echo in the darkness of his subconsciousness. The creaking of rope against wood. That plopping sound—like thick drops of viscous rain. Braxton shook his head and took another drag from his cigarette.

He couldn't deny it any longer. No matter how hard he tried. No matter how much he drank. Deep within he knew the bodies he saw that early August night was no hallucination. And no amount of booze could erase what he just saw at the Holman estate. The acrid smell of burning remains, laden with chemical-preservatives. The same kind of chemicals purchased by Mitchell's winery.

And now there's a crime scene about thirty-five miles downriver. Where they're going to find the last traces of the other missing couple, Elle and Aaron. Right on par with his working theory.

Braxton had reached the point of crisis. He had to decide. Either get the hell out and live in fear, or get to the bottom of it before finding himself in an interrogation room, jail cell, or worse. After a few silent curses, he resigned himself to the tedious work in front of him. He had to go all in. The truth must be uncovered, despite the potential dangers ahead.

THREE DAYS LATER

Under the afternoon sun, SAIC Richter stood confidently outside the FBI building. The press, gathered eagerly, focused on him and the special agents flanking him on the podium. The setting, with the FBI's emblem in the background, added gravitas to the moment.

Richter's voice broke the silence, announcing a breakthrough in the Elle Harris and Aaron Stewart case. "After rigorous investigation over the past month, our team has confirmed that the last known whereabouts of the missing couple was the Rogue River Ranch." His words echoed off the building's facade, signaling the importance of this discovery.

The remote location of the ranch, yet another enigma in the case, was now a pivotal piece of the puzzle. As Richter fielded questions from the press, the gravity of the situation was palpable. His responses were measured, revealing only what was necessary, while Riley and the other agents at his sides underscored the seriousness of the investigation. This major development, a turning point in the case, promised to lead the investigation down new paths. Or, at least that was the hope.

During the press conference, Braxton was absorbed in his research at the Medford library, unaware of the significant update being delivered. It was only on his drive home that he heard the news about the confirmation of Elle Harris and Aaron Stewart's DNA at Rogue River Ranch. This revelation brought a complex mix of emotions for Braxton. On one hand, he felt a sense of thrill, as this information validated his own theories about the case. On the other hand, it also deepened his sense of unease, as the reality of his entanglement in this grim situation became more tangible.

FIFTEEN DAYS LATER

Nestled on a bench in the serene courthouse garden, the folder in his bag bulged with the fruits of his two-week research marathon, filled with pages of carefully chosen cases, each potentially a key to unlocking his complex theory. In a moment of impulse, he dialed Jason. They hadn't been seeing much of each other lately, and he missed their little chats. Not to mention, particularly since Riley ghosted him, he had come to realize how good a friend Jason had become.

The call connected, and instantly Braxton could tell Jason was swamped. Amidst the cacophony of construction—the rhythmic hammering and distant shouts—Jason's voice came through, rushed yet polite.

"Hey, Braxton, sorry, can't really talk. I'm right in the middle of something," Jason said, his words almost battling the noise around him.

"Understandable," Braxton responded, trying to mask his disappointment. "Was just curious about some rafting details for my book, but it can wait."

"Tell you what," Jason offered, "I'll pass your number to the best rafter we've got. He's the go-to guy for any river questions."

Braxton appreciated the gesture. "Thanks, Jason. That'd be awesome."

With a quick exchange of pleasantries, they concluded the call. Braxton turned his attention back to his papers, the brief interaction with Jason providing a momentary escape from the weight of his research.

Braxton carefully extracted the latest batch of courthouse records from his bag, his attention immediately drawn to a document titled "Multilateral Venture Compact." It was buried deep within one of the scores of motions filed in the Emerson v. Hoffnung case, yet contained only a table of contents. As he scanned the page, his phone buzzed with an incoming call.

"Hello, this is Braxton," he answered.

"Hey, it's Adam, Jason's rafting buddy. Heard you had some questions about the Rogue River?" Adam's voice was clear and friendly.

"Yeah, hey, thanks for calling, Adam. So, I don't know what Jason has told you, but I'm working on a book about local history and need some insights on navigating the Rogue River. Like, how far down can an experienced rafter go?" Braxton inquired, his tone eager yet professional.

Adam's reply came with a note of caution, "Well, in the right conditions, you could make it all the way to the Pacific. But, man, it's risky without proper gear, especially a satellite phone. You don't want to be stranded out there."

"So," Braxton ventured, "have you ever done it?"

Adam chuckled for a moment before answering. "Nah, can't say I have. Furthest I've gone was about halfway—to Rogue River Ranch. It's a fun trip, but it can get pretty technical at certain points."

"Really," Braxton said, trying to mask his intrigue. "So, how long did that take?"

"Oh, you can get to the ranch in about a day if you know what you're doing."

Appreciative of Adam's advice and straightforward manner, Braxton replied, "Thanks, Adam, that's really helpful info."

"No problem, happy to help a friend of Jason's. He's my brother from another mother," Adam responded warmly.

Braxton ended the call, quickly packing his papers. He had to move fast to avoid a parking ticket. As he hurried to his car, Braxton's mind was abuzz, weaving Adam's insights into the complex tapestry of his research.

As Braxton settled into his car, he connected his phone, took a sip from his flask, and merged into the traffic heading toward Jacksonville. His mind worked tirelessly, weaving together the cryptic clues uncovered in his research.

He pondered over the cryptic pseudo-Latin terms he had uncovered in the court cases, noticing a pattern where terms like "Ab Initio" intersected with "Prima Imperator," and "Prime Ascendant" linked to "Supreme Executor." This was further compounded by his findings in the Jacksonville historic archives, where the initials "PI" and "SE" recurred alongside the names Emerson and Hoffnung, suggesting a deeper, generational link between the archives and the court cases.

Glancing in his rearview mirror, Braxton's eyes narrowed, zeroing in on the ominous silhouette of a black Mercedes SUV lurking a few cars back. A gnawing suspicion, fueled by the sight of its persistent shadowing since he hit the highway, tightened his grip on the steering wheel. The road ahead constricted to two lanes, the lingering tang of alcohol on his breath a palpable reminder that outrunning him wasn't an option. As the familiar outskirts of Jacksonville loomed, he made a split-second decision and veered off the main route, his heart pounding as the SUV ominously echoed his maneuver.

With a calculated burst of speed, Braxton used a momentary straightaway stretch to put some distance between them. Then, with a mix of dread and determination, he pulled the emergency brake. The car obeyed, tail swinging out in a controlled arc, a dance of metal and momentum as his world spun in a breath-stealing 180-degree swivel, leaving him facing the oncoming SUV. Adrenaline peaking, he snapped the brake loose and sped away, catching a brief, yet vivid, glimpse of the driver—a fortyish man with thinning blond hair and a broad physique, cramped by the SUV's confines.

His heart threatening to break free from his chest, Braxton floored the accelerator, propelling his car back onto the highway in a desperate bid to reclaim the distance. The ensuing minutes stretched into eternity, each second a test of his resolve. Constant rearview glances revealed nothing but the empty road behind him. Relief, cold and sweet, cascaded through him as he coasted into the safety of Jacksonville's embrace. The encounter left him unnerved, a cocktail of fear and exhilaration coursing through his veins, yet there was an undeniable spark of vitality igniting within, the rush of survival rekindling his resolve.

After the nerve-wracking encounter, Braxton parked in the lot near the Saloon. His heart still racing, he took solace in the warmth of the bourbon, its burn offering a momentary escape. Doubts nagged at him about the SUV—was it just a coincidence or something more sinister? The risky maneuver he had pulled loomed over his thoughts, intensifying his need to share his burdens.

Stepping into the Saloon, he found the familiar, comforting presence of Stacey behind the bar. He ordered a bourbon on the rocks, the ice clinking softly in the glass. Seeking out Jason, he casually asked Stacey about his whereabouts. Her response, that Jason was out getting supplies for the Saloon renovation project, left Braxton introspective, his mind adrift among the clues he had pieced together. The weight of his solitary investigation pressed heavily on him as he sipped his drink, lost in the labyrinth of his investigation.

"Having a bad jay?" Stacey's playful remark broke through his solemn mood, sparking a light-hearted exchange. They bantered about the ups and downs of daily life, with Stacey's quick wit matching Braxton's dry humor. The conversation danced around topics from the mundane to the absurd, each taunt and retort drawing a more relaxed smile from Braxton.

Then, in a moment of jest, Braxton said, "You know, if I were ten years younger, I might have tried my luck with you." Stacey's response was a combination of amusement and intrigue.

She winked and said, "Well, they don't have to be my age. Or even my gender."

Braxton chuckled. "Duly noted," Braxton replied with a wistful shake of his head, "or should I say *dooby* noted."

This playful interaction lightened the atmosphere, leaving Braxton feeling a bit more buoyant. As he finished his drink, he expressed his gratitude to Stacey for the enjoyable banter before preparing to leave, his spirits markedly lifted.

Leaving the Saloon, Braxton noticed the lights were on at the historical society building. Compelled by a hunch, he grabbed his bag from his car and entered the building. The clerk at the front desk greeted him with a familiar smile, half-joking about his expertise surpassing hers in the archives.

Acknowledging her comment with a friendly nod, Braxton found a quiet corner to delve into the archives. Surrounded by the musty scent of old records, he began his meticulous search through the County Clerk records, seeking further clues that might be hidden in the depths of Jacksonville's history.

After a hyper-focused half-hour in the archives, Braxton uncovered a pivotal detail: the entire Hoffnung family had legally changed their surname to "Holman" by the early 1900s. This revelation was the missing piece in his puzzle, indicating that the Hoffnungs hadn't been eradicated by the Emersons but had instead changed their surname, likely due to the rising xenophobia during the lead-up to World War One. Energized by this confirmation, Braxton photographed the crucial pages with his cell phone, capturing this vital evidence for his investigation.

Basking in the revelation about the Hoffnung family's name change, Braxton pulled out the document that he had printed out earlier at the courthouse—the table of contents of the so-called Multilateral Venture Compact. As he examined the contents, his initial curiosity was quickly replaced by a growing sense of unease.

The words *"Article 13—Of Retribution: Reciprocal Termination Clauses"* leaped out at him, casting a grim pall over the already foreboding document. This clause hinted at a dark, almost draconian web of provisions binding Jacksonville's elite in secretive and potentially lethal deals.

Sitting alone with this knowledge, Braxton felt the chill of danger closing in. The secrets he was unearthing were not just dusty relics of history but possibly the motive behind the recent bloody events in Jacksonville. He understood the perilous path he was treading—unmasking truths meant to remain shrouded in the town's enigmatic past could place him squarely in the crosshairs of a dangerous game.

Leaving the building with a deliberate calm he didn't feel, Braxton reached his car, his hands unsteady as he swallowed a few shots from his flask. The alcohol did little to soothe his frayed nerves. As he sat there, the enormity of what he had uncovered hit him. He was tangled in a web that could make him the next target. Starting his car, he drove off, the weight of history and the threat of the present heavy on his mind as he calculated his next move.

CHAPTER TEN

PAYING TRIBUTE
AT THE FEET

FRIDAY, OCTOBER 12, 7:01 AM

Three days on, the onset of fall brought a crisp chill to the air. Even after a warm-up jog, Braxton still felt the bite of the morning as he arrived at Britt Gardens. The early sun crested the eastern mountains, casting faint, long shadows through the scattered clouds.

His breath, visible in the cool air, trailed behind as he transitioned to a walk amidst the frost-kissed surroundings. He continued down the park's brick pathway until it ended. To his left was a small stone bench; to his right, a dirt path wound into the forest, a blend of evergreens and deciduous trees. The latter were shedding their multi-hued leaves, paying tribute at the feet of the Siskiyou Mountains.

He walked down the dirt path, reflecting on the hours he had spent going through the archives, piecing everything together over the past month. Keeping a low profile and saying that it was all for his (nonexistent) book.

He knew that he was either going insane, or someone was keeping tabs on him. The missing clothes, how his drawers had been rifled through, his gun moving from its usual place, the disarray of his notepads, and doors that locked and unlocked by themselves. It was something that hung heavy in his mind. But he kept to his usual patterns so as not to raise suspicion.

Deep down, Braxton had hoped to avoid this juncture. Returning to the scene of a past crime was the last thing one should do. But the time had inevitably arrived.

Braxton's heart raced as he fixed his gaze on a large oak tree, about forty feet into the woods. Its sturdy boughs arched against the somber morning sky. Shaking, he pulled out his phone, snapping a few photos. Each step toward the tree quickened his pulse, the ground sloping downwards. Under its sprawling branches, he halted, breath caught in his throat.

The bark had been stripped bare in places. *Those are rope marks.* The realization hit him like a physical blow, the world tilting as he stumbled forward, grasping the oak's trunk for support.

A harsh gust of wind whipped through the trees, rattling the frostbitten leaves. Overwhelmed, Braxton bent over, vomiting beneath the creaking boughs. He sank to the ground, resting his forehead against the rough bark, shivering, as the last spasms wracked his body. Memories, unbidden, flooded back—fragments of a past he'd tried to bury.

Wiping his face, Braxton took deep breaths, steadying his racing heart. Despite all of his research and preparation, the reality of it all was overwhelming. His panicked brain raced for an explanation, ranging from multiverse theory to an elaborate twisted practical joke.

Regaining his composure, Braxton stood, the nausea subsiding, replaced by an odd sense of calm. All his time and effort had borne out the truth—that *Ab Initio* and *Prime Ascendant* were more than just a legal term and a brewery name.

He wasn't delusional or paranoid. The paper trail bore it all out. There was a plausible explanation for the murder cases. One involving powerful forces that Braxton would rather not trifle with. Or maybe he was insane. After all, his theory seemed stranger than fiction.

Either way, he was way out of his depth. And for a brief inspirational moment, Braxton was ready to swear off drinking for good and get his shit together.

"Okay." He pulled out his flask and took several long pulls. "Just act normal and go home," he muttered to himself, slowly making his way back to civilization.

A quarter of an hour later, Braxton found himself back on South First Street. As he walked, he tried to distract himself from the lingering anxiety. His mind wandered to the peculiarities of Oregon's street naming system—the compass bearings like "W" or "E" preceding street names, sometimes even combined as "NE" or "SW." He mused over how these directions often seemed more confusing than helpful, especially when the streets veered in unexpected directions.

After making a right turn onto Main Street, Braxton crossed over East California Street. The early morning atmosphere in downtown, following the tourist season, was far from its usual bustling self. Occasionally, media crews made token appearances, providing "at-the-scene updates" that mostly consisted of regurgitated content. Shop owners along the main thoroughfare took their time opening up for the day, and a work van's engine hummed as it idled before merging onto the street.

Braxton made a right turn onto West C Street, only to find it transformed into East C Street just a block later. His musings on the confusing nature of compass-oriented street names deepened as he continued. He couldn't help but wonder if this system became even more bewildering when applied to alphabetically named streets. A nagging curiosity tempted him to walk further down the road and check if the sign read "East E Street" or perhaps even "E E Street." It was precisely at this moment that he noticed the off-white GMC work van rolling slowly behind him.

Half a block down West D Street, Braxton's ears caught the van's low hum as it made a right turn, continuing to shadow him discreetly. His heart quickened, and he increased his pace, making a quick right turn at the end of the block, heading back into town. The ominous sound of the van's engine growing louder filled his ears as it accelerated, but it remained on its course, proceeding straight along D Street.

After quickly scanning his surroundings and confirming that he was in the clear, Braxton let out a few nervous breaths. He reached into his pocket and took a couple of quick swigs from his flask, trying to calm his racing nerves. With renewed determination, he continued walking at a normal pace toward C Street until he reached the crosswalk. But as he approached it, dread washed over him—there was the van, accelerating directly toward him.

"What the fuck, dude?" Braxton hissed through clenched teeth. The van slowed its approach, but the harsh morning sunlight prevented Braxton from getting a clear view of the driver. Without hesitation, he broke into a run.

The van continued to trail closely behind and a surge of bile hiccupped into Braxton's mouth as he drew deep, searing breaths through his teeth. Despite the rising panic, he forced himself to maintain an ordinary running pace for a couple more blocks, the persistent sound of the van's engine a constant reminder of the threat behind him. Then, as he made a slight right turn into Doc Griffin Park, Braxton kicked in the afterburners, leaving the van in his wake.

Braxton halted near a gray house, raising his arms to take slow, deliberate breaths, mimicking the posture of someone who had just completed a routine jog. He placed his palms against a nearby telephone pole, methodically stretching his calf muscles one at a time. The van rumbled past, approximately a block away from his position. Braxton continued his stretching routine until the sound of the van's engine faded into the distance.

"Damn," Braxton said under his breath, "that literally just happened." Leaving nothing to chance, he stretched a couple more times in front of the Jacksonville police station—which looked like any other house in the neighborhood—before walking back to Doc Griffin Park.

After regaining his breath, Braxton resumed his run, weaving a zig-zagging path toward home. Despite the lingering anxiety and paranoia, Braxton couldn't help but admit that this was one of the fastest mile-per-minute paces he had ever clocked.

A few hours later, Braxton had shaved, showered, and yet the anxiety persisted. He cautiously peeked through his window blinds, finding nothing out of the ordinary. Armed with a drink in one hand and his phone in the other, he slumped onto the couch and composed an email to Riley's private address:

Hey, it's been a while. I hope you're doing well. I need to discuss something, and I promise it's not about us.

Then he sent her a text message to check her inbox.

In an effort to keep himself distracted, Braxton reached for his laptop to attend to some bills. As he finished his drink, mostly to quell the anxiety stemming from his dwindling resources, he promptly poured another.

His phone vibrated, displaying a blocked number. Braxton hesitated for a moment before answering, feigning nonchalance. "Hello?"

"Brax? It's Riley."

"Yeah. Hey, how's it going?" Despite his racing heart's best efforts to betray him, Braxton kept his tone breezy.

"First, I just want to apologize for ghosting you," Riley began. "Basically. . .it's complicated. I was figuring out how to respond to your messages, but," she sighed, "Like I said, it's complicated."

Braxton interjected: "Go ahead and delete those messages. I mean, yeah, you dropped off pretty abruptly there. And I may have said some things. . .so please don't—"

"It's fine, Brax," Riley reassured him. "Stop overthinking it. Work has really swamped me, so my social life's been nonexistent. I'm glad you reached out, actually." She paused. "So, what's going on with you? You wanted to talk about something?"

"I mean, honestly, I'd rather talk in person. Can we meet up somewhere for coffee or something?"

"Ummm. . . sure," she replied. "Can you meet me in Medford in about an hour? I can text you the address."

"Yeah, I can do that. That sounds good. Would really appreciate it." He hoped he didn't come off too eager. But, in fairness, it took almost becoming roadkill before asking to see her.

"Okay, you should be getting the text." Braxton felt the phone vibrate against his cheek.

"Yeah, I think I just got it. I'll see you then. Thanks again for getting back to me, Riley." After exchanging goodbyes, Braxton ended the call.

He scuttled over to the kitchen window and took another peek through the blinds. Nothing out of the ordinary.

Braxton went with a dose of Adderall instead of THC, downing the pill with a gulp of bourbon. After taking stock of things, including the topped-up hip flask, he headed out the front door, pretending like it was just any other day.

He scanned the street after starting the car. Nothing out of place. A couple of regulars walking their dogs, and that was about it. After making sure his work product was secured in his bag, Braxton took a moment to reflect. It was all happening so fast, but at least it was coming together. Riley getting back to him was one of the biggest wildcards.

ONE HOUR LATER

Braxton sat at one of the small tables positioned against the coffee shop's interior brick wall, facing the front entrance. The place had an unmistakable hipster vibe, evident in its music, employees, and most of its clientele. But the coffee was strong, so strong that Braxton had to double down on his flask injections just to taste the bourbon.

He kept his eyes locked onto his phone, pretending not to notice Riley as she entered. The sound of her placing an order reached his ears, and by the time she took a seat across from him, he had no idea what the document on his phone was saying.

"Hey," Riley greeted with an upbeat smile. Braxton couldn't help but return the smile.

"Hola." Braxton tried to keep things casual and relaxed, despite his mach-speed heartbeat. He took a sip from his spiked coffee, feeling its soothing warmth traveling from his esophagus down to his stomach and then up his spine into his brain.

"I'm really glad you reached out to me," Riley said. Her words sounded sincere, though Braxton couldn't be entirely sure. Nonetheless, she was sitting right there in front of him, which meant something.

"No worries, no worries," Braxton replied, feigning a laid-back demeanor. "Just don't hold those messages against me. It was a bit abrupt, and I was kind of seeking feedback, I guess? I know, I know, I overthink things," he added with a smirk.

"So, what's going on?" Riley cut through the awkwardness.

Braxton paused, considering where to begin. He felt the need to pro-vide some context before diving into the weird surveillance-van shit. "Well, ummm, let me start by asking, is this place clean?"

Riley looked puzzled. "What do you mean?"

Braxton leaned closer and lowered his voice. "I mean, can anyone overhear us right now? If not, we should be fine. Otherwise, we might need to go for a walk." He discreetly slid a folded note across the table to her.

Riley accepted the note, her expression shifting from curiosity to surprise and then concern. "So. . ." she began, uncertain.

Braxton nodded. "Yeah. But don't worry, it's not a big deal. It's not like I've been totally forthcoming to you, either." He let the message on the note sink in. "So, can we continue our conversation here?"

Riley read the note again, which contained a straightforward mes-sage: "I know you're FBI. Please be straight with me."

With a deep breath, she responded, "Yeah, we're good. It's just me."

"Can I have that back, please?" Braxton eyed the paper clutched in her hand. She gave it back to him. "Thanks." He started ripping it to tiny shreds under the table.

"How long have you known?" she asked.

"What part?" said Braxton, "that you're a special agent? Pretty much from when we first met. Granted, I had a little help from the Saloon's peanut gallery that night."

"What other part is there?" Riley asked.

"That we met before," Braxton smiled. "At the San Francisco field office. Remember? We chatted for a bit because all the other applicants were pretty much ex-military. You and I were the only attorneys there. It took me a while to make that connection, by the way. I didn't remember you being so— Ah, fuck it, I'll just say it. I didn't recall you being so hot back then."

Riley smiled and turned her head a little, trying to hide the blush. "I'll be straight with you, Brax. I knew that we had met earlier, too. The third time we hung out." She took a sip of coffee. "You know, I feel kind of relieved that we both know that we know. Because—I mean it was also genuine. But, you know, with my job and everything, well. . .it's complicated."

"Okay. Cool. Now that we got that unresolved awkwardness out of the way, I need to talk to you about something." Braxton balled up the bits of paper and dropped them into his coffee cup. "But I need to hit the head real quick, if that's okay."

"Do you really have to go? Or do you just need some shots from your flask?" Riley said without judgment. Braxton felt the blood surface hot on his face. Giving up altogether, he gave her a devious grin.

"Well, in the spirit of full disclosure." Braxton pulled the flask from his jacket pocket and downed a few swigs with no one the wiser.

"Thanks. I usually don't start so early in the day," he lied, "but some crazy shit has been going down. Especially today." He licked his lips. "So, I have to ask. Do you guys have a surveillance team on me?"

"You know I can't get into—" Riley began, but then she interrupted herself. "No," she said, lowering her voice, "Not to my knowledge. You're nowhere near anyone's radar. Why? Should you be?"

"That's a really good question," Braxton replied, his tone contemplative. "Because I'm pretty sure that I'm on someone's watch list. So, if it is you guys, I want to surrender myself for questioning right now." He paused for a moment, the silence feeling like an eternity, until Riley shook her head indicating that it wasn't the case.

"Because if it's not you guys," he continued, "then I'm in way over my head. Something deep," he surmised, surprising himself with how calmly he conveyed his predicament. "Okay," he added, "just so you know, you're the only other person who knows about this shit."

"What kind of shit?" Riley inquired.

Braxton scanned the coffee shop, taking in the upbeat indie pop music playing at a decent volume, which added a surreal touch to the moment. He observed the other customers, mostly in their twenties or forties, busy with their Apple devices.

"You've been off-grid with me, right?" Braxton inquired. "Please be honest about that. Because if I find out I'm anywhere in your notes or if my name ever came up. . . well, I guess I'll just. . ." His voice trailed off.

Riley took a moment before responding. "Look," she said, "can we agree that I'm clearly not cut out for undercover work? I'm just a standard field agent. And by the way, sleeping with someone to gather information isn't part of my job description. I made up the whole pharmacy rep cover story to keep a low profile. That's it. If I ever thought you were involved in something, we wouldn't have. . . well, you get the idea. It's not in my playbook."

"So, that's a 'no' then?" Braxton sought clarification. Riley nodded. "And you're not feeding me a line, right? Is that a 'yes'?"

"Yes," Riley affirmed.

The litigator in Braxton started to emerge, causing him to step back and reevaluate the situation.

"Maybe I'm being super paranoid," Braxton sighed. "I mean, I don't want to get you involved if that's going to mess with—"

"Brax!" Riley hissed, her tone urgent. She took a moment to compose herself, massaging the bridge of her nose. "Look, you're overthinking this. I haven't said a word about you to anyone. Not to colleagues, not to family, not to friends, nobody." Braxton nodded, realizing the irony in how her denying any connection with him was the best outcome. "Have you told anyone?" Riley ventured.

"No, not really," Braxton responded. "I mean, not that I didn't want to. But I figured that whatever this thing we had going on between us wasn't a 'sanctioned op' or anything like that. So, I wasn't going to say anything until—well, until the right moment, I guess." He reflected for a couple of beats, fixated on the coffee-soaked shreds of paper at the bottom of his cup, as if reading tea leaves.

"All right," Braxton continued, leaning in. "Let me get into it: do the terms 'Prime Ascendant' or 'Ab Initio' mean anything to you?" Riley gave him a blank stare. He tried not to get lost in her turquoise eyes. "Okay," he said, regrouping. "Okay, right. The bodies that were discovered in the cemetery. Were they embalmed or anything like that?" Riley couldn't hide her surprise this time.

"Shit. I knew it," he said. "Okay. Can we drive to Jacksonville? I need to show you something."

CHAPTER ELEVEN

INTO THE DARKNESS BEYOND

FRIDAY, OCTOBER 12, 11:27 AM

"Looks like they took the exit," Braxton remarked as they drove along OR 238, his eyes on a van that had been trailing them. Earlier, before leaving the coffee shop, Braxton had insisted that they take their separate cars to a parking garage before continuing to Jacksonville in Riley's gray sedan.

Riley reassured him, saying, "I told you, Brax, we're clean. Just sit back and let me do my job." Braxton found it hard to decide which was more unsettling, his own anxiety or Riley's calm demeanor. "If it helps, go ahead and take a shot. I won't judge."

Braxton chuckled, saying, "Well. . .it's not every day I get permission to drink in a federal law enforcement vehicle." He noticed a hint of disapproval in her expression as he reached for his flask. "Sorry," he quickly added after taking a generous sip. "Didn't mean to sound so cavalier. I tend to resort to humor to cope, even if it comes off as a bit mean-spirited. That's not my intention."

Riley offered a reassuring smile. "Relax, Brax. You're overthinking things again," she said, her tone nostalgic.

"You're absolutely right," he conceded. "I am a bit on edge right now. But it's a relief to share this with someone, even if you probably think I'm some kind of conspiracy nut."

Riley gently teased, "Well, that did sound a bit mean-spirited, Braxton."

He couldn't help but grin. "Ah, you got me there. Well played." They parked in the lot between the cemetery and the old town.

"Alright," Riley said as she unbuckled her seatbelt. "Where to?"

Ten minutes later, as they walked along the narrow road winding up to the hilltop cemetery, Braxton and Riley slowed down, and Braxton took a moment to get his bearings. Riley was all too familiar with the area, given the hours she and her colleagues had spent combing through it since the Holman remains were discovered there.

"Okay," Braxton said, pointing ahead. "It's this way."

They began to walk northeast, passing by the Masonic order and Oddfellows plots clustered in the center of the graveyard. Riley had mixed feelings about the entire situation. She found Braxton to be a decent guy, even dating material, but his alcohol-fueled spontaneity posed a significant liability. It was the main reason she had ghosted him. Which was too bad, because he was smart, insightful and—while not movie-star gorgeous—a good-looking guy. Their physical chemistry was undeniable, and his spontaneity could yield some endearing moments.

Riley recalled their last evening at Braxton's, with "Labyrinth" in the background. Suddenly Braxton vanished into his room, only to reappear as David Bowie's famed dance scene began. Sporting an unabashed grin, Braxton launched into a hilariously accurate rendition, his pelvic thrusts exaggerated for comedic effect. By the third thrust, Riley's laughter broke free as it clicked: Braxton's quick bedroom retreat was to bolster his shorts with at least three pairs of socks to mimic Bowie's on-screen bulge. This playful spectacle, a glimpse into Braxton's unguarded joy and creativity, had momentarily deepened their connection through sheer silliness.

Pulled back to the present by the somberness of their surroundings, Riley stifled her chuckles, thankful Braxton hadn't noticed. As they navigated the quiet paths, his confident voice cut through her reflections, "We're going the right way, aren't we?" His assurance, laced with a hint of challenge, tethered her back from her daydreams. The litigator in him was making a resurgence.

Riley had observed this side of him earlier at the coffee shop—a sharp, concise demeanor with a hint of the kind of attorney she disliked the most: the type who would poke holes in a case and add a dash of arrogance for good measure.

Feeling conflicted, she sighed and replied, "Brax, that's hard to say when I don't know your destination. No offense, but we've combed this place way too many times to count."

They continued to walk in silence, heading toward the cemetery's eastern boundary. Braxton eventually came to a stop, and they found themselves in an open, grassy field. Uphill, to their north, stood two elaborately adorned, monument-sized mausoleums dedicated to the area's prominent families.

Braxton raised his arm and pointed to a large, rectangular granite memorial a few yards away. On its face was a sizable plaque that read: "WE REMEMBER in 1996. These persons, *INTER ALIOS*, buried in the Pauper Section of this cemetery." Below the inscription were scores of names and dates spanning from 1870 through 1910, listing some of the deceased interred in the common grave.

Braxton gestured toward the serene grassy field that stretched to the southern end of the cemetery grounds.

"This is where you found the bodies, right?" He posed the question, his tone more inquisitive this time.

Riley smirked and gently shook her head from side to side. "You know I can't delve into undisclosed details without approval, Braxton," she held her ground.

"*C'mon*, Riley," he pleaded. "This is just a conversation between you and me, as human beings. I'm asking for an honest answer, a simple yes-or-no."

He paused, taking a breath, and lowered his voice. "You found the Holman couple right here in the Pauper Field, right?"

There was a prolonged silence, and then Riley nodded.

"And they were embalmed, weren't they?" Braxton continued.

Riley was perplexed by how much Braxton seemed to know. It didn't matter much anymore; her reaction at the coffee shop had already given away that detail.

"Trust me, I wish I didn't know," Braxton grumbled as he removed his hat, his voice trembling slightly. He ran his hand through his hair, blinking rapidly as his eyes welled up with tears. "God damn it!" He opened his flask and took a few swigs, trying to steady his emotions. His shoulders shook as he fought back the tears threatening to escape. "Okay," he exhaled deeply, his voice cracking, "just give me a moment to process this and get my shit together."

Riley moved closer and embraced him, wrapping her arms around him tightly. "Relax, Brax," she whispered soothingly in his ear, her voice filled with empathy. "Stop overthinking it," she urged softly. "I've got you, Brax. I'm right here. It's okay, I've got you."

She could feel his body trembling against hers, and she held him even closer. "Relax," she repeated, her own tears now flowing freely, "I've got you." And there they stood, embracing in a moment where the laws of time and space seemed suspended, holding each other as the rest of the world disappeared around them.

Something strange was happening. Chanting in the distance, growing louder with each heartbeat.

"*In Terra Lios, In Terra Lios. . .*"

The voices had returned, emanating from everywhere yet nowhere as their surroundings seemed to melt away into darkness.

"*In Terra Lios, In Terra Lios. . .*"

The hypnotic chanting was pulling them toward its source. Their hearts raced, their breaths grew ragged.

"*In Terra Lios, In Terra Lios. . .*"

They were drawn to it, a force compelling them inward. The chanting echoed and boomed, drawing them deeper into the realm beyond.

The chanting reached its climax as Braxton and Riley remained connected, as if they were one being, mutually experiencing formative moments of their lives, until some unknown force pushed them into the unknown.

Then there was silence. Braxton saw himself streaming down a river of light surrounded by darkness. Total entropy. He saw other light particles arcing through the stream, some propelling themselves with negative force until disappearing forever into the surrounding nothingness; others passively staying in their lane; and those which found themselves in the torrent's energy-rich center, the part forming galaxies and life therein.

He saw how the last group positively bonded, moving from one connection to the next, clustering together until creating such mass that they gravitated into the thriving center, beaming through all of infinity.

It occurred to him that by only focusing on where he wanted to be, he had lost sight of what he was doing in the now.

He admitted that—given the universe's incomprehensible complexity—no amount of planning would put him where he wanted to be.

He came to realize that he was part of something infinite, powerful, and mysterious; something that no amount of processing power could ever reverse-engineer. Indeed, going down that path would lead to madness. Into the darkness beyond.

It dawned on him that there was no master plan. That all he could do is connect in the now. To make positive bonds with good intentions. To let go of the illusion of control, and have faith that he would end up in the torrent's center. Where life, experience, and true self-awareness could flourish.

That by doing good in the now, he could do well in the future.

He released his ego and was absorbed into the current. Drifting ever faster until the light around him phased from white to yellow to a vibrant blue. Awakening in the depths of Riley's eyes as she peered back at him.

They were back in the cemetery. Two more lost souls in the Pauper Field. Holding one another tightly. Weeping as the universe swirled around them. Both connecting in the now.

THIRTY MINUTES LATER

The drive back from the cemetery was awkward for both Riley and Braxton. Neither could deny that they had experienced something together in the Pauper Field, something that felt otherworldly. Each also admitted that, until that moment, neither had felt so closely connected to another human being before. But due to the dynamics at hand, neither was willing to say it for fear that the other didn't feel the same way.

Hence the awkwardness.

"I'm assuming there's no standard protocol for. . .this kind of situation?" Braxton broke the silence.

"That's a fair assumption," said Riley. "Especially when I have no idea as to what 'this kind of situation' even means."

"Okay. How can we do this, Riley?" Braxton took off his glasses and started wiping them. "The last thing I want to do is make things difficult for you. How about this—and I'm really trusting you here—I'll just start saying things. And you stop me when it's something you guys don't know about. Fair?"

"Fair," Riley agreed. "And if you say anything that you shouldn't know about, I'll let you know that I didn't quite hear you. So don't repeat it."

"Even better," Braxton leaned back in the passenger seat. "So, here goes. Over the course of Jacksonville's history, two fraternal orders came to power: Prime Ascendant and Ab Initio." Riley nodded.

"Okay," Braxton continued, "Elle Harris was Ab Initio through her mother's side." Riley nodded again. "Let's make this easier. I'll stop itemizing things and you tell me when to stop. Cool?"

"Cool," Riley took a left onto the county road leading back to Medford.

"Okay. Don't ask how I even got involved with this, and we should be fine. All right?" Braxton didn't wait for Riley's response. "Ab Initio was the only game in town until the 1870s when a new fraternal order, Prime Ascendant, splintered off." He took a moment to gather his thoughts.

"Prime Ascendant was formed by one of the top dogs of Ab Initio, a guy named Paul Hoffnung. Incidentally, the Hoffnung family changed their last name to Holman just over a hundred years ago. Did you know that?"

Riley nodded. "A lot of people did that back then to avoid anti-German sentiment during World War One."

"Yeah, but they did it en masse before the war even started," Braxton explained.

Riley shrugged. "Some people are more informed than others, especially the rich."

"I suppose," Braxton said. "Anyhow, where was I?"

"Prime Ascendant splintered off from Ab Initio," Riley replied seamlessly.

"Right," Braxton continued. "Everything seemed civil enough until Ab Initio's leader died from a lightning-fast case of 'quick consumption.' I have no idea how their rules of succession work, but I do know that a young widower named William Emerson was ultimately appointed as the first Order's *Prima Imperator*. Emerson retained control until dying of natural causes in 1936."

With muscle memory, Braxton reached for his flask but thought better of it and slid it back into his pocket. "William Emerson is Mitchell Emerson's paternal great-great-grandfather."

Riley maintained her composure. "I've heard everything so far. And—how should I put it?—you're bringing up a theory that's been labeled 'fringe at best' amongst my colleagues. I wish I could say more. . ."

"No, that's perfect, Riley, thank you!" Braxton replied with enthusiasm. "The less I know, the better, frankly. And I'm thinking the less you know about my situation, the better for you. The last thing I want is for you to deal with a polygraph session with the Office of Professional Responsibility."

"I didn't hear that, Brax," Riley smirked.

"Ha-ha, totally. Okay, Emerson reign covered," he said, taking a moment to collect his thoughts before continuing. "After a host of ailments causing premature death within both circles, both fraternal orders came up with a set of rules concerning their operations."

"I can only speculate as to the specifics," he continued, "but Ab Initio seems to control the business infrastructure—banking, transportation, trade conduits, and the like. They're the money guys. They make sure the goods get to where they need to go and profit at every step. Prime Ascendant, on the other hand, is all about resource production. They grow the food, harvest the timber, own the factories, and control the workforce. In sum, Prime Ascendant controls the means of production, and Ab Initio controls the flow of commerce. Ya with me?"

"Yep, I've heard that," said Riley.

Braxton delved deeper into the complexities. "The written code of conduct between the entities, called the 'Multilateral Venture Compact,' has an entire article titled 'Of Retribution: Reciprocal Termination Clauses,' consisting of twenty-plus pages." He noticed Riley tensing up.

"We didn't know that," she admitted.

"No way, really?" Braxton's excitement was evident. "I'm kinda having a legal geek-gasm right now!"

Riley chuckled. "Okay, so how the hell do you know that? Or is it better that I don't know?"

"No, it's totally fine," Braxton reassured her. "Without getting into the absolute living hell-on-earth anguish caused by poring through old-timey nineteenth-century case law, I found that out via public records."

"The Compact's table of contents was attached to a motion submitted by one of Prime Ascendant's attorneys. I have a copy of it, actually. But it's just a table of contents. Nothing substantive. Still, though, I was pretty stoked on finding that little relic. It was tedious, to say the least."

"I can imagine," Riley commiserated. "Anything else you want to tell me?"

"I mean. . . I don't know," Braxton drifted.

Riley pressed on, her tone earnest. "Why were you so paranoid this morning, Brax? Talking about surveillance and being followed and such-like?"

"Well, yeah, there is that," Braxton admitted. "Something weird happened this morning, that's for sure. And it really happened; I didn't make something up just to see you again or anything. . . though I did miss you," he added honestly. "Basically, I thought some dude in a work van was following me. I shook him off after pulling some tricks out of my runner's hat. But after seeing you today, I'm beginning to think that maybe he was just lost or something. Thank you, Riley. Seriously. I mean it."

His tone carried genuine sincerity. He wanted to share more with her—the funeral procession, the burning corpses, the embalming chemicals purchased by Mitchell's winery, and the haunting sight of two hanging bodies the night before Elle and Aaron were reported missing. But the lawyer in him knew that such disclosures would lead to an interrogation room, and he needed to keep Riley's deniability plausible.

"Well, I don't know what I did exactly," said Riley, "but I'm glad you're feeling better. You were kind of a wreck." She pulled into the parking garage. "And you shouldn't have to feel like making something up to get a hold me. The way I left things between us was bad. I just didn't know how to explain it to you, even though—unbeknownst to me—you knew. So, for what it's worth, I'm sorry."

Braxton chuckled softly. "It's a mad, mad world out there, Agent McAvoy," he said with a shake of his head. "Hey, while we're at it, can I ask you a question?" Despite the dubious look on Riley's face, he pressed on. "Was there anything unusual about the young couple's DNA samples found at Rogue River Ranch a few weeks back?"

"Not really," Riley replied confidently. "We're absolutely certain it was their DNA, with minuscule chances of it being otherwise. I can vouch for the lab testing. It was a perfect match."

"Of course." Braxton nodded. "Well, hypothetically, would one use samples collected by local authorities in a case like this?"

"Our standard procedure is to preserve DNA samples from missing persons immediately upon assignment. We cross-check against samples from close relatives like parents, siblings, and children if available. The samples and tests were pristine. It was undoubtedly their DNA," Riley explained.

"Got it," Braxton said. "Forgive my curiosity, but what's more effective for cross-checking: parents or offspring? I'm not asking for specifics—"

"Okay," Riley interjected, choosing her words carefully. "So, *hypothetically*, there wouldn't be a need to test their child's DNA in this instance. Each victim's parents and siblings provided samples for cross-checking, and the matches were indisputable. My superior was somewhat relieved by that. The Hunter case has been complex. But, yes, the results are rock-solid. Nothing 'unusual' in that regard."

"Cool," Braxton acknowledged. "Go ahead and drop me off by my car. I've had enough tradecraft for the day."

Riley pulled into the space next to his car and turned off the engine, catching Braxton off guard.

"Okay, I owe you some candor, Brax," Riley said. "I can't deny that we have a connection. I've never felt the way I felt when we embraced back there. Never—"

"Holy shit, me too!" Braxton blurted.

"Brax," she intoned, "I adore you, but please just shut up for a second so I can say this to you, okay?"

Due to his heart nearly exploding after hearing "I adore you," Braxton promptly shut up.

"The best word I can use here is 'conflicted,'" Riley continued. "I'm conflicted by this innate feeling of trust and comfort I have with you, even though you know things that only a person of interest would know. I mean. . ." She unbuckled her seat belt.

"I mean, I think I've fallen for a jaded attorney with a chronic drinking problem, which is something I need about as much as a hole in my head. And I won't even get into the train wreck that is my personal life. FYI: I don't have one. You were basically it, and I think we can both agree that I managed to fuck that up right and proper."

"It's all good, Riley, seriously," said Braxton.

"Just please shut the fuck up and let me get this out," she put up her index finger. "On one level, we both know that there's no way that this could work out. I'm on a specific trajectory, and I'm not going to let my codependence get the best of me again." Her voice tremored for a bit.

"Say what you want about the FBI," she galvanized, "and I'm the first to admit that there's some shady shit going on in the bureau. But I'm dedicated to its purpose. To do good. To prevent harm to society. That is my agency. On the other hand, I'm also being nudged to settle down, have kids, a family. You know, have it all.

"And I realized something. Back at the Pauper Field. If I don't have kids, what will become of me? What mark will I leave behind? Will it just be my name on a plaque? And is it weird that I'm okay with that? So, yeah. I'm conflicted." They both sat in silence for a few seconds. "Now get out of the car so I can make sure you're not too impaired to drive."

Braxton looked at her, stupefied, until hearing himself say: "Seriously?"

"No, Brax," said Riley with an extra dose of sarcasm, "I'm totally fine with you driving your car around while stumbling-over drunk."

Braxton gave her a befuddled smile and opened the passenger door. He turned around to tell her something, and was surprised to see that she was already walking toward the back of her car.

"Oh, shit, she was being serious." Braxton got out and walked over to where Riley was waiting, penlight at the ready.

"Well, yeah," Riley said after administering a horizontal nystagmus test, "you're less impaired than I would've thought. But I'm not condoning it." She pocketed the penlight.

They looked at each other again, and both moved in to embrace. They sealed their embrace with a kiss that neither wanted to end. And when that moment did come, their lips parted with such perfect synchronicity that it felt like maybe it never really could completely end.

"Okay," Braxton said. "Okay," he repeated. It was the first time they had made physical contact since being in the Pauper Field, and something had come over him.

"Look, I need to be real with you. I want you to know that I'm way out of my depth here. Like, with everything. I mean, I know we have no future together. You don't think I know that?" he marshaled his thoughts.

"I've been living my entire life based on other people's expectations," he went on. "And you know what else? I honestly have no idea who I am. It's like. . .the only way I can see myself is through the lens of how others see me.

"So, who is Braxton Hayward at his core? I have no idea. Do you? I know so little about him that it took thirty-plus years to ask the right question: that beneath the pomp and circumstance of my performance, is there anything else? Any soul, or spark? Or am I supposed to be an empty vessel to be filled with society's expectations?

"Because if it's the latter, that not only means I have no personal meaning, it also means that the very core of my being is worthless when society's gaze deems me a failure. That's a pretty messed-up life philosophy, don't you think? And I literally just figured this out."

Braxton drew a breath, letting the words flow out. "That totally explains why I alter my state of consciousness. I drink and smoke and indulge to fill the void and to numb the sting after the inevitable fallout. All I need to do is fill that vessel with some earnest self-worth. To become comfortable in my own skin. I need to find a way to take control away from that smartass envy-driven know-it-all ego of mine and be grateful for everything good that life has given me.

"But here's the even crazier part: despite this epiphany—which was triggered by what could only be described as having an out-of-body experience with a soulmate—despite all of that, I know that I'll go back home and drink until I pass out. So, trust me. I get it. I'm feeling conflicted, too.

"But know this, Riley: I will give you whatever you ask for." His voice started to tremble. "I will go wherever you want me to go, whether it's with you or away from you. I will do everything in my power to make your life better, even if that means that I not be part of it."

Braxton removed his glasses and wiped away his tears. They locked eyes and hugged again. After unentangling, Riley gave Braxton a reassuring pat on his shoulder, and then got into her car. Braxton likewise started for his car but stopped short and turned around.

He knocked on Riley's window, which she rolled down.

"Sorry," Braxton said, "one last thing. If I get the urge to drunk-text you later because I want to spend every living minute together with you, I'll remind myself to shut the fuck up until you're ready to tell me where you're coming from." He gave her a self-deprecating smile. Riley smiled back, shook her head from side to side, and started rolling up the window.

"Fuckin' Braxton," she said, turning her face away to hide her blush.

As Braxton watched Riley drive away and descend into the parking structure's lower level, he reached for a cigarette, placed it between his lips, lit it, and took a slow, contemplative drag while absorbing the view.

At that moment, he began to reflect on the day's events, each one captured by his memory, frame by frame. It was as if the shutter controlling his photographic memory had remained in the "open" position. He could recall every detail, from Riley's license plate number to the names and dates inscribed on the Pauper Field memorial placard.

Yet something even more peculiar began to occur. Instead of internalizing the usual anxiety and self-loathing brought on by life's chaos and uncertainty, he found himself letting go of all that negative energy, handing it back over to the universe from whence it came. It occurred to him that at that moment of time, there was nothing he could do to predict what may or may not happen. So, there was no reason to dwell on it in the first place. Braxton realized there was no reason to dwell on what may or may not happen; he couldn't predict it anyway.

A sense of calm washed over him, coursing through his body and mind. His breathing slowed, and his heartbeat became steady and easygoing. He couldn't help but recall a similar feeling from over half a decade ago in San Francisco when he had locked eyes with the Dalai Lama, who had blissfully smiled and waved from his humble motorcade.

"Hmm," Braxton mused as he settled into his car, "could this be what serenity is supposed to feel like?"

With the engine idling, he took a moment to process everything. The clarity he experienced was unlike anything he had felt before. Braxton reached for his phone, ready to send a message.

Instead of crafting an eloquent text with proper introductory and closing clauses—which would have required numerous reviews and edits to ensure it didn't look like he was drunk—within seconds, Braxton typed and sent the following:

ATTORNEY-CLIENT PRIVILEGED COMMUNICATION: This is Braxton Hayward. We need to talk. Meet me at the Saloon no later than noon tomorrow. Please advise as to the specific ETA. Thank you.

He dropped the phone into the cupholder and put the car into gear. Seconds later, his phone buzzed with a text notification.

ATTORNEY-CLIENT PRIVILEGED COMMUNICATION: Confirming receipt. Will be at Saloon at 10:30 AM tomorrow. See you then.

Driving back to Jacksonville, Braxton grappled with the unsettling truths he had unearthed. He had delved into the world of the powerful and secretive, individuals who could make him disappear at will. Braxton felt he stood on the brink of a profound shift, torn between the allure of familiarity and the uncertainty of what lay ahead, all while knowing his typical routine awaited him: return home, open a bottle, and drink until he passed out.

CHAPTER TWELVE

OF RETRIBUTION: RECIPROCAL TERMINATION CLAUSES

SATURDAY, OCTOBER 13, 10:27 AM

The next morning, Braxton found himself at a corner table in the bustling dining area. The Saloon had recently introduced its late-morning brunch specials, which had quickly become popular among tourists and locals alike. Tony the chef's talent for crafting simple dishes using fresh local ingredients, Amanda's no-nonsense service, and Stacey's expertly made Bloody Marys and mimosas all contributed to its success. Luckily, Braxton had arrived early enough to secure a table.

Before him sat a cup of coffee and an empty shot glass, evidence of his early morning indulgence. He had decided that if Riley knew about his day drinking, there was no need to hide it from anyone else. It was one less thing to worry about.

Braxton took another sip of his spiked coffee, gazing into the distance. Just then, the door swung open, and another customer entered. Their eyes met, and a nod of acknowledgment passed between them. It was Mitchell, heading straight for Braxton's table.

"Nothing beats a morning run followed by an Irish coffee, huh?" Mitchell commented as he took a seat.

"Yup," Braxton replied, studying his own disheveled appearance. It seemed like he had a rough night. Braxton was dressed in running gear and a black puffy jacket that hung unevenly over his frame. His head was bare, his hair unkempt, and he hadn't bothered to shave.

"I have a hard stop at eleven, just so you know," Mitchell began, setting the tone. "What's on your mind?"

Braxton took another sip of his cream-colored coffee and spoke with a hint of sarcasm, "You know, Mitch, that's one thing I appreciate about you. No beating around the bush. Why bother with pleasantries when everything's just hunky-fucking-dory, right?"

Mitchell looked concerned, leaning in slightly. "Are you feeling okay, Brax? Because, honestly, you don't look too great," he remarked. "Sorry if that sounds blunt, but it's a busy time of year, and I've rearranged my schedule to meet with you. So, can you tell me why I'm here? Because—"

Before he could finish, Amanda approached the table.

"Sorry, Manda," Braxton slurred. "My bad. Looks like we won't have time for breakfast after all. Just let me know what I owe you, and we'll be out of your hair as soon as I'm done with this." He gestured toward his coffee mug, which he clumsily swirled with his other hand. "Unless you want anything?" Mitchell declined, and Amanda promptly left.

Braxton broke the silence, "Let's go for a walk once we settle the bill."

"I'm fine with that," said Mitchell. The two men sat in silence as Braxton finished his drink.

"Ah, perfect timing," said Braxton as Amanda reappeared with the bill. "I've got it right here." He pulled a wad of cash out of his pocket and peeled off fifteen dollars.

"I think you only meant to give me—"

"Nah, nah, it's all good," Braxton interjected. "It was a triple shot, remember? And that extra five-spot is the tip. Thanks. And it's great to see that the whole breakfast/brunch thing has taken off. Toodles!" he lushed. Amanda backpedaled away with a baffled look on her face.

"Okay," Braxton said. "Shall we?" Both men stood up and headed out the front door, nodding to Jason on their way out.

Despite the warm morning air, Braxton kept his jacket on as they walked westward.

"We headed anywhere in particular?" asked Mitchell.

"Can you tell your driver that you'll call him when you need him? I don't like being tailed," Braxton said. Mitchell came to a stop.

"Oh, come on, dude," Braxton went on. "Enough with the cloak and dagger. I know you've been keeping tabs on me. Call off the dogs and let's have a friendly chat."

Mitchell gave Braxton a once-over and gestured at his right-front jacket pocket. "You ditch the heat, and I'll call off the dogs."

"Fair," Braxton agreed. "I'm parked around the corner. Walk with me."

The two resumed their walk, making their way to the silver BMW. Braxton popped the trunk and casually tossed his jacket inside. There was an audible thud when the Glock compact pistol, a compensation from another client, landed in the trunk. Realizing that it wasn't a good idea to toss around garments containing firearms, Braxton winced a little.

"It's not loaded. But still—oops." He put on a lightweight jacket and closed the trunk. Mitchell chuckled and shrugged as if to say "meh."

Braxton turned to Mitchell, who remained on the sidewalk. "Okay. That's all I have, unless keys and cigarettes count." He placed those items on the car and patted his pockets. "You can call them off now."

"Confirmed," Mitchell said with a nod. Braxton turned around to see two men rolling by in the black late-model European SUV he had evaded earlier that week. He recognized its beefy driver, who nodded back and roared off in a rather melodramatic fashion, in Braxton's opinion.

"Where to?" Mitchell asked.

"It's a beautiful morning. How about we head to the gardens?" Braxton armed the car alarm, and they both crossed the street. "While ill-advised, I'm going to put this out there," said Braxton after crossing the street. "But contrary to all the indicators, I don't think you're the malicious asshole that you've been made out as."

"That's funny you say that," Mitchell replied, "because I come from a strong family lineage of malicious assholery." The tension released, and both men laughed as they wound their way past the music festival grounds into Britt Gardens.

"So, how's business?" Braxton asked.

"Oh, you know," said Mitchell. "It's going. Thanks again for going over those docs. That kind of work gives me a migraine. Between you and me, I barely passed my UCC sales class at Stanford."

"Yeah, no problem," Braxton replied. "Actually, I'm kind of impressed."

"About what?" Mitchell asked.

"How you waited almost thirty minutes before reminding me that you went to Stanford," Braxton chuckled. "Just messing with you, dude."

"Ha," Mitchell scoffed. "I got those Harvard boys beat by twenty-nine minutes and fifty-five seconds."

As they ventured deeper into the park, Braxton couldn't help but notice Mitchell's growing discomfort. His face became more stoic with each step along the brick-laid pathway, and the unease was palpable, especially as they reached the end of the path.

"We're walking into the forest?" Mitchell pointed at his feet, his voice tinged with concern. "I'm wearing Italian leather." Braxton rolled his eyes in response and forged ahead. Mitchell sighed audibly and reluctantly followed, each footfall deepening the silence between them. The unspoken tension hung heavily in the air, casting a shadow over their otherwise tranquil surroundings.

The path eventually began to slope down, leading them to the massive oak tree that had been their destination all along. Braxton halted, turning his attention to the thick branch where the bark had been stripped away by the ropes.

"I'm sure you already knew that this was the destination," Braxton remarked after they stopped. He pointed at the distinctive branch. "See anything unusual there?"

Mitchell's expression tightened as he glowered. "Maybe some kids tied up rope swings?"

Braxton's patience wore thin as he scowled. "Let me tell you where I'm at, Mitch," he began, his tone becoming more serious. "Despite rigorous efforts to the contrary, I have reconciled with the fact that I saw two bodies hanging from that tree during the wee hours of August seventh. I also know that the last time anyone saw your ex-girlfriend and her fiancé was the night of August sixth. Thing being, my recollection of that night was. . .foggy to say the least. So, I can't ID the bodies. It could have been anyone, for all I know." Braxton paused, taking a deep breath, and continued, "Like Andrew and Susan Holman, for example."

Mitchell was momentarily caught off guard, his eyebrows raising for a microsecond before he regained his poker face. He smirked at his own tell, disguising it as disdain, and then let out a disbelieving chuckle while shaking his head.

"I think you've been taking too many hits from that flask of yours, Brax," he condescended. "I mean, your timing is all off. The Holman murder happened weeks after Elle and Aaron's disappearance."

Unfazed, Braxton pressed on. "How do you know when they were killed?" he asked.

"Read the news, dude," Mitchell quipped. "They were reported missing on August sixteenth, like a couple of weeks after Elle's disappearance."

"Correct. And then their corpses were found at the cemetery the next day. But how do you know *when* the Holmans were murdered, Mitchell?" Braxton repeated.

Mitchell sighed heavily and responded, "So, wait—let me make sure I understand. You're saying that after kidnapping, killing, and doing

God-knows-what to an elderly couple for a couple of weeks God-knows-where, the perpetrator suddenly has a 'come to Jesus' moment and lays their bodies to rest at a cemetery? C'mon, Brax. None of this makes any sense."

Braxton shot back, his tone sharp, "How many times did you practice that line in front of the mirror, Mitch? The delivery is convincing—I'll give you that. But, I mean, you realize how flimsy that sounds, right?"

Mitchell's expression iced over, mirroring the same cold demeanor he had when Braxton pointed out the purchase order for embalming chemicals.

"Do you want to know what I think?" Braxton continued, his voice unwavering. Mitchell remained silent, prompting Braxton to proceed. "I'll take that as a yes. Here's what I think: you're in way over your head. I think that you have things so tightly wound that the slightest of breezes will untether it all.

"I think that for the first time in your life, you don't have control over everything, and it's eating away at you minute by minute because there's no way you can map everything out. Trust me, I know that feeling. But you know what else? I don't think you're the type who commits senseless homicide. I think that—perhaps unlike your predecessors—your moral compass is still intact."

Braxton paused, letting the words sink in. "As for me, I have no idea why our paths intersected. That is something beyond our control. What is within our control is which way we go. So, going against all interests of self-preservation, I'm taking a leap of faith." Braxton mustered his will.

"Mitchell Emerson, I am informed and believe that you are the *Prima Imperator* of *Ab Initio* via your bloodline to William Emerson. I know that you're involved with the Harris and Holman cases."

Mitchell's expression remained unreadable, giving nothing away.

Braxton continued, "I also know that the Hoffnung family changed their last name to Holman by the early 1900s. Andrew Holman descends from Paul Hoffnung, the founder and first *Supreme Executor* of *Prime Ascendant*."

Mitchell's eyes narrowed slightly, a flicker of recognition or perhaps irritation crossing his face. Braxton pressed on, sensing he was getting somewhere.

"I also know that your ex-girlfriend Elle Harris is Ab Initio by bloodline.

"So, let's put it all together. Elle Harris, Ab Initio's beautiful, effusive darling and your former lover, disappears with her fiancé under mysterious circumstances. Yet their child is found safe and sound. Around two weeks later, two high-standing members of the other Order—Prime Ascendant—are reported missing."

As Braxton recounted the gruesome details, a chilling sensation crept up his spine, causing the hairs on the back of his neck to stand on end. His voice trembled with a mix of horror and conviction as he continued. "A couple of days afterward, the elder couple's embalmed remains are found at the cemetery. Those chemicals you bought weren't just for cleaning wine tanks, Mitchell. They were for embalming." Braxton felt a shudder run through his body, not of fear, but of the grim reality he had faced.

"When I saw the bodies hanging from this tree," Braxton went on, his voice hardened, "I could hear the blood plopping onto the dead leaves below. So, the night your guys must've found me passed out over there," Braxton pointed at a small boulder that was about twenty feet away from them, "the bodies hadn't been embalmed yet. That was the next step. And after being preserved, they were laid to rest at the cemetery about two weeks later." His words carried the weight of undeniable truth, and he looked at Mitchell with unwavering resolve, ready to face whatever reckoning lay ahead.

Braxton took a breath while visualizing the document he was about to quote. "Of Retribution: Reciprocal Termination Clauses." Mitchell blinked that time. "You see where I'm going with this, right?"

"Braxton," Mitchell had found his voice. "I'm not sure you want to continue this conversation. I don't think you're ready to find out where this rabbit hole could lead you."

"I'm going to take that as a lead-in and not a threat," Braxton swiped. "Because, guess what? Everything you tell me is privileged information that I must take to the grave. We have an ongoing attorney-client relationship. The FBI is leading the investigation, which means I can advise you on federal law. Hell, I could represent you in federal court *pro hac vice*—but I'd advise against it," he scoffed.

"Point being," Braxton pressed on, "if the cops ask either one of us anything about what we talk about, the unassailable answer is 'confidential privileged information.' Which is actually pretty brilliant, now that I think of it. . ." Braxton's voice trailed off. Then he started to laugh. "Ah, fuck you, Mitch," he chuckled again, "you *are* an asshole."

"What?" Mitchell feigned innocence, doing nothing to prevent the grin from spreading across his face.

"You brought me into this on purpose, didn't you," Braxton went on. "Jesus Christ, I can't *believe* it took me this long to figure that out. Could have saved a LOT of tedium if that light flicked on earlier, that's for sure." He shook his head in disbelief. "But it all makes sense. I mean, I thought that you were throwing me some billables as a gesture of goodwill for Jason. But now that I think about it, you don't want any of this mess to land on a local lawyer's desk, do you?"

"You passed," Mitchell said, and Braxton blinked in confusion.

"It took a slight nudge, but you passed," Mitchell repeated. "You see, there are sacrosanct covenants governing who can have knowledge of Ab Initio's inner workings. All initiates are granted compartmentalized access through a specific set of rules that I won't bore you with, as they don't apply to you. That's because the only way to become an initiate is by bloodline or marriage. Ascendants, on the other hand, use a hybrid induction method. . ." Mitchell's voice trailed off as a couple of hikers headed their way. "Let's take a walk to your car. I want to show you something." Mitchell was already in motion.

As they strolled back toward civilization, Mitchell remained tight-lipped about the matters they had just discussed. Instead, he filled the time with intriguing tidbits about his hometown. He pointed out buildings that had served as backdrops for a cowboy movie filmed by a production company in the 1970s. Soon enough, they found themselves standing next to Braxton's BMW.

"So, I have to ask," Mitchell said, "how did you sober up so quickly? You were pretty sloppy when we left the Saloon. I mean, if I didn't know you better, I wouldn't think that you're even drunk right now."

"Huh?" Braxton feigned ignorance as a sly grin spread across his face. He retrieved a cigarette from his pocket and lit it. "Maybe it's my lightning-fast metabolism?" He took a leisurely drag. "Or maybe that was regular cream in my coffee? I'll let you decide."

"I mean, that's actually pretty damn funny, but why would you. . . I can't even. . ." Mitchell stammered.

"Ugh, that was pretty embarrassing now that you mention it," Braxton cringed as he recalled the scene he had caused at the Saloon. "But I had no idea what I was walking into. So I needed something to work with if things went south. You know, something that might keep your guard down. I went with what I knew.

"And you have to admit, it kind of worked. Did you stop and wonder why my car was parked so close by? You know I live less than half a mile away. And given how your boys have been tailing me, something tells me that you have a pretty good idea of my running habits."

Mitchell's smirk confirmed Braxton's theory about who had been keeping tabs on him for God-knows-how-long.

"So, you haven't had anything to drink today?" Mitchell asked.

"Nope. That was all improv. Though I think my performance landed me on Amanda's permanent shit list. 'Glad the whole breakfast/brunch thing really took off. . .*toodles!*'" Braxton mocked himself.

Mitchell shook his head, rolled his eyes a little, and sighed. "Fuckin' Braxton," he chuckled.

"Yeah, I get that a lot," Braxton said. "So, what's the plan?" he asked after tossing his cigarette butt into the trash. "I don't think we're done talking about things, so—"

"Right, right, back to business," Mitchell said. "Well, would you mind giving me a ride to my place? Some asshole deprived me of my wheels. It's like a ten-to-fifteen-minute drive from here."

"Sure, hop in," Braxton unlocked his car doors. The two got into the BMW and headed toward the rolling hills to their north.

About five minutes later, Braxton opened up the throttle on Old Stage Road, the engine growling with a newfound vigor. Mitchell, on the other hand, swiped through his smartphone, his fingers dancing across the screen as he managed his clandestine empire. Pocketing his phone, Mitchell finally allowed himself to take in the scenic view that surrounded them. Pastures, vineyards, and forest groves dotted the landscape with rustic pops of orange and yellow. This picturesque countryside was framed by the majestic alpine peaks of the Rogue River Siskiyou Mountains, which ran their granite gauntlets westward until dissolving into the Pacific shoreline some seventy-five miles away.

"We've got a few miles yet. It's the left after Livingston Road. I'll remind you," Mitchell said, breaking the silence. He shifted his gaze to Braxton, recognizing that the man had a lot on his mind, given the new dynamics of their post-disclosure relationship.

Mitchell couldn't help but wonder what thoughts might be running through Braxton's head about him. Perhaps Braxton viewed him as some sort of James Bond villain—a secret-society mastermind calling in erasures, laundering money for powerful oligarchs, or even running arms and contraband via subterranean tunnels beneath the mountains. The last one was probably his favorite—an exhilarating fantasy but entirely impractical.

"So, let me ask you this," Mitchell broke the silence. "When did you first start putting the pieces together?"

Braxton squinted at something ahead of him. "Are we being recorded?"

Given his earlier whimsical Bond villain thought and Braxton's hushed tone, Mitchell burst into laughter.

"I'm sorry. . . I'm sorry," Mitchell said, noticing that Braxton didn't share his amusement. "Bad timing for that train of thought. I wasn't laughing at you," Mitchell reassured him. "There's no audio or video device in your car that we know of. We'll remove the GPS tracker once we get to my place."

Braxton sighed, his voice carrying a hint of amusement. "Is it strange that I know he's not joking about the GPS tracker? And did I really just say that out loud?" They both chuckled, recognizing the surreal nature of their conversation. All things considered, Mitchell had to admit that Braxton was taking it all in good stride.

"To answer your question," Braxton continued, "I had my suspicions since pointing out those 'tank cleaning' chemicals to you." He air-quoted "tank cleaning" with his right hand, emphasizing the euphemism. Mitchell nodded.

"Well, yeah, that's why you're here. That's one of the reasons why you passed. You found the needle in the haystack. And once you discovered the rope marks, I figured it was time to give you a little nudge," Mitchell explained. He felt the car reduce in speed after passing Livingston. "It's that next left coming up in a few hundred yards. Then bear left at the last fork."

The car exited the main road and wended its way up a street that terminated at Mitchell's security gate. He got out, punched in the code, and got back in the passenger seat as the ornate metal gate granted access. The BMW followed the private drive that curled its way up to the rectangular multilevel modern architecture Sunset magazine-caliber dwelling constituting Mitchell's lair.

After clearing the gate, Braxton did his best to contain his awe at the sight of the dream home that lay before him. It was situated on a ten-acre spread consisting of orchards, vineyards, and natural-style landscaping surrounding a main house and its grounds. The property included an indoor/outdoor pool, a pool house, a gymnasium, and various sporting areas behind and flanking the main residence.

The area from the pool to the front of the house featured native flora, crushed-rock pathways, grassy pads, and tasteful minimalist sculptures in sand gardens. These elements were all crisscrossed by several streams branching from a main creek that ran along the acreage.

To keep his cool, Braxton pretended that he hung out with one-percenters at such places all the time. It wasn't a total lie, given the parties thrown by the wealthy wine family kids back in his bougie high school days. Even then, Mitchell's place made those vineyard-baron estates look like McMansions.

Mitchell directed Braxton to park on the spotless cement pad in front of the right-hand garage door, one of five that ran along the five-thousand-square-foot parking structure perpendicular to the house. Braxton felt obliged to warn him about his car's oil leak.

"No worries," Mitchell reassured him. "Just park right in front over there." Slowing to a stop, Braxton saw someone wearing coveralls emerge from the garage building.

"Just leave it running," Mitchell instructed. "He needs to roll it onto the lift to remove the tracker." He nodded to the coveralled man, who waved back and posted himself at a respectful distance.

Judging from his face and shocks of thinning gray hair, the man looked to be in his early sixties. Braxton estimated his height at five-nine, and despite his paunch, he appeared powerfully built. The man's eyes and body language conveyed an energetic and curious mind, ready for engagement.

Braxton returned his gaze to Mitchell, blinked a few times, and burst into laughter. It was such a spontaneous and hearty laugh that he had to remove his glasses and rub his eyes to regain composure. After a few aftershocks, due in part to Mitchell's polite yet confused expression, Braxton managed to compose himself.

"Are you fucking serious?" he asked amidst chuckles. "What are you, some sort of Bond villain? A lair *and* minions?" Braxton couldn't help but find the situation absurd. "Let me guess. He's German, and his name is Otto. Am I right?" He suppressed a nervous giggle.

"Not exactly," Mitchell replied with a grin. "He's German, but his name is Gunther. The other auto mechanic applicant's name was Otto, but I thought that was a bit too much on the nose." They both burst into laughter again, finding humor in the unexpected turn of events.

They stayed in the car for a while, regaining their composure. Braxton remained behind the wheel, still a bit hesitant about the whole situation. Mitchell unbuckled his seat belt, raised his body from the seat, and pulled a holstered .45-caliber Heckler & Koch USP Compact handgun from his inner waistband. He dropped the firearm onto Braxton's lap.

"There's a loaner for ya if you're worried about anyone getting the drop on you inside," Mitchell offered.

Braxton looked down at the gun, picked it up, and removed it from the holster. After studying it for a moment, he slid out the magazine, confirmed its full capacity, and checked the chamber. He cleared the loaded round, reloaded the magazine, and cupped the unspent cartridge in his hand.

"Pretty ballsy to keep it chambered like that," Braxton remarked as he dropped the unspent round into Mitchell's open palm. "That's some OG kind of shit right there." He re-holstered the handgun, unbuckled his seat belt, and slid the weapon into his waistband.

Mitchell flashed a satisfied smile, gave a quick thumbs-up, and reached for the door handle. However, Braxton stayed in place, lost in thought. Mitchell leaned back into the gray leather passenger seat, and both of them sat there for a moment, contemplating the new developments.

"I can understand this all being a bit overwhelming," Mitchell empathized. "Just so you know, the groundskeeper and his wife are on a trip right now, and my security detail only comes here when I ask them to. That leaves you, me, and Gunther—by the way, he goes by Gordon; Gordo for short. His living quarters are on the third story of the garage. The guy is an absolute genius Applied Sciences engineer. He's first generation, born in the 1950s and raised in Menlo Park, California, of all places."

Braxton loosened his grip on the wheel, trying to adapt to the unique situation he found himself in. Mitchell continued his storytelling as Braxton gazed off into the distance.

"Gordo's dad, Hans, was a wunderkind rocket scientist—one of Wernher von Braun's protégés—developing weapons for Nazi Germany during World War Two. So, naturally, Uncle Sam brought him over to the U.S. as part of Operation Paper Clip. Hans worked for JPL and then for NASA Ames up at Moffett Field.

"There he struck up an unusual friendship with a custodial worker named Alberto, a middle-aged Hispanic gentleman known for his reliability and easygoing smile. Alberto took as many shifts as possible, working doubles so his kids could get an education and live the American Dream." Mitchell paused, taking a breath.

"You see, unlike Calculus and Applied Physics, English didn't come easy to Hans. He found a workaround by memorizing the English word for every component used to assemble his spacecraft and launch systems, by order of installation. So, despite being the only person on the planet who could tell you in English how to build a spacecraft and its engines from memory, Hans's English remained conversational at best. This remained so for the better part of a decade. He didn't mind so much until noticing his lesser-qualified former subordinates ascend into the upper ranks of the space program, or others making obscene amounts of money in the private sector. Hans, on the other hand, kept on being passed over.

"Then, during a political mixer with the bigwigs holding the purse strings, it dawned on him. Hans was doing his usual thing, standing in the background, nodding pleasantly and laughing along, praying to God that nobody tried to start a conversation with him. Then he focused on his former underlings working the room, cracking jokes in fluent English, using their cute scientific-sounding accents to charm the politicians into funding their pet projects."

Engrossed in the story, Braxton hadn't noticed that Gunther had retreated back into the parking structure.

"So," Mitchell continued, "burning the midnight oil one night, Hans stepped out for a smoke break to clear his head. But he couldn't smoke because his lighter had crapped out. Then Alberto approached with his disarming smile and handed Hans his lighter. They had a pleasant chat, and Alberto insisted that Hans keep the lighter. While walking back to his station, Hans realized that that was the first time he felt comfortable speaking English with someone."

Mitchell cleared his throat.

"You see, neither could speak the other's native language, so they had no choice but to speak in English. Alberto must have felt the same way, as, over the next couple of months, they would seek each other out to practice their English, ultimately realizing that they enjoyed each other's company.

"As their friendship solidified, Hans was invited over for dinner. There Hans met Alberto's family at his modest home, which included eldest daughter Renata, a young woman with gentle features and inquisitive eyes who—two years earlier—was valedictorian of her high school class. She was offered, but then was denied, full-ride scholarships to Berkeley and Stanford. As you can guess, both offers were revoked due to 'missing paperwork.' You see, she wasn't documented."

"Well, it's pretty easy to guess where this goes," Mitchell summarized as the garage door began to open. "After several prompts from his wife at the dinner table, Alberto explains that he's taught Hans everything he knows and that the time has come for him to find a better instructor. As it turns out, Renata has a particular gift for languages. Indeed, after graduating from high school she gained fluency in French and German, basically for shits and giggles." Mitchell nodded in Gunther's direction as he started emerging from the garage.

"As a result of this coupling, Gordo's dad ended up being integral to the Apollo project and basically spearheaded the space shuttle program until retiring in the eighties. His mom ended up teaching English, French, German, and Latin American literature at Berkeley and then Stanford."

Mitchell concluded the biography as Gunther returned to his post outside, maintaining a respectful distance. Braxton's hands had dropped from the wheel, his right one resting on the gun snugged in his waistband.

"The point being, Brax," Mitchell leaned forward, his tone serious, "is that Gordo passed his test the same way you did. He demonstrated having a particular set of skills and abilities in response to the testing protocols directly administered by the PI." He paused briefly. "The PI is shorthand for the person in charge of Ab Initio, it means Prima Impera—"

"I fucking know what PI stands for," Braxton hissed, feeling the weight of the situation pressing down on him.

Mitchell continued, undeterred, "Look, Gordo can leave anytime he wants. That building in front of us is the incubator for his ideas. We provide him with all the time, equipment, and materials he needs. No red tape or committee oversight. Including the stuff that—how shall I say it—can't be acquired through normal commercial means."

Braxton's mind raced, trying to process the revelation Mitchell was sharing. He felt a strong urge for a stiff drink to calm his nerves.

"If it were up to him, he'd spend every waking hour in his workshop. He's one of those kind of guys. Anyhow, his innovations get registered with the patent office through one of Ab Initio's shell companies. We provide the means, license the tech, and Gordo gets ten percent of the cut. In perpetuity. He may not look the part, but the guy's a multimillionaire."

Mitchell turned to face Braxton, his expression a blend of amusement and pride. "I trust you've heard about the all-electric cars with those revolutionary motors and batteries being made in Silicon Valley?"

Braxton's eyes widened in recognition. "Yeah, bro," Mitchell pointed at Gunther, "that's the guy right over there."

Braxton was left in a state of disbelief as he tried to process the incredible information he had just received. Before he could respond, Mitchell opened the passenger door and put one foot out, presenting Braxton with a choice.

"So," Mitchell said, "you have two ways to go: option A is to drop me off, turn around, and drive to your girlfriend's to report the tracking device. Or there's option B, which is to follow me inside and let Gordo do his thing."

Before Braxton could think of a response, Mitchell was out of the car, exchanging greetings and discussing what to do with the car. Eventually, Braxton drew himself out of the BMW, reluctantly backpedaling to let Gunther get in. He slid into the driver's seat, disarming Braxton with a reassuring smile.

Braxton stood motionless as his car entered the garage, still gripping the handgun snugged in his waistband. He glanced back at Mitchell, who was already striding toward the mansion, a structure worthy of Architectural Digest.

Braxton resigned himself to the inexorable course of events, clutching the concealed weapon as if it were his sole anchor to reality. With determination, he followed Mitchell into the enigmatic lair, ready to confront the mysteries that lay ahead.

CHAPTER THIRTEEN

AB INITIO WAS THE ORIGINAL

SATURDAY, OCTOBER 13, 1:01 PM

At Mitchell's urging, Braxton freshened up in one of the house's expansive bathrooms. Noticing their similar sizes, Mitchell selected an array of "casual" designer clothes from his extensive walk-in closet and offered them to Braxton for a change.

While Braxton was away, Mitchell prepared a selection of wholesome fare. He arranged an assortment of bread, cheese, and fine charcuterie on the kitchen counter. These were all selected from the large Sub Zero fridge, which was a standout among the suite of premium stainless-steel appliances in the kitchen, resembling more of a professional chef's domain than a typical home kitchen.

When Braxton returned, they settled down to the inviting spread. As they began to eat, Mitchell seamlessly picked up their conversation from where it had paused in the park.

Mitchell delved into the history of the secret orders. "Ab Initio was the original, the first of its kind," he began, "but it was the divisive issue of induction practices that led to the birth of Prime Ascendant." Ab Initio strictly adhered to a policy of lineage-only membership, with no room for exceptions.

He then brought up the 1860s, a pivotal era for Ab Initio. "Paul Hoffnung, second-in-command at the time, pushed for a radical change," Mitchell recounted. Hoffnung proposed infusing new blood and ideas into the Order, sparking a heated debate that split the members down the middle. This deadlock put the onus on the Prima Imperator, or 'PI,' to make a decisive call or step down.

"The then-presiding PI acted more like a figurehead, relishing in prestige rather than decisive action," Mitchell continued. As a result, the matter remained unresolved, lingering in a state of uncertainty through his tenure and that of the next three successors, each of whom met with untimely deaths.

Finally, the narrative reached William Emerson. "Emerson was different—methodical, ambitious," Mitchell described. "He ascended to power as a father and widower, having recently lost his wife to quick consumption—one of several maladies that had been thinning the Order's ranks at an alarming rate." Emerson's ascension marked a crucial turning point for the Order, his leadership distinctly shaped by both personal loss and a keen strategic mind.

Upon becoming PI, Emerson's inaugural act was to confront the contentious issue dividing the Order: Hoffnung's proposal to abolish the bloodline-only mandate. The vote was split, and with decisive authority, he voted against changing the policy.

This decision heightened internal conflicts within Ab Initio, leading to legal and trade disputes, exacerbated by the mysterious rash of illnesses and deaths decimating the Order. Emerson, addressing these challenges, convened a special board meeting to propose new bylaws. These bylaws would allow for non-bloodline inductions under specific conditions.

Hoffnung opposed Emerson, demanding compliance with his proposal and threatening an economic shift to Medford, jeopardizing

Jacksonville's financial standing. Emerson, unfazed, pushed his bylaws through with a decisive supermajority vote. He then gave Hoffnung's followers an ultimatum: reconcile within six weeks or be excommunicated from Ab Initio.

Reflecting on these events, Hoffnung would later concede, albeit grudgingly, that Emerson's masterful tactical plays in forcing negotiations were, in his words, "an occasion in which one had no choice but to love the art, notwithstanding the artist."

The intense negotiations culminated in a memorandum of understanding, leading to the formation of Prime Ascendent, mirroring Ab Initio in all but induction practices. Following the agreement, the mysterious deaths that had plagued the orders remarkably began to decline.

"Article Thirteen!" exclaimed Braxton, his excitement palpable. Having had their fill in the kitchen, he and Mitchell had settled into a common room adorned with expansive views of the surrounding mountains and valley.

"Article Thirteen of the Compact, 'Of Retribution: Reciprocal Termination Clauses,'" Braxton continued, his legal research enthusiasm shining through, bolstered by his unusually sharp photographic memory.

Mitchell, eyebrows raised, responded with a smile, "That's right. You surprised me earlier with that reference. How did you come across it?"

Braxton, eager to share, said, "I found the Compact's table of contents attached to an old legal brief in the courthouse archives. Sorry, didn't mean to interrupt."

"No problem," Mitchell replied, sipping his aged scotch while Braxton opted for sparkling water. "Sometimes, I do tire of my own voice," he chuckled.

Regaining his train of thought, Mitchell mused, "You know the saying, 'A camel is a horse designed by a committee'? That's what happened with the Compact. It had its flaws and gaps, leading to two decades of legal wrangling. And during that time, despite some underhanded tactics, something else occurred, didn't it?"

Braxton ventured a guess, "A lot of lawyers and judges got filthy rich?"

Mitchell acknowledged, "Well, that's technically true, but I was referring to something else—"

"Illuminati members stopped dropping like flies?" Braxton interjected. "I mean, no disrespect. But that's accurate, right?"

Mitchell nodded in agreement. "Correct, and no offense taken," he said, taking a sip of his scotch. "The Compact, you see, aims to foster peace and prosperity. When the mysterious deaths ceased, both factions interpreted this as divine approval of the Compact and their respective doctrines, merging enterprise with spirituality for all Initiates and Ascendants."

Braxton, trying to process this theo-capitalist ideology, felt something amiss. "But, wasn't anyone suspicious that these 'acts of God' might not be so random? There seems to be a more logical explanation. . ."

Mitchell dismissed the idea with a wave of his hand. "Oh, of course, they were assassinating each other. But that's beside the point. The Compact, particularly Article Thirteen, is revered as a holy covenant, the unalterable Word of God."

He then probed Braxton, "Just out of curiosity, what's your take on Article Thirteen's content?"

Braxton, unsure, gestured openly. "This is just speculation, but I believe it outlines 'rules of engagement' for when a member of either Order dies or disappears under suspicious circumstances." He scrutinized Mitchell, who maintained a neutral expression.

"Say an Ab Initio member is found dead," Braxton continued. "Article Thirteen might dictate that Prime Ascendant is held accountable, regardless of the truth. Ab Initio then has to retaliate. There are probably guidelines on the execution method, handling of remains, and so forth, signaling that vengeance has been served—a temporary truce until the next incident."

After a brief pause, Braxton added, "I suspect that part of the ritual involves hanging, embalming, and interment in the Pauper Field." He noticed a fleeting change in Mitchell's expression.

Mitchell responded, "That's an intriguing theory, though it has its flaws."

"More than a few, I'd wager," Braxton acknowledged.

"For instance," Mitchell countered, "why would anyone consent to such drastic retribution for a crime they likely didn't commit?" Braxton took a sip of water, remaining silent. "That wasn't a rhetorical question, Brax," Mitchell pressed.

Braxton, after a moment of thought, replied, "Well, it's harsh, but it makes sense from a global perspective. First, if you know you'll get hit back for attacking the other side, you're less likely to start trouble. Second, everyone has to work to keep things peaceful, which keeps everyone safer. Third, being careful means you live longer and do better in the long run."

Braxton continued, "Also, it means you really have to check out anyone new joining. If you don't and something goes wrong, it could backfire on you or your loved ones. That's why secrecy is so important."

Mitchell nodded and then questioned further, "What about when there's trouble inside an Order? Why would one Order ever agree to pay a price for infighting going on in the other?"

Braxton thought for a moment, "Yeah, that's tricky. But I think there's a way to show that an accusation is wrong or that a death isn't suspicious. Also, there must be rules about what kind of deaths actually count for this. Like, an old person dying naturally wouldn't count. Each group probably has a way to handle its own problems without dragging the other into it. That's how I'd set it up, at least."

"Very impressive, Braxton," Mitchell acknowledged. "But how did you figure out 'Prima Imperator' is the title for Ab Initio's leader?"

Braxton replied, "It was a bit of detective work. I used my legal search tools to look up that term after seeing it in some old court cases.

Cross-referencing the cases and names in local historical archives led me to it—including William Emerson's name. It was mostly guesswork, really."

Mitchell, impressed yet limited in what he could share, said, "That's quite resourceful of you. Unfortunately, I can't show you the Compact or other secret documents. It would attract too much attention." He finished his drink and set the glass aside.

"That's alright, Mitch. I've had my fill of decoding old texts for one day. But I feel there's more to why I'm here," Braxton said, sensing a deeper purpose to their meeting.

Mitchell stood up. "You look like you could use a smoke. Let's go outside." Braxton, very much feeling the need for a cigarette, followed him to the second-floor balcony. Settling into the modern patio chairs, Braxton lit up and relaxed, taking in the scenic view.

"So," Mitchell began, "where do you want to start?"

Braxton, ready to unveil his theories, exhaled a cloud of smoke. "There's a lot on my mind," he said. "Like how Elle and Aaron might have staged their deaths, and the Holmans' plans for their own end." He paused, looking directly at Mitchell. "And then there's the matter of you being Hunter's biological father, not Aaron."

Mitchell, visibly surprised, gave a knowing smile. "You're full of surprises, Braxton. Since that night in Britt Gardens, you've turned into quite the sleuth. Keep the clothes, they're yours. Things got messy getting you into the van that night. Good thing you had your address on that Post-It in your wallet."

Braxton, nodding, shared his thoughts. "I don't remember anything after I blacked out, but it's good to know what happened. Losing my entire outfit was a first for me. Next time, I'll wear my address, just to make things easier," he joked, taking a drag from his cigarette. "And hey, maybe your guys should snap a photo before rearranging my stuff or messing with my locks when they check up on me."

Mitchell, looking thoughtful, asked for a cigarette. Lighting it, he inhaled deeply, then coughed slightly as he gazed over the valley. "The main thing now is Hunter. I was supposed to take him after Elle and Aaron's disappearance, and I'm clueless about why he was moved out of state. The guardianship documents I have aren't being honored. And there's the FBI; they're not supposed to be involved. If you can get law enforcement off my back and get me custody of Hunter, Braxton, you'll be set for life."

Braxton paused, weighing Mitchell's words against a tumult of thoughts and emotions. The offer, drenched in implications, hung in the air like the smoke from Mitchell's cigarette. And at that moment, he grasped the full weight of that parable about Honest Abe throwing that guy out the window. He glanced at Mitchell, the gears in his mind turning. This was a pivotal moment, one that called for a careful balance of tact, strategy, and integrity.

"Set for life, huh?" Braxton finally responded, his voice laced with a skepticism that didn't quite mask the undercurrent of intrigue. He stood, pacing a few steps, absorbing the vastness of the valley before them as if drawing inspiration from the view. "Mitchell, 'set for life' is a tempting pitch, but what's at stake is more than just my future. It's Hunter's well-being and the legacy of two families caught in a tangle of secrets." He stopped, facing Mitchell squarely. "But if it's the truth you're ready to share, then I'm all ears. Let's uncover the whole story, not just for my sake, but for Hunter's. And if that path leads to justice and safety for him, then we have a deal."

Mitchell drew a long, final drag from his cigarette, the weight of Braxton's words pressing in. With a slow exhale, he snuffed out the cigarette, a silent acknowledgment of the pact they were about to forge. The air between them charged with a new gravity, signaling the start of a crucial collaboration.

The conversation evolved at the slow, measured pace of a chess match, with each participant taking turns to share, probe, and reveal. Braxton's mind worked fervently, etching each word and nuance into memory as they untangled the web surrounding the homicides, Hunter's custody, and the enigma of Elle and Aaron. The descent of the afternoon sun, transitioning the sky into a canvas of autumnal hues, echoed the progress of their dialogue—from initial confrontation to mutual understanding and strategy.

As their meeting drew to a close, the sun hovered just above the horizon, bathing the valley in a warm, golden glow that softened the edges of the day. They had navigated a complex maze of facts and theories, finally reaching a consensus, with the drama of their conversation underscored by the tranquil beauty of the lingering daylight.

With the day's agenda now behind him, Braxton handed Mitchell's handgun back and stepped into the crisp afternoon air. His next stop was Gunther's garage, a haven of mechanical precision and the tang of oil and metal. The familiar cadence of German greetings filled the space as Braxton and Gunther exchanged pleasantries, their voices reverberating off the garage walls.

The garage lights cast a clinical glow over Braxton's BMW, raised on the lift like a display piece. Gunther, with the satisfaction of a job well done, gestured toward the workbench where the GPS tracking device— once clandestinely lodged in the car's underbelly—now lay deactivated. Together, they examined the car thoroughly. Gunther assured Braxton, with a nod of professional pride, that the vehicle was now free of any surveillance devices.

As they walked around the vehicle, Gunther highlighted the additional improvements he had made: new tires and a wheel alignment, an oil leak patched up, fresh brake pads, and an updated engine control monitor. His enthusiasm for the E39 series shone through his technical explanations, revealing not just a mechanic's skill but a true enthusiast's passion.

Braxton listened, appreciating the work but feeling the familiar twinge of discomfort at owing someone. He had always preferred to keep his debts, whether of money or favors, to a minimum.

Gunther, handing the keys back to Braxton, beamed with satisfaction. "Gern geschehen," he said warmly. "I have a soft spot for the E39s—own a couple myself. They're a driver's dream. All you need to do is look at where you want to go, and then you're there."

As Braxton drove along the meandering country road, the BMW felt smoother than ever. However, this did little to ease his mounting anxiety. His mind was a whirlwind of thoughts and speculations, especially about Mitchell's intentions regarding Hunter. Mitchell's reluctance to file a parentage case, citing reputational concerns, seemed suspect to Braxton. And why was Hunter with Prime Ascendant instead of with Elle's Ab Initio family? The pieces weren't fitting together.

As a wave of anxiety threatened to engulf him, Braxton felt a sudden urge for a stiff drink to quell the rising panic. But then, a profound shift occurred within him. It was as if a switch had been flipped, releasing the tension from his body. He let go of his swirling thoughts, surrendering them to the vastness of the universe.

A comforting warmth spread through him, bringing a realization that was both simple and profound. The future, with all its unpredictability and design, held no power over the present moment. Nothing he could do or say right at that instant would alter the course of events to come. His goal, he understood, was straightforward yet meaningful: to do good, to avoid causing unnecessary harm to others, and to refrain from envying those who seemed to have more.

Opening the sunroof, he took deep, measured breaths, soaking in the magnificence of the world around him. The scenery came alive in vivid detail, each element standing out with remarkable clarity. He felt an alignment with the "now," a serene connection to the present moment that grounded him in a profound sense of peace.

As Braxton drove into downtown Jacksonville, his mind was abuzz with the myriad details of his recent discoveries. He felt on the cusp of a major breakthrough. Speaking to himself, he began piecing together the puzzle: "Ab Initio. . . Prime Ascendant. . . Multilateral Venture Compact. . . Supreme Executor. . . Prima Imperator. . .Multilateral. . ." His voice faded as an epiphany dawned on him. The answer had been there all along, just waiting to be seen.

A few minutes later, Braxton was at his familiar spot in the Saloon. He ordered a ginger beer as Jason wrapped up with another patron. "Good to see you, Jason. We need to chat, from the beginning. . . Or, in legal terms, *ab initio*."

Jason's face shifted subtly, blending acknowledgment with a hint of wariness. "Likewise, Braxton," he replied, though his tone seemed a bit strained. "Actually, there's something I need to attend to out back." He motioned toward the rear of the building, where all the construction activity had been taking place. "Hang tight for a bit. Stacey will take over here in just a moment."

Braxton sipped his drink, his brain still racing with theories. "Well, the issues at hand are of *prime ascendance*," he remarked with a playful smirk.

Jason gave a brief nod and moved to assist another customer. Unable to hold back, Braxton added, "Some may even say that they're of *prima imperat—*"

Jason interjected softly, yet with an edge of firmness, "I grow what you're toking about, Braxton. I get it."

Braxton reclined in his chair, a wry smile playing on his lips. "Fuckin' Braxton, always pushing the envelope," he thought out loud. "No rush, Jason. I'll just be over here, piecing it all together."

As Braxton leaned back, his gaze swept across the Saloon, absorbing the warmth and familiarity of the scene. The sunlight filtered through the windows, illuminating the dust motes dancing in the air—a serene backdrop to his tumultuous thoughts. Amidst the gentle hubbub of conversation and laughter, the occasional sound of construction from the back pierced through, a subtle reminder of the ongoing changes Jason was spearheading. It was a sound of progress, of something new emerging from the old, much like the revelations unfolding in Braxton's own quest.

Braxton's contemplation was cut short as Jason returned, the anticipation in his stride as palpable as the dust on his clothes. "Sorry about the wait," Jason began, his voice carrying a blend of excitement and caution. "Things are really shaping up back there. It's been a long time coming, but it's going to bring a whole new vibe to the Saloon. I can't wait for you to see it."

The idea of transformation, of revealing something new and unexpected, resonated deeply with Braxton at that moment. "I'm looking forward to it," he responded, his curiosity sparked not just by the prospect of the Saloon's physical changes, but by the metaphorical layers they seemed to represent. Just like the Saloon, Jacksonville, and even Braxton himself were undergoing a period of significant change, with old facades being torn down to make way for new truths to surface.

It struck Braxton then, the realization that he was sitting at the very heart of a nexus of change. The renovations, his own investigations, the enigmatic dance of the secret societies—all were threads in a larger tapestry that was slowly being woven together. And as each thread was pulled, the picture that emerged was one of complexity, danger, and undeniable intrigue.

Braxton allowed himself a moment to reflect on the journey that had brought him here, to this pivotal point. The challenges and revelations that lay ahead were daunting, but also exhilarating. With a newfound resolve, he understood that the path forward was not just about uncovering the secrets hidden in the shadows of Jacksonville but about shaping the outcome of the story itself.

CHAPTER FOURTEEN

A GOD-GIVEN RIGHT

SUNDAY, OCTOBER 14, 9:57 AM

As Braxton pulled into the Medford Costco parking lot, the crispness of the early autumn morning was unmistakable. He found a parking spot just as the radio DJ announced a day-long Justin Timberlake tribute in honor of his wedding. Braxton, rolling his eyes at the celebrity gossip, switched off the car and the radio in one swift motion.

Stepping out of the car, Braxton paused, the remnants of his initial annoyance with the radio announcement lingering. Yet, as he closed the car door behind him, a moment of reflection washed over him. It wasn't just about Timberlake or the celebrity hype, but the recognition of effort and achievement in any field. While his music wasn't Braxton's style, there was no denying the man's talent and hard work. *Good for you, JT,* he thought, a newfound respect tempering his tone, *and congrats.*

Inside the store, after flashing his membership card, Braxton grabbed a cart and began stocking up on essentials: toilet paper, paper towels, trash bags, and, following Jason's recommendation, a case of nonalcoholic beer.

As Braxton wove through the Costco aisles, a familiar voice pierced the hum of shoppers. "Braxton?" Pivoting, he spotted Emily maneuvering a heavy flatbed cart, its load a mix of Halloween festivity and faux horror. He smiled, pushing his cart over to assist, noting how her preparations seemed to span the gamut from delightful to downright ghoulish.

Catching his amused look, Emily chuckled, brushing a lock of hair from her face. "You caught me. I'm on a mission to host the most epic Halloween party the Rogue Valley has ever seen. Kids, adults, and maybe a few friendly ghosts."

Glancing at the bale of toilet paper in his cart, Braxton responded with a wry smile, "Are mummies invited too? If so, it looks like I've got my costume all wrapped up."

Emily's infectious laughter at his impromptu dad-joke echoed through the vast warehouse lightened the moment, deepening the ease of their encounter. Given the enormity of her loaded cart, Braxton offered to switch with her. "Let me help," he insisted, testing the hefty load with a good-natured chuckle. Emily gracefully accepted his offer.

As they walked together, Braxton inquired about her phone, leading to a brief exchange about the events of that night. Emily's smile, radiant and genuine, lifted Braxton's mood. Their conversation flowed easily as they discussed Emily's preparations for her upcoming Halloween party.

While undertaking the formidable task of maneuvering her cart, Braxton enjoyed a glimpse into Emily's life revealed by its contents. It was a veritable treasure trove of party supplies, overflowing with kid-friendly snacks and cereals, alongside bulk packages of baking essentials like flour, sugar, and chocolate chips—a clear sign of a household that loved to bake. Amidst the family-friendly items, there were also several handles of liquor and craft beer, setting the stage for a festive celebration.

As they went through the aisles, Braxton and Emily playfully strategized how to maneuver the "monster cart" without causing traffic jams. They added two cases of sparkling wine—or "bubbles," as Emily called them—and beef jerky snacks for Braxton.

The conversation flowed effortlessly. Emily shared her plans for the "low-key" bash she was hosting, complete with multi-phased decorations and themed treats. They laughed about the inevitable Costco phenomenon: no matter what you plan to buy, you always end up spending a small fortune.

Their banter continued in the checkout line, where Braxton recounted a recent technology mishap. He had tried using voice recognition to find NW A Street, only to be serenaded with lyrics from NWA's iconic rap songs. "So there I was, lost in a sea of 'Gangsta Gangsta' and 'Fuck tha Police' among other Original Gangsta tunes, still clueless about my actual destination," he joked.

"You're outta control!" Emily's laughter filled the air, her amusement contagious. As they reached the cashier, the clerk, a rustic woman in her fifties, peered over her glasses at Braxton. "I don't accept tips, honey," she said with a smirk.

Confused, Braxton followed her gaze to Emily. "She asked to put all your items on one bill while you were lost in your 'Straight Outta Compton' rap nostalgia," the clerk explained.

Braxton, processing this, couldn't help but smile. "First off, that was awesome," he said, acknowledging the clerk's shared appreciation for OG rap. "And second." He turned to Emily, "sneaky, but well played."

Emily's laughter, as light and invigorating as the autumn air outside, filled the space around them. Braxton, riding the wave of her amusement, felt an exhilarating sense of camaraderie. As they locked eyes, there was a spark—an electric charge of mutual recognition and intrigue. It was an acknowledgment, silent but powerful, of the unexpected bond being forged under the bright lights of Costco.

"It's the least I could do," she said, her voice tinged with a hint of mischief, pulling Braxton back from the brink of deeper contemplation.

"Then I guess this makes us partners in crime—or at least in shopping," Braxton quipped.

Their gaze held for a moment longer than necessary, a silent conversation in the midst of clattering carts and the beeping of the clerk's scanners. It was in these brief, unguarded moments that Braxton felt the thrill of a challenge; not the kind he was used to in courtrooms, but something altogether more personal and intriguing. Here, in the most ordinary of settings, he found himself engaged in a subtle dance of personalities, each step revealing a bit more of the intricate layers behind Emily's smile and the laughter that seemed to pull him deeper into her orbit.

Outside, Braxton and Emily quickly transferred her purchases into the trunk of her European navy-blue crossover, laughing as they juggled the bulkier items to fit everything snugly. "Quite the haul," Braxton remarked. "I trust your girls are going to help stow all this booty once you're home?"

Emily shot him a playful glance that sparkled with that same kind of mischief as earlier. "The girls are with their dad today. And you," she tapped him lightly on the arm, "agreed to be my partner in crime, remember?" Her wink echoed her words, a silent pact sealed as the trunk hummed shut.

"It's just a quick drive, about fifteen minutes." She pointed to a spot where he could park. "Park over there, and you can follow me."

As Braxton headed back to his car, he couldn't resist calling back, "Okay, BRB!" His voice danced across the parking lot, intertwining with the lingering notes of Emily's laughter—a melody that hinted at the unexpected adventure just beginning to unfold between them.

ABOUT FIFTEEN MINUTES LATER

Emily's home, nestled in the Jacksonville foothills, was a striking contrast to Mitchell's opulent lair. The modern ranch-style house, with its five bedrooms and three-and-a-half baths, radiated a sense of warmth and comfort. Its deep blue facade, accented by crisp white trim, made the wraparound porch stand out invitingly. Nearby, a matching two-story garage with a windowed upper level hinted at the possibility of a cozy granny unit.

Set among a cluster of houses on a private circular road, the home struck a perfect balance between privacy and community—a style that resonated well with Braxton's preferences.

As they began unloading, Emily efficiently directed where each item should go, while Braxton took on the task of ferrying the goods from car to house. Emily had designated her arts and crafts room as the staging area for the upcoming Halloween party, making Braxton's job of sorting the items easier. He found himself momentarily distracted by Emily's agile movements—whether she was perched on a stool or reaching into high cabinets—her effortless grace and energy endearing her to him even more.

With the last of the groceries and party supplies carried in, Braxton paused to wash his hands in the kitchen sink. As he dried off, his gaze inadvertently landed on an item that seemed out of place amidst the orderly chaos of the kitchen—a thick envelope bearing the Cedar & Sterling Law Group logo, prominently labeled "Confidential." The law firm's name sparked recognition; it was the same firm that had rebuffed attempts from Mitchell's attorney to access Elle's trust documents. Addressed to Emily, the envelope's presence alluded to hidden depths within her story, intertwining her narrative with the ongoing mystery of Elle and Aaron's disappearance. Braxton considered bringing it up but opted against it, wary of overstepping. His hesitation wove another thread into the complex tapestry of their developing connection.

Turning, he discovered that Emily had not only stowed away all the groceries but had also prepared an inviting spread of charcuterie and cheese. The sight prompted a light-hearted thought about the widespread appeal of such platters within the secret societies, almost as if charcuterie served as a universal emblem of hospitality among the Initiates and Ascendants.

"Would you like a drink?" Emily offered, drawing his attention to a demi-bottle of sparkling wine on the kitchen island, its contents already contributing to her glass. The inviting fizz of the bubbles seemed to echo the light, anticipative atmosphere between them.

Preferring to stay clear-headed, Braxton chose sparkling water, which Emily poured into a glass with a generous serving of ice. Their glasses chimed in a casual toast, an exchange of glances over the rims sealing an unspoken agreement to enjoy the moment. They sipped their drinks, allowing the ambiance of shared understanding to deepen as they began to sample the assortment on the charcuterie board.

"Well, I have to say," Braxton said, "that was pretty flawless all around. I didn't see anyone tailing us. Did you?"

"Nh-nh," Emily shook her head no.

"Because it really seemed like the two of us just happened to bump into each other. I was kind of believing it myself after a few minutes."

In truth, Jason had set up their encounter the night before and Braxton didn't know what to expect. But Emily's charm and easygoing attitude put him at such ease that it almost felt like they were a couple out on a shopping trip.

"Ever dabble in acting back in high school?" Braxton inquired, a hint of curiosity in his voice.

Emily's response was a burst of genuine laughter, the sound bright and unguarded. "Oh, no, not at all," she replied, still chuckling. "My life was all about academics. I was buried in books at OHSU in Portland, then continued at U-Dub in Seattle for med school." She recounted this without a trace of pretension, her tone simply matter-of-fact. "That's where I crossed paths with Erik, the girls' father."

Braxton looked surprised. "Really? I had you pegged as a marketing guru for the brewery."

"That's been my recent focus, along with raising my daughters," Emily explained, her voice warm. "I've kept my medical license up to date, but I haven't formally practiced in years. Erik's always been the one in the clinic."

Braxton's interest deepened as he leaned in. "What area were you specializing in?"

"Pediatrics," Emily replied, a hint of nostalgia in her voice. "I had big plans in that field, but life took a different turn after marrying Erik." She deftly topped a cracker with brie and salami, her movements as fluid and natural as the conversation itself.

She took a sip of her sparkling wine, reflecting. "Life has its own plans, doesn't it?"

"Indeed," Braxton agreed, reaching for a slice of prosciutto.

Emily continued, her tone becoming more contemplative. "Jason mentioned you've learned quite a bit about our little slice of heaven up here." She finished her glass and refilled it, her movements thoughtful. "I suppose there's no harm in sharing more with you now. . ."

Braxton remained silent, sensing the importance of what she was about to reveal.

"After Zoe was born, I had envisioned joining the pediatric practice with Erik and his father. But instead, I found myself overseeing the medical marijuana program for Prime Ascendant." She paused, taking a sip. "I was responsible for writing medical use recommendations, certifying caregivers, and overseeing grow-ops. It was deemed safer for Erik's reputation if I took on that role—after all, my credentials were more expendable."

As she spoke, her gaze drifted to the window, lost in thought. "But it wasn't all in vain. I genuinely helped many people improve their lives. I fully support both medical and recreational use." A sense of pride flickered in her eyes. "Working off the grid, I also became a discreet healthcare provider for our members, dealing with everything from STDs and mental health issues to prescribing Adderall and managing terminal illnesses."

Her voice wavered slightly, then steadied. "Life carried on. To the outside world, we were the perfect family: successful careers, beautiful kids, a dream home, vacations out of a magazine. The whole package."

Braxton noticed the tension in Emily's hand as she tightly gripped her glass, her knuckles turning white. "Sounds like you were white-knuckling your way through it," he commented softly, his voice laced with empathy.

Emily gave a weary nod, emptying her glass before pouring another. "I'm sorry, this isn't typical for me. The last time I indulged like this was on my birthday. It's not really who I am."

Braxton raised his hands, palms facing her in a gesture of peace. "No worries, no judgment here. Remember, we met at a bar, in broad daylight. I totally get it. I'd usually join in, but I'm on a different path at the moment." He gently steered the conversation back. "So, what happened after the divorce?"

Emily sipped her drink, her demeanor softening. "It's been a mix, really. I actually get along with most of Erik's family. His mom's a total bitch, but his dad's a gem—very forward-thinking, especially for a supreme executor. He stepped in after Andrew Holman retired."

"Andrew and Susan Holman, they were special people. Grounded, despite their status. Andrew could always find the silver lining, and Susan, well, she had a way of speaking her mind that was both direct and kind. They were quite the pair." A fond smile flickered across her face.

"They were instrumental in me leading their brewing and distillery projects. And I think they played a part in keeping my mother-in-law at bay, especially during. . ." Her voice trailed off.

"The divorce?" Braxton interjected softly.

"Yup," Emily confirmed with a sharp pop of the "p." "As the 'out spouse', I was bound by a nondisclosure agreement, but they ensured I was taken care of. It's a standard practice—providing support until the children are grown or for half the duration of the marriage, whichever is longer. Most times, it works out amicably. And I still hold a place within Prime Ascendant, as long as I fulfill my role."

She thumped her fist lightly on the counter, a determined glint in her eye. "But I've always been one to cover my bases. I've kept thorough records of everything."

Braxton nodded, absorbing her words. "Smart move," he acknowledged, sensing the underlying meaning in her words.

Emily leaned back slightly, her expression softening but still earnest. "Just to be clear," she began, "most people in both Prime Ascendant and Ab Initio are genuinely good, well-meaning folks. There's room for all sorts of discussions and beliefs. We enjoy the same freedoms as anyone else."

She took a reflective pause. "Personal autonomy is actually a core tenet of our beliefs. It's all about fostering innovation, which in turn drives prosperity, right?" A hint of sarcasm tinged her voice.

Emily's demeanor grew somber. "But, truthfully, it's a complex web. It's all under the guise of a God-given right, but at its core, it's about leveraging human, political, and financial capital." She shook her head, disillusionment evident in her tone. "As long as you play by their rules, don't challenge their beliefs or expose their secrets, you're safe. But the moment you cross those lines, that's when the cleanup crew arrives."

Braxton hesitated, then took a slow sip from his glass, the haunting images from that night flooding back. "Seeing what I did that night, after I dropped you off. . . It left no doubt about how seriously Prime Ascendant takes its rituals."

A shiver ran through him, the vivid images of the flames consuming the Holmans' bodies refusing to fade. "I can't seem to erase that scene from my mind," he confessed, his eyes reflecting the turmoil within. "It's a memory I wish I never had."

At his words, Emily's expression softened with empathy. "You were there? You saw that?" Her voice was laced with concern as her eyes searched his face. Without hesitation, she reached out, pulling Braxton into a comforting hug.

In the closeness of their embrace, a moment of shared vulnerability emerged. They stood there, connected in their mutual understanding, the world around them momentarily fading away. As they slowly pulled back, their eyes met, conveying a depth of emotion that went beyond words.

There was a brief pause, a fleeting moment where their closeness lingered, hinting at something more. Yet, almost as quickly as it appeared, the moment passed, leaving a subtle but undeniable awareness between them. They stepped apart, each tinged by the brief but meaningful exchange, the air around them charged with a newfound understanding.

"Erik had arranged for the kids to be dropped off that night," Emily began, breaking the silence. "That's why I was there when you dropped me off. I never intended for you to witness. . .that." Her voice carried a hint of regret.

Braxton paused, a thought crossing his mind. Had Emily intended for him to witness the Prime Ascendant funeral, maybe to buy time for someone to search his home? But he chose to believe her words. Besides, Mitchell had already admitted to keeping tabs on him. And if any other Ascendant had seen Braxton at the Holman compound that night, it was unlikely she would've agreed to meet him again. Emily was careful, not careless.

"Yeah, that scene was. . .overwhelming," Braxton admitted, opening up. "The hooded figures, the chants, the fire. . .it felt almost medieval."

"Yes. Yes, it is," Emily confirmed. "Isn't it barbaric? Ugh. And especially with the embalmed bodies. It's so. . .mortifying."

Emily's hand paused as she tipped the bottle, the last drops of wine falling into her glass. Her voice grew softer, tinged with a mix of relief and vulnerability. "It's been such a relief to talk openly about all this. With Jason, everything's shrouded in secrecy, filled with coded signals and 'need to know' boundaries. It's been a long time since I've had the chance to really share. . .especially since. . ." Her words faded into a thoughtful silence.

"Since?" Braxton prompted gently, sensing the importance of what she was about to divulge.

There was a moment of hesitation, a deep breath taken before she spoke. "Since Elle disappeared," she finally whispered, her voice barely above a murmur.

She lifted her head, her eyes meeting Braxton's squarely, a trace of resolve in her voice as she repeated more firmly, "Yes, since then."

As Emily uttered those words, a somber weight settled in the room. Her confession hung in the air, a poignant acknowledgment of the shadows cast by the young couple's disappearance. Braxton could see the mix of relief and sorrow in her eyes, a reflection of their shared burden of secrets and unspoken truths.

In the quiet of the kitchen, with only the soft clink of their glasses punctuating the silence, they both recognized the significance of this moment. It was more than just an exchange of words; it was an opening of worlds, a bridging of solitary journeys. A silent promise of trust and understanding passed between them, marking an uncharted path in their intertwined stories.

CHAPTER FIFTEEN

LAID TO REST

FRIDAY, OCTOBER 19, 7:53 PM

The week had been a grueling maze of investigation and strategic planning for Braxton. Now, he stood beside his car, indulging in a solitary smoke a few blocks away from the bustling center of Ashland. As the twilight deepened, the air turned cool, heralding the evening chill.

Braxton flicked his cigarette butt into a nearby trash bin and freshened up with a breath strip. He quickly spruced himself up in his BMW, a spritz of fabric odor remover followed by a dab of hand sanitizer, before stepping back into the street.

He spotted Riley's car approaching and locked his own vehicle, ready to meet her. The time for secrecy and subterfuge felt over; he was weary of the covert tactics.

Riley pulled up and parked nearby. Stepping out, she broke away from her usual field agent attire. Instead, she sported black denim skinny jeans and a light-colored U-neck long-sleeve blouse that flattered her teardrop bustline and svelte build. She let down her hair, which fell in soft waves around her face, the gesture highlighting her effortless beauty. Even the Glock 23 at her waist seemed to move in harmony with her.

Braxton found himself transfixed, his gaze lingering on Riley. There was an unmistakable allure in her appearance, a blend of effortless grace and an underlying edge brought by the sidearm at her waist. Realizing he was staring, Braxton quickly shifted his eyes away, taking a moment to compose himself.

"You still carrying the forty-cal S&Ws?" Braxton asked, nodding toward her concealed sidearm.

"Better stopping power," she replied casually, then noticing his puzzled look, she added with a smile, "The forty-caliber rounds, I mean."

"Right, right, of course. Well, looking good as always, McAvoy," Braxton said, recovering his composure. He grabbed his jacket from his car, the streetlights casting a stark silhouette against his lean frame.

As they crossed the street, Riley's hand found his, an unexpected but welcome gesture. Braxton felt a rush of exhilaration, a swarm of butterflies ascending from his stomach to his head, leaving him both thrilled and slightly disoriented.

They chose a refined sushi restaurant known for its elegant rolls and fresh sashimi, a far cry from the more extravagant, gimmicky sushi places. Following Riley's lead, they began their meal with a bottle of sake.

Braxton, having maintained sobriety for the past few days, hadn't encountered any significant withdrawal symptoms. This reassured him that his relationship with alcohol was more habitual, tied to social contexts rather than a physical dependency. As he pondered over a night of indulgence, he rationalized that a brief return wouldn't necessarily throw him off course. After all, there was nowhere else he'd rather be than here with Riley. That thought alone was intoxicating, eclipsing any other desire—well, almost any other.

After savoring their meal and another bottle of sake, Braxton, feeling a sense of chivalry, insisted on covering the bill. They stepped out into the crisp night, the air refreshing after the warmth of the restaurant. Riley, always aware of the local haunts, suggested a high-end bar nearby, a spot often frequented by tourists opting for spirits over Shakespeare.

At the bar, Braxton secured a cozy cocktail table while Riley fetched their drinks: a vodka martini for herself and a top-shelf bourbon Manhattan for him, garnished with a natural glazed cherry—his favorite.

As the evening unfurled, Braxton was caught between his affection for Riley and the necessity of guiding her away from the secret society's shadow over the murders. Each laugh and shared glance deepened his conflict. Wanting her trust while needing to mislead her felt like walking a tightrope. Without letting on, he gently nudged their light-hearted talk, aiming to shift her focus from the society's involvement. His feelings for Riley made the deception weigh even heavier on his conscience. Yet Riley deftly kept the conversation light.

"How did languages start?" she pondered, her drink in hand. "Just random sounds until they meant something?"

Braxton laughed. "Or an alien lesson in linguistics, preparing us for. . . an intergalactic harvest?"

Her laughter sparkled, amused. "Pitch that novel, and I'm claiming five percent of the royalties."

"I'll remember that," Braxton grinned, shifting gears. "Ever think about airport security? Tight until baggage claim, where it's suddenly a free-for-all. What's up with that, anyway?"

Riley's laughter rang out, her tone playfully imitating SAIC Richter's. "That kind of intel, Mr. Hayward, is way above your pay grade."

As the night deepened, Braxton found himself mirroring Riley's pace, drink for drink, though he always kept just a tantalizing step ahead as they ventured out of the bar. Their stroll through Lithia Park was charged with an electric undercurrent, their banter weaving effortlessly between the light-hearted and the profound. Braxton rode the wave of energy between them, each topic a dance closer to something more intimate.

In a moment of raw honesty, under the cloak of twilight that made every secret seem sacred, Riley shared a piece of her past. "When I aimed for the FBI analyst spot, my psych eval hinted at codependency," she confessed, her voice a blend of vulnerability and defiance. Her revelation wasn't just words; it was an invitation into the labyrinth of her inner world.

She leaned in closer, her gaze locked on Braxton's. "I bypassed therapy, opting instead to dissect those psych tests with help from a gray-ops analyst," she admitted, her voice dropping to a conspiratorial whisper. The moonlight caught the mischief in her eyes, transforming it into a challenge, a spark. "I mastered those tests so well, it was like holding a secret map to navigate my way into being a field agent."

Braxton, captivated by the rebel spirit she wielded so effortlessly, found himself drawn in by the gravity of her story and the allure of her resilience. The air around them seemed to thicken with unspoken promises, each word a thread pulling them inexorably closer. The space between them charged with the potential of what the night might yet unveil.

Braxton felt an irresistible pull to share his own shadows, not just as confessions but as bridges drawing them closer. As he recounted the personal and professional storms he'd weathered, his voice carried the resonance of shared struggle, the intimacy of their surroundings amplifying each word.

"I was caught in a cycle, burdened by law school debt in a system I once believed in," he murmured, leaning closer, his breath mingling with hers. The moon above lent a confessional glow, casting their shared vulnerabilities in a light that felt both raw and beautiful. "My faith in justice. . . it unraveled with a single judge's decision, pushing me to the brink, into bankruptcy. It was as if my entire worth was reduced to nothing in the eyes of the world."

At that moment, the space between them felt charged, not just with the pain of past betrayals but with the electricity of mutual understanding. Braxton's revelations, far from casting a shadow, seemed to pull them into an orbit of their own making, where each shared secret was a thread binding them tighter.

"And just like that," he continued, his gaze locking with Riley's, "everything I worked for was torn away, leaving me to question my place in a world I thought I understood." The intensity of his gaze invited her into the depths of his experience, making it palpable, almost tangible in the cool night air.

Their conversation, a tapestry of revelations, wove around them a cocoon that felt both intimate and isolating, as if for a moment, the rest of the world ceased to exist, leaving only the truth of their shared experiences.

Braxton's revelations took a more personal turn as he delved into his family history. He shared stories of his spirited grandmother, known for her threat of high colonics to deter overly familiar patients. He then recounted his father's journey from seminary school to earning both a PhD and an MD, driven by profound faith and discipline. How meeting Braxton's mother had redefined his father's calling, prompting him to leave the monastic life. "So, I guess that makes my brother and me living embodiments of the first deadly sin," he quipped with dry humor.

Riley, with a curious tilt of her head, ventured into uncharted territory.

"Braxton," she started, her tone soft yet probing, "what was it like, growing up with a psychiatrist for a dad? And how your parents glazed over the things your brother did to you. . .how did you even manage?"

"Well," Braxton began, his voice steady but laced with a pain he'd long buried, "Chase had this twisted sense of humor. He'd mess with my head in ways. . ." He paused, gathering the courage to expose wounds long hidden. "He convinced me once that I had undergone a sex change as a newborn. Of course, I didn't believe him. Still though, the way my parents played along—thinking it was all in good fun. . .it just didn't sit right."

The confession hung heavy in the air, a testament to the psychological games that had been a staple of his upbringing.

"He'd shove our dog's butt in my face, even get his friends involved. He'd call me a 'poser,' a 'nerd,' constantly belittling me, telling me I'd never be worth anything to anyone. That I'd never get married or have kids because I was such a loser." Braxton's laugh was hollow, devoid of real humor. "I spent my childhood putting up this facade for him and my parents, pretending everything was fine, so they wouldn't dive into my mind and uncover all those insecurities and feelings of worthlessness that only seemed to resolve when. . .when I felt valued by others."

Riley listened, her expression conveyed a sense of anger and sorrow for Braxton.

"It led me down some dark paths," Braxton continued, the words tasting bitter. "Hence the substance abuse, drinking. . .anything to dull the constant noise in my head, a voice that echoed with cynicism, telling me I was nothing."

The raw honesty of his admission bridged the gap between them, the shared darkness of their pasts forming a connection that was as profound as it was painful.

Riley reached out, her hand finding him in the dim light. "Braxton, I. . ." Her voice trailed off, but her grasp tightened, a silent promise of understanding and acceptance.

As the surge of the moment passed through him, Braxton grew puzzled. He didn't recall ever telling Riley about what his brother had done to him—nor his parents' implicit acceptance of the same.

Braxton paused, taken aback. He had never mentioned these details, had he? His confusion must have shown because Riley leaned in, concern etching her features.

Before he could ponder further, a memory surged within him—a vivid, almost intrusive flash of a young girl, her face a mirror of fear as shadows danced menacingly around her. It was so clear, so poignant, he couldn't hold it back.

"You know, Riley, there's this scene that keeps playing in my head," Braxton ventured cautiously. "A little girl, terror in her eyes as she watches. . ." He hesitated, unsure. ". . .hiding in the closet from her drunk and unpredictable father. It's like I was there, but I. . ." His voice trailed off, lost in the vividness of the memory.

Riley froze, her eyes wide, a storm of confusion and alarm brewing in their depths. "What are you talking about, Braxton?" The tremble in her voice was new, vulnerable. "I never told you about any of that. How could you possibly know?"

Braxton was just as bewildered. "I thought you did. Maybe after a few drinks?" he suggested uncertainly. "And I don't remember ever talking about my brother's antics either, unless I was too inebriated to recall."

Braxton felt the weight of her gaze, heavy with unspoken questions and a dawning realization of something deeper, something unexplained between them. The connection at that moment was electric, charged with the mystery of shared secrets neither had voiced.

"I-I just don't know," Braxton admitted. "It's like I could see it, Riley. As if your memories somehow became mine."

The air between them thickened, charged with the implications of their shared experience. This wasn't just a conversation; it was a revelation, a moment that transcended the ordinary and hinted at a connection far beyond what either of them could have anticipated.

They walked in silence for a moment, crossing a bridge over the creek. The dense tree canopy shrouded them in darkness, blotting out the stars. Riley's voice broke the quiet, her tone tinged with unease. "This place gives me the creeps," she admitted. "It reminds me of a nightmare I had—something about ghostly figures hanging from ropes, then bursting into flames."

Braxton stopped in his tracks, a chill running down his spine. "What did you just say?" he asked, his voice barely above a whisper.

Under the dim park lights and the soft glow of the moon, Riley's face took on an ethereal quality. As they exchanged glances, a shared memory from their time in the Pauper Field surfaced unbidden. In unison, almost as if compelled by an unseen force, they whispered, "In terra lios."

The world around them receded, leaving only the magnetic pull drawing them closer. Without a word, they moved toward each other, as if guided by a force beyond their comprehension. Their embrace was inevitable, a collision of souls rather than mere bodies. As their lips met, the air itself seemed to thrum with the intensity of their connection, each kiss a heartbeat echoing through the vast, starlit expanse above them. Time suspended, wrapped in the warmth of their shared breath, the night whispered secrets only they could understand.

Continuing their walk through the park, each step seemed to echo the intensity of their shared moment. It was as if they were moving through a dream, the world around them distant and hazy. Eventually, they made their way back to their cars. Riley, ever the agent, suggested she'd cover him as they drove back to his place.

Once settled in his car, Braxton's phone rang with a call from Riley. He answered on speakerphone, their conversation filling the car, making the drive seem shorter, more intimate. Soon enough, they were at his doorstep, Riley by his side.

Stepping inside, Braxton's attempt at hospitality was interrupted by Riley's decisive step into his arms, her initiative igniting a spark that quickly flared into an inferno of desire. As they moved together toward the bedroom, it was as if each layer they shed was not just of clothing but of any remaining barriers between them. They collapsed onto his bed, a whirlwind of discovery and desire, exploring each other with a fervor that was both carnal and deeply emotional. They reached a crescendo of passion that transcended the physical—a profound melding of souls, marking a zenith of passion and connection neither had known before.

The narrative of their night continued with Braxton's spontaneous decision to join Riley as she took a postcoital shower—what began with a touch of annoyance quickly blossomed into laughter and an unexpected encore of their earlier passion. It was a whimsical, yet deeply intimate coda to their evening, a manifestation of the spontaneity and depth of their connection.

Hours later, in the quiet of Braxton's kitchen, as the remnants of the night lingered, time seemed to stretch and contract, reluctant to march forward. Riley, standing by the counter with a cup of strong coffee cradled between her hands, appeared as an oasis of warmth in the cool predawn light filtering through the window. The rich aroma of the brew mingled with the fading traces of their earlier intimacy, a sensory reminder of the night's depth.

The kitchen, usually just a room, had transformed into a sanctuary of shared secrets and laughter, now echoing with a poignant silence. Riley's attempt at casual conversation, her voice light and teasing, seemed to dance around the gravity of their parting. Braxton found himself caught in the moment, his responses automatic as he struggled to memorize the curve of her smile, the way her hair tumbled over her shoulders, and the lively spark in her eyes that had captivated him from the start.

As they navigated this tender moment, the space between them was charged with an unspoken acknowledgment of the night's transformative power. Braxton no longer cared about his objective—to convince her not to pursue his theories about secret societies and Mitchell's involvement. Instead, he watched Riley move in the familiar space of his kitchen, feeling a bittersweet pang at the thought of the impending goodbye. Every gesture, every shared glance, was imbued with the weight of a connection that had deepened unexpectedly, binding them in ways neither had anticipated.

Their banter, a veneer of normalcy, couldn't fully mask the undercurrent of wistfulness tugging at their hearts. The magic of the night, so vivid and all-encompassing, was giving way to the harsh reality of daybreak, a reminder of the separate lives waiting beyond the door.

Braxton's gaze lingered on Riley, capturing the nuances of her expression, the comfortable ease with which she occupied his space, as if trying to etch this image into his memory. The way she laughed, head thrown back, carefree and genuine, stirred something within him—a desire to freeze time, to remain suspended in this bubble where the complexities of their lives outside could not breach their newfound sanctuary.

In the dim light, as Riley edged toward the door, a silence enveloped them, heavy with unspoken words and shared experiences. She hesitated, her hand on the handle, and turned to face Braxton. Her eyes revealed a tumult of emotions—sadness, acceptance, and a silent plea for understanding. It was a gaze that transcended words, laying bare the depth of what they had shared and the pain of impending separation.

"Brax," she whispered, her voice a delicate blend of resolve and vulnerability. "We need some space, for now." Her words, though expected, struck Braxton with the force of a physical blow. He nodded, the gesture a mask for the turmoil within.

Riley's gaze never wavered as she continued, her voice firmer now, though tinged with regret. "Chasing shadows and theories of Illuminati vendettas will lead us nowhere. And off the record," she leaned in closer, lowering her voice, "but the leading theory about these cases points to a serial killer with a medical or pathology background and a mentor—protégé dynamic. This profile has roots in several cold cases from the past. So, unless we find compelling evidence to the contrary, this will be the focus of our investigation."

She squared her shoulders, her tone firm yet caring. "That said, I know you're involved in something big, Braxton. And while I trust you'll do the right thing, I can't compromise my integrity for our relationship, no matter how deep our connection."

The moment stretched, filled with a poignant blend of professional integrity and personal longing. Then, tenderly, Riley gave Braxton a soft, tearful kiss goodbye. Braxton wished he could stop time, to stay in this moment forever, but reality beckoned.

After their lips parted, she reached up to brush away a tear Braxton hadn't felt escape, her touch a bittersweet echo of their connection. "But how did you piece it together? The cemetery, the embalming?" Her question hung between them, a silent homage to their intricate dance of revelation and concealment.

After recovering from the moment, Braxton responded with a smirk, "I found out from you."

Riley's confusion deepened. "But how?"

"I pieced it together," Braxton explained. "The embalming part I got from another source. But the cemetery's side entrance, the proximity to the mausoleums, it all pointed to a respectful, perhaps traditional act. And your reactions, first at the coffee shop and then at the cemetery, confirmed it."

Riley's lips pursed, a mix of frustration and admiration in her eyes. "Well, as much as I hate being the one who gave it away, I have to admit that I'm impressed. If you ask me, the bureau really missed out on a great investigator."

Braxton's face brightened. "Thanks, Riley. That means a lot." Then his smile turned playful. "But you, Agent McAvoy, might want to stick to your day job. Undercover work doesn't seem to be your forte."

Riley let out a laugh, echoing Braxton's sentiment. "Fuckin' Braxton," she repeated, half in jest, half in exasperation. They leaned in for a final kiss, a moment that seemed to hang in the air, brimming with unspoken emotions and wishes for more time.

As their embrace finally ended, Braxton stood in stunned silence, watching as Riley vanished into the night. The reality of the moment hit him hard, and he found himself stumbling into the bathroom, tears streaming down his face. Bent over the toilet, he was a portrait of raw emotion, silently pleading for relief from the weight of his broken heart spilling out.

THE NEXT MORNING

Braxton's car rolled to a stop in front of the liquor store on the raw, overcast morning. Nursing a mild hangover, he hesitated before stepping out—not quite needing the "hair of the dog," but drawn there nonetheless.

Inside, the hard liquor aisle beckoned. Braxton's fingers traced over premium bottles, each a testament to splurging temptations. Settling for a budget-friendly option, he examined its label, a frugal compromise.

Then, an unusual sensation overtook him—a palpable warmth enveloping his back, as if a large, ethereal hand had gently settled there. In the midst of the liquor store's mundane ambiance, a voice resonated, clear and profound, emanating from both within and all around: "I've got you, Brax. And you've got this."

Startled yet enveloped in a profound sense of comfort, Braxton placed the bottle back on the shelf, feeling his actions being guided by the reassuring presence of the unseen hand. As he made his way out of the store, the world around him seemed to slow down, every step feeling lighter, almost as if he was floating toward his car. The gentle pressure on his back, a comforting reminder of the unseen support, slowly faded, but its warmth remained, enveloping him in a serene embrace.

Reaching his car, Braxton paused, feeling as though time itself had momentarily stilled. The usually loud, self-critical voice in his head, prophesying regret for not purchasing the bottle, was now just a distant echo, drowned out by a newfound sense of peace. Sunlight filtered through gray clouds, casting a patinated beauty over the mundane parking lot, revealing a serene elegance he hadn't truly appreciated before.

Braxton stood there, rooted in the moment, deeply aware of the extraordinary shift within him. In this moment of reflection, Braxton faced the darkest shadows of his past head-on—the allure of a permanent escape from life's relentless grip, the firearm in his bedroom serving as a siren call during his lowest ebbs.

Yet now, he consciously relinquished that darkness, surrendering it back to the universe. The urge to succumb to old habits diminished, eclipsed by the emerging strength and purpose that had guided him to this awakening.

The voice returned, this time as a soft, yet unmistakably powerful echo in his mind: "Do good in the now, and you can do well in the future." The words resonated deep within, finding a permanent home in his soul.

A profound calm embraced Braxton. His once-racing thoughts decelerated to a serene pace; his heartbeat in a steady, reassuring rhythm. As he ignited the car's engine, a sense of readiness washed over him. The challenges of tomorrow loomed, yet he felt equipped with a clarity and resolve he hadn't experienced in years.

CHAPTER SIXTEEN

THE DEVIL THAT YOU KNOW

SUNDAY, OCTOBER 21, 2:03 PM

That afternoon, Braxton settled into his familiar haunt at the bar, becoming an island of calm in the midst of the Saloon's pre-event hustle. Around him, the place hummed with the energy of a select few regulars who had the privilege of staying during the setup for that evening's exclusive gathering.

Stacey was everywhere at once, a dynamo balancing the art of stocking shelves and preparing the bar, all while issuing directives to Jason. Her movements were a ballet of efficiency, a dance she performed with ease. Jason, for his part, navigated through Stacey's list of tasks with a determination that matched his stride. Amanda took charge of transforming the Saloon's space, her presence fleeting yet impactful, as she flitted from corner to corner ensuring perfection in every detail.

Braxton, nursing a ginger beer, found himself momentarily detached, an observer within his own life's swirling activity. It was as though he was a fixed point in a fast-forward world, the flurry of preparations casting the other patrons and crew in a blur of motion around him. Across the bar, Earl and Donnie were engrossed in their own world, their occasional looks in Braxton's direction punctuating their deep dive into discussion. Acknowledging their unspoken camaraderie, Braxton lifted his glass in a quiet salute, a gesture they mirrored before getting lost in conversation once again.

The moment was broken when three men entered. Stacey started toward them, ready to inform them of the closed setup, but stopped short upon recognizing one of them—Mitchell. Braxton gave a nod and started to rise from his stool, but Mitchell gestured for him to stay put, signaling he'd join soon.

As the trio approached, Braxton's earlier suspicions were confirmed—these were the men he had seen during his last meetup with Mitchell. Rising from his seat, Braxton noted their more imposing statures. "Salt," the driver of the black SUV he had previously encountered, loomed at six feet three inches, his frame carrying around two hundred and fifty pounds. His build, suggestive of a history of physical power, had softened slightly, hinting at a life eased into comfort.

His partner, "Pepper," offered a striking contrast with jet-black hair and Mediterranean features. Younger and slightly shorter, Pepper's physique was leaner and more defined, suggesting a disciplined fitness regime. He gave the impression of being a newer recruit to Mitchell's entourage. Both were dressed in casual flannels and open-front jackets, subtly concealing the handguns at their waists.

Jason emerged from the back, acknowledging Mitchell with a nod. He gestured toward a couple of vacant stools at the mid-bar area for the accompanying duo. With a subtle nod from their chief, Salt and Pepper smoothly transitioned from their sweep formation to the designated stools, sitting back-to-back. Stacey, in her usual efficient manner, served them waters, receiving appreciative nods in return.

In the meantime, Jason disappeared into the kitchen, and Mitchell advanced toward Braxton, who rose to greet him with a friendly handshake. They exchanged warm greetings, a few casual taps on the back sealing their camaraderie. Braxton then turned to Salt and Pepper, raising his palms in a playful surrender, his smile disarming.

"Hey there, leadfoot," Braxton teased, extending his hand toward Salt. The latter's head shook in a sheepish "you caught me" grin before giving Braxton's hand a firm, almost overpowering shake.

"Yow-za," Braxton exaggeratedly shook his hand in the air, "maybe 'leadfist' suits you better," he joked, earning a chuckle before turning to Pepper.

"Great to officially meet you," Braxton extended his hand to Pepper, a playful edge in his voice. "I'm Braxton, but 'Action Braxton' works too!" he quipped. Pepper responded with a broadened smile, grasping Braxton's hand firmly. As he started to introduce himself, a cautious look from Salt made him pause mid-sentence. This brief interaction, subtly orchestrated by Braxton, unveiled the dynamics and hierarchy at play within their group.

Seizing the moment, Braxton suggested, "Let's check out the new setup at the back. Jason's done an amazing job, and it's all set up for an event tonight. It's quiet back there now. Shall we?"

Mitchell agreed, "Sure, lead the way." As Braxton began to guide them through the bar, he paused, noticing Salt rising from his stool.

"Do you need your guys to sweep the area first?" Braxton inquired, his tone considerate. Salt paused, half-risen, while Pepper maintained a relaxed posture on his stool.

Mitchell waved off the notion with a casual air. "No, that won't be necessary."

With Mitchell's assurance, Braxton proceeded, weaving through the Saloon with familiar ease. They moved beyond the main area, entering the bar's back hallway, which led to the newly revamped outdoor space. This area, Jason's labor of love and ingenuity, awaited its first impressions in the quiet before the evening's buzz. It was a hidden gem, now unveiled under Jason's creative vision—a vision that had breathed new life into the old space, transforming it into an enchanting setting for the night's affair and future events. Braxton was eager to share this transformation with Mitchell, a preamble to the profound changes that had unfolded since their last encounter, hinting at the broader implications and challenges each was poised to face.

"So, what do you think?" Braxton gestured expansively as they entered. The space was impressively large, effectively more than doubling the Saloon's footprint. It was bordered by a towering thirty-five-foot brick wall, a relic from a Western movie set of the 1970s. The wall, imposing yet imbued with a touch of cinematic history, enclosed the area, which had remained unused due to its open sky.

Jason had poured considerable effort and resources into reimagining this once-neglected space. Though most of the transformation had been accomplished early on, the final touches were ensnared in an eighteen-month ordeal, wrestling with city bureaucracy and red tape before he could complete the work essential for full operations. Braxton moved toward a wooden table, admiring how its rustic aesthetic harmoniously merged with the updated elements of the area.

The area was warmed by portable gas heaters, strategically placed. The concrete floor had been covered with pavers and composite decking, creating cozy seating areas interspersed with large planters bursting with greenery and artistic topiaries.

Braxton's eyes then moved to the performance stage, set against the brick wall, and the second-story mezzanine that encircled the area. The old Saloon roof had been repurposed into a secondary bar, an audio-visual booth, and a VIP section. Above, a new roof with a large skylight bathed the area in natural light, enhancing the open-air feel.

Mitchell settled into the seat opposite Braxton, his eyes roving over the innovative outdoor space. "This is really awesome," he commented, impressed by the transformation. At that moment, Stacey, effortlessly juggling her duties, approached with two steaming cups of coffee. She placed them on the table, along with a shot of Bailey's next to Mitchell's cup, offering a quick but warm smile before returning to the bar.

"Thanks for the quick setup," Mitchell said, breaking the momentary silence after Stacey's departure. "I appreciate the effort."

Braxton's smile was relaxed, yet there was a hint of calculation in his eyes. "Of course. Jason wanted you to see the new space, and it seemed like the perfect opportunity to meet. You know, efficient use of time and all that."

"Definitely. It's good to see Jason's efforts come to fruition." The conversation paused as they both took a moment to sip their coffee, the atmosphere charged with unspoken intentions. "So, what's the news?" Mitchell prompted.

"There's the Mitchell I know and love. Always cutting to the chase." Braxton's expression became more focused. "Well, it seems like there might have been a few gaps in our last conversation. Not suggesting you left them intentionally, but there are still pieces missing in this puzzle."

Lighting a cigarette, Braxton leaned back, the smoke swirling above them. "For instance," he continued, "we didn't really delve into the dynamics between you and Elle. That's where I'd like to start."

Mitchell shifted uncomfortably, looking for a way to divert the conversation. "As I've mentioned, it's too soon to give you direct access to the Compact and other scriptures. And taking a picture or copying them is forbidden."

Braxton released a thoughtful plume of smoke. "Understood. But I'm more interested in the personal side of things. Specifically, when did you learn that Hunter was your son?"

Mitchell looked momentarily taken aback. "I'm not sure how that's relevant to our—"

"It's very relevant, Mitch," Braxton cut in smoothly. "Every piece you give me helps build the whole picture. So, indulge me."

Mitchell exhaled deeply, his gaze shifting to the shot of Irish cream beside his coffee. After a moment, he mixed the two together. "Alright," he conceded. "I found out when Hunter was just a few months old."

"How did you find out?" Braxton transitioned into a question-and-answer format. It felt like he was taking Mitchell's deposition, except instead of a stenographer, it was his memory that was recording all the information.

Braxton leaned in, his demeanor shifting. "So, did you and Elle conduct DNA tests to confirm Hunter's paternity?" he asked directly.

Mitchell nodded, his expression somber. "Yes, we did. The tests were anonymous, but they confirmed I'm Hunter's biological father."

Braxton pressed further, "And this was over three-and-a-half years ago? Back when she and Aaron had been together for about a year, right?"

Mitchell took a sip of his coffee, now mixed with Irish cream. "Yes, it was a little while after Hunter was born."

The conversation then veered toward the paternity test results. "Elle and I both had access to the results. It was a shared online link with an automatic expiration for privacy," Mitchell explained. "To the best of my knowledge, the results came directly from the lab. Elle couldn't have tampered with them."

The nature of Mitchell's relationship with Elle at that time was the next topic. "Things were on and off between us when she got pregnant," Mitchell admitted. "But finding out I was Hunter's father wasn't a complete shock."

Braxton then delved into the reasons for their breakup. "Apart from her leaving you for Aaron, what were the other reasons?"

Mitchell's expression darkened as he recounted Elle's transformation. "It was subtle at first. I thought it was just her dry sense of humor. But then, her heretical views against Ab Initio escalated. She would talk about how she felt brainwashed, how the whole narrative of a fairytale princess finding her handsome prince was a ploy, a form of grooming by the Order. She saw it as misogynistic, a way to control her and her sister. It was more than just disillusionment; it was a fundamental challenge to everything Ab Initio stood for."

He paused, the weight of his words hanging in the air. "These were not just mere comments. They were outright dangerous, given my position within the Order. Elle's statements were tantamount to suicide if any other Initiate overheard them. It was a huge red flag for me." Mitchell's tone conveyed a mix of concern and frustration as he reflected on the precariousness of that time.

"And you were the Prima Imperator at this time?" Braxton queried.

"Yes, I was the provisional PI then, formally coronated a year later," Mitchell confirmed.

"Apart from Elle's shift in beliefs and her subsequent involvement with Aaron, were there any other reasons that caused the two of you to break off the relationship?" Braxton inquired.

Mitchell's response carried a tone of reflection spiked with a tinge of regret. "She became fixated on leaving Ab Initio, on vanishing from our current lives. She had this elaborate plan to live off the grid in Alaska, utilizing Gunther's advanced solar and wind technologies for cryptocurrency mining. It was her way of breaking free, a complete departure from everything we were part of."

He leaned back, a hint of exasperation in his voice. "I tried to reason with her. Suggested we spend a year fulfilling my duties as PI, then take a month off to decompress and reevaluate. But Elle was relentless. Her ideas became more radical, her behavior more erratic. Each day, her demands grew, turning into a liability I couldn't afford to entertain. It wasn't just a simple disagreement; it was a fundamental clash of our visions for the future." Mitchell's recounting painted a picture of a relationship strained to its breaking point, caught between loyalty to an Order and a partner's desperate bid for freedom.

Braxton shifted his focus, laying out the key issues at hand. "So, we have Aaron, heretical beliefs, and Elle's desire for escape as the main factors in your breakup. Anything else significant? Any instances of domestic violence, police involvement, or involuntary holds? I'm just trying to cover all bases here."

Mitchell shook his head, a note of solemnity in his voice. "No, nothing like that. There was no abuse, no allegations. Elle did threaten to harm herself a couple of times, but I saw it more as melodramatic expressions, especially in the context of everything else going on."

Braxton then circled back to Aaron. "So, Elle and Aaron got together quite soon after your breakup, didn't they?"

Mitchell nodded, a hint of resignation in his tone. "Yes, there was a brief overlap. Elle was upfront about it, though. In hindsight, it was somewhat of a relief, given the circumstances. Anyhow, we agreed not to openly date anyone for a few months and just let things cool down."

Braxton probed further. "So, the breakup didn't cause much stir within the Order? Just the usual gossip?"

"Correct," Mitchell affirmed succinctly.

Braxton placed his elbows on the table and leaned in. "Can you walk me through the conversation when Elle first told you about her and Aaron that day?"

Mitchell stirred his coffee, taking a reflective sip. "Well, it was actually the night she told me."

Braxton pressed on. "And you two stopped being intimate right after that conversation?"

Mitchell nodded. "Yes. Our last intimacy was about an hour before she disclosed. . .her infidelity."

Braxton sought clarity. "What exactly did Elle say that night?"

Mitchell corrected, "Actually, it was in the evening."

Braxton's tone sharpened. "Cut to the chase, Mitch. Tell me about the conversation that evening when Elle revealed her infidelity shortly after you two were last intimate."

Mitchell sighed. "Elle started by reiterating her criticisms of Ab Initio. Then she mentioned having a 'spiritual awakening' at the cemetery with Aaron, which led to their physical relationship. She said that after our last intimate moment, she realized her path was with Aaron, not me."

Braxton nodded empathetically. "That must have been tough to hear."

Mitchell responded with a half-smile. "Yeah, it stung. But I wasn't losing my cool over it."

Braxton reassured him. "I get it, Mitch. It's clear your relationship wasn't abusive. No need to justify it."

Mitchell looked relieved. "Thanks. That topic was heavily scrutinized after Elle disappeared. Guess it's become a reflex."

Braxton listened intently. "So, aside from the obvious ego-bruising, what happened after she told you that your most recent performance sealed the deal for her? That she was going to be with Aaron instead of you?"

Mitchell's response was measured. "Well, yeah when you put it that way, it wasn't easy, but our relationship was already shaky. Elle's heretical comments had been a major stressor. So, we cooled things down. I played along with her narrative of a 'spiritual awakening in the Pauper Field' to maintain harmony. We presented a united front to our families, saying it was a mutual decision to part ways. Despite the underlying strain, we managed to remain civil. Then Elle started openly dating Aaron about six weeks later."

Braxton narrowed his eyes thoughtfully. "Okay, so I'm curious, Mitchell. What's your take on Aaron?"

Mitchell shrugged nonchalantly, hands spread wide. "Well, you know, I don't really have much of an opinion on him," he said, evading a direct answer.

Braxton pressed further. "Was there anything concerning about him? Like, was he ever abusive toward Elle or Hunter, or did he have any substance abuse problems?"

Mitchell leaned back, his expression contemplative. "Our acquaintance wasn't under the most ideal circumstances," he admitted. "At first, their relationship irked me, especially since it became public so soon. But then Elle's pregnancy made sense in terms of timing. Overall, Aaron's a decent guy, a good father. He's solid, both in Ab Initio's vetting records and in person. I know he underwent counseling for PTSD, which aligns with his military background. We're not close, but whenever our paths crossed, things were always amicable."

Braxton angled forward, his curiosity piqued. "Where exactly in the cemetery did this so-called spiritual awakening happen with Elle and Aaron?"

Mitchell shifted uncomfortably. "It was in the Pauper Field," he replied. "You know, the section for the unknown, unclaimed, or indigent."

"Indigent or indigenous?" Braxton quizzed, seeking clarity.

Mitchell chuckled dryly. "Probably both. Among many others without means or next of kin."

Braxton continued, probing deeper. "Is there any other significance of the Pauper Field to you, aside from what you and I discussed at your place?"

Mitchell shook his head. "No, nothing more than what I've already mentioned."

"You've never had any profound experiences there? Spiritual awakenings, shared memories, anything out of the ordinary?" Braxton pressed on.

"Not that I'm aware of, no," he replied, his expression a blend of caution and disbelief. Mitchell's dubious look seemed to challenge the line of questioning.

"So, if you had experienced anything unusual there, you'd know it, right?" Braxton asked pointedly.

Mitchell nodded in agreement. "Yes, Brax, that's correct. I'd be aware."

Braxton shuffled his notes, ready to piece together the puzzle. "Let's quickly debrief on what we covered earlier, make sure I got everything right," he proposed, his tone businesslike.

Mitchell nodded, though he seemed slightly impatient. "Okay, Braxton, but I have another commitment soon—"

Braxton cut in, "We should be done well before your next appointment. So, a couple of years after learning Hunter was your son, you and Elle hatched a plan, correct?"

Mitchell adjusted his posture. "More accurately, she crafted the plan. I simply followed along, as she deemed it the only viable option."

"So, during this period," Braxton pressed forward, "the dynamic between you, Elle, and Aaron was relatively stable, right? I mean, you weren't best buddies, but things were amicable?"

Mitchell's expression softened, a faint hint of nostalgia crossing his features. "Yes, that's accurate. We weren't close, but things were generally smooth between us."

As Braxton exhaled a stream of smoke, his gaze fixed intently on Mitchell. "You were okay with not being recognized as your own son's father?" The question hung in the air, laden with the weight of unspoken emotions.

Mitchell's face, a canvas of inner conflict and resignation, mirrored the complexity of the situation. "Honestly, it wasn't easy to come to terms with the fact that Hunter would never know I'm his actual father. Elle had a way of stirring up trouble with her words, and claiming paternity would have only aggravated things within the Order. By the time Elle brought her plan to me, I had reluctantly accepted that Hunter would grow up without knowing about me. I trusted Aaron would be a great dad, and despite our differences, Elle was a phenomenal mother. She dedicated most of her time to him, despite the nanny support. Yet, the reality of not being a part of my son's life in any significant way. . .it's a wound that never really heals."

Braxton flicked ash off his cigarette, his demeanor shifting to one of keen interest. "So, this plan you had with Elle—was Aaron or anyone else involved in it?"

Mitchell adjusted in his seat, his countenance revealing a hint of caution. "Not directly, no. Elle mentioned she had a back-channel connection with someone from Prime Ascendant, the other Order, who handled their side of things. And she used Jason and the Saloon as a kind of signaling hub for the different stages of the plan. You know, the old 'one by land, two by sea' approach. I myself never had direct talks with Aaron or anyone else for that matter. At least, not that I was aware of." Mitchell's account hinted at a labyrinth of hidden channels and covert operations, weaving through the intricate webbing of their secret societies.

Braxton exhaled another stream of smoke, his demeanor serious yet composed. "So, let's simplify this," he started, "According to the Multilateral Venture Compact between Ab Initio and Prime Ascendant, any mysterious deaths in one Order triggers the death of equal-ranked members in the other. Correct?"

Mitchell gave a slow nod. "Broadly speaking, yes."

Braxton continued, piecing together the narrative. "Elle couldn't take it anymore and needed an out. She comes up with a plan, a way to escape the brutal reciprocity of the Orders. She confides in you about the Holmans' terminal illness and their plan for a joint suicide—which is forbidden in both Orders. So, this was unknown even to their closest kin."

Mitchell listened, his expression unreadable.

"Elle knew when the Holmans planned to end their lives—a sin within both Orders. So, she syncs this with her wedding date to Aaron. The plan: Hunter is found safe, oblivious to the events. Your role? Go to the Holmans' campsite, make it look like an execution, while they're already dead from self-euthanasia. This maneuver bolsters your standing in the Order and keeps the Holmans' suicide under wraps."

Mitchell remained silent as he nodded, his eyes fixed on Braxton.

"The Compact's rituals are barbarous and gruesome," Braxton pressed on. "More specifically: 'The body is to be hung in a public space adjacent to the cemetery, but at no elevation higher than said cemetery itself. Upon hanging the body, the blood of the dead shall be drained and soaked into the soil beneath. After said blood has been fully drained, the noose shall be removed from the body's torso and the remains taken to an appropriate facility for disembowelment and embalmment. Then at such time deemed appropriate by the avenging Order's leader, which cannot exceed twenty-one days from the initial mysterious death or disappearance, such embalmed bodies shall be shrouded and laid to rest in the Pauper Field. Whereupon, the initial loss is deemed equalized.'"

Mitchell's expression hardened. "I don't have it memorized, but that sounds almost exactly like it says. I don't remember being that specific with you the other day."

Braxton took a final puff of his cigarette and stubbed it out, his eyes locked on Mitchell. "So, staying on point. The embalming hid any traces of the medication the Holmans used for their suicide, right?"

Mitchell nodded, "Correct, that's what I understand."

Braxton continued, his tone tinted with incredulity and pragmatism. "Okay, so Elle's plan not only covers up the Holmans' suicide, but it also ensures you get custody of Hunter. Everyone benefits from this batshit-crazy logic. The Holmans' suicide is concealed, there's no link between you and them, and Hunter's left with no memory of the ordeal. You get plausible deniability for both Elle and Aaron's disappearance and the Holman case. It's a win-win situation, at least until things go sideways with Hunter. That's about the size of it, isn't it?"

Mitchell's face tightened up, conveying both acceptance and annoyance. "Factually, yes, that's a fair summary. But I take issue with how you're framing the Order's actions."

Braxton leaned back, a sardonic grin playing on his lips. "No offense intended, Mitch. But here I am, Braxton Hayward: the cliché of a jaded, divorced, bankrupt, hard-drinking attorney. Given my less-than-stellar academic credentials, I'm guessing you saw me as a desperate candidate for some sort of trial by fire, to see if I'm cut out for Ab Initio. If I pull it off, no more money worries, right? Just need to deflect the heat from you and secure Hunter's custody, and I'm in."

Mitchell gave a wry smile, tinged with a hint of respect. "You're being too hard on yourself, Braxton. But yes, that's essentially it."

Braxton's expression turned more serious. "Well, just so you know, I've already handled the first part. Without getting into my work product methodology, I've steered law enforcement away, suggesting they focus on a theory involving an aging serial killer with medical know-how, now training a protégé. That should throw them off your scent. But remember, you didn't hear this from me."

Mitchell's smile broadened, a visible sense of relief washing over him. "Understood," he said, clearly grateful for the update.

Braxton narrowed his eyes slightly, adopting a more thoughtful tone. "So, the remaining task is securing legal custody of Hunter for you. Elle left you guardianship papers, but her estate lawyers now claim ignorance. That's my problem to solve."

He paused, studying Mitchell's reaction. "I've done my homework, even without access to the Order's documents about the fate of children in assassinated members' families. I think I've pieced together what we need. But before I proceed, is there anything else you need to disclose? Anything at all?"

Mitchell spread his hands in a gesture of openness. "Aside from what we've already discussed, there's nothing more to add."

Braxton leaned forward, his demeanor serious. "Just to be clear, Mitchell, in my practice, I've had clients who presented facts in their favor, omitting crucial details. Things would be going smoothly until contradictory evidence is dropped like a truckload of dog shit into the grinding wheels of justice, wrecking the case. I want to avoid that here. So, this is your chance—anything else you might have left out?"

Mitchell met Braxton's stare evenly. "No, Braxton. You've got everything. There's nothing else."

Braxton's posture relaxed as he shifted the conversation to a more analytical tone. "Now, let's address what happens when children are involved in these reciprocal terminations," he said thoughtfully. "You've previously mentioned that children are placed according to the guardianship nominations left by a deceased or disappeared parent. But what about scenarios involving a surviving parent who's been excommunicated? Or cases where no guardianship nominations exist? These seem to be significant oversights, yet both Ab Initio and Prime Ascendant tend to be meticulous in their rules. I mean, if I thought of that, there's no doubt in my mind that the brilliant but twisted-as-fuck founders wouldn't factor in such contingencies."

Mitchell listened, a look of contemplation crossing his face as Braxton continued.

"So here's what I discovered," Braxton continued. "Turns out Elle and Aaron updated their guardianship documents. This means the copy you showed me, the one you were banking on, is now void. The revised paperwork doesn't name you as Hunter's guardian."

Braxton paused, allowing the gravity of the situation to sink in. "But it's not the end of the road. We're in the modern era, and legal avenues are still open to you. Filing a paternity action and obtaining a court-ordered test should be straightforward, especially since Hunter has no surviving parents. There's no explicit deadline to start this process in Oregon. Sure, there might be some ruffled feathers and pearl-clutching within some circles, but that's a manageable challenge."

Braxton leaned back, a confident glint in his eye. "So, that resolves the Hunter situation, right? Mission accomplished, I would say. Now, about my induction into Ab Initio," his tone shifting to one of negotiation. "Let's talk about the compensation. Are we looking at a 'consigliere' type arrangement, where I'm paid a monthly nonrefundable retainer to keep everything in order? Or are we talking about specific billables through a loan-out company?"

He paused for a moment, contemplating his preferences. "Personally, I'd lean toward the retainer model. Maybe something like thirty grand a month plus expenses? And we could set a review in about six months to see how things are going." Braxton's expression turned slightly pragmatic. "Of course, if it's more tax-efficient to go with billables, I understand. But that would likely mean an additional five thousand a month for the extra accounting services."

Mitchell raised his hands, signaling a need to slow down. "Hold on, Braxton, just pump the brakes a bit," he said. "I'm not sure pursuing the parentage angle is a practical option."

Braxton's eyebrows furrowed in confusion. "Is there something I'm missing here?"

"No, it's not that," Mitchell replied, his tone reflecting concern. "It's just. . .the potential backlash, the negative publicity it could generate. It's problematic."

Braxton drew forward, his voice firm yet persuasive. "But think about it, Mitchell. You'll handle the publicity just fine. In fact, I'd say it could even boost your standing, showcasing the 'no-nonsense' approach of the Emerson ethos within both Orders. Picture this: you personally fulfilling your execution duties, then taking swift and decisive action to claim your son once you realized the possibility of his paternity. It's the epitome of a man of action, securing Ab Initio's lineage and its future prosperity."

Mitchell's face remained stoic, a subtle tension creeping into his features as Braxton pulled out his phone. "Just a sec, let me check something," Braxton said, his fingers swiftly navigating the screen. His brow furrowed in concentration, a hint of anticipation coloring his tone.

Reading aloud, Braxton's voice took on a note of revelation. "Okay, here we go," he began, "Section 13.22 of Article Thirteen of the Compact clearly states, 'any minor child who survives the suspicious or reciprocal termination or disappearance of both or either surviving parent(s), as defined in section. . .'" He skimmed through the text, then found his mark, "shall immediately become a ward of the other Order, unless otherwise stated by a lawful written nomination executed by the surviving child's parent(s)."

He paused, his gaze lifting from the phone to meet Mitchell's. "And here's the real kicker," he continued, "'any member of any Order who openly challenges in court the guardianship or wardship of any child displaced by a suspicious or reciprocal termination shall forthwith be forever excommunicated from membership of, and in, either Order.' So, if you were to file for paternity, you'd effectively be expelling yourself from the Order."

As the gravity of his discovery settled in the air, Braxton took a casual sip of coffee, his demeanor nonchalant. "It's pretty ingenious, when you think about it. It encourages young couples to keep their estate plans updated post-childbirth while simultaneously discouraging the targeting of families with children. I have to admit, those old-timey sociopaths were perverse, but they were undeniably brilliant."

Mitchell's face contorted with irritation. "Hold on a second," he interjected sharply. "I'd watch what you say next. Your ongoing criticism of the Order and its sacred principles is crossing a line. Despite that, I've been lenient with you."

He paused, his expression turning grave. "But then you read parts of the Compact right off your phone. Unsanctioned duplication of our holy scriptures? That alone is a surefire way to get excommunicated. It's a shame, Braxton. I actually liked having you around. I know you're no fool, so I trust you'll understand the need to keep this. . .uncomplicated. As much as I acknowledge the strides you've made, you've failed the ultimate test. You're now persona non grata. I'll arrange for a nondisclosure agreement for you to sign and give you two weeks to leave town. And because I genuinely do like you, I'll cover the advance you paid on your lease."

Mitchell's right hand casually rested near his waist, a subtle hint at the power he wielded. With his other hand, he took out his phone, ready to summon Salt and Pepper. The air was charged with tension, a silent standoff between two men who had reached an irrevocable crossroads.

Braxton maintained a composed facade, though his mind raced with the unfolding events. "I thought bringing weapons to neutral ground was a bit taboo," he remarked, a hint of sarcasm lacing his words.

Mitchell waved off the comment with a dismissive gesture. "Look, Brax, I mean it when I say I've enjoyed our time together. I'm not just saying that. I like you, and our discussions have been enlightening. But unfortunately, this just wasn't meant to be. I can't overlook any more heresy or desecration within my inner circle. I'm relieved, though, knowing you're smart enough to avoid any drastic actions from my side regarding your departure."

Braxton, undeterred by Mitchell's veiled threats, continued, seeking clarity. "I just want to make sure I understand the full picture," he said calmly. "Indulge me for a moment. You played a key role in facilitating a victimless exit for Elle and Aaron. If it stays under wraps, it would've served multiple purposes: silencing Elle, boosting your leadership credibility, and ultimately bringing your son back into your life.

"Then, post-execution, while still on the radar of a high-profile investigation, you encounter issues with Hunter's custody. That's where I came in. You needed someone to divert law enforcement's attention and secure the guardianship documents from the Prime Ascendant contact Elle had used. And throughout all this, you were betting on me overlooking a crucial detail."

Braxton paused momentarily, his voice steady yet laden with the significance of his deduction. "That, in fact, *a third organization* exists, established by the Compact itself." His words hung in the air, heavy with implication.

As the back door of the Saloon slammed shut, Mitchell rose, ready to leave. He exchanged a brief, charged glance with Braxton, a scoff escaping his lips as he turned to signal his departure to his associates.

His stride halted abruptly, surprise etching his features as he found Jason and Tony, not his own men, blocking his path. Tony's demeanor was relaxed yet assertive. "Your boys got a little tied up while hanging out at the bar with Donnie and Earl. You know how it is when they get going. Quite the captive audience," he remarked casually, his tone masking the undercurrent of control he exerted. With a final rub of his bruised knuckles, Tony retreated into the Saloon, leaving a clear message without uttering another word.

As Jason assumed his protective stance, Mitchell's defeat was palpable. The once-assertive leader now appeared diminished, his usual confidence replaced by a sense of resignation. His slumped posture was a silent admission that the tide had turned against him.

Braxton, seizing control of the conversation, began to lay out his understanding of the situation. "Both Orders had a good run over the last decade, but there's a piece of the puzzle you withheld. The Compact established a third entity, Inter Alios, with two key objectives: to prevent harm to the public and to avoid mutual destruction between the Orders."

He gestured toward Jason. "Here's the Justice of the Peace of Inter Alios. Jason's been holding the fort, but he lacks the legal qualifications for the Principal Magistrate role. This position needs someone with legal expertise."

Braxton continued, "The last Principal Magistrate was an old-school civil rights attorney. His retirement a decade ago left a void that wasn't filled. It's clear why both orders might have preferred it this way. Without its Principal Magistrate, Inter Alios is effectively handicapped, leaving both orders unchecked."

He paused to take a sip of his coffee, letting his words sink in. "So, it seems to me that Inter Alios has been waiting for someone with the right legal background to take up the mantle of Principal Magistrate. Without that leadership, it's like the proverbial cat's away, and the mice will play. And it looks like they've been playing for quite a while." Braxton's tone was matter-of-fact, his analysis sharp and to the point, cutting through the complexities of the situation with ease.

After another sip of coffee, Braxton continued, his tone laced with irony and revelation. "It's not exactly a position you can advertise on job boards, right?" He chuckled dryly. "Given the Orders' deep connections in the legal world, finding an impartial local lawyer or judge would be near impossible. A convenient setup for both Orders, really. Pay the dues to Inter Alios and make a shit-ton of money off the rest of us, at our expense."

Jason, playing his part seamlessly, placed an embossed document before Mitchell. Braxton, with a hint of theatricality, announced, "Mitchell Emerson, third of his bloodline as Prima Imperator of Ab Initio, consider this your formal notice. I, Braxton T. Hayward, unanimously approved by Inter Alios, hereby accept the appointment as Principal Magistrate."

Allowing Mitchell a moment to digest the document, Braxton continued, "You'll see at the bottom, the notice of appointment has been served to each Order as mandated by the Compact."

Mitchell, visibly shaken, shot a look of disbelief at Jason. Braxton, however, was unrelenting in his delivery. "I could've played along, even helped you with Hunter, to join your Order. But, to be honest, the more I learned about each Order, the more disillusioned I became. The faith required in your belief system. . .it's nothing but greed and exploitation disguised as divine commandments. The abuse of power is staggering."

As Braxton spoke, his voice wavered, hinting at a deeper internal conflict. The clarity he had gained was now clouded by the realization of the Orders' true nature. His photographic memory, recently a reliable ally, seemed to flicker, reflecting the turmoil of his thoughts.

Braxton, absorbed in his phone, continued, "And there's more. The Principal Magistrate needs to have what the Compact calls 'a healthy disregard for the beliefs held by Ab Initio and Prime Ascendant at all times.'" He glanced up, a wry smile playing on his lips. "You might twist it however you like, Mitch, but even the Compact's founders knew what kind of destruction money-worship can cause. That's why they established a third Order. To keep the peace and prevent you all from killing each other."

As Braxton put down his phone, he caught Mitchell shooting Jason a look filled with bitter disdain. The air was thick with unspoken recriminations and a history of complex allegiances.

Mitchell's voice broke through, tinged with betrayal and disbelief. "Really, Jason? After everything. . .all that I've done for you?" His words echoed a sense of profound letdown.

Jason met Mitchell's eyes steadily, his expression resolute yet tinged with regret. Jason spoke, his voice calm yet firm. "Mitch, I've got great respect for our history, for all that we've been through. But this time, my decision isn't about sticking with the devil that you know. It's about taking a leap into the unknown. And my gut's telling me it's the right call."

Jason's words echoed in the charged silence, cementing a moment that was both pivotal and transformative. It transcended a mere alteration in dynamics between two men; it was a seismic shift in the complex ballet of power and control that had long ruled their world. This critical juncture, heavy with unspoken consequences, heralded not just a turning point for Mitchell and Jason, but a profound realignment in the intricate lattice of alliances, secrets, and machinations they were enmeshed in. It was a watershed moment, signaling the dawn of an uncertain yet undeniably new era.

CHAPTER SEVENTEEN

INTER ALIOS . . . AMONG OTHER PEOPLE

SUNDAY, OCTOBER 21, 3:01 PM

In the aftermath of Mitchell's departure, Braxton found solace in the serene atmosphere of the Saloon's atrium. The echoes of the day's tensions reverberating through his mind as he sat in quietude. Meanwhile, Jason busied himself, preparing the Saloon for the evening's private event. It was an intimate gathering, primarily comprising close friends, family, and a selection of local musicians with whom Jason occasionally shared the stage. Despite its informal nature, Jason's attention to detail underscored his dedication to hosting a memorable affair.

Having set the stage for the night, Jason advised his staff to take a well-deserved break, promising to cover their hour's absence. Donnie and Earl, having wrapped up their part in the day's events, also made their exits. Jason then ventured to his car, retrieving several worn binders—the keepers of records and procedures crucial to the Order's operations.

With the binders in tow, he secured the Saloon's doors from the inside, ensuring privacy for what was to follow. Jason's steps led him to the outdoor area, where Braxton awaited, lost in thought amidst the quiet aftermath of their recent encounter. The air was charged with a subtle energy of change and new beginnings, setting the stage for the crucial discussions that lay ahead.

Jason, armed with his binders and a casual demeanor, approached Braxton, who appeared visibly on edge. The stress of the recent confrontation had left its mark; Braxton was chain-smoking, a clear sign of his internal turmoil.

Jason attempted to lighten the mood with a bit of reeferese. "So, how's it growing?" he asked, but the question did little to cut through Braxton's apparent anxiety.

Braxton, trying to shake off the residual tension, admitted, "Well, I guess it could have gone a lot worse. You know? It's always weird after a full-on cross-examination, regardless of the outcome. But it's been a while since my hands shook like this afterwards." He glanced down at the sweat marks his palms had left on the table, chuckling wryly, "Damn. I sure picked the wrong week to stop drinking."

Jason's concern was evident as he inquired about Braxton's well-being, particularly in relation to any withdrawal symptoms he might be experiencing. "Right? How are you doing with that, by the way? Any DTs or other withdrawal stuff? Because no judgment if you need anything to help taper off. . ."

Braxton quickly brushed off the concern, attributing his physical symptoms to the day's stress and his recent decision to quit drinking. "Nah, I'm good," he said, though his demeanor suggested otherwise. He then changed the subject to focus on the tasks at hand. "So, what's on the docket, JP?" he asked, using a shorthand for Justice of the Peace.

Jason, settling into his role, opened the least worn of the binders. "So, we need to record last month's induction. . .for Stacey, I mean," he said, thumbing through the pages. "And then we need to come up with the minutes formalizing your Principal Magistrate appointment. Then everyone will sign off once they get back."

Braxton, lost for a moment while shifting through his notes, glanced up with an appreciative smile. "Nice play on the 'stick with the devil that you know' quote earlier, Jason. Despite the implications, it was a nice touch."

Jason chuckled, a bit self-deprecating. "Just sort of came out, you know? Maybe not the best choice of words, but. . ."

"No, it was perfect. Really," Braxton interjected, his tone sincere. "And thank you, for everything."

Jason shrugged, a wry smile on his face. "Might be a bit of Stockholm Syndrome talking, but you're welcome." He redirected their attention to the task at hand. "So, no objections to Stacey's induction?"

Braxton nodded affirmatively, his endorsement clear. "No objection. Appointment wholeheartedly endorsed." He looked back at Jason, ready to move forward. "What's next on the agenda?"

"We need a summary of your qualifications and background for the Principal Magistrate role," Jason explained, his tone professional.

Braxton exhaled softly, gathering his thoughts. "Well, I've got a law degree and over five years of legal practice under my belt. That should tick the boxes for the basic requirements, right?" Jason acknowledged with a nod, diligently recording Braxton's words.

"And for the factual summary?" Jason inquired, looking up from his notes.

Braxton hesitated, realizing his photographic memory had returned to its standard haywire mode. "How detailed should we go here?" He pondered for a moment. "Perhaps it's best to start at the beginning and distill from there."

Jason agreed, pen ready. "Start from wherever you feel is best. We can refine it as needed."

"Whereas. . ." Braxton started, then hesitated. "Let's keep it plain and simple. Hope you're ready for a long story," he said, gathering his thoughts.

"So, after the Saloon closed on August sixth, I found myself drunkenly stumbling into Britt Gardens, where I saw two bodies hanging from a tree. At first, I wasn't sure if it was real or just a drunken nightmare. I tried to block it out, but as the news unfolded, I felt compelled to unravel the murder-disappearance cases," Braxton explained, lighting a cigarette.

"As I started piecing things together, I learned about Elle, Aaron, and the Holman couple. Despite my initial denial, I was driven to discover the truth behind this seemingly perfect community."

Braxton paused, taking a drag of his cigarette. "We had these high-profile local couples disappearing, and then Elle and Aaron's child, Hunter, found safe at a Medford hospital. I found it odd that Mitchell Emerson, Elle's ex, was arrested at that same hospital."

Braxton continued, his narrative unwavering despite the turmoil beneath. "Coincidences piled up. I ended up managing a Saloon for a bartender I barely knew," he said, taking another drag of his cigarette. "Then this woman, Emily, leaves a custom beer at the Saloon, labeled 'Prime Ascendent.' That same day, I receive a curious call from said bartender about the darkness of Emily's beer, and soon after, the Holman couple's bodies turn up in the cemetery. It was all starting to connect." As he spoke, Braxton's voice wavered slightly, a flicker of unease crossing his features. Memories of the chilling images he had seen—sewn-up mouths and blank, empty eyes reflecting back at him from a metal bowl—flashed through his mind, unspoken yet profoundly disturbing.

Braxton flicked ash into the tray, his gaze becoming distant. "That's when I was introduced to Mitchell, Elle's ex, recently arrested at Medford hospital. He wanted to hire me," Braxton said, his voice tinged with irony.

"At his winery, I noticed Mitchell's expertise, but something else caught my eye. Emails between his lawyer and Elle's estate-planning attorney detailed unusual circumstances and legal obstacles regarding her estate. Then there was an invoice for embalming chemicals, allegedly for cleaning wine tanks. His explanation was plausible, yet it left me with lingering doubts."

"Diving into local archives and court records, I stumbled upon odd uses of 'ab initio' in legal terms. Then, I met Emily, who I found out is connected to the Holman family. One thing led to another, and I ended up witnessing a bizarre funeral ritual at the Holman estate."

Braxton shifted in his seat, a pensive look crossing his face. "And then there's Riley McAvoy," he said, his voice taking on a softer tone. "Our relationship. . .it's been anything but straightforward. I found out early on, through my bartender friend, that her pharmaceutical rep persona was a cover. She was actually an FBI agent, working on the high-profile cases we've been discussing."

Pausing, Braxton's eyes seemed to look inward. "Despite everything, being with Riley. . . it brought something back into my life. After a few encounters, it dawned on me that we had crossed paths before, back when I applied to the FBI. I chose not to bring it up, not wanting to risk what little we had. But she figured it out and, well, distanced herself by September. In a way, her ghosting me propelled me further into my research, trying to stay connected to her orbit by unraveling these cases."

He glanced at the pack of cigarettes, then opted for a sip of water instead. "That's when a drone flyer stumbled upon what looked like a murder scene at Rogue River Ranch. It made me face reality. No matter how much I wanted to dismiss the macabre visions of that drunken night as a nightmare, the truth was staring me in the face at the Holman estate. I couldn't ignore it any longer. I had to dive deeper, to connect the dots and intensify my research."

Braxton's narrative continued, detailing his encounters and discoveries. "During this time, I felt like I was being watched. Things out of place, like locks being unlatched, clothes missing, notepads and drawers in disarray. After confirming my suspicions at Rogue River Ranch, things escalated."

Braxton delved deeper into the peculiarities surrounding Elle and Aaron's disappearance, his analytical mind piecing together the disparate elements. "The discovery at Rogue River Ranch was a linchpin in this case," he explained, his voice steady. "It's an isolated spot, yet likely to be stumbled upon. So, I started connecting the dots," he took a moment to collect his thoughts.

"The last sighting of Elle and Aaron was in Grants Pass, around nine-thirty p.m. on August sixth. From there, their car surfaced a hundred miles south in Weed, California—roughly a two-hour drive. But then, their DNA turns up at Rogue River Ranch, which is at least another four hours north of Weed. This place, tucked away in the wilderness, yet not entirely off the grid, seemed curiously chosen."

He pitched forward, emphasizing his point. "It got me thinking. If I were planning to vanish, that's exactly where I'd fake my death. Far enough from my car to create a mystery, yet in a place bound to be discovered eventually. The goal being to leave enough time to disappear completely before the evidence is found. It's too calculated, too convenient to be mere coincidence."

Braxton took another moment to gather his thoughts, his eyes reflective. "The deeper question that nagged at me was the motive," he continued. "Why would Elle and Aaron, a successful couple with everything seemingly going for them, even contemplate faking their own deaths? It's a drastic step. And abandoning their child in the process? That's not something you expect from loving parents. The easiest explanation might be some sort of mental breakdown, but it didn't sit right. There had to be a stronger force at play, something compelling enough to drive them to such extremes."

He exhaled slowly, his gaze distant. "This is where the puzzle pieces didn't align with the usual narrative. What pressures, what unseen forces, could push them to such a decision? This wasn't just a simple case of running away from life's problems; it was something far more intricate and, possibly, sinister."

He took a slow, contemplative drink of water. "That's when my thoughts took a turn toward the conspiratorial. Jacksonville's not just a quaint town; it's steeped in history, including ties to masonic orders. The cemetery itself has sections dedicated to them. It got me thinking: what if Elle and Aaron staged their own deaths to escape some sort of clandestine cult?"

Braxton's tone shifted to one of discovery. "It was like pieces of a puzzle falling into place, almost serendipitously. I dove deeper into legal research, paying extra for a subscription that allowed me to conduct a Boolean search on terms like 'ab initio' and 'prime ascend!' in Oregon cases from the late 19th century. An exclamation point in the search term, by the way, helps find root-word derivatives."

He leaned in, the excitement of the chase evident in his voice. "I had already stumbled upon the Hoffnung v. Emerson case from the Oregon Supreme Court records. That led me to dig deeper, to sift through old case files. That's how I uncovered the appellate brief with the Multilateral Venture Compact between Ab Initio and Prime Ascendant. It was like unearthing a hidden chapter in the town's history, a secret saga that spanned generations."

Braxton's recounting of his research in the historic archives revealed a fascinating twist. "Once I pieced together the case records, I dived further into local history. That's when I discovered that all descendants of Paul Hoffnung, the founder of Prime Ascendant, had changed their surname to 'Holman' before the 20th century. It seemed they anticipated the turmoil in Europe and adapted their name for more... palatable business dealings, especially with World War I looming. That's my theory, anyway."

He paused, then continued, "So, the stage was set with two key players: Ab Initio, under the Emerson family's banner, and Prime Ascendant, helmed by the Holman family, originally Hoffnung. Elle's deep ties with Mitchell suggested her allegiance to Ab Initio, and my research confirmed it. As for Aaron, he was an outsider with no ties to the local legacy."

Braxton's voice carried the weight of his discoveries. "What struck me as too much of a coincidence was the simultaneous disappearance of two prominent couples from each Order. It reeked of a reciprocal, almost vendetta-like maneuver. An eye-for-an-eye scenario playing out in a modern setting, cloaked in the guise of random disappearances."

"Hey, Braxton?" Jason interrupted.

"Yeah?" he looked up.

"I sort of jotted down some notes from the other day's discussion. You know, after your meeting with Mitchell at his place?" Jason flipped through his notepad. "Would you prefer that I go over those to make things easier? You're doing great, but I thought I'd put that out there."

"Please do," Braxton let out a sigh. "I've been doing a lot of talking today, so I'd appreciate the assist."

"Okay," Jason had found the right page. "Well, this one's easy. So, after your meeting with Mitchell, you came here and briefed me on everything. That's when I introduced the concept of Inter Alios and its need for a Principal Magistrate. You didn't hesitate to accept, which gave you access to the Compact and other confidential records. But something intrigued me—even before I mentioned Inter Alios, you were adamant about the existence of a third entity. How did you piece that together?"

Braxton nodded, recalling the moment. "Yeah, my research was pointing toward something bigger than just Ab Initio and Prime Ascendant. There were just too many unanswered questions, too many inconsistencies. So, I started making educated guesses, treating them as facts in conversations to see how people reacted. It was a bit like throwing darts in the dark, but surprisingly, it worked. For instance, I had this theory about the Holmans being embalmed and left to rest in the Pauper Field. I presented it as a fact to Riley, and her reaction confirmed it."

Braxton paused, reflecting on the critical moment of revelation. "About the existence of a third Order—that hit me out of the blue, yet it made perfect sense. It dawned on me when considering the Compact's full title: the Multi-lateral Venture Compact. If it were only about Ab Initio and Prime Ascendant, it would logically be titled a Bi-lateral Venture Compact. It was a subtle clue hiding in plain sight, indicating the involvement of more than two parties."

He sat back, his expression one of excitement and realization. "It was a moment of clarity, where all the disparate threads began to weave into a coherent picture. That's when I knew there had to be another entity, a third Order, part of this intricate web." Braxton's tone conveyed both the thrill of the discovery and the gravity of its implications.

Jason, with a hint of amusement, interjected for clarification. "Quick question, if you don't mind. How did you piece together my involvement in all this?"

Braxton crossed his arms, a knowing look crossing his face. "Well, it just clicked, you know? Several puzzle pieces fit together perfectly. The incident with Emily and the craft beer labeled 'Prime Ascendant' was a start. Then there was you, entrusting me with the Saloon, almost like a subtle test. You also introduced me to Mitchell and consistently dropped nuggets of insider info."

Jason, nodding in understanding, smoothly transitioned the conversation. "Alright, let's move on. What's your take on what happened to Elle and Aaron?"

Braxton, absentmindedly pulling another cigarette from the pack, delved into his theory. "Remember our talk about the rafting trips you guys used to take? How Aaron was adept at navigating the rapids, and considering Elle's activism, she's no stranger to roughing it out there."

Lighting the cigarette, he continued, "Here's my thought: Elle and Aaron set off from the Grants Pass area in a raft or drift boat, heading down the Rogue River toward Gold Beach, where the river meets the Pacific. The Rogue River Ranch? It's strategically located halfway between Grants Pass and Gold Beach. Perfect spot for them to make a brief stop, leave behind some deliberately planted evidence—stained clothes, personal effects—and then continue their journey downstream."

Exhaling a cloud of smoke, he leaned back. "Once they reached the coast, they ditch the boat, vanish. Given Aaron's law enforcement background and Elle's resources, odds are high that they could secure credible credentials. A calculated, but not impossible, escape." Braxton's theory, detailed and well-reasoned, painted a vivid picture of their potential disappearance.

Jason attentively listened to Braxton's hypothesis, jotting down notes. "Interesting angle," he remarked, an eyebrow raised in intrigue. "But how do you explain Hunter and their car turning up in Weed?"

Braxton, deep in thought, considered the implications. "The key here is their accomplice," he stated. "Someone took their car and took care of Hunter, probably starting in Grants Pass." He paused, considering the various suspects he had pondered, including Jason.

"Think about the timeline," Braxton continued. "Elle and Aaron were last seen on August sixth. They were reported missing two days later, and their car and Hunter were found in Weed on the ninth. They wouldn't have started their journey on the river at night, so they likely camped near the launch site with Hunter for their last night together."

Braxton's analysis became more profound. "This means the accomplice had to keep Hunter hidden and quiet for nearly forty-eight hours. The person would need to be single, with a private place to keep Hunter and the SUV without drawing attention. I had a few suspects in mind, even you at one point," he said with a half-smile.

Braxton's voice took on a tone of revelation. "It wasn't until last week when I figured out the one person who connected all the dots in this intricate situation. She's the same person unwittingly named as Hunter's guardian in Elle and Aaron's revised will. The same one who sent the coded message through the Prime Ascendant stout bottle. And, remarkably, she was also involved in procuring the necessary medications for the Holmans' chosen exit." Braxton paused, letting the significance of his words settle. "Emily was the key figure, the central element in this entire web of events."

Jason responded with a hint of admiration in his voice. "Emily is truly remarkable. If I wasn't—well, let's not digress. The point being I knew she was Elle's contact within Prime Ascendant. Our business dealings were a convenient cover, but I always maintained a 'don't-ask-don't-tell' policy regarding the specifics of Elle's plan." He gave a nod of acknowledgment. "Coordinating your meeting with her was the right move, it seems."

Braxton, intrigued, leaned in. "So, this beer-bottle code, how does it work?"

Jason chuckled lightly. "It's surprisingly simple. Pale ale or a light brew signifies everything is fine. A dark beer, like a stout, indicates complications. And an amber brew is a warning to brace for the worst. Quite elementary, really."

"I see, old school but effective," Braxton noted, appreciating the code's simplicity.

"Right," Jason nodded, ready to delve deeper. "Now, about Hunter being Mitchell's son. How did you piece that together?"

"It began with Mitchell's arrest at Medford hospital, coinciding with Hunter's discovery. And then there was that unforgettable out-of-body experience I shared with Riley in the Pauper Field." Braxton paused, the memories vivid in his mind. "After that, she confirmed that Hunter's DNA wasn't used to match with the findings at Rogue River Ranch. And finally, during my face-off with Mitchell at his lair, he validated my suspicions," Braxton explained, his voice tinged with reflection.

"Okay," Jason looked through his notes. "So, if I understand correctly, you encountered four dead bodies. The two hanging from the tree, and the two that were cremated at the Prime Ascendant funeral. That's a total of four bodies. How do you explain that?"

Braxton worked to piece it all together, his thoughts falling into place. "Well," he started, "it's been a bit of a blur, but I'll do my best to recount everything in order.

"As you're aware from the Compact, a reciprocal kill involves a specific method to signal the other Order that the score has been settled. The bodies are hanged and drained of their fluids, then embalmed and laid to rest in the Pauper Field. Since Elle and Aaron are likely still alive, there's only one logical conclusion: I must have seen the bodies of Susan and

Andrew Holman twice." Braxton extinguished his cigarette in the ash-tray, the final wisp of smoke foretelling the closure of a complex puzzle.

"Bear in mind," he continued, "that they were reported missing on August sixteenth. But they left for their camping trip on August fourth. Through Elle, Mitchell knew that the Holman couple planned on taking their lethal doses on August sixth. So, after the two passed away, Mitchell and his goons went to the Holman's campsite. Mitch went into their camper trailer alone, and later told Salt and Pepper that he smothered them to death. Then they removed the bodies and hung them across from the cemetery near Britt Gardens. And I just happened to be in the wrong place at the wrong time . . ."

"Wait a minute," Jason interjected. "Elle, Aaron, and Hunter weren't reported missing until August eighth. And you're saying Mitch and his team did all of this on the night of August sixth through August seventh. So, how could it be 'reciprocal' when no one even knew about Elle, Aaron, and Hunter's disappearance until August *eighth*?"

"I know, right?" Braxton said, raising an eyebrow. "Quite the conundrum. Mitchell not only had to keep people in the dark about the Holman's euthanasia, he also had to make it look like he issued the kill order after Elle, Aaron, and Hunter were reported missing. So, I asked Mitchell the same question. And I've got to give it to the guy, it was pretty ingenious. A total Emerson move, through and through. But of course, I never said this to you."

"Of course," Jason replied, putting down his pen.

"I guess around July thirtieth," Braxton began, "Mitch put Salt and Pepper on 'Level One' lockdown detail. That's when the security team shelters in place with him twenty-four-seven. Security has no internet, phone, radio, or TV access—local network only—so they're not distracted from the camera feeds. And since someone always needs to be awake, they work overlapping sixteen-hour shifts. As you can imagine, time starts doing weird things under those conditions."

Braxton cocked his head up to the skylight, squinting at a songbird exploring the space's upper awnings.

"Well," Braxton continued, "to make a long story short, Mitchell had them beta-test Gunther's prototype smartwatches that could override their phones and computers. This allowed Mitchell to make time adjustments over the next several days so that by the time he told them that Elle and Aaron went missing on the sixth, Salt and Pepper's personal time-zone said it was August eighth. It served as a perfect alibi for Mitchell within his own Order. Pretty fucking brilliant, actually."

"For sure," Jason agreed. "Total Emerson move all the way." Jason glanced back down at his notes. "So, what should we do about Mitchell?"

"What should we do about Mitchell?" Braxton echoed, his brow furrowed in thought.

"Yeah," said Jason, his voice tinged with frustration.

"What do you mean?" Braxton inquired, his gaze drifting back up to the skylight.

"I mean, he's been so manipulative," Jason explained, his tone filled with concern. "He was using you to get custody of Hunter through golden carrots and half-truths. He didn't tell you about Inter Alios. He lied about the Compact's rules. That's what I mean."

"Oh, that," Braxton acknowledged with a nod. "Well, first off, you have to realize who you're dealing with. Mitchell was born and raised to be that way. When presented with a situation, his instinct is to maximize personal gain. It's unfortunate, to be honest. Because as I grew to know him, I could see that there was some decency stirring within.

"And let's not underplay Elle's role here," Braxton continued, shifting gears. "She most likely believed that promising Hunter to Mitchell was the only way he would go along with the plan. That promise was the keystone. For all she knew, her life hinged on that promise. A promise Elle planned to break.

"But for her, it was justified. She was not going to let Hunter be brainwashed by Ab Initio. She put the child's interests above her own integrity. So, in the end, she gave Hunter to Emily instead of Mitchell. And I think that's how she reconciled cutting all ties, to be honest." Braxton raised his arms and stretched his back.

"But let's look at it from Mitchell's perspective," Braxton said, adopting a contemplative tone. "There he was, in a serious relationship with Elle. He loves and faithfully sticks by her, despite her sacrilegious criticism of their spiritual beliefs. He tries to make it work. Then—right after making love—Elle tells Mitchell that she and Aaron just had mind-blowing sex, and she terminates their relationship. Still, Mitch does the decent thing, and they part on civil terms.

"Soon she starts dating Aaron, and a baby's on the way. Hunter is born, and Mitchell finds out he's the baby-daddy. But the birth certificate will state otherwise. And, Mitch makes peace with that. Then a couple of years later, Elle reopens that wound to get Mitchell on board with her risky high-profile exit-plan.

"Then after following her plan to a tee, Mitchell finds out that his guardianship papers are bunk, meaning that Hunter will be raised as a Prime Ascendant. I mean, that's pretty fucked up, right? The mother of your child doing that kind of shit to you? When all you've been doing is trying to be decent about it? *Of course*, you're motivated to do whatever it takes to get custody of your kid. Even if it means resorting to unconventional means. As a fellow human being, I can't blame Mitchell for having such a visceral reaction."

"Well, yeah . . ." Jason ran a hand through his hair, deep in thought. "Considering all that, I can see where you're coming from. It's just that Mitchell always comes across as unflappable, put-together, and strictly business. It's easy to forget that he has any emotions at all. You've got to be on your toes with him because it feels like he's constantly plotting . . ."

"Absolutely," Braxton nodded in agreement. "I wouldn't trust him any farther than I could throw him. What I'm getting at is that beneath all the intricate chess moves and power plays, there might be a glimmer of decency. So, regarding your question about what we should do with Mitchell, my plan is to appeal to his better nature without giving away the whole farm."

Jason took a moment to review his notes one last time. "Well, since you brought it up earlier. . .what's your perspective on the whole Pauper Field phenomenon?"

"I'm sorry?" Braxton momentarily lost focus.

"Pauper Field," Jason reiterated, "what's your take on it?"

"Dude. . ." Braxton took one of last cigarettes from the pack. "Normally I'd object to that question as vague, ambiguous, and calling for speculation. But, I mean, you're asking what's my take on it?"

"Yeah," Jason said.

Braxton lit a cigarette and leaned back, speaking thoughtfully. "Honestly, man. . .It's a tough one. I typically steer clear of anything theological or metaphysical because the complexities of reality are baffling enough. But I can't deny that something inexplicable happened between Riley and me up in the Pauper Field."

He finished his glass of water and swirled it around, lost in the patterns forming at the base.

"But it's probably just a quirk of biochemistry," Braxton continued. "You know, a surge of dopamine that synchronized our brains in a peculiar way at that precise moment? It's not a complete explanation, but it's the closest rationalization I can come up with."

"How is it not a complete explanation?" Jason used the familiar tactic of turning a statement into a question to delve deeper.

"Okay, sure," Braxton conceded. "Let me explain further. For instance, I swear to God I never mentioned to Riley about seeing any dead bodies hanging from a tree or being set on fire. But she brought up both of those things during our last conversation. Also, I don't recall Riley discussing her father's abusive past when we talked. But I have this vivid, visceral memory of her experiencing that. So, I mean, did we genuinely exchange unspoken memories?" He rubbed his chin and gazed into the distance, lost in thought.

"Or," he continued with a touch more confidence, "we might have simply forgotten the conversation when we revealed those things to each other. That memory I had of her could've been from an '80s TV show about domestic violence, for all I know. It's obviously the most rational conclusion, especially since most our relationship involved sharing genuine intimacies while keeping disclosures to a minimum. What I find most intriguing is that Elle and Aaron had a similar experience in the Pauper Field. . ."

"Really?" Jason sounded genuinely surprised.

"Absolutely," Braxton confirmed. "Oh, that's right, you weren't here when Mitch mentioned that today. I'm not sure if you knew, but apparently, Elle and Aaron had a Pauper Field moment too. That's what led to her breakup and, ultimately, their departure from Ab Initio."

"No kidding?" Jason responded. "I had no idea."

"Well, that's what Mitchell told me," Braxton said, taking a drag from his cigarette, its tip sporting about an inch of ash. "Though, it's quite a beautiful notion when you think about it."

"Yeah?" Jason inquired.

"Absolutely," Braxton replied, flicking the ash into the tray. "Consider this: how long does your existence remain known after you pass away? It varies widely, doesn't it? If you're a schoolteacher with no children of your own but you're leaving an impression on a new group of ten-year-olds every year, theoretically, your legacy could extend for some eighty years after you retire. If you're a public figure involved in historic moments, you might be remembered for millennia. Yet, for most people, memories of their existence fade after their grandkids or great-grandkids pass away. Then, they become nothing more than a name on a headstone."

Braxton took another puff, his gaze distant. "It's not the most pleasant thought, to be sure," he continued. "But it's especially disheartening for the nameless souls in the Pauper Field. They were deemed so insignificant by society that their existence was entirely erased. No grave marker, no remembrance."

"So, part of me wants to believe that perhaps those forgotten souls in the Pauper Field channel some kind of energy," Braxton mused, exhaling another stream of smoke. "An inter-dimensional force that guides anyone receptive to it onto a different path. A path that might even alter the course of destiny. . ."

"Maybe," he continued, "just maybe, the purpose of those unfortunate souls' fate wasn't what they could accomplish in life, but what they could influence after life." Braxton extinguished his cigarette, emphasizing his contemplation.

"It is nice notion," Jason conceded, "in twisted sort of way. I can't argue with that."

Braxton's eyes widened suddenly. "Oh my God," he exclaimed, his energy surging. "Are you frickin' kidding me?"

"What?" Jason inquired, curious about the abrupt change in Braxton's demeanor.

"The Pauper Field memorial plaque," Braxton continued, his excitement growing. "The monument that lists the names of those buried there. It was dedicated in 1996. Did the previous Principal Magistrate have something to do with building that monument?"

"Dude, you're just realizing that now?" Jason couldn't hold back his laughter, and it resonated through the atrium, causing a nearby songbird to take flight in surprise.

Braxton quickly retrieved his phone and started swiping through some photos until he found the one he wanted to show. "Right there," he pointed out on the screen. "'We remember in 1996. These persons, INTER ALIOS, buried in the Pauper Section of this cemetery. . .'" He read the inscription aloud, emphasizing the Latin terms.

"Oh my God," Braxton sighed, his amusement unmistakable. "The plaque clearly says 'Inter Alios' on its face, and I'm just now making this connection? That's actually hilarious," he chuckled.

"Among other people," Jason chimed in. "Isn't that what 'inter alios' means?"

"Exactly," Braxton confirmed. "At least, that's how lawyers and judges use it. There's 'inter alia,' which means 'among other things,' and then there's 'inter alios,' meaning 'among other people.' It's incredible how it was hiding in plain sight." Braxton smiled, shook his head in amusement, and turned to Jason. "Is there anything else?"

"I think that pretty much covers everything," Jason replied, handing over his notepad. "Do you want to take a look at what I've got? Excuse the poor penmanship."

Braxton accepted the notepad and began reviewing the notes, all neatly written in Jason's handwriting. He read through them attentively, a smile gradually forming on his face. "Nicely done," Braxton complimented. "Honestly, I couldn't have done it better myself."

"Okay," Jason reached out to retrieve his notepad. "Let me read it out loud for approval, and then I'll get a clean printout for everyone to sign once they get back. Cool?"

"Cool," Braxton agreed. "I'm ready when you are."

Jason cleared his throat and began reading aloud, "WHEREAS, the Board finds that BRAXTON T. HAYWARD satisfies the educational and professional requirements of the position, and is duly qualified to act as Principal Magistrate of and for INTER ALIOS."

He continued, "WHEREAS, for conspicuous gallantry and intrepidity at the risk of his life above and beyond the call of reason in the course of investigating suspicious disappearances and homicides concerning four (4) members of AB INITIO and PRIME ASCENDENT ('Orders'). Disregarding all sense of self-preservation through his interactions with other members of said Orders and law enforcement agent(s). And after demonstrating full candor to the Justice of the Peace by disclosing such facts and findings, his unwavering courage and steadfast devotion to the cause of INTER ALIOS being duly affirmed, it is:

"RESOLVED, that the undersigned have unanimously appointed and approved BRAXTON T. HAYWARD as Principal Magistrate of INTER ALIOS."

Jason concluded, "And that's basically it."

"Sounds about right," Braxton agreed, feeling a renewed sense of energy. "It's specifically vague, without being too overbroad. I have to say, you've got a real knack for this." Braxton began gathering his belongings that were scattered across the table.

"You're sticking around for the party tonight, right?" Jason asked.

"Well. . ." Braxton engaged in some silent deliberation, "normally I would say hell, yeah. But I'm thinking it's best that I go for a run and then chill at home for the night. No offense. I don't think I can trust myself to say no if someone offers me a drink, you know?"

"Say no more, dude," Jason said. "All good. And good on you, Brax. I mean it. Call me if you need anything."

"Cheers," Braxton grinned. "Greatly app-reefer-ated."

"Ha," Jason retorted. "Dooby honest, that reeferism weeds a little work there, bud."

"Nice. A triple-hit. No pun intended," Braxton said. "Move to adjourn?"

"So moved, and ratified," Jason confirmed. "Meeting adjourned."

Braxton had packed up all of his things, and the two men were standing by the table. "Hey," said Braxton, "now that we're off the record, can I ask you something kind of personal?"

"Of course," said Jason. "What's up?"

"I mean, not that it makes any difference," Braxton went on, "but when were you planning on telling me that you're gay?"

"Dude," Jason blinked a few times. "Who told you that? Was it Stacey?"

"No, it wasn't Stacey," said Braxton.

"Then who was it?"

"It was you. Just now," Braxton smiled. "You see what I mean about my random deductions ending up being true? It's actually kind of scary."

"Well, now you've got my attention," Jason had regained his composure. "What led to that deduction in particular?"

"I mean, it kind of dawned on me a couple of days ago," Braxton explained. "You're a total catch and still single. But then you said two things today that tipped me off:

"First, when you said Emily was a remarkable person—something we agree on—you caught yourself before saying something like 'if I wasn't gay.' Then later, you said you had a 'don't-ask-don't-tell' policy in terms of Elle's escape plan. The don't-ask-don't-tell policy was in effect for homosexual servicemembers back when you served. So, based on those prompts I stated my theory as a fact, and you confirmed it for me. Pretty crazy, right?"

Braxton patted Jason's shoulder. "Just so you know, you can be open with me about that kind of stuff. I don't judge. In fact, if I wasn't straight, I'd be your twink any day of the week."

Jason rolled his eyes. "Wow. Within minutes of appointment, and you're already trying to seduce the staff. Just. Wow." Jason chuckled and shook his head. "Fuckin' Braxton. . ."

Jason began clearing the table of the coffee cups and glassware, efficiently stacking them on a tray. Braxton continued gathering his multiple files, each one representing the culmination of his tireless efforts in solving the complex cases that had brought him to this point. The accumulation of his work and dedication weighed both physically and metaphorically in those files.

A couple of minutes later, Jason returned, and together, they walked from the atrium back into the familiar confines of the Saloon. As they entered, Braxton was met with an unexpected sight. The entire Inter Alios team, including Stacey, Donnie, Earl, Tony, and Amanda, were gathered there. They all wore smiles of anticipation.

Before Braxton could process the scene, they began clapping, their applause echoing through the Saloon. Braxton felt a lump in his throat, his eyes glistening with tears. It was a moment he had never expected, a moment where he finally felt like he belonged somewhere, a moment where he realized he had found a purpose in life.

Overwhelmed with emotion, Braxton's facade of stoicism cracked, and tears streamed down his cheeks. He had come to Jacksonville as a stranger, an outsider, but now he was part of a family—a family of individuals who shared a common mission and had come to accept him as one of their own.

He wiped away his tears, his voice quivering with gratitude. "Thank you," he managed to say, his words filled with sincerity. "Thank you all."

The applause continued, the sound of unity and acceptance, as Braxton Hayward, Principal Magistrate of Inter Alios, had not only broken free from the dark and perilous web that had ensnared him but also discovered something he had spent his entire life searching for—a profound sense of belonging and purpose. He felt as if his journey had come full circle, yet now he was now equipped to do good and truly be well.

WINTER

CHAPTER EIGHTEEN

FROM ONE PAUPER
FIELDER TO ANOTHER

SUNDAY, DECEMBER 17, 10:41 AM

FIVE YEARS LATER

The pale morning light filtered through the clouds, casting a soft glow over the I-5 as Braxton cruised northward in his new hybrid Acura MDX. He savored the car's quiet comfort, a welcome contrast to the chill outside. The nearly empty road was a rare luxury, offering a fleeting moment of tranquility in his otherwise hectic life.

His car signaled an incoming call, the screen displaying a name that brought a smile to his face. "What's cooking, good-looking?" Braxton greeted, leaning into the familiarity and warmth that characterized their exchanges.

Riley's laughter rang clear, a sound that never failed to stir something within him. "Starting the day with your best lines, huh?" she teased, her amusement evident. "I saw your missed call from earlier. To what do I owe the pleasure?"

Braxton's gaze drifted to the road ahead, his mind momentarily reflecting on the complexity of their relationship. "I wanted to thank you for connecting me with your contact at the Bureau of Land Management. That was a solid favor."

"No worries," Riley's voice softened, a mock seriousness creeping in. "But it's gonna cost you dinner once I fly back next week."

The corners of Braxton's mouth twitched upwards. "Wow, that seems kind of steep. I'd hate to know what an FBI rendition goes for these days. Should I plan on taking out a second mortgage?"

Their laughter mingled through the airwaves, and their conversation flowed naturally, filled with the kind of playful banter and mutual teasing that had always marked their relationship. As the call wound down, Braxton felt a tinge of nostalgia mixed with something he couldn't quite name. "Looking forward to that dinner I owe you," he said, the words holding more weight than he intended.

"Me too. Take care, Braxton."

As he ended the call, Braxton's thoughts lingered on Riley—the history they shared and the paths their lives had taken. He merged onto the Grants Pass exit, the familiar route offering a moment of reflection. Each mile brought him closer to his speaking engagement, mingling anticipation with memories.

The transition from the freeway to the streets of Grants Pass felt familiar, each landmark a reminder of the many roles he had played in this small corner of the world. Parking his car, Braxton stepped into the crisp morning air, his conversation with Riley fading as he approached the modest, shopworn community center.

Standing behind a well-worn lectern in the softly lit room, enveloped by a quiet air of expectant stillness, Braxton found himself facing about fifty people. They sat in metal folding chairs, their attentive eyes anchoring him to the moment. Lifting a small, disposable coffee cup, he savored a sip, the bittersweet coffee blending seamlessly with the gravity of his opening words, each one a vessel for the experiences and insights he was about to share.

"Truth be told," Braxton began, his voice resonating with sincerity, "when I first moved up here about five years ago, I told everyone that my plan was to write the next 'great American novel' or whatever. But in reality, my plan was to fuck off and drink until insolvency or death— whichever came first. Alcohol's cunning, baffling, and powerful grip on me was so insidious that death was preferable to quitting." Braxton cleared his throat, the room hanging on his every word.

"And the funny thing about it is that even though it's been over four years since I had a drink," he continued, referencing his last relapse, "that craving still crops up out of nowhere. I mean, here I am, living in this gorgeous place with a smart, beautiful, awesome wife in a great house with kids that I love and adore. . .even when they're being complete and total pains in my ass." A wave of understanding swept through the crowd, punctuated by scattered chuckles that tittered like a gentle breeze on a calm sea.

"And I have no doubt that I'd have none of that if I kept on drinking. Yet, just the other day, I found myself on a Friday afternoon ahead of schedule. So, I decided to start the weekend early and get more familiar with this cool drone I got as a birthday gift a couple of months back. And about ten minutes into this wonderful drive under the best of circumstances, it popped right in there: 'You know what would be perfect right now? A nice end-of-the-week Manhattan. Top-shelf bourbon. Make it a triple. Craft cherry coated with extra syrup.'" Braxton paused, taking a breath as he visualized the drink's allure. In response, several heads in the audience nodded almost in unison.

"Ironically, most of my livelihood is derived from the sale and consumption of alcohol," Braxton continued, his gaze shifting above the audience members' heads to maintain his concentration, "but I know for a fact that any attempt to have 'just one drink' with my colleagues would inevitably yield rock-bottom results."

Braxton paused, his voice carrying the weight of hard-earned wisdom.

"Now, if it were the pre-sobriety Braxton who had that Friday Manhattan thought," he reflected, "he'd have already flipped a U-turn and be headed to the nearest watering hole at a high rate of speed. Indeed, there was no other choice but to do that.

"And to be clear, my poison is booze, bourbon in particular. But it doesn't matter what your pick is: be it pills, rails, hits, you name it. In either event, I've come to realize that no matter what kind of day I'm having there is no such thing as having 'just one.'

"And then it occurred to me," Braxton shared his epiphany with the room, "The only way you can have a choice in the matter is to choose *not* having that first taste. Whether it's to amplify the moment or numb the pain, the second I take a swallow, that first drink will be bottomless. . .at least until I hit bottom, that is."

As he shifted his gaze back to his notes, Braxton continued with a profound insight, his voice resonating with the shared experiences of those listening.

"The main reason why I drank was to stop myself from future-tripping," he admitted, prompting numerous nodding heads in the audience. "You know, how one thought goes to the next to the next to the next until you think that you're gonna end up dead anyways, so you might as well enjoy another drink while you can?"

Braxton paused, allowing the weight of his words to settle in the room.

"Compare that to now," he urged contemplation, "where I acknowledge that there is no way to predict how the rest of my life will play out. All I can do is have faith that by doing good in the now, I may find myself doing well in the future. And why *not* take that route? Because once you decide not to do something that is certain to cause destruction, the options as to what you *can* do become unlimited."

With that, Braxton yielded the rest of his time to the meeting's secretary, who opened the room for other shares, leaving the audience with food for thought and hopefully some guidance.

After spending a good half-hour engaging with both familiar faces and newcomers, Braxton wrapped up the final conversations and prepared to leave. These speaking engagements scattered across the Rogue Valley were not just commitments on his calendar; they were something he looked forward to, opportunities to connect and grow alongside others walking similar paths. This particular Sunday morning recovery meeting resonated deeply, touching a special place in his heart reserved for moments of shared journeys and collective resilience.

Embarking on his homeward journey, Braxton drove southward along the ribbon of I-5. The noonday air was crisp, a chilly reminder of winter's grip. Here and there, patches of ice glistened on the asphalt, catching weak sunbeams that struggled through the winter sky. Such minor challenges seemed trivial against the capabilities of the brand-new SUV, a vehicle as ready for the elements as Braxton felt for the road ahead.

As the miles unfurled before him, Braxton found his thoughts anchored firmly in the now, the rhythm of the journey harmonizing with his post-meeting reflections. "Call Honeybee," he voiced into the calm of the SUV. The affectionate nickname for his wife brought a smile to his lips with its fond familiarity. After a brief series of rings, her voice came through, a sunburst of warmth in the wintry air.

"Hello?" Her greeting, simple yet imbued with the promise of connection, filled the cabin.

"Am I on speaker?" Braxton inquired.

"What? Hang on, let me take this off speaker so I can hear you better. Hello?" Her voice came back, clearer now, and he dove right in.

"Yessshhh. . .hellllo, Pushy," Braxton playfully quipped, his voice taking on the unmistakable but arguably the worst Sean Connery James Bond impression ever attempted.

Her infectious laugh erupted from the speakers, filling the cabin of the car with warmth and mirth. "You're outta control!" Emily's voice chimed in. Braxton could almost envision her rolling her eyes, silently reproaching herself for indulging in a recent marathon of old-school Bond movies with him just the other night.

"Anyways, done with the meeting and heading back down," Braxton updated. "Just wanted to check in to see what's happening on your end."

Emily paused briefly, mentally juggling household activities. "Ummm. . .let's see," she began. "Zoe is off with her boyfriend, the twins and I are here at home baking, and Hunter is off ice skating with Uncle Mitch. So, yeah, it's actually a pretty low-key day."

"Oh, that's right," Braxton recalled. "Mitch has Hunter today. For a second there, I thought it was still Saturday. Okay, well, I'll be on the road for a bit. Do you want me to pick anything up from the store on my way home?"

Emily pondered for a moment before responding, "We're running low on brown sugar, and we could use some powdered sugar and graham crackers. Also, could you grab some lactose-free and almond milk? Come to think of it, perhaps some—"

Braxton interjected politely, "Maybe you could text me the list so I don't forget anything?" Emily chuckled and agreed to do so.

Their conversation flowed, encompassing updates on their day and the final logistical details for the upcoming Christmas celebrations. After about ten minutes, they bid each other farewell. Braxton's phone soon buzzed with a series of text messages as Emily continued to refine and expand upon the shopping list.

Navigating the frost-kissed road, Braxton's mind wandered through the maze of memories that had steered him to this unforeseen juncture in his life. The unpredictability of his journey struck him with a profound sense of wonder. He dwelled on the days he and Riley had strived to salvage their relationship, seeking solace in each other's company, only to face the harsh reality of her transfer to the Portland field office. The shadow of their inevitable separation had plunged him into despair, a darkness so deep it led him to seek solace in alcohol, losing himself until the world faded to black.

It was in the aftermath of those darkest moments that Braxton acknowledged the need for change, reaching out for support and beginning his journey toward recovery in meetings that offered a semblance of hope. Despite the distance and the separate paths their careers had taken—Riley's impending elevation to SAIC of a Task Force in Denver being the latest milestone—they remained connected, their conversations about work and life a bridge between their past and their present, an enduring bond that, despite everything, continued to link their lives together.

This reflection led Braxton to ponder the pivotal role Inter Alios had played in his journey, not just as a sanctuary but as a force of transformation. The organization had stepped in at a critical juncture, erasing his student debt with an interest-free loan. Recently repaid in full, Braxton chose to continue contributing the monthly stipend, a gesture of his deep commitment, driven by a desire to aid Inter Alios in its ongoing efforts to recruit and expand, reflecting his gratitude and dedication to the group that had offered him a second chance.

Then, there was the unexpected turn in his life when he had gotten to know Emily more intimately as they continued to cross paths. It started with him helping her set up a corporation for the brewery and distillery business that the Holmans had left to her—a twist of fate that had surprised Emily more than anyone else.

Their journey had taken them from friends to dating, to cohabitating at her place, and eventually, they had moved into one of Inter Alios' properties with a charming wraparound porch that was closer to town. Braxton fondly remembered how they had decided to tie the knot, making him a proud stepparent in their blended illuminati family. Their bed, adorned with decorative pillows when not in use, symbolized the warmth and love that now enveloped his life.

Braxton had proven himself adept at balancing the diverse interests required by his job. It just sort of happened, one day at a time. The Saloon's live concert venue had become a resounding success. It attracted musicians already playing at the Britt Festival, and word of its unique acoustics and down-to-earth atmosphere spread throughout the industry, drawing even more talent to both local venues. Braxton handled the transactional side of the operation, skillfully brokering and finalizing deals, including booking renowned performers like JT and a couple of artists straight out of Compton. These deals significantly contributed to keeping Inter Alios' coffers at sufficient levels.

On another front were his Principal Magistrate duties. After addressing some initial challenges following his impromptu appointment, Braxton had begun to find creative ways to offset the exploitative enterprises of each Order. These measures included requiring generous endowments to local nonprofits, healthcare clinics, education programs, and similar causes. Braxton had even contemplated implementing a carbon toll to fund open wildlife spaces and reduce pollution, although he knew that Inter Alios woefully lacked the resources to execute such an ambitious project.

Despite the vast disparity in assets between Inter Alios and the several billion-dollar fortunes amassed by Ab Initio and Prime Ascendant over the last century-and-a-half, Braxton, Jason, and the dedicated members of Inter Alios were making remarkable strides with the resources they had mustered.

Immersed in thought, Braxton almost missed his exit. The Sunday store crowd wasn't too bad, but locating items and reconciling Emily's extensive shopping lists, which came in six separate texts, took extra time. Nonetheless, he was soon back on the road.

About five minutes from home, his car signaled an incoming text. Assuming it was another "if you haven't left the store yet, could you get. . ." message from Emily, he decided to ignore it, given his proximity to home.

He backed into the driveway in front of the detached garage, which housed a second-story unit recently occupied by his oldest stepdaughter, Zoe.

With brisk efficiency, he made two round trips between his car and the house, relocating most of the grocery bags to the front porch of the main residence. Returning to the SUV, he grabbed the last bag and hit the button to close the rear tailgate. As the tailgate lowered, he pulled out his phone.

The message was from an unfamiliar number that had occasionally sent him texts over the past several years. Initially wary of potential phishing schemes, he had left the texts unread. However, curiosity got the better of him this time, and he tapped on the message icon. It appeared to be the same mix of links and encrypted gibberish he had received from that number in the past.

But this time there was a message below the coded data:

"FROM ONE PAUPER FIELDER TO ANOTHER: Wallet set up for INTER ALIOS. We have been mining for years. U may want to cash some out now. A final 20K (in trust for Hunter) will be dropped into wallet by end of year. The rest is up to you, PM. -EH/AS"

Staring at the screen, the initials, references to Pauper Field, Inter Alios, and PM (Principal Magistrate) left Braxton in a state of shock. With trembling fingers, he clicked on the link, the rear door of his car locking into place as he did so. His surroundings blurred as he blinked at the information displayed on the screen, half-expecting hidden cameras to capture his reaction, thinking it might be an elaborate practical joke.

With his phone still in hand, Braxton hurriedly dropped the bag on the front porch and quick-stepped his way up the stairs. The girls were in the kitchen, streaming music and baking Christmas goodies with enthusiasm. Their curly-haired dog briefly acknowledged his presence before returning to her vigilant watch for any stray crumbs.

Braxton let out a small yelp after knocking his elbow on the second-story stairway banister. Reaching the master bedroom, he retrieved his laptop from the nightstand and fumbled with his pin code, cursing under his breath when he made a mistake. The computer seemed to take an eternity to load, adding to his growing anxiety.

Once the laptop finally came to life, he opened a browser and painstakingly retyped the link from his cell phone, along with the encryption codes. What he found was a digital wallet containing one hundred thousand Bitcoins.

Rubbing his chin in disbelief, Braxton opened another tab to check the present value of a single Bitcoin, assuming it might be worth only a couple of hundred bucks at most after years of not hearing about cryptocurrency.

While his laptop's browser tab loaded, he used his phone's calculator to multiply the Bitcoin value by 100,000. His brow furrowed in shock as the result stared back at him, and he cleared the calculator, double-checking his input, but the number remained the same.

He repeated the calculation using his laptop calculator, yet the number remained unchanged, further deepening his shock. Head cocked, Braxton began counting the digits to the left of the decimal point, his vision blurring around the seventh digit. Panic set in as he realized he had forgotten to breathe during the calculations. His surroundings grew foggy, and an eerie whispered chanting seemed to emanate from everywhere and yet nowhere.

"*In Terra Lios, In Terra Lios,*" the chant weaved through the air, a spectral whisper that seemed to draw the very strength from Braxton's limbs. He found himself sinking onto the bed, the world around him fading as the haunting refrain enveloped him, the decorative pillows beneath him unnoticed in his growing weakness.

But then, as if the air itself shifted, the chant morphed subtly, the words bending in Braxton's weary mind. "*Inter Alios, Inter Alios,*" it now seemed to say, the sounds blurring and reshaping into the name of the very organization he had come to lead. The realization struck him with the force of a revelation, a clarifying moment amidst the swirling confusion.

His consciousness teetered on the edge of oblivion as the voices intensified, the chant now unmistakably clear. "*Inter Alios, Inter Alios,*" it resonated, not just around him but within him, anchoring him to this pivotal point in his life.

Just as the enormity of the situation threatened to overwhelm him, a voice pierced the veil of his faltering senses. "Holy shiii—" it exclaimed, a startled acknowledgment of the profound revelation that lay before him. The voice seemed to come from far away, yet it was unmistakably his own, reacting to the ten-figure amount displayed on the calculator's screen.

The first sensation that broke through Braxton's haze was the warm, damp touch of his dog's tongue across his face, a feeling that slowly brought him back to reality from his foggy reverie. Beside him stood Emily, her eyes mirroring a mix of worry and care. "Are you okay?" she inquired, her voice cutting through the lingering fog of his consciousness.

Slowly, Braxton gathered his thoughts, and although he felt strangely invigorated, he still felt caught in a surreal dream. "I'm fine," he replied, attributing his dazed condition to the excess coffee consumed at the meeting.

Emily looked over at the laptop screen, where the mind-numbing billion-dollar sum still gleamed. Her face lit up with excitement. "Oh, good," she said, "you finally got her message." She leaned in, caressing him and planting a tender kiss on his forehead, assuring him that there were still some freshly baked cookies awaiting him in the kitchen.

As Emily left the room, Braxton remained lying in bed, his eyes tracing the familiar cracks and contours of the ceiling above. In this moment of solitude, his mind ventured beyond these four walls, reaching out to the vast, unending universe. Guided to its energy-rich core, the part forming galaxies and sparking with life, he felt an overwhelming sense of tranquility as he let go, allowing himself to be drawn toward the thriving center, beaming through all of infinity.

This wasn't an escape but an alignment, a reminder that life, with all its chaos and clarity, was inherently intertwined with the cosmos. The challenges he had faced, the voices that once echoed with mystery, had been guiding him toward a newfound understanding. They whispered of continuity and change, of being part of a greater whole.

Drawing a deep breath, Braxton felt the weight of the recent developments lift, replaced by a sense of purpose that was both humbling and empowering. It dawned on him how Inter Alios, once just a name, had become his calling, a bridge between his past and the future he was ready to shape. It stood as a means of connection—not just between individuals but across the expanse of time and space.

Rising from the bed, the room seemed to embrace him, the light through the window casting long shadows that spoke of the day's potential. Moving toward that light, Braxton carried with him a quiet determination and an open heart, ready to face the journey ahead with a spirit renewed by understanding and acceptance. In embracing the present and stepping into the unknown, Braxton found not just a sense of serenity but a vibrant hope. The universe, in all its infinite wonder, felt closer than ever, a constant reminder of the ironic beauty in the journey and the unspoken connections that bind us all—*inter alios*.